DARK SKYE

BOOKS BY KRESLEY COLE

The Immortals After Dark Series

The Warlord Wants Forever
A Hunger Like No Other
No Rest for the Wicked
Wicked Deeds on a Winter's Night
Dark Needs at Night's Edge
Dark Desires After Dusk
Kiss of a Demon King
Deep Kiss of Winter
Pleasure of a Dark Prince
Demon from the Dark
Dreams of a Dark Warrior
Lothaire
Shadow's Claim
MacRieve

The Game Maker Series

The Professional

The Arcana Chronicles

Poison Princess
Endless Knight

The MacCarrick Brothers Series

If You Dare
If You Desire
If You Deceive

The Sutherland Series

The Captain of All Pleasures
The Price of Pleasure

KRESLEY COLE

DARK SKYE

GALLERY BOOKS
New York · London · Toronto · Sydney · New Delhi

G

Gallery Books
A Division of Simon & Schuster, Inc.
1230 Avenue of the Americas
New York, NY 10020

This book is a work of fiction. Any references to historical events, real people, or real places are used fictitiously. Other names, characters, places, and events are products of the author's imagination, and any resemblance to actual events or places or persons, living or dead, is entirely coincidental.

First Gallery Books hardcover edition August 2014

GALLERY BOOKS and colophon are registered trademarks of Simon & Schuster, Inc.

For information about special discounts for bulk purchases, please contact Simon & Schuster Special Sales at 1-866-506-1949 or business@simonandschuster.com.

The Simon & Schuster Speakers Bureau can bring authors to your live event. For more information or to book an event contact the Simon & Schuster Speakers Bureau at 1-866-248-3049 or visit our website at www.simonspeakers.com.

Manufactured in the United States of America

10 9 8 7 6 5 4 3 2 1

Library of Congress Cataloging-in-Publication Data

Cole, Kresley.
Dark Skye / Kresley Cole.
pages cm.—(Immortals after dark ; 15)
1. Fantasy fiction. 2. Love stories. I. Title.
PS3603.O4287D37 2014
813'.6—dc23 2014019025

ISBN 978-1-4516-4994-9
ISBN 978-1-4516-4996-3 (ebook)

Dedicated with much love
to all the ladies on the
"Belles on Wheels" bus tour.
What a wild, awesome ride that was!
(can we do it again?)

EXCERPTED FROM

THE LIVING BOOK OF LORE . . .

The Lore

". . . and those sentient creatures that are not human will be united in one stratum, coexisting with, yet secret from, man's."

- Most are immortal and can regenerate from injuries, killed only by mystical fire or beheading.
- Their eyes change with intense emotion, often to a breed-specific color.

The Sept of Sorceri

"The Sept forever seek and covet others' powers, challenging and dueling to seize more—or, more darkly, stealing another's sorcery. . . ."

- A breed-line broken from the enchantment caste of the House of Witches.
- One of the physically weaker species in the Lore, they used elaborate armors to protect their bodies. Eventually they held metals—and especially gold—sacred.

The Vrekeners

"Death descends on swift wings. The righteous reckoning of the Lore, they strike like a plague from the heavens, their wings blocking out the light of the sun, casting the land in shadow."

- Mortal enemies of the Sept of Sorceri, most of whom they consider wicked and unclean.
- They live in the Air Territories, a realm consisting of floating islands, hidden above the clouds. Their royal seat is Skye Hall. They refer to their home as the Territories or simply *the Skye.*

The Demonarchies

"The demon dynasties are as varied as the bands of man. . . ."

- Most breeds can *trace,* or teleport, like vampires.
- The rage demonarchy is located in the plane of Rothkalina, ruled by King Rydstrom the Good.

The Order

"The immortal takers. Once captured by the Order, immortals do not return. . . ."

- A multinational mortal operation created to study—and exterminate—nonhumans.
- Possesses several secret holding facilities, where Loreans are imprisoned, examined, and executed.

The Accession

"And a time shall come to pass when all immortal beings in the Lore, from the Valkyrie, vampire, Lykae, and demon factions to the witches, shifters, fey, and sirens . . . must fight and destroy each other."

- A kind of mystical checks-and-balances system for an ever-growing population of immortals.
- Two major alliances: the Pravus Rule and the Vertas League.
- Occurs every five hundred years. Or right now . . .

PROLOGUE

Deep within the Alps, mortal realm

ROUGHLY FIVE CENTURIES AGO

Crawling along a meadow on her hands and knees, Lanthe scoured the grass for berries or dandelions—anything to dull her hunger pangs as her stomach seemed to gnaw on itself.

Her older sister, Sabine—or Ai-bee, as Lanthe called her—would soon be back from the nearby human village, where she'd gone on a desperate food run. Lanthe had wanted to accompany her, but Sabine said nine was too young.

So Lanthe waited in this meadow, her favorite spot below the high mountain abbey where she lived with Sabine and her parents. A fir-tree forest surrounded the small clearing, and a placid lake reflected the sky like a mirror. Her dress hem continually danced with swaying wildflowers.

Here, she could coax rabbits to share dandelions with her, naming the creatures and talking to them. Other times, she'd spend hours lying in the grass, gazing up at puffy white clouds to spot shapes.

But today was cloudless. Which was why she frowned when a shadow passed over the sun.

She shielded her eyes to peer upward—and saw . . . wings. Deadly wings. They belonged to a boy, one who looked as shocked as she was.

He was a Vrekener! An enemy to her kind.

As she scrambled to her feet, their eyes met. His had gone as wide as hers. They stared, right up until the moment he flew headfirst into a tree.

Spell broken, she hiked up her dress and ran for her life. Before she'd made the cover of forest, he dropped in front of her, spreading his wings.

She gasped, momentarily stunned by the sight of them. Vrekener wings were jagged—more dragon than dove—with a tapering flare at three points along the bottom. The flares farthest from the body on either side were tipped with talons. *Scary* talons.

She whirled around to flee in the other direction, skirting the lake. Though she was as fast as a fey, he again caught up with her, corralling her with those wings. On the inside, they were gray, with lines of light forking out all over them.

Lanthe and the boy stared at each other, his gaze flicking over her face. Whatever he saw there made him exhale a sharp breath. *Puh.*

No use running. And no one would ever hear her scream. Her parents were all the way up in the abbey, a pair of recluses. Would Sabine find Lanthe's mangled body down here?

Not if I use my sorcery. At the thought, she began to tremble. Lanthe didn't want to call on her powers. It seemed every time she did ended in disaster. But she would against a Vrekener.

Even if he was the most handsome boy she'd ever imagined.

Looking to be a year or two older than she was, he had vivid gray eyes, tanned skin, broad cheekbones, and sandy brown hair that tumbled over his forehead and around his horns. Those jutting spikes were smooth and silvery.

He had even, white teeth, with a pair of fangs! She had the mad urge to tap one of those points with the pad of her forefinger—

"I smell magics on you," the Vrekener said, narrowing those gray eyes. "Are you a little Sorceri?"

There was no denying her species, so she raised her hands threateningly. Power easily leapt to them, swirls of dazzling blue light sparkling in her palms. "I am the Queen of Persuasion, a great and terrible sorceress," she said in an ominous voice, even while fighting the urge to bite her fingernails. "If you come any closer to me, Vrekener, I will be forced to hurt you."

He didn't seem bothered whatsoever by her show of sorcery. As if she hadn't spoken, he said, "Or maybe you're a little lamb. From the sky, you look like one, crawling around in a white frock and eating flowers."

She drew her head back, sputtering, "Wh-what?" Was he jesting with her?

Yes, his eyes gleamed with amusement. While she was fearing for her life—and threatening his—he acted as if he'd just stumbled upon a new playmate.

One he'd been longing for.

"What's your name, sorceress?"

She was so startled she found herself saying, "Melanthe. Of the Deie Sorceri family."

He sounded out her name. "Mel-anth-ee." Then he pressed his hand over his chest. "I'm Thronos Talos, Prince of the Skye." His tone was filled with importance.

"Never heard of you," she said, casting a glance over her shoulder toward the abbey. If Sabine caught this boy here with Lanthe, her overprotective big sister would kill him with her fantastical powers.

Lanthe didn't like things to be killed, not even handsome Vrekeners.

As the Queen of Illusions, Sabine could make her victims see anything she chose, changing the appearance of their surroundings. She could also reach into a person's mind, draw forth his worst nightmare, then present it to him.

Unlike Lanthe, Sabine never hesitated to use her powers. . . .

"Is that where you live?" the Vrekener asked, interrupting her thoughts. Was he following her gaze to the mountaintop?

"No! Not at all. We live far away from here. I walk leagues to get to this meadow."

"Really?" He clearly disbelieved her, but didn't seem angered by her lie. "Strange that I sense sorcery from that direction. *Lots* of it."

Vrekeners tracked Sorceri by scent—and by power outlays. Lanthe would have to get her parents to use more caution. Or try to. They were consumed with creating ever more gold. "I don't know what you mean."

He let it go. "So what's persuasion?"

She glanced down at her palms, startled to see how much sorcery she wielded. Did she really mean to hurt him? He didn't seem as threatening anymore.

Pursing her lips, she called back her power. "I can make anyone do anything I tell them to do. It's called persuasion, but it should be called commanding."

Years ago, when she'd first used it, she'd crossly told Sabine to shut her mouth. For an entire week, no one had understood why Sabine hadn't been able to open it. Her sister had almost starved.

"That sounds impressive, lamb. So you're as powerful as you are pretty?"

Her cheeks heated. He thought she was pretty? She gazed down at her frayed dress. Though faded nearly white from repeated washing, it used to have color. Sorceri loved color. Her feet were bare because she'd outgrown her boots. She didn't feel very pretty.

"I'm sure you get called beautiful all the time," he said confidently.

No. She didn't. She rarely encountered anyone besides her family. If Sabine complimented her, she'd remark on Lanthe's ability, not her looks. And sometimes her parents didn't seem to see her at all—

The boy started striding toward her.

"Wait, wh-what are you doing?" She tripped back until she met a tree.

"Just making certain of something." He leaned his face in close to her hair, and then he . . . he *scented* her! When he drew back, he wore a cocky grin, as if he'd just won a prize or discovered a new realm.

For some reason, that grin made her feel as if she'd run all the way up the mountain. Her heart pounded, and she couldn't seem to catch her breath.

"You smell like sky. And *home.*" He said this as if it was significant—a weighty and undeniable truth.

"What does that mean?" Gods, this boy confused her.

"To me, you smell like no one else in the world ever has, or ever will." His gray irises glowed silver with emotion. A breeze ruffled his sandy brown hair. "It means you and I are going to be best friends. When we grow up, we'll be . . . more."

She focused on the words *best friends,* and ached with yearning. She'd always wanted a friend! She loved Sabine, but her sister was twelve and usually had grown-up stuff on her mind, like how to get warm clothing for the coming winter, or enough food to feed four.

Lanthe supposed someone had to be concerned with those things—since their parents were always preoccupied. When Lanthe had been a baby, she'd called for *Ai-bee* over their own mother.

But Lanthe could never be best friends with a Vrekener, despite how intriguing she found him. "You should go, Thronos Talos," she said, just as her stomach growled, embarrassing her and deepening his amusement.

"You might be a great and terrible sorceress, but you can't eat sorcery, can you?" He spread those spellbinding wings. "Will you stay here if I go find food for you?"

"Why would you do that?"

His shoulders went back, his silvery eyes alight—as if with pride. "That's my job now, lamb."

She sighed. "I don't understand. We're *enemies.* We're not supposed to be like"—she waved from herself to him—"this."

He winked at her. "I won't tell if you don't."

Four months later

Thronos . . . told.

And then Lanthe made him pay for it.

"Sorceri are licentious, gambling, paranoid hedonists; their love of wine-swilling and carousing is matched only by their delight in thievery. For Sorceri powers to go unchecked would be disastrous."

—Thronos Talos, Knight of Reckoning, heir to the Skye

"Meaningless sex is like eating the worm at the bottom of a tequila bottle: fun in the moment, but not something you'd want to repeat over and over."

—Melanthe of the Deie Sorceri, Queen of Persuasion

ONE

An island, somewhere in the Pacific Ocean

MODERN TIMES

As Lanthe sprinted down a shaking, smoky tunnel, she focused on her friends ahead: Carrow, a witch, and Carrow's newly adopted daughter, Ruby. The witch was holding the seven-year-old girl in her arms as she ran headlong for an exit out of this godsforsaken maze.

Lanthe followed, gripping her sword with a gauntleted hand, her metal claws digging into the handle. She tried to smile for Ruby, who was frowning back at her.

Carrow—or Crow, as Ruby called her—and Lanthe had attempted to turn their dire escape into a fun-filled adventure for her. Snarky and adorable Ruby clearly wasn't sold.

Charging into the tunnels had seemed like such a good idea at the time, a way out of the Order prison they'd all been jailed in—and an escape from other immortals. After tonight's cataclysmic overthrow, Loreans stalked the fiery halls, hunting for prey. Carrow's estranged husband, who might or might not be evil, hunted for her.

Another quake rocked the tunnel, grit raining down over Lanthe's black braids. Unfortunately, Lanthe had her own stalker—Thronos, a crazed, winged warlord who'd been obsessed with capturing her for the last five hundred years.

But Vrekeners feared enclosed spaces; anything underground was a forbidding landscape, much less a failing tunnel. He'd never follow her into this subterranean maze.

Explosions sounded somewhere in the distance, and the tunnel rumbled. *Seemed like such a good idea.* She gazed up, saw the immense ceiling supports bowed from strain. No wonder. New mountains were sprouting from the earth all over this prison island, courtesy of Lanthe's fellow Sorceri.

A boulder dropped in her path, slowing her progress. Rock dust wafted over her like a grainy curtain, spattering her face and Sorceri mask. Carrow and Ruby grew indistinct in the haze. The two turned a corner, out of sight.

As Lanthe increased her speed, she gave a frustrated yank on her *torque,* a treat from the humans for all their immortal captives. The indestructible collar prevented them from using their innate abilities, neutralizing strength, endurance, and healing.

Some of the prisoners—all of the most evil ones—had had theirs removed this night. Lanthe still wore one, which wasn't fair, since few would consider her "good."

Without that torque, she would have been able to command stronger beings to protect her and her friends. She would have been able to read an opponent's mind, run with supernatural speed, or create a portal to step through—away from this island nightmare forever.

Away from Thronos.

Lanthe hiked up her metal breastplate—not ideal for running for one's life. Nor were her metal mesh skirt and thigh-high stiletto boots. Still she sped forward, wishing her thoughts would stop returning to her age-old foe.

During their captivity, she'd had the shock of her life when guards had dragged Thronos by their cell. He'd let himself be seized by the Order and taken to her prison—Lanthe knew it. With malice in his eyes, he'd grated to her, *"Soon."*

When Carrow had asked about that, Lanthe had been sparing of the details: "Would you believe that Thronos and I were childhood friends?"

Later, Carrow had pressed, so Lanthe had admitted, "He's broken because of me. I 'persuaded' him to dive from a great height. And not to use his wings." Most of his skin had been slashed and scarred, the bones of his wings and limbs fractured—before his immortality had taken hold, before he could regenerate.

What more could Lanthe say? How to explain the bond she and Thronos had shared? Until he'd betrayed her fragile trust . . .

Well, Carrow, Thronos led his clan to my family's secret lair one night. His father killed my parents, lopped their heads right off with a Vrekener fire scythe. My fierce sister Sabine retaliated, taking the father's life. When she was nearly murdered, I gave Thronos wounds that would last an eternal lifetime, then left him to die.

Alas, since then, things have gone downhill.

"Air's getting fresher!" Carrow called from somewhere ahead. "Almost there!"

At last, the smoke was clearing. Which meant Lanthe needed to catch up. Who knew what could be awaiting them out in the night? Thousands of immortals had escaped.

Had this many enemies ever been so concentrated in one inescapable place?

She readied her sword. A vague memory arose of holding her first one. Mother had absently handed each of her daughters a golden sword, telling them, "Never depend solely on your powers. If you and your sister want to survive to adulthood, you'd best get handy with one of these. . . ."

Now Lanthe kept her weapon poised for—

Pain on her ankle?

Body reeling forward?

One second Lanthe had been sprinting; the next she was on her face, sword tumbling in front of her. Something had her! Claws sank into her ankle, piercing the leather of her boot. She screamed and thrashed, but it hauled her back.

Ghoul? Demon? Wendigo? She stabbed her metal claws into the ground, scrabbling for purchase, looking over her shoulder.

Her own nightmare.

Thronos.

His scarred face was bloodied, his towering body tensed. A maniacal glint shone in his gray eyes as his wings unfurled—they seemed to flicker in the dim tunnel. A trick of light.

The bastard had actually braved an underground shaft. *Vrekeners never abandon their hunt.*

"Release me, you dick!" She kicked out with more force, but she was no match for his strength. Wait, why didn't he have a collar? Thronos was akin to an angel, a warrior for right.

She knew he'd become a warlord. Had he turned evil over these centuries?

"Let her go, Thronos!" Carrow yelled, charging. She'd parked Ruby somewhere, returning to take on a Vrekener.

For Lanthe. *I knew I liked that witch.*

Before she could reach Lanthe, Thronos had used one of his wings to send Carrow sprawling. The witch scrambled up again, drawing her own sword.

Lanthe continued to thrash, filled with dread. Thronos was too strong; like Lanthe, Carrow still had her collar.

When the witch charged again, a wing flashed out once more, but Carrow anticipated the move, hunching down to slide under it. She shoved her sword up, piercing the wing, leaving her weapon to hang like a giant splinter.

He gave a yell, releasing Lanthe to pluck the sword free. Blood poured from him, pooling in the gravel.

Carrow lunged for Lanthe, snaring her hand. Before she could get Lanthe up and running, Thronos seized Lanthe's leg again, wrenching her back—but Carrow and Lanthe kept their hands locked.

It was a losing proposition. Ruby was vulnerable without Carrow. And for all the grief, heartache, and pain Thronos and his kind had dished out to Lanthe over the years, she didn't believe he could murder her in cold blood.

She chanced another look back. No matter how much he'd looked like he was about to.

His blood-splattered face was as grim as a reaper's, his lips thinned, his scars whitening. The age-old question arose: did he want to abduct her or kill her? Or abduct her to torture then kill?

No, no, he couldn't hurt her; Lanthe was his fated mate. Hurting her would hurt him.

The tunnel quaked again. In the distance, Ruby called, "Crow!"

"Save Ruby!" Lanthe cried. Smoke thickened, rubble building around them.

Carrow shook her head, digging in determinedly. "I'll save you both."

In a deafening rush, rocks began to tumble down from the ceiling, filling the space between Carrow and Ruby.

Ruby screamed, "Crow! Where are you?"

Carrow screamed back, "I'm coming!"

"Save your girl!" Lanthe yanked her hand free, allowing Thronos to haul her away. "I'll be okay!"

Carrow's stricken face disappeared as he dragged Lanthe into the smoke.

After three weeks of imprisonment at the hands of vile humans, Lanthe had been caught again—by something she hated even more than mortals who enjoyed vivisecting their captives. "Let me go, Thronos!" Her body lurched with each of his limping steps.

Almost at once, he veered into a smaller off-shoot tunnel that she hadn't seen when speeding past it.

"You're going the wrong way!" She dug her metal claws in, raking furrows into the ground. When a cloud of gravel erupted in front of her face, she coughed up grit. "Damn it, Thronos, turn back!" Blood continued to pour from his wing, leaving a trail beside Lanthe's furrows. "We were almost at an exit before!"

She and Carrow had been hoping to reach the shore. Now he seemed to be ascending. Leave it to a Vrekener to make for the high ground.

"Centuries I've waited for this," he grated, never loosening his viselike grip around her ankle.

Another quake rocked the tunnel. When a boulder crashed down beside her, she stopped clawing with her gauntlets, instead crying, "Faster, idiot!"

As if she weighed nothing, he yanked her up from the ground and into his arms in one fluid move. He'd grown taller than any Vrekener she'd ever seen. He must be nearing seven feet in height, looming over her five and a half feet. With his gaze boring into hers, he squeezed her against his chest.

His hair—too light to be black, too dark to be brown—was streaked with ash, the matte gray matching his eyes. But as he beheld her, his irises turned to that brilliant silver—like lightning. Like his ghostly wings.

"Let me go!" she yelled, slashing at him with her claws.

He dropped her to her feet—just to shove her against the wall. With his rigid body pressed against her, he leaned in, tilting his head creepily.

Was he going to kiss her? "Don't you dare!" She moved to strike him again, but he pinned her wrists above her head.

A heartbeat later, he took her mouth, dumbfounding her. He slanted his lips more aggressively, burning away her shock.

She bit his bottom lip. He kept going. She bit harder.

He squeezed her wrists until she thought he would snap her bones. She released him, and he finally drew back, smirking with bloody fangs.

"Now it begins." With his free hand, he swiped his fingers over his bloody mouth, then reached to smear her lips with crimson.

She jerked her head away. *Dear gods, he's been maddened.*

Another quake; more rocks joined that huge boulder, blocking the way they'd come.

"Just brilliant!" She was trapped with Thronos, her survival tied to his. She gazed back at those rocks. Had her friends made it out alive?

Reading her worry, he sneered, "I'd be more concerned about *your* fate." She faced her enemy with dread. "Which has at last been sealed. . . ."

TWO

I have her. Thronos just stopped himself from roaring with triumph. *I bloody have her.*

With her wrists still pinned, he ripped her mask away, his gaze taking in her face. Her wide blue eyes were stark against her soot-marked skin. Dust coated the wild, raven braids that tangled about her cheeks and neck. His blood painted her plump lips. Even in this state, she was still the most alluring creature he'd ever seen.

And the most treacherous.

He tore his gaze away, focusing on their survival. This ungodsly tunnel would fail soon. Out in the night, dangers would lurk in every shadow. Most species on this island hated his kind.

He released Melanthe's hands, just to yank her back into his arms.

"Hey! Where are you taking me?"

Earlier, Thronos had scented saltwater and rain-steeped air—must be an exit from this maze. With her trembling body squeezed against his chest, he began running/limping in that direction, blocking out the grueling pain in his lower right leg.

Pain from just one of the injuries she'd given him.

Get her to safety; refrain from murdering her.

In a short while, the smoke started to thin. Fewer rocks fell.

Melanthe peered around her. "It's clearing! Faster, Thronos!"

Instead he stopped dead in his tracks, kicking up gravel. He'd caught a scent. *Can't be right.*

When he set her to her feet, she demanded, "What is wrong with you? The way back is blocked; we're almost out!"

But the threat was already *in.*

"Is something coming? Tell me!" Her sense of smell wasn't nearly as keen as his.

An eerie howl echoed down the tunnel. Others joined it.

"Are those ghouls?" she asked, a quaver in her voice.

Even immortals beware their bite. The mindless beasts grew their numbers by contagion. A single bite or scratch . . .

The ground vibrated from their approaching footfalls. *Must be hundreds of them.*

He would have to fight a swarm of ghouls—underground. Did Lanthe comprehend the danger they faced? Had he captured his prize only to lose it?

Never. He shoved her behind him, flaring his wings.

"You brought me this way! You've doomed us." Oh, yes, she understood the danger. To herself, she muttered, "I was so close to escape. As usual, Thronos ruins my plans. My life." She snapped at him, "My EVERYTHING!"

He swung his head around, baring his fangs. "Silence, creature!" His old familiar wrath blistered him inside—the wrath that sometimes made him wonder if he mightn't just kill her and spare himself this misery.

Melanthe is *misery.* He knew this well.

"All my life, I've just wanted to be left alone," she continued. "But you keep hunting me . . ." She trailed off when an eerie green light began to illuminate the shaft. The glow of the ghouls' skin as they neared.

From behind him, she said, "I wish to the gods that I'd never met you."

With all his heart, he told her, "Mutual."

There was no way she and Thronos could get past this throng without a single contagious injury.

Though he was now a battle-tested warlord, attacking hotbeds of Pravus in between his searches for her, he was weaponless, about to fight in his least advantageous surroundings. Lanthe's powers were neutralized; she didn't even have her sword. She splayed her fingers out of habit—to wield sorcery she couldn't tap—and awaited an unstoppable attack.

In these seconds, she swept her gaze over Thronos, as she hadn't been able to do for years.

He had on dark boots and broken-in black leather pants that molded to his muscular legs. His white linen shirt had cutouts in the back—they buttoned above and below the roots of his wings. The humans must have taken his customary trench coat.

She glanced up at his silvery horns. Though many demons had two, Vrekeners usually sported four. But two of Thronos's had been removed—probably because of how damaged they'd been in his "fall." The remaining pair were larger than normal, curving around the sides of his head like those of a Volar demon.

He lowered his hands, his black claws curling past his fingertips. As all the muscles in his body tensed for combat, he brought his wings close to his sides. The top joints were so gnarled, she could almost *hear* their movements catching and grinding.

When he was young, he'd been able to pin his wings down along his back, until they were undetectable under a coat. Now, because of his injuries, those flares jutted by his sides.

His formerly black wing talons had been "silvered" once he'd become a knight—honed, smoothed, and sharpened until they'd turned color.

Few of her kind ever got close enough to a Vrekener to know what those wings truly looked like; well, at least not the Sorceri who'd lived to tell about it. She remembered how startled she'd been to discover what covered the backs—

One bloodcurdling howl sounded from ahead. A ghoul battle charge?

A tidal wave of contagious, vicious killers flooded toward them, their watery yellow eyes burning with rage. They climbed the walls, scrabbling over each other to reach their prey.

The ghouls were fifty feet away. *Forty.*

Thronos's wings rippled, as if with eagerness. Lanthe's last sight on earth might be a Vrekener's wings. *Not a big surprise.*

Thirty feet away. Twenty . . . then . . . striking distance.

One of his wings flashed out, then the other.

Beheaded ghouls dropped in place. More than a dozen gaping necks pumped their blood, a syrupy green goo.

Her lips parted. "What the hell?" The silver talons of Thronos's wings dripped green; they'd sliced through throats like a razor blade.

Like his father's fire scythe.

Eyes wide, she sidled along the wall to get a better look at him. She hadn't known Thronos was that fast—or that his wings were so deadly.

The scent of ghoul blood fouled the air and made the next line of them hesitate. Never ceasing their wails, they stared down at the twitching bodies of their kind, then up at Thronos, confusion on their faces.

When another wave decided to shoot forward, he used his wings again. Goo splashed the walls, striping the fallen bodies. A pool of green seeped toward her and Thronos.

His wings moved so fast she could barely see them, could only feel their backdrafts over her face. Headless bodies piled up, and Lanthe felt . . . hope.

Back when she'd allied with the Pravus Army, Lanthe had observed soldiers sparring—vampires, centaurs, fire demons, and more. They'd always grunted and yelled when they struck. Thronos was eerily silent. One male against a horde of baying monsters.

Gods, he was strong.

Technically he was a demon angel—though Vrekeners vehemently denied any demon blood in their line. Right now, he looked seriously demonic. Watching him like this, she realized that in their confrontations over the last few centuries, Thronos had been pulling his punches.

He might not have wanted to kill his mate, but he could've taken out Lanthe's protector, her sister Sabine. Yet he hadn't. Earlier, Thronos could've killed Carrow without a thought. Instead, he'd spared her life. Why?

As the bodies accumulated and poisonous blood crept toward her boots, Lanthe grew queasy. A quake sent her stumbling against the rock wall. The force shuffled the mound of ghouls, sifting corpses. The sheer number of slain was mind-boggling.

When his next strike felled yet another line of them, no more advanced around the corner. They sounded as if they lay in wait outside the tunnel.

Thronos turned to her, broad chest heaving, his grave face covered in grit and sweat. His collar-length hair was damp, whipping over his cheeks.

She grudgingly admitted that he looked . . . magnificent. For so long, she'd focused on his scars, his weaknesses. She'd underestimated this male.

He grated one word: "Come."

One of Lanthe's favorite mottos was the simplest—*when in trouble, leave.*

Seeing no other choice, she crossed to him. He lifted her into his arms, one looping around her waist, the other coiling around her neck.

Unbidden, memories of her childhood arose, when his expressions had been open, his words kind to her. When he'd nicknamed her and taught her to swim.

He'd been a fascinating mix of cocky and vulnerable; one minute he'd be flashing a teasing grin, the next his cheeks would heat with a blush. . . .

"Hold on to me, Melanthe."

She could only nod and comply.

He booted bodies away, then took off in a limping sprint. She knew what he planned. To evade the ghouls just outside the mine, Thronos would run to the very edge, then leap into flight.

He'd taken her into the sky before—when she'd been a girl who'd trusted him utterly. Years later, she'd witnessed a Vrekener fly Sabine to a great height, just for the pleasure of dropping her to a cobblestone street below.

Sabine's head had cracked open like an egg, but somehow Lanthe's sorcery had wrenched her from the jaws of death.

Ever since then, Lanthe had had nightmares about flying.

Could Thronos even carry her? According to rumor, he suffered inconceivable pain whenever he flew, his twisted wings not working right on the best of days; surely they were exhausted from beheading scores of foes. The left one still bled from Carrow's sword.

Tightening her arms around him, her metal claws digging into his skin, Lanthe squeezed her eyes shut—which only increased her awareness of *him.*

His heartbeat thundering as he ran.

The rippling of his surprisingly large muscles.

His breaths in her ear as he clutched her close, like a coveted treasure.

She had no warning before he shoved his legs down, swooping his great wings. Her stomach dropped when they shot into the sky.

As raindrops hit her uncovered skin like bullets, she peeked down; ghouls leapt for them, but Thronos had flown too high to be reached.

So high. The ground grew smaller . . . smaller . . .

"Ah, gods." *I'm going to vomit.*

THREE

Free of the tunnel!

Thronos sucked in breaths of fresh air as he ascended. At last, they'd emerged from smoke and offal to clean rain and gusting ocean breezes.

Struggling to ignore the agony flying always brought him, he outlined his plan. *Focus: survival, escape, then revenge.*

On the other side of the island, he had the means to leave this place, but reaching that distant coast wouldn't be easy, not with so many bloodthirsty foes in play.

There were winged Volar demons who would attack in the air as a pack. Sorceri could wield their powers from the ground. Even in this rain, fire demons could launch their flames, grenades that seared flesh away like acid. The mortals of the Order would likely send ground reinforcements—or air strikes.

Now Thronos would have to elude any threat, yet already his wings screamed with pain—both old and new. His bones grated on each other like cogs with no notches, the muscles knotted around the joints. He avoided flying whenever possible, but saw no way around it; the ground was a free-for-all.

All across the landscape, Vertas allies lay beheaded or wounded. Cerunnos slithered after fey; vampires took down members of the good demonarchies. The Pravus were wiping them all out.

Just as they had the mortals.

For all his life, Thronos had been a sword for right. But not tonight. No matter how badly he craved to fight alongside his allies, he wouldn't jeopardize his catch.

It struck him again: *By the gods, I* have *her.*

He adjusted his grip, inhaling sharply from the feel of her against him. He hadn't held her since they'd been innocent children. Despite his excruciating pain, his thoughts were anything but innocent.

Most of her curvaceous figure was on display in her shameless Sorceri garb. Aside from her gauntlets, she wore only a metal breastplate and a minuscule skirt configured of mesh and strips of leather. When he'd dragged her through the tunnel, it'd ridden up to reveal a shockingly small black thong and the flawless curves of her ass. . . .

Now the molded cups of her breastplate pressed against him. Her waist and hips were so damned womanly, eliciting lust.

This was the body he should have been enjoying for the last five hundred years. The body that should have given him offspring ten times over. *Wrath welling.*

"Take me down!" she suddenly screeched.

"You want down? I should open my arms—let you feel what it's like to plummet!" *As I learned from you.*

"D-don't drop me!" She was shaking against him. Her claws dug in deeper, tiny hooks in his flesh. More pain to put with the rest of it. "Is that your plan? To torture me before you kill me?"

Kill her? "If I wanted you dead, you would be so."

She lifted her head from his chest. Her rain-dampened face was drawn, her plump bottom lip quivering. Amidst her panic, she seemed to be taking his measure, determining whether he was telling the truth. "But torture's still on the table?"

"Perhaps."

When he sensed an air current and abruptly dipped to catch it, she cried, "Take me to the ground, or I'll vomit!"

Thronos knew she would stop at nothing to get free. But to act as if she would be sick? She used to love it when he took her into the air, would laugh with delight. He'd flown with her often, back when he'd been addicted to the sound of her laughter.

"I can't take this height, Thronos! I swear to gold."

They were only a few hundred feet in the air. Yet her vow to *gold* gave him pause. She would consider it as sacred as a vow made to the Lore.

"Oh, gods." A second later, she heaved, throwing up a concoction of gruel, water, and dirt on his shirt.

A growl sounded from his chest; hers heaved once more.

If his arms hadn't been full, Thronos would have pinched his brow in disbelief. Not only did his fated, eternal mate have no wings, she now suffered from a fear of heights.

Yet another way the wicked sorceress was all wrong for him. In addition to the fact that she despised him as much as he despised her, Melanthe was a light-skirted liar and thief who'd proved malicious to the bone.

But she hadn't always been that way. He remembered her as a sensitive girl—though already mischievous.

He spotted a grassy plateau, high above the ocean. No creatures in sight. He descended, landing without particular care.

When he released Melanthe, her right leg stepped left, then her left leg stepped right. He predicted her fall and readily allowed it. When she landed on her knees, she heaved again.

Exhaling with impatience, he used the time to wipe away her sick from his shirt and check himself for ghoul wounds.

No marks.

From her spot on the ground, Melanthe said, "I thought Vrekeners were supposed to keep the Lore hush-hush from humans. If so, bang-up job you're doing!"

Since memory, Vrekeners had been tasked with stamping out evil in the Lore—and with hiding its existence, punishing anyone who threatened the immortals' secret.

Yet all the while, this human enclave had kept its acquisitive gaze on Loreans.

Getting captured by them had been as easy as Thronos had expected.

Melanthe eyed him. "If all the good immortals still have their collars, why don't you?"

"The better question: How could you possibly have retained yours?"

FOUR

Lanthe swiped the back of her forearm over her mouth. "I wondered that myself."

Earlier, Lanthe, Carrow, Ruby, and two other Sorceri had been whiling away time in their cell, awaiting their turn at vivisection, when suddenly they'd felt a presence; a sorceress of colossal power had descended on this island, La Dorada the Queen of Evil.

That female had liberated all the evil beings, popping their collars off—members of the Pravus like Lanthe's cellmate, Portia the Queen of Stone.

Portia had used her goddesslike control over rock of any kind to raise mountains up through the center of the prison. The force had crushed the thick metal cell walls like tin cans.

Her accomplice, Emberine the Queen of Flames, had lit the place up like an inferno. Immortals had flooded out, overpowering the Order's various defenses.

Then . . . *pande-fucking-monium.*

Humans—and collared Loreans—had been gutted, drained of blood, infected by ghouls or Wendigos, raped to death by succubae, or eaten by any number of creatures.

The Queen of Evil, a freaking fellow Sorceri, had left Lanthe helpless in the midst of that chaos. *Real solidarity there, Dorada.* And yet she'd freed Thronos, a Vrekener? He was a "knight of reckoning," the equivalent of a Lore sheriff.

Lanthe raised her face to the rain, collecting a mouthful to rinse. Then she turned to him. "Maybe you lost your collar because you've become evil over all these centuries."

"Or maybe my mind was filled with evil imaginings." Another flash of his fangs. "You have that effect on me."

Lanthe worked her way to her feet, swaying dizzily. He'd dropped them onto a sliver of land, hundreds of feet above the ground. From this unsettling vantage, she scanned the night. Though a Sorceri's night vision wasn't as acute as most immortals', she could see a good deal of the island, even in the darkness.

Skirmishes were breaking out all over, and the Pravus were dominating. The island teemed with them. She didn't remember this many Pravus in the cells. She'd bet that alliance was teleporting reinforcements here to pick off the helpless, collared Vertas.

Like me. A year ago, she and Sabine had switched sides, helping King Rydstrom the Good reclaim his kingdom of Rothkalina.

Prior to that, the sisters had been all Pravus, all the time. Once Lanthe got free of Thronos, maybe she could try to slide back to her former alliance, at least until Sabine came and saved her.

Her big sister must be worried sick over her weeks-long disappearance. Before leaving their home to hunt for a new boyfriend, Lanthe had left her a note that merely read: *Out getting some strange, XOXO.*

In fact, Lanthe was surprised Sabine hadn't found her by now. She always had in the past. They'd never been separated for this long—

Her eyes widened. From this height, she'd spied Carrow, Ruby, and Carrow's new vemon husband, Malkom Slaine. Though that vampire/demon was one of the deadliest, most fearsome beings in the Lore, he appeared to be shepherding them to safety.

Guess he decided against killing Carrow.

Lanthe's heart leapt to see them safe, and she drew a breath to call for them, but Thronos slapped his calloused hand over her mouth.

She kicked back with her boots, struggling against him; he held her with minimal effort. He waited until Carrow was out of earshot before releasing Lanthe.

"They're going to worry about me!" She strained to keep them in sight.

"Good. If the witch is foolish enough to care about someone like you, she deserves woe."

Someone like me. "Speaking from experience?" She whirled around on him, eye level with his chest. The wet linen of his shirt clung to his muscles, draping over his pecs, showing hints of the scars beneath.

Why haven't I ever noticed his muscles are so defined? Probably because each time she'd seen him, she'd been running for her life.

She craned her head up to peer at his face, at the raised scars there. *All caused by me.* A deep one twisted along his chiseled jawline, while four shorter ones slashed diagonally down his cheeks, like Celtic war paint.

Once a body became immortal, it was unchangeable for the most part. Though a Lorean like him could buy a glamour from the witches to camouflage those marks, he would always have them.

Despite his scars, females would still find him handsome. Very much so.

"What are you looking at?" he snapped, seeming disturbed by the perusal. But then, he seemed disturbed in general.

"My lifetime enemy." She'd spent that long constantly fleeing Vrekeners. Now she was trapped with the object of her fears. Not exactly helping her Vrekener PTSD.

But she'd escape sooner or later; she always did.

And then he'd just come after her again, as *he* always did. "Well, you've got me, Thronos. Now what happens?"

She thought she saw a flicker of shock in his eyes, as if he could barely accept his success after so long.

"Now I'm going to get us off this island."

"How? It's thousands of miles from land, surrounded by shark-infested waters." The humans had been prepared to prevent escape. Well, prepared for everything *except* a really piqued La Dorada. "You can't fly that distance."

Though he'd tried to hide it, she'd seen his pain from just a short jaunt—his face had grown drawn and waxen, his lips a thin line.

Considering that others of his kind could fly hundreds, if not thousands, of miles at a time, she wondered what his limit was. "Especially not with me in tow."

He looked like he was biting down rage—as if just the sound of her voice was setting him off. "I have other means of escape."

"Uh-huh. Listen, there's a key to my torque down there." Of sorts.

Each collar was locked and unlocked with the thumbprint of the warden, a troll named Fegley (not *literally* a troll). When Lanthe and company had stumbled across the trapped warden, Lanthe had cut off his hand for ease of use. But before Lanthe could free herself, Emberine had stolen the grubby thing and incinerated the rest of Fegley!

Which had forced Lanthe and her friends to hit the tunnels. . . .

"If you help me get this collar off," she told Thronos, "I could create a portal to wherever you want." Or she could command him to repeatedly stab himself in the dick. Then she'd run away as fast as she could manage—seeing as she would be laughing really hard.

This was assuming her sporadic persuasion worked, but she was hopeful; after all, she'd been storing up a lot of it over the last three weeks.

Thronos pinned her gaze with his own frenzied one. "You'll wear that collar for the rest of your immortal life. That you retain it is a stroke of fortune."

She knew he was serious. Which meant she had to get away from him and find that hand. "You always wanted me biddable, didn't you? Like Vrekener females?" Lanthe had heard they never laughed, drank, danced, or sang, and always wore drab, full-coverage clothing.

A world away from merry, hedonistic Sorceri females with their racy metal garments, brightly colored masks, and bold makeup.

And, horror of horrors—Vrekeners disdained the wearing of gold.

For a gold-worshipping sorceress like Lanthe, this was blasphemy. "You always wished I'd been born meek and powerless."

"You might as well have been powerless. Over these centuries, you could hardly use your abilities—even without the collar."

Burn. Worse, he was right. Though persuasion was her root power—the one she'd been born with, akin to her soul—she'd almost extinguished it by healing her sister from repeated Vrekener attacks.

Each time the winged menace found them, Sabine would charge into danger. Each time, Lanthe would clean up the damage, commanding Sabine's body to mend itself.

Lanthe's ruined power was well-known. While Sorceri had stolen other abilities from her, there'd been no takers on her defective soul.

"Look at your glittering eyes. Sensitive about this, creature?"

She reminded herself that she had managed a few spurts of persuasion in emergency situations. On one night, the stars had aligned, and she'd rendered Omort—a nearly omnipotent sorcerer—temporarily powerless.

Long enough for the demon King Rydstrom the Good to fight and kill him. Without Lanthe's help, Rydstrom never could have freed all the rage demons of Rothkalina from Omort's oppression.

How badly she wished for everyone in the Lore to know about that! Then they'd respect her.

She narrowed her eyes, recalling another time she'd conjured persuasion. "I used my sorcery *on you* the last time we met."

Thronos clearly didn't like to be reminded of that. A year ago, he'd set a trap around one of her portals, lying in wait for her to return. When she'd come upon him and his knights, she'd eked out some sorcery—enough for her to get through the portal.

"If you recall, I resisted your commands!"

Just as she'd been sealing it, he'd managed to shove his boot through the door. Alas, the portal closure had *severed his foot.*

Because of him she'd failed to rescue her sister from a perilous situation, so naturally Lanthe had kicked his foot around her room, screaming at it.

She slitted her eyes up at him. "I vow to you I'll get this collar off me, and when I do, I'll demonstrate how powerful I've gotten!" The rain continued to pour; ghouls howled below. But Lanthe was too pissed to pay them any mind; she had eons of pain to vent. "I'll command you to forget I ever lived!"

A muscle ticked in his clenched jaw, and those slashing scars on his cheeks whitened. "Never!"

"Why not, *demon*? Every day I wish I'd never been in that meadow when you flew over."

He unfurled his wings to their terrifying full length, a span of over fifteen feet. "I'm no *demon*."

"Uh-huh." *You keep telling yourself that.* He looked to say more, so she cut him off. "Even if you manage to get me off this island, you can't just keep me. I have friends who will come for me." King Rydstrom—now Lanthe's brother-in-law—was ferocious about Sabine's and Lanthe's protection, vowing to slay anyone who thought to harm either sister.

He understood that without Lanthe, his beloved wife Sabine wouldn't have survived all those years, and he felt indebted to her. But Rydstrom and Sabine didn't know the truth: Lanthe had caused the Vrekeners to descend on them in the first place—because she'd stupidly befriended Thronos, a fact that she'd never revealed to her sister.

"And what friends would those be?" Thronos grated.

"Perhaps you've heard of my brother-in-law Rydstrom, the ruler of Rothkalina, master of Castle Tornin?"

Rydstrom had alerted the king of the Air Territories—Thronos's brother—of his protection. Any plot to harm either of the sisters would be considered an act of war against all rage demons. "Rydstrom is my protector."

"I have no fear of him. Just as I had no fear of your previous protector. *Omort the Deathless.*"

She could only imagine what Thronos had heard about Omort. Once he'd stolen Rydstrom's crown, Omort had instituted a reign of terror in

Rothkalina. Though she and Sabine had resided with their brother—*half* brother—in the seized Castle Tornin, that didn't mean they'd shared Omort's sickening behavior.

They would've escaped, but he'd had lethal controls in place, forever forcing them to return to him.

She remembered telling Sabine, "I'll scream if he beheads another oracle." He'd butchered hundreds of them, peeling their heads from their necks with his bare hands.

"What can we do?" Sabine had said, sounding as blasé as ever. "Take it up with management?"

Anyone who contradicted Omort was slaughtered. Or worse.

Lanthe had a brief impulse to explain to Thronos what things had really been like with Omort. To explain that she'd lived in Castle Tornin under two kings—and now thanked gold for her new life under Rydstrom's reign. But then she recalled that she wouldn't be around Thronos long enough to waste the effort. Not that the Vrekener would believe her anyway.

So she returned to intimidation. "If you don't fear Rydstrom, then maybe you'll fear Nïx the Ever-Knowing." The three-thousand-year-old Valkyrie was a soothsayer, rumored to be on her way toward full-blown goddesshood. Though Nïx was insane—seeing the future and past more clearly than the present—she was steering the entire freaking Accession, that great immortal killing time.

"Nïx, then?" he scoffed.

Okay, so maybe she and Lanthe weren't tight, *per se* (they'd scarcely spoken). But Nïx had been in on the plot to kill Omort, had aided Sabine, Lanthe, and Rydstrom. Rydstrom considered her a good friend. "Yes, the Valkyrie is one of my best friends."

"With so much practice, sorceress, I thought you'd be more skilled at deception." He drew his lips back from his fangs. "Who do you think told me how to find you?"

Lanthe rocked on her feet—either from shock or because the ground was moving again. "She wouldn't." Lanthe should've known better than to trust a Valkyrie!

"She would and she did. Along with some advice concerning you."

"Tell me."

His answer: a smirk.

"Then you did let yourself get caught by the Order?" He had to have—how else could mortals have captured a male who could fly?

But then, how the hell had they taken half of these beings? She'd probably been their easiest catch. When Lanthe had left Tornin, heading to the mortal realm to find a lover after her long sex drought, a woman on the street had offered her discount gold; Lanthe had followed like a slavering dog—right into a trap.

"That's a big risk, based on a mad Valkyrie's word," Lanthe said.

He raked his gaze over her. "My reward is commensurate. As will be my revenge."

Squeezing her temples, Lanthe began to pace the small expanse of land, steering clear of the edges, while keeping away from Thronos's imposing presence. She'd spent ages bolting at the sight of him; now this proximity was messing with her mind.

Unrelenting Vrekener attacks had affected Lanthe and Sabine in different ways. While Sabine had been left deadened to fear, Lanthe had grown chronically nervous, always expecting another surprise strike. Now her every instinct for survival was on high alert just from his nearness—

The plateau suddenly split open like halves of a log chopped in two. She screamed as a gorge yawned between her and Thronos.

When the motion stilled and she could clear her vision, she saw they were on opposite sides of a brand-new chasm.

Those rising mountains were making all the earth around them shed away, like chunks from glaciers. "You're going to get me killed up here!" she yelled, but Thronos was already in flight.

The ground disappeared beneath her feet; before she could fall, he snatched her close as he took to the air once more.

"Ah, gods. This is happening. This is actually *happening*." She buried her face against his chest. *I hate this, I hate this. . . .*

"Your fear of flying inconveniences me. When did this develop, sorceress?"

"When one of your knights took Sabine high into the air—then *dropped* her. She was fourteen." At the memory of Sabine's head exploding, Lanthe heaved again.

"What lies are you telling now? No Vrekeners attacked your sister."

She fell silent. Was *he* lying? Or did he truly not know his knights had hunted her and Sabine? As prince of the Air Territories, Thronos was the Lord General of Knights, in command of their staunchest warriors.

Did some of those men have their own secret agenda?

If Thronos forced her back to his home of Skye Hall, then what was to stop those knights from pitching her over the side?

When he slowed, she cried against his shirt, "Yes, not so fast!"

He turned in place, inhaling sharply.

Curiosity demanded that Lanthe raise her head. "Oh, my gold."

That new mountain jutted from the center of the prison, sloughing off the structures. Each chunk of concrete that fell was swept up to circle the peak like a tornado. Portia's work. How much she must be enjoying this!

Ember's towering flames wreathed the entire thing. The sorceress's fires burned so strong, they grew in the rain, heating the drops to steam.

They were two of the most powerful Sorceri ever born. Their abilities were in a league even with Sabine's illusions.

Part of Lanthe couldn't help but marvel, as she might at a work of art.

"Offendments," Thronos hissed near her ear. The Vrekener word for wrongdoing. "This is the work of your people. Your . . . ilk. And you wonder why Vrekeners were entrusted to battle the Sorceri?"

The mortals' former prison was now a picture of hell.

Thronos didn't regret the defeat of the Order—he'd found these humans contemptible—but now a greater evil reigned. As he watched the flames climb higher, the show of Sorceri might called to him.

To vanquish it.

For now, their actions would serve as a timely reminder of what he was dealing with. Melanthe's sorcery wasn't awing, but hers was more insidious. Everything about her was. Already she was trying to sow dissension, lying about Vrekener attacks.

He turned away from the spectacle and swept forward, gritting his teeth against the pain.

"I hate this, I hate this, I hate this," she chanted, her face tucked back against his chest.

He hated it too. The only Vrekener in history who despised flying—and it was because of his own mate.

During those four childhood months he'd spent with Melanthe, he'd once encountered a crazed sorceress who'd told him, "Melanthe will never be what you need her to be."

At the time, Thronos had thought that he and Melanthe would prove her and everyone else wrong.

How naïve he'd been.

His mate couldn't be more unsuitable for him. In addition to all their history—and all her offendments—Melanthe was a Sorceri, a species that confounded him with their counterintuitive ways.

They covered up their faces with masks, calling it ornamentation—instead of concealment. They didn't trust their own kind, had no unity. They loved to revel with other Loreans, but if they possessed something of value, they would hole up in faraway keeps like hibernating dragons. They could be brave when facing a violent enemy, yet debilitated by their fear of losing one of their precious powers.

Though Melanthe's sinister persuasion wasn't lost, it was *contained*—a step in the right direction.

She wanted that torque off? It would ring her neck for eternity!

"Where are we going now?" She was no longer shaking. Her body *shuddered* in his arms.

He forecasted more sorceress vomit directly. "I told you. I have means to leave the island."

Thronos had information others didn't. His cell in the prison had been near a guard station, and he'd heard them talking about the Order's escape plans in case of an emergency.

There were rumors of a ship on the far side of the island.

All the members of the Order were dead. No mortal would've lived to take Thronos's ship. And even if other Loreans happened to hear of it, they wouldn't be able to cross the mountainous terrain of the inner island before he could.

He didn't expect the berth to be visible from the air—the Order had been clever with cloaking their structures—but Thronos would be able to scent the craft's engines. Once the rain stopped pouring.

He would use the vessel to get himself and Melanthe close enough for him to fly back to the Skye. There, when he was thinking more clearly, he would decide her fate.

She'd asked if he planned to kill her. Never. But that didn't mean he should honor her by making her his wife and princess.

Maybe if he could eventually teach her right from wrong, he would use her—his mate and therefore his sole option—to continue his line. He felt a duty to reproduce since his family had been winnowed down. Even now, he was his brother King Aristo's heir.

But that would mean Thronos would have to marry Melanthe first. He couldn't even explore her body until then. The mere kiss he'd taken from her was an offendment.

He peered down at her in his arms. How could he wed her after everything he'd heard about her? When he didn't know the extent of her involvement in the atrocities under Omort's reign?

He remembered Aristo telling him centuries ago, "Your mate and her sister have allied with their brother Omort the Deathless, leader of the Pravus. Reports filter out from their hold. Thronos, what their family is doing . . . it's beyond appalling."

Incest, blood orgies, child sacrifices.

Melanthe—the sister of Omort and possibly his concubine—mother to my offspring?

WRATH. He felt like he was drowning in it. Engulfed in it.

"You're hurting me!"

He found his claws digging into her. He didn't loosen his grip.

"What are you thinking of to make you so enraged?"

He clenched his jaw, unable even to speak. He listened to her heartbeat, focusing on it. *Get control, Talos.* Early in his life he'd seen the tragedies even a brief loss of control could wreak.

Glass shards like fangs flaying my skin. He gave his head a hard shake, increasing his speed.

In a softer voice, Melanthe said, "Nïx wouldn't have sold me out if she'd known you were going to hurt me."

Debatable. He'd met the Valkyrie a year ago in the mortal city of New Orleans, when he was still regenerating the foot he'd lost because of Melanthe. Nïx hadn't seemed to be tracking reality when she'd told Thronos where to be to get captured—and when to be there, just a week ago. All those months spent waiting since then had been punishing.

"What did that Valkyrie tell you about me?" Melanthe asked. "What was her advice?"

It'd been one cryptic sentence: *Before Melanthe became this, she was that. . . .*

The female would say nothing more, no matter how much he'd pressed. "She mentioned nothing about my treatment of you," he grated as the pain in his wings intensified steadily.

With the pain came equal parts wrath.

Because of the creature in his arms, he'd had lifetimes of both.

FIVE

Numbed to the drizzle and cold, Lanthe was lulled into a kind of exhausted stupor as the flight went on and on and on. When they'd crossed over an expansive forest, the noises of the battles grew dimmer.

She dared a glance back, could still see bursts of spectral light. Soon that melee would spread outward all over the entire island. Thronos had to know that.

His face was tensely set—as if he were concentrating on blocking out his pain. There'd be no talking. *Think about something else, Lanthe. Anything else.*

Yet now that she was his captive (temporarily), she found her mind mired in thoughts of him. A memory arose of their first day together, when he'd tried to feed her—his idea of courting.

Unfortunately, he hadn't known she was a vegetarian.

"For you." Thronos proudly dropped a carcass of bloody meat at her feet.

She burst into tears.

"Why do you cry?" Despite all his confidence, he looked confounded—and pained, as if her tears tormented him. "You don't like my gift?"

"Th-that was my bunny!" One of the woodland creatures that she called friend.

"It's decent meat. And you're starving."

Her face heated. "I am not!"

"Are too. You were scrounging for twigs, lamb."

"They're b-berries! I like to eat berries."

The next morning, when curiosity had driven her back to the meadow, she'd found it littered with piles of berries. Thronos had been standing among them, with his fingers stained, his chin up, and that cocky look back on his face. Delighted, she'd leaned up and pecked his lips. His wings had snapped open, a reaction that had seemed to embarrass him.

After that rocky start, they'd grown to be best friends, just as he'd promised.

Later on, he'd asked her why her parents didn't buy food. She couldn't make him understand that her mother and father worshipped gold more than anything it could purchase. Not to mention that they'd deemed Lanthe old enough to begin stealing her own way through life—

Thronos's grip was loosening in midair! "Wait!" she cried.

But he'd only repositioned her in the cradle of his arms. Apparently he was adjusting her for the duration—and wasn't about to dump her like an armful of firewood. After a moment she relaxed slightly.

Though she had recurring nightmares about Vrekeners sweeping down on her, she was now trapped directly under a pair of wings. Talk about immersion therapy.

She stared up at them, spread in flight, wind whistling through his healing sword wound. As a girl, she'd been obsessed with his wings, touching them all the time.

She'd been fascinated to discover the backs were covered with scales like those of a dragon. As if in a mosaic, Thronos's black and silver scales had made slashing designs that resembled sharp feathers.

During the day, the undersides were dark gray. At night, they turned black, stark against the electrical pathways that forked out along the bones. Each of those pulselines shone as bright as phosphorescence.

One night when they'd secretly met, he'd spread his wings, showing her how the pulselines moved. It'd looked like he'd been surrounded by lightning wings. He'd demonstrated how he could use tricks of light to camouflage his wings so they'd be invisible in the dark.

When he'd grown embarrassed by her wide-eyed stare, those pulselines had quickened, like a blush.

"I never knew these were scales instead of feathers," she told him. "I guess none of my kind have gotten a good look at the backs of Vrekener wings."

He appeared troubled. "That's because no Vrekeners ever retreat from Sorceri."

Now Thronos's wings were contorted in places. She'd always imagined the bones had been set badly, but up close, she could see that they'd mended true, in strong straight lines. Maybe the muscles had bunched, growing off-kilter?

Biting her bottom lip, she dared to reach up and touch a pulseline. Its beat accelerated, and his grip tightened on her.

The first time she'd ever voluntarily touched him as an adult.

When he cast her a killing glance, he again resembled a reaper, every inch a "righteous reckoning." His silvered talons glinted, as ominous as a sword blade. "Why did you do that?" he demanded.

"You used to like me to touch them."

Voice brusque, he said, "You assume I remember that far back?"

What if he didn't? His mind might have been injured. For some reason, the idea of that made her chest ache. She remembered every second of those four months. Regardless of their history, she found herself thinking of them—of him—far too often.

As they gained altitude to crest another mountain, her ears popped. Rain fell even harder, drops pelting her, winds buffeting them. She heard crashing waves. They'd reached the far coastline? She blinked against the rain, saw he was following the shore north. Or south. Who knew with her wretched directional skills?

He looked as if he were trying to scent something. He flew them to a point, hovered, then returned down the coast, flying farther in the opposite direction. Again he repeated his pattern, clearly growing more frustrated.

"Even if your senses are as keen as a Lykae's, you can't scent through pouring rain."

"Silence." He dove to circle a tree at the very edge of the storm-tossed peak.

The tree swayed in the winds, the top like the deck of a pitching ship. Yet the bastard tossed her onto a thrashing limb! She clawed her gauntlets across the wood, scrabbling for a hold.

If she fell, she'd tumble down the mountain, her body dashed to pieces. Apparently he'd forgotten how susceptible to injury Sorceri were!

Or maybe he hadn't forgotten.

Once she'd steadied herself, she eased around to crawl along the limb, the wood slick beneath her hands and knees. Kneeling before the trunk, she stabbed her gauntlet claws into it, then peered up, blinking against the downpour. No leaves screened her from the gale. Above, bare limbs spread out like veins, as if they were stretching for the sky's arteries of lightning.

Thronos stood at the very top, easily balanced, rising to his full height to ride the movement. A hand shielded his gaze from the horizontal rain.

As she put out a prayer to the gods that he got struck up there, her teeth began chattering. She soon shook until her head bobbed, and not just because of her fear of heights. She hadn't had more than an hour or two of sleep at a time for three weeks, and had rarely eaten the gruel they'd been served.

Right now, she should be tucked in bed in her warm tower at Tornin, watching DVDs on her solar-powered TV and enjoying sumptuous foods and sweet Sorceri wine—while waited on hand and foot. Instead, she was trapped with her worst nightmare, strangling with the need to kill him.

A burst of hysterical laughter left her lips. *Lanthe and Thronos, sitting in a tree, k-i-l-l-i-n-g. . . .*

Damn it, why the hell hadn't Sabine found her? Maybe the double-dealing Nïx had steered her wrong—while giving Thronos detailed directions to find Lanthe.

If Sabine found out he had her sister, she would unleash hell.

That night so long ago, when Thronos had led others to the abbey, Sabine had noted the way he'd stared at Lanthe: "The young Vrekener looked at you with absolute yearning. His people must have somehow discovered you are his fated mate. They attacked our family to secure you for the hawkling's future, to groom you. To *break* you. As they do with so many other Sorceri children."

Which Lanthe had supposed was true. But she'd remained silent, and to this day, Sabine had no idea of her sister's connection to Thronos.

What was he planning for Lanthe once he'd gotten her off the island? Did he expect to have sex with her? She recalled the way he'd kissed her in the mine.

Oh, yeah. He expected it.

She heard a swoop of wings as he returned to stand behind her. She chanced a look over her shoulder, hating how he was totally in his element. As the tempest raged all around them, flashes of lightning illuminated his horns, wings, and fangs.

A true demon.

She remembered calling him one when they were young. He'd been horror-struck, hadn't come back to the meadow for three days. Later she'd realized he'd flown home with the question: "Mom, Dad, am I a demon?"

When he'd finally returned to Lanthe, he'd been quick to present all the information he'd gathered about how Vrekeners were completely, utterly, without a doubt different from savage demons.

Vrekeners couldn't teleport like demons, their eyes didn't grow black with emotion, and males didn't mark their females upon claiming. While demon horns had a function in that species' mating rituals (Thronos had blushed at that), Vrekener horns were only for menacing show, to terrify wrongdoers. Their wings were for swift capture of prey, to stamp out evil as quickly as possible—because evil could spread.

She'd rested her chin in her hand and asked in a saucy tone, "And your fangs? Do they stamp out evil too?" He'd looked troubled for the rest of the day. . . .

Seeing him in this lightning, his species was plain to her—just as it was to many others in the Lore. When Loreans called Vrekeners *demonic angels,* it wasn't because they *resembled* demons.

She recalled Sabine and Rydstrom debating Vrekener origins. Rydstrom had said, "They are sanctimonious, maniacal, and deluded. My kind claims no affinity with theirs."

Now Lanthe blinked, and Thronos was gone. As thunder rocked the night, he moved from limb to limb, an eerie predator. He alighted on one above her. From there he could have spread his wings, blocking the worst of the storm for her, but he was content to watch her suffer.

She couldn't remember the last time she'd felt this helpless, this powerless. The key to her collar was on the other side of the island. Thronos had separated her from her only shot at getting this thing off her neck. Not that she could simply walk up to Emberine and Portia and ask for it back. But Lanthe could've planned a sneak attack, *anything.*

Her portal power sure would come in handy right now.

He moved to a nearby limb, hanging from his arms to bring their faces inches apart. "I told you that I'd have you soon."

"You also told me you knew a way off this island. But you can't find it, can you?"

"We'll reach it in the morn."

"Uh-huh." *Bully for us.* When she turned away, he vaulted to the other side, leaning in once more.

"In the tunnel, you let go of the witch's hand so she could protect her young. Why would someone like you be moved to help her?"

Again with the *someone like you*? "Why should I tell you anything? You won't believe a word I say."

"Lies do spill so readily from those red lips. But I learn much from the very untruths you speak."

She dared to loosen one gauntlet to give him a vulgar hand gesture. "Learn *this,* demon."

Between gritted teeth, he said, "Call me that again, harlot."

She detested that word! With all the countless immortal and mortal languages, why was there no male equivalent?

A gust of wind drilled rain against her, sending her into a fit of coughing.

His voice a harsh grate, he said, "A male shouldn't be heartened to see his mate's misery. But this pleases me well."

"Mate? I'll die first."

He brought one of his wings closer to her, easing that talon to her face. The silver length was rounded, smooth as ivory on the outside of the curve—but she'd witnessed how sharp the tip was.

"I could have killed you so easily, so many times." He ran the back of the talon across her throat, letting the threat hang between them.

"Instead, you sent your knights to do it!"

"These lies again?"

Did Lanthe ever lie? Of course. In the noble pursuit of gold, she pulled out all the stops. She also lied to avoid trouble. Those outside her new family might get an earful now and again. But few things irritated her more than disbelief when she was actually telling the truth.

"You foul Sorceri pride yourselves on falsehoods!"

Foul Sorceri . . . Someone like you. "I'm so sick of you! You'd think after five hundred years that you could take a hint. I will never want you like you want me!"

"WANT?" His claw-tipped hand slashed the tree, his fury bubbling over—as if she'd hit an exposed nerve. "Do not ever mistake my interest in you! Fate has saddled me with you, cursing me with a female I find lacking in all ways!" His voice continued rising with every word. "Instinct compels me to pursue you, to protect you. Otherwise I'd take your head myself! I want you like a man with a badly set limb wants his bone rebroken. It's a bitter necessity. *You* are the bitterest necessity."

His words didn't hurt Lanthe. She'd been scorned by men before. Why would she care what a scarred, maddened Vrekener thought of her?

She didn't care at all. He mattered not at all.

When she just blinked up at him, he seemed to rein in his fury. "What either of us *wants* is immaterial. I've taken you because that's what fate decreed. You're mine by the laws of the Lore, the laws I uphold."

"And you always follow the laws? You act like Vrekeners are so righteous? I've seen more evil in your kind than in most Sorceri I've met."

"Now I know you lie! You resided with Omort!"

With each Accession, a warrior for ultimate good, or ultimate evil, was born. Lanthe's half brother had been that warrior a few Accessions ago, bringing evil to the Lore for centuries. After her mother, Elisabet, had given birth to him, she'd been cast out in shame by the noble family of Deie Sorceri. By the time Lanthe and Sabine's father had come into the picture, Elisabet had been . . . troubled.

This Accession, twin girls had been born for ultimate good, daughters of Rydstrom's brother, Cadeon, and Cadeon's Valkyrie wife, Holly. Lanthe was a doting auntie to them.

"You remained with Omort," Thronos grated, "during his reign of child sacrifices, orgies, and incest."

Omort had hosted orgies and made a willing concubine of his half sister Hettiah, who'd died the same day he had. Toward the end of his reign, when Omort had demanded sacrifices, he'd yelled, "Something *young*!"

Until that one fantastical day when Lanthe had challenged Omort, she'd been helpless to stop him. She would be haunted forever by the things she'd seen him do. *Take it up with management.*

"I did remain with him," Lanthe admitted. "For ages."

"Then what evils do you think Vrekeners have perpetrated to measure up to that fiend's?"

"Torture, murder, thievery. Even you know your kind steals Sorceri powers." The fire scythe his father had wielded wasn't good only for parent beheadings; it also drained powers from its victims, a process Sorceri derisively termed *neutering.*

It was rumored that some "benevolent" Vrekener had ordered the knights to siphon sorcery, *instead* of taking lives. Yet in the last century, the knights had begun doing *both*—so that those abilities could never be reincarnated. . . .

"We harvest and store them, preventing them from being used for evil."

"To us, a root power is like a soul. You're stealing souls!"

"Sorceri steal each other's powers, like cannibals feeding! How many have *you* stolen?"

She didn't answer, was guilty as charged. She'd had no choice, since hers kept getting poached by smooth-talking Sorceri males. How many times had she fallen for one's seduction, only to discover he'd used sex to lower her guard?

But she never stole from decent-minded Sorceri, the ones who only wanted to be left alone to drink, fornicate, gamble, and worship any gold they'd swindled, swiped, or conjured.

"Yet you had to steal, didn't you?" Thronos bit out. Fat drops of rain pummeled them, batting against his wings. "Since yours were continually robbed?"

She hadn't known he was aware of that. No one would want her worst enemy to know she'd been a dupe.

"Was that how you got caught by the mortals?" He canted his head in that foreboding way. "Were you away from Rothkalina seeking another power?"

"I don't think you really want to know the answer to that question."

"Tell me, or I'll toss you down the mountain myself." He reached forward, his fingers making a cage over her throat, his expression promising pain.

He was a monster, a world away from the boy he'd been when he fed her and held her—and she'd sighed words she could never take back.

Oh, well, he'd asked for it. "I was seeking something else entirely. After losing a wager with my sister, I had to go without sex for a year. I was on the hunt for a new lover when I got nabbed."

He gave a curt yell, lifting her by her jaw. She dug her gauntlets into his forearms, but he didn't seem to feel them. "Wh-what are you doing?"

In the bobbing tree, he held her body aloft, so her gaze was level with his.

Mother of gold, he *was* going to toss her! She couldn't stifle a whimper of fear.

His head rushed toward her body. She braced for a vicious strike of his horns. Instead of hitting her, he rubbed the base of one over her shoulder and neck, marking her with his scent.

As if by doing so, he could pry her out of some faceless male's arms.

The behavior was blatantly demonic.

When he finally pulled back, his eyes gleamed with rage. "You crippled me. For centuries, you cuckolded me over and over again. The pain you gave me in the past wasn't enough for you? You wish to deliver more?"

Right now? Desperately! She wanted to claw his eyes out, to rake her gauntlets down his scarred face! "Because you deserve it!"

He flung her back down to the limb. "Look what you wrought, Melanthe!"

As she scrambled toward the trunk, he ripped open the front of his shirt, revealing scars she hadn't seen before, marks jagging along his rigid torso. He pounded a fist over the center of his chest, over the raised scar there. "Does this one look like it was deep? Half an inch closer, and it would have pierced my heart!"

She blinked against the rain, against tears that seemed determined to fall. But not out of pity, out of impotent fury.

"Every second I fly is hellish! Because of you!"

"I'd do it all over again!"

He threw back his head and gave a roar up to the lightning-strewn sky. When he leveled his gaze on her, she shrank under the savagery she saw there. "Gods damn you, sorceress! You have no reason to hate me as I do you!"

"No reason?" she sputtered. "Do you know what it's like to feel panic whenever a cloud passes over the sun? To hunch down, gasping for breath, pulse racing? You and your scarred face are the star of every nightmare I've ever had!"

Melanthe's eyes blazed with hostility. He stared into them as lightning reflected across those blue depths.

He was his mate's bogeyman? Fitting.

She was his bane.

Melanthe is *misery*. He shook his head hard, ignoring the weird ache in his horns, preventing himself from rubbing them over her again. He could barely reason, his thoughts a snarl in his mind.

Control. If he couldn't maintain it, then she would wind up dead. Which would end his plans for continuing his line.

Without that, and without the chase, what reason would he have to live?

Lose control, lose your mate.

Yet keeping her alive didn't mean he had to prevent her suffering. So why had he experienced the impulse to shelter her with his body? He needed to remind himself of all he'd lost. Of all his agony.

He'd implied to her that he didn't remember their childhood time together. In fact, he recalled every moment with a blistering, crystal clarity. Earlier, when she'd stroked his wing with her eyes full of wonder, it'd brought him right back to the first time she'd touched him. . . .

Biting her bottom lip, she tentatively reached in, tracing a pulseline. His wings had flared uncontrollably, embarrassing him, making the back of his neck heat.

"There," she murmured with a grin. "You're not so scary, then. What's it like to fly?"

He took her hand. "I could show you."

And Thronos remembered those agonizing days after his fall, when he'd fought not to succumb to his injuries. He'd heard his mother's voice saying, *"Don't you understand what she's done to you?" He must have been calling for Melanthe. "What her kind have taken from us? Your father is gone." Then, lower: "And so too will I be."*

He remembered attempting to fly once more; his atrophied wings had been unable to support him. The humiliation had burned worse than the unbearable pain. He'd ignored the whispers when his people had dubbed him their "tragic prince," forever cursed to desire the wicked sorceress who'd nearly murdered him.

He'd told himself it would all be worth it—once he had Melanthe again.

Bile rose in his throat as he remembered seeing her as a woman for the first time. He shook away the memory—*lest I murder her.*

For centuries, he'd vowed *she* would be worth all his pain. He craned his head up at the trunk of this tree.

Never forget. . . .

SIX

Lanthe woke to the feel of her stomach lurching as her body tumbled from the tree.

She unleashed a scream, fumbling to latch onto a limb; her arms wouldn't respond, filled with pins and needles. Falling! The drizzly fog was so dense she couldn't see what was below her—

She landed with an *oomph*.

Thronos had caught her in his arms. Breathless, she stared up at him as his wings held them aloft.

After the freezing night she'd just spent in the tree, his body was a hot haven. Warmth from his damp chest seeped into her, dulling some of her alarm.

Yesterday she would've sworn she could never sleep with a Vrekener nearby. But apparently, she'd been out.

As rain softly fell, his gaze roamed over her, and when his eyes began to glow with something other than rage, she swallowed. Though she was loath to admit it, chemistry sparked between them.

She might be the bitterest necessity, but his instincts were doubtless screaming inside him, commanding him on a loop: *MATE FEMALE!*

Which was never going to happen. A: She didn't do males she hated.

Just a rule she had. And B? She was in the fertile time of her infrequent Sorceri cycle, could all but *look* at seed and get knocked up.

She had to trust that he wouldn't force her. She wished she could probe his thoughts, reading his mind, but her collar prevented it. He'd probably developed mental blocks anyway. . . .

Her gaze was drawn behind him, and her lips parted.

While she'd dozed, he'd clawed slashes into the tree. The marks were all around the same size, lined up and patterned along the trunk.

She'd bet there were roughly five hundred slashes, one for every year he'd gone without his mate. "You're insane," she whispered. She'd been around enough crazed males to last an immortal lifetime. She gazed up at this one with wary eyes.

She recalled the things she'd told him last night—*I'd do it again!* Maybe she oughtn't to poke the bear so much.

Yet even as he drew his lips back from his fangs, he seemed less frenzied today; still simmering, but perhaps the night had been cathartic for him. "You're one to speak of insanity, when your line is tainted with it."

Had he found out about her mother, Elisabet? Or just assumed this because Omort came from Lanthe's family? She averted her gaze. "I don't know what you're talking about."

"Untruth," he grated. "Tell me another, and I'll throttle you." He shot into the sky.

"Where are you taking me?"

He headed north away from the coast back toward the island's interior. Or maybe he headed south. East?

He didn't answer her question, asking one of his own: "If you believed yourself to be targeted by Vrekeners, why not communicate with me in our few encounters?" He sounded almost normal.

"You always looked murderous. I couldn't be sure that you weren't on board with their plan to out and out kill me."

"On board to murder my fated *mate*?" he said, as if she'd spoken nonsense.

"So you're saying you had no idea that we were targeted?"

"I know what you're trying to do, and your divisive tactics won't work. I sought—and received—the sacred word of Vrekener knights that they would visit no harm upon you or your sister. I will always believe that over the accusations of someone like you."

"You made them vow that?"

"I knew well that Sabine's death would destroy you. I wanted revenge against you, not against a broken shell of a mate."

Though this was surprising to Lanthe, it didn't change their situation today. "It happened, Thronos. Whether you want to believe me or not."

"You sound like *you* believe what you're saying. No doubt, typical Sorceri paranoia. Your kind are notorious for it. You probably mistook a Volar demon for a Vrekener."

"That's the other reason I never tried to communicate with you—I knew you'd never believe me."

On edge, Thronos didn't reply. He just scented other immortals. They must have overrun even this farthest edge of the island.

Earlier, when he'd finally picked up the vessel's scent, he'd begun cutting across a forest to reach it, which was proving to be more of a risk than he'd expected.

He needed to concentrate on their escape, but now that he was thinking more clearly, he couldn't stop replaying Melanthe's words from the night before. Why would *he* be her nightmare all these years? Why would she fear when a cloud crossed the sun?

Unless she'd actually been attacked.

"Why did you say that about my line?" she asked. "Being tainted?"

Melanthe didn't know this, but Thronos had briefly met her mother when he was eleven. And it had scared the hell out of him. "I'll answer as soon as you admit it's true."

She didn't bite, instead saying, "Speaking of communication, did you ever think about contacting me when I was in Rothkalina?"

"You know that demon realm is out of my reach. The portals have been guarded by armies for the last two reigns."

"You could've sent a message to a letter station at one of the portal gates."

"What should I have written? *Dear Harlot, rumor has it that you are very happy with your new life in Rothkalina with your beloved brother Omort. I hear that you have all the gold you could ever want, and I know how much you always enjoyed a good blood orgy. Well done, Melanthe! By the way, would you like to meet for a rational discussion about our future?*"

"Well. I *did* have a lot of gold."

Do not strangle her!

In a matter-of-fact tone, she said, "I'm just pointing out the sole true detail about your pretend letter. Oh, and you should know . . . if you keep calling me *harlot,* sooner or later I'm going to have a rage blackout, and then I'll wake up to find you—awfully sadly—dead."

"You threaten *me?* A powerless, physically weak sorceress?" he sneered. "I must amend my treatment of you forthwith."

"You've turned into a sarcastic, unbalanced, judgmental dick." To herself, she muttered, "Man, can I pick 'em."

"If you take issue with the term *harlot,* then perhaps you shouldn't have slept with half the Lore."

"Half?" she scoffed. "Three-quarters for the win!"

How could she sound so bloody uncaring, when he was insulting her character?

"Besides, I don't take issue with the term as much as the fact that *you* feel you can judge me. I despise judgmental people."

"As do most creatures who deserve to be judged."

"You got me. I'm a *ho fo sho.*"

What did that mean? "You speak like a human."

She nodded, as if that hadn't been an insult as well. "I watch a lot of TV."

Yet another thing they didn't have in common. "Naturally, you choose pointless pastimes."

"I did so much reading in my first couple of centuries—when I was in hiding from Vrekeners—that I figure I can skate a little now."

"I marvel that you had time for anything other than your conquests."

"So I'm a TV-watching harlot who deserves to be judged?" She gave a disheartened sigh. "Thronos, you have to know that I'll never be what you need me to be."

He scanned the ground for movement within the stands of trees. "I was told this long ago. I also heard that I'd never survive the injuries I sustained. Then they said I'd never fly again. Yet I did, and I do. Once I get you to my home, you will *become* what I need."

"I like myself!" she cried. "Did you never consider becoming what *I* need, Thronos?"

"I'm confused about your preferences. Should I emulate a drunken fey? Or a slick-tongued sorcerer who beds anything that moves?" Or maybe she preferred them like her first: a leech.

Don't think of that memory. . . . "In the Skye, I will make you understand the value of loyalty, honesty, and *fidelity* to a single male."

"You just confirmed what we've always heard: that Vrekeners kidnap and brainwash bold, independent Sorceri females, turning them into blank-eyed slaves to their men."

"It isn't like that! Sorceri young are happy among us, accepted as our own." As soon as they were disempowered.

"Uh-huh," she said. He was beginning to recognize that was her way of indicating *untruth.* "They're trapped in a dismal floating realm filled with grim, self-righteous killjoys. They are in our version of *hell.*"

"Since you'll soon see the truth of my words for yourself, there's no sense in arguing about it."

"Because you're taking me to Skye Hell? You think I'll be happy among you? Accepted as your own?"

"I said other Sorceri were," he pointed out. "Not you. You don't deserve happiness. You deserve the full force of my revenge."

"Revenge? After that night in the abbey, I never *tried* to hurt you, Thronos. I've just lived my life. I wish to all the gods that you could learn to live yours without your *bitterest necessity.*"

His rage had been so intense the night before, he only vaguely remembered calling her that. But he couldn't regret it. Considering his still-seething wrath, his words could have come out much worse. His actions as well.

As he soared over one mountain peak, heading for another, his gaze shot downward.

Fire demons had gathered in wait. For him, their enemy. Their hands were aglow, filled with flames.

They attacked, streams of fire burning through the fog and rain. Thronos's wings had been swooping, gaining altitude; at once he brought them closer, arcing his body down, gathering speed to elude their strike.

Against his chest, she cried, "Don't drop me, Vrekener!"

If he could dive down behind the mountain ahead . . . He picked up speed. Almost there—

A trap. They'd driven him into a broadside from another waiting group. Fire began to crisscross in all directions, flames zooming through the air toward them. A kill zone.

There was nowhere to fly, trails of fire showering all around him.

Impact. A sphere of flames, large as a cannonball, struck him in the wing. Like a hammer of the gods, it sent him reeling into another group's volley.

His wings were fireproof, but the flames clung to his scales, as if he'd been doused with oil.

"Thronos!" Melanthe screamed in pain. The fire was wrapping around him to lap at her. "My legs!"

When he smelled her seared skin, he had no choice but to separate her from the fire. He did all he could; he wrapped his wings around her body, covering her as he dove evasively. The speed might help him shed the flames.

No way to stop his descent. The base of a mountain rushed closer, fringed with jagged boulders. His mate screamed again, this time in terror.

Had the fire subsided? At the last second, he opened his wings, sculling them forward like oars in thick water. *"Ahh!"* he yelled against the pain as he scooped air, slowing their descent into the boulders.

Boom!

Another fire grenade blasted him square in the back, exploding flames all over them, accelerating his velocity even more.

He gritted his teeth, knowing he had only one chance of keeping Melanthe unharmed: fold her within his wings and take the impact on his back.

He turned in the air, praying to every deity in the heavens. . . .

SEVEN

Lanthe hadn't stopped screaming. Heat had scorched her until Thronos blanketed her body, but then they'd dropped.

Her stomach plunged as they fell, yet she could see nothing from the cocoon of his wings.

All she knew was that they were going to crash—hard. When even he tucked his head at the last instant, fear robbed her of breath.

They hit, the craggy ground punching them like a giant fist. The force of impact sent them bounding into the air once more, a flaming skipping stone.

Vertigo overtook her, confusion. She heard bones snap! Not hers?

They crashed down again and again. Then something pierced the cocoon directly by her face; a jut of rock tore through the skin of his wing, the momentum ripping flesh away.

They came to an abrupt stop, like the finale of a fatal car pileup.

Thronos made no sound. Unconscious?

Dizzy and panicked, Lanthe scrambled away from him. She shoved against his imprisoning wings, making him groan in pain.

Freed, she stumbled to her feet, staggering on the stony terrain. She shook off her dizziness, taking stock of her own injuries. Burns only.

Thronos had taken the full brunt. Flames still flickered on his back, hissing in the light rain. He'd broken bones, and that one wing lay wasted.

Which she didn't care about. Because he'd put her in that situation in the first place. It was his duty to mitigate the fuckup!

She gazed around warily. Why had those fire demons targeted one Vrekener? Yes, Thronos was a Pravus enemy, but fire demons often acted as lackeys, hired guns.

They'd be coming for him, and she needed to be gone when they did. She spied a natural path through the field of boulders, had just taken her first step when she heard another groan.

In a pained rasp, Thronos called her name.

Don't look back at him, don't look back. The last time she had, she'd been tormented by what she'd seen for all her days.

Against her will, she found herself turning.

His matte gray eyes were awash in misery as he grated, "Do not run . . . from me."

The world seemed to shrink down, morning turning to midnight in her head. All at once she was back in the mountainside abbey, on the night her parents had been slain, the night Lanthe had first used her powers to save Sabine's life. . . .

"Wake, Lanthe." Sabine clutched her hand, wresting her from her bed. "Don't make a sound."

"What is it, Ai-bee?" Lanthe whispered sleepily.

"Just hurry." As if to herself, she said, "I warned Mother and Father to move us from here, but they refused to listen."

Sabine hated their troubled mother and distant father. She blamed the pair for everything: not providing food or shoes or new dresses. She railed against them for their constant sorcery outlays that put the entire family at risk: *If even Lanthe insists that you're using too much . . .*

Lanthe knew the two weren't as good as other parents

seemed to be, but her heart was filled with love—why not give it to them?

"And now Vrekeners are in the abbey," Sabine murmured.

Here? "Mayhap they aren't here to fight." Thronos was her secret best friend; he would never let his kind attack her family!

"They're here to kill our parents and abduct us. As they always do with Sorceri." They'd heard the tales. Sorceri who broke the laws of the Lore were executed, while their children were fostered in stern Vrekener families.

Even with Sabine by her side, Lanthe was terrified as they stole through the abbey, lightning striking all around the mountain.

They stumbled into their parents' room. Mother and Father were curled together in sleep. Towering stained-glass windows allowed in the glow of lightning, distorting it. She blinked. For a second, she'd thought her parents appeared . . . headless.

When the scent of blood hit Lanthe, her legs buckled.

Their bodies *were* decapitated; the heads lay at unnatural angles, inches from their necks.

Sabine threw up; Lanthe collapsed with a scream, her vision going dark as she hovered on the verge of unconsciousness.

Mother and Father were dead. Never to return.

Mother with her gaze frenzied as she beheld her precious gold. Father with his lost look whenever he beheld his crazed wife. Both dead . . .

Lanthe dimly comprehended that the room had filled with Vrekeners, their wings flickering in the lightning-filled night. The leader held a fire scythe with a blade of black flames.

Then she saw Thronos. His eyes were wide, and he was trying to reach her, but one of the men held him back.

How could Thronos have led these killers here? After all the time they'd shared?

After my confession just this morning . . . ?

To Sabine, the leader intoned, "Come peaceably, young sorceress. We do not wish to hurt you. We wish to put you on the path of goodness."

Sabine, the Queen of Illusions, gave a chilling laugh as she called up her power. Her amber eyes started to glimmer like shining metal, stark against her fire-red hair. "We know what you do to Sorceri girls. You plan to turn us into biddable, grave crones like your sour-faced women. We'd rather fight to the death!" She began creating her illusions; at once, the soldiers hunched down, as if they believed the ceiling was pressing down on them.

Even betrayed like this, Lanthe wanted to ask Sabine to spare Thronos, but her lips moved soundlessly. *Mother and Father are dead.*

Had her parents ever even awakened tonight?

Sabine raised her palms toward the leader, using her sorcery to make him see his worst nightmares. He fell to his knees, dropping his scythe to claw at his eyes.

With a smile, Sabine snatched up his weapon. She swung for his neck, was still smiling when blood spurted across her beautiful, ruthless face.

Thronos gave a grief-stricken yell as the Vrekener's head rolled to Sabine's feet.

Was the leader Thronos's father?

Lanthe's sight was dim, but she thought Sabine's illusions were . . . fading? Her sister would be facing these foes alone, all bent on avenging their leader.

Lanthe found her voice just as a Vrekener sidled up behind Sabine.

"Ai-bee, behind you!"

Too late. The male had already struck. He slit Sabine's throat, blood painting the walls as her small body fell.

Lanthe's daze burned away. She scrambled to her feet, shrieking, *"Ai-bee?"* She ran for her sister, kneeling beside her. "No, no, no, Ai-bee, don't die, don't die, don't die!" Lanthe's own sorcery was manifesting itself. The air grew warm, as electric as the lightning surrounding them.

Sabine is leaving me. Because of Thronos and these men. *My entire family taken from me in one night.* A clarity such as she'd never known swept over her.

My family dies; the Vrekeners pay.

No longer would she hesitate to use her power. No mercy—for any of them.

She commanded the soldiers, "Do not move! You stab yourself! Fight each other—to the death!"

The room was thick with whorls of sorcery, and the abbey quaked all around them, the ancient rock walls groaning. A fracture forked along one of the stained-glass windows. In an earsplitting rush, it shattered.

She turned to her betrayer, the boy she'd thought she loved. The boy who'd led these fiends straight to her home.

He was wending his way around bodies to reach her, now that the adult who'd guarded him was dead.

Voice breaking, she sobbed, "I *trusted* you. Sabine was everything to me." Then, louder, she commanded him: "Jump through the window"—the one hundreds of feet above the valley floor—"and do not use your wings on the way down!"

His silver eyes pleaded for her not to do this thing, so she turned back to her sister's body, refusing to watch.

He never made a sound all the way down.

"Live, Ai-bee!" Lanthe screamed, but Sabine's glassy gaze was sightless, her chest still of breath. *"HEAL!"* she commanded, using all the power she possessed. The room quaked harder, jostling furniture. Mother's head hit the floor and rolled, Father's right behind hers. "Don't leave me! LIVE!"

More sorcery, more, more, *MORE* . . .

Sabine's eyes fluttered open—they were bright, lucid. "Wh-what happened?"

While Lanthe was utterly emptied of sorcery, Sabine bounded to her feet, appearing rested.

I brought her back. She's all I have now.

They fled from the abbey into the night. Yet in the valley, Lanthe trailed behind Sabine. She looked back over her shoulder, saw Thronos on the ground, clinging to life.

His body lay broken, limbs and wings twisted, skin flayed.

Somehow he raised his hand off the ground to reach for her with yearning in his eyes. . . .

Now, hundreds of years later, Thronos raised his hand off the ground to reach for her once more.

Just as she'd done that night, Lanthe turned from him and ran.

EIGHT

Hoping to find Carrow and her crew, Lanthe headed for low ground. In the steady rain, she sprinted over uneven terrain. Though her lungs began to burn, she kept up a punishing pace, slowing only to hide when she sensed other immortals.

All the while, she tried not to think about Thronos. So why did she keep seeing his scars, his misery?

She *refused* to feel guilt about leaving him behind earlier, much less for making him jump as a boy.

If Thronos hadn't betrayed her, then that Vrekener leader—who was his *father,* the king—wouldn't have murdered her parents. Over the years, Sabine wouldn't have needed so much of Lanthe's sorcery to repeatedly cheat death.

Lanthe could be one of the most feared Sorceri alive—instead of a power-on-the-fritz punch line. Hell, even Thronos had ridiculed her!

To be the Queen of Persuasion was to be the queen of nothing.

And in the Lore, perceived weakness was considered an invitation for enemy species to attack.

Sabine had recently voiced a new theory about Lanthe's persuasion: since Vrekeners tracked Sorceri by their power outlays, perhaps she feared drawing them down on her, and her fear was causing performance issues. Maybe her ability was intact, but her anxiety over the winged menace undermined it—even in Rothkalina, where they were sure no Vrekeners would ever come.

Lanthe didn't figure her Vrekener PTSD was *helping* things.

At least her portal ability still worked. If she could lose this collar, she could walk straight into Castle Tornin's court.

The only problem? If conditions weren't ideal—such as not having adequate time to concentrate—she had little control over where her threshold opened. And most other planes were not quite so welcoming as this one. Worse, she could only create a portal every five or six days. So if she screwed up with a destination, she couldn't do a quick fix.

A huge risk. Yet so was staying on this island.

Damn it, what had Thronos been thinking to try to capture her? If he'd succeeded, Rydstrom would have traced an army of rage demons to the Air Territories. Well, Rydstrom would if someone could finally find that domain in the heavens, one that was mystically concealed and moved throughout the year.

The only reason the Sorceri had never struck back against Vrekener aggression was because they couldn't find the Skye, or capture any of its inhabitants.

Maybe that was what made Thronos so daring—he knew there'd never be recourse against his kind.

Lanthe was so caught up with thoughts of him, she heard the log whooshing toward her face too late.

Her last thought before she blacked out: *One more thing to blame him for. . . .*

Lanthe dreamed of a voice. Only a voice. It belonged to a female, pleasantly cadenced.

"You'll move through worlds," the female murmured, as if imparting a secret to Lanthe. "In one realm, hurt. In one realm, leave. In one realm, cleave. In one realm, *shine.*"

"I don't understand," Lanthe said in her dream. The voice sounded familiar, but after an immortal's lifetime of acquaintances, she couldn't place it.

"Just think of your upcoming journey as the Four Realms of Samhain Past."

"That doesn't even make sense." Lanthe's frustration level was rising. "What are you talking about?"

"Whisper, whisper, whisper."

"Oh, come on! Now you're just whispering *whisper*!"

"Be my spark," the voice said, "and send worlds aflame. Now, wake, before it's too late. . . ."

"Ow, OWWWW." Lanthe came to by degrees, groaning from the pain in her face. "Who the hell hit me?" she croaked, wondering how long she'd been out.

And where was the woman? Had that truly been a dream? It'd seemed so real!

As Lanthe sat up, blinking around her, she pinched her broken nose. With a wince, she tweaked it back in place. Overcast daylight crept through spindly conifer needles, disorienting her. When her vision cleared, her face fell.

Pravus. In number. *Oh, shit.*

There were all kinds surrounding her: vampires, centaurs, demons, Invidia—demigods of discord—and Libitinae, winged castrators. They'd gathered in a clearing in the forest, within an encampment of rock—enormous square slabs had been stacked upright like Stonehenge, part deux. Only one person could effect that.

Lanthe craned her head around. Sure enough, Portia sat upon a stone throne, gazing at Lanthe on the ground. The sorceress's eyes were bright behind her jade-green mask, the spikes of her pale yellow hair jutting as boldly as the mountains she'd created.

Beside her, the smoldering Emberine, Queen of Flames, had draped herself over the rock throne's armrest, as a consort would. Apparently they were presiding over their new capital of This-Is-So-Fucked Island.

Some said Portia and Ember were sisters, while others said lovers. After spending a week in the same cell with them, Lanthe was leaning toward lovers.

She'd wanted to get closer to the key, but not like this. She gazed past them toward the outer edge of the clearing. More stones formed floating cells, caging a wood nymph, a fox shifter, an animus demon.

Thronos.

His capture didn't surprise her, considering the sheer number of the fire demons. Plus he'd been injured. She could almost pity him—a prince of Vrekeners imprisoned by Sorceri.

They would torture him to learn the location of his home. Afterward, they would . . . keep him—as a plaything, ensorcelled to do their every bidding.

She knew well the kinds of acts they'd force him to do. What they'd force him to *be*.

Why did that make her bristle?

His gaze was focused on Lanthe, and he looked frenzied to reach her. One of his wings was back to nearly normal, still gnarled. The one that'd been shredded had bits of flesh trying to grow.

"It took you long enough to wake," Portia told her. "Exactly how weak are you?"

Lanthe made it to her feet, brushing leaves off herself. Why would the great Portia care? Lanthe had a sinking suspicion: maybe the fire demons hadn't been targeting Thronos at all.

Despite her power, Portia never would've captured her in the past. Sabine's reprisal was too feared. Now? Just because the sisters had helped assassinate Omort, the Pravus leader, Lanthe was fair game for Sorceri?

Still, she regretted nothing. Her brother had had it coming. "Did you have to attack me, Portia? You know I would've come willingly." *I never would've come willingly.*

"We fortuitously found you on the ground, unconscious."

Then who hit me?

Ember added, "As if someone had left you on our doorstep, like a cat with a savaged mouse."

Lanthe cast a worried look at Ember. Both females were diabolical. But while Portia at least listened to reason, Ember was akin to the flames she wielded—volatile.

"What did I miss?" a male voice asked.

Lanthe turned to see a sorcerer in full gold regalia striding into the clearing, a man she'd hoped never to see again.

"Has my Melanthe arisen?" Felix the Duplicitor asked, his striking face lit with a smile, his gold gleaming seductively. His Sorceri ability enabled him to make anyone believe any lie he told. She would know.

Her face heated as she remembered his fervent vows to her. When he'd promised her a future together—with gold, his protection, gold, children, and more gold—light-skirted Lanthe had been a lock.

In the throes, she'd ceded her clairsentience and battle sorcery. She hadn't possessed her portal power yet, and he hadn't wanted her tainted soul.

Portia turned to him. "Your pet's only just woken."

His pet? Lanthe ground her teeth.

He turned the full wattage of his smile on Lanthe. "It's been an age, Mel."

After sex, when Lanthe had asked him about a wedding date, he'd released her from his spell, chucking her chin, and remarked, "Though you tempt me sorely, there'll be no wedding for us, dear. But wasn't the sex enough of a reward?"

No, Felix. No, it was not. She'd slunk away, burning with humiliation, dreading how to tell Sabine that she'd lost even more powers. *I'm such an idiot,* she'd railed at herself, *such a dupe!*

"You look as ravishing as ever," he said now, but he hadn't used his power, so she was free to disbelieve him.

Ravishing? Her recently broken nose was swollen like a balloon, and she probably had two glaring black eyes. "And you're the same duplicitous male you always were, Felix." Sorceri weren't a forthright species to begin with; needless to say, Felix was a favorite among them. "Looking no worse for wear from your prison stay." That gold armor really was to die for.

"I've only recently arrived. Had a vampire friend trace me to this island for the 'sport.' "

Just as Lanthe had suspected.

"I'd found it yawn-worthy—until I heard about your capture."

His interest put her even more on edge.

Portia said, "You have something we want, Melanthe."

Why now? They'd had her, Carrow, and Ruby in their sights earlier when they were all escaping the prison. Yet they'd spared the trio, merely stealing the hand that Lanthe had harvested from Fegley—the grubby one that now hung from Portia's gold belt.

The key to Lanthe's freedom. "I'm all ears."

"With so many helpless Vertas trapped here, we've decided to eradicate them, bringing more Pravus to the island. To get a jump on the Accession."

Every few centuries the Accession rolled around, a supernatural force that fueled conflicts between factions, drawing them into battles, culling immortal numbers. Accessions could last decades or longer. Some said this one had already started with the renewed vampire clashes a few years ago.

"We've had our allies teleport more soldiers here," Portia continued, "but what we need is an army of reinforcements."

Lanthe could read the writing on the wall. "You want me to create a threshold." Ensuring the doom of all the Vertas here?

Like Carrow and Ruby.

Think fast, Lanthe. Portia would have to remove her collar. If Lanthe could manage persuasion, she could command them to release her.

"Bravo, Melanthe," Portia said. "We want a door to the centauri lands so thousands of them can march directly here."

"They already have a portal." Most dimensions had at least one—but the quality varied.

"It's being utilized for a new top-secret offensive," Portia said, eyes flickering at the thought of carnage.

Who were the centaurs targeting? "Well, Portia, I can't do anything with my current accessory." She yanked on her torque. "So . . ."

"But we can't trust you." Ember flipped her long red and black locks over her shoulder. "Not after your actions in Rothkalina last year."

"Mel, did you really behead Hettiah?" Felix's tone was admiring.

Hettiah had been Omort's half sister and consort—a pale, evil imitation of his unrequited desire: Sabine. Lanthe had battled Hettiah and narrowly prevailed.

In answer, she shrugged.

"You did!" He looked overjoyed. "Then the other rumor must be true. You ensorcelled Omort!"

She'd wanted everyone to know about the part she'd played and respect her. Now she wished her involvement had been kept secret.

Because Felix appeared to be on another power hunt.

For her very soul.

He could tell her she'd always loved him, that he'd given her all he'd promised over these years—and she would believe him. . . .

NINE

Captive of the Sorceri.

This would have galled Thronos had he not been confident of his impending freedom. He'd seize it soon enough.

No, he was more enraged that Melanthe had fled him—though he hadn't expected anything different. Long ago, when he'd seen her turn away and run, he'd thought his world had ended. He'd thought he had no reason to live.

Now? He lived for vengeance. He would attack these foes—punishing whoever had battered her face—then recapture his mate.

He swung his gaze around toward the sorcerer, adding another target for punishment: Felix, the male who'd spoken to Melanthe.

An ex-lover, no doubt. How many of them populated this island?

The blond male wasn't nearly as tall or muscular as Thronos and wore ostentatious gold armor. His manners were practiced, his skin unscarred. So that was the type of male his mate preferred.

The opposite of me.

At the thought, fury surged through Thronos. He shoved against the slabs holding him, but there was no budging them. Portia, that sorceress of stone, was too powerful, and he was weakened from regeneration. His bones had mended, but he'd only reformed the barest covering across his right wing.

He'd been no match for the twenty fire demons who'd descended upon him.

Once healed, he'd strike. For now, he kept his mouth shut and listened, trying to glean information—such as why Melanthe would have ensorcelled Omort. Probably a rank power grab. *Sometimes, Omort, Sorceri paranoia is warranted.*

"If you can't trust me," Melanthe told Portia, "then what do you propose?"

The sorceress of fire, Emberine, tittered. "We've been deprived of color for so long—let's do something bright."

What did that mean?

"Be done with this, ladies," Felix said. When a fleeting ray of sunlight reflected off his gilded armor, every Sorceri gaze was magnetically drawn to it, including Melanthe's.

Most Vrekeners believed the Sorceri's claims of gold worship were just a disguise for rampant greed—as if the Sorceri would care how others viewed them. But Thronos knew they genuinely revered all metals, especially gold. The element was talismanic to them. Even at nine, Melanthe had been obsessed with it. *Her mother as well . . .*

Portia said, "You rush our fun, Felix?"

"I'm keen to renew my attentions to the Queen of Persuasion."

The hell that would be happening. Surprisingly, Melanthe's expression matched Thronos's thoughts.

Emberine gave an exaggerated frown. "I'm afraid our friend Lanthe is already smitten—with the demon angel."

Smitten?

Melanthe's blackened eyes widened. "He and his knights have hunted my sister and me, killing Sabine over and over, forcing me to burn through my persuasion to save her life."

Again, she repeated her claims? Though he'd told her about his knights' vows?

Emberine tsked at Thronos. "Naughty knights oughtn't to have brained Sabine in front of young Lanthe."

Melanthe turned to him, her face tight with rage. "Yet that one doesn't believe me!"

This one . . . is starting to. At least about attacks actually happening. Maybe some kind of offshoot group had targeted the sisters.

In a contemplative tone, Portia asked, "Do you think it's possible that our handsome prince doesn't know what his kinsmen do to our kind when they're drunken and frustrated?"

Vrekeners never imbibe, he thought automatically, though he knew that wasn't true. He had but once in his life, yet his brother secretly carried a golden flask, one stolen from a sorcerer he'd defeated.

Aristo loved few things better than warring with Sorceri. Just as their father had. It was a source of contention between the brothers.

Portia faced Melanthe once more. "Such an infamously hostile past between you and the Vrekener. Your sister beheaded his father, and you personally crippled him, even though you're his mate." How indifferently the sorceress spoke of tragedies! "Then Vrekeners hunted you. Which was why your reactions over the last week perplexed us."

Melanthe's head swung up, confusion in her eyes. Instead of demanding to know what that sorceress was talking about, she snapped, "Let's just get to this—"

"Shall we tell you, Felix?" Emberine asked coyly. "Every time the Vrekener was even mentioned, Lanthe's cheeks would heat, her eyes turning metallic."

Thronos stilled. Could it be true?

"That emotion was *hate,*" Melanthe spat, but he got the impression that her feelings were far more complicated than that.

He had no delusions about his own feelings. Like a stream carving a groove through rock, her actions had forever transformed him. He would always despise her.

Portia said, "Then you won't mind if we skin him? Crush him under the weight of a mountain?"

Melanthe gave a snort of disbelief. "Be—my—guest. And do save me a seat."

Or perhaps she hated as deeply as he did.

Emberine stroked the backs of her metal claws across Portia's bared thigh as she addressed Melanthe: "You gave him his wounds before he could regenerate. Did he find you as a boy then?"

Of not even twelve.

"It's known that a Vrekener will never stray from a mate." Emberine laughed as she said, "Tell us, Lanthe, is the mighty warlord a virgin? Is the angel pure as driven snow? Or was the demon in him an early starter?"

Thronos set his jaw. *Not—a—demon.*

Melanthe didn't answer. At least she refused to join in their ridicule.

Emberine's gaze roved over him, desire plain on her face. "I must initiate him!"

He could remain silent no longer. "Try it, slattern. Free me, and try it."

They tittered at that. "Oh, Portia, I know I could get him to stray!"

Best of luck. You think I haven't endeavored to? He glanced in Melanthe's direction. How would she feel about him being with another?

Though her face was blank, her eyes shimmered.

"We can't waste time on that, Ember." Portia seemed . . . jealous? "We move on with our plans."

With another laugh, Emberine sprinted to Melanthe, faster than Thronos's eyes could follow. In a heartbeat's time, she'd crossed the clearing, stopping behind Melanthe to position a blade at her slender throat, hovering above that collar.

"No!" Thronos bellowed, his instinct screaming for him to protect his mate.

The metal was simmering red from Emberine's hold. It would slice through Melanthe's flesh. She swallowed, wincing from the heat.

Portia rose, riding a cloud of pebbles toward the two females, readying a *severed hand* for the torque removal.

Felix—the as-good-as-dead sorcerer—followed, seeming amused by the proceedings.

Emberine told Melanthe, "You're about to do precisely as we say, or you'll die. But before Portia releases your powers, we're going to ensure that you can't call out any persuasive commands." She gripped Melanthe's cheeks. "Now, stick out your tongue like a good little queen."

TEN

Lanthe's thoughts were in turmoil.

Encountering Felix again after all these years was throwing her. Not to mention seeing Ember's lust for Thronos. The fire queen's need to seduce him had affected Lanthe in surprising ways, ways she'd have to think about later.

For now, she was a mite busy preparing for an amputation. Sweat dripped down her forehead and neck, pooling against her damned collar.

"Lose your tongue, and gain your freedom," Ember sneered.

Thronos bellowed at that, his wings flaring inside his cage. As if he cared about Lanthe. He acted this way because of uncontrollable instincts—despite hating everything about her.

Was Thronos that much different from Felix? Two males wanted something from her; yet neither cared about her. They only saw what she could give them, how they could use her.

"Be quick about it," Felix said, earning a scathing look from Lanthe. "The sooner Mel's tongue goes, the sooner it regenerates." Flashing white teeth, he quipped, "I know just how she's going to want to break in her new one."

Lanthe shuddered. He could make her believe she loved every minute of her violation.

"Open wide!" Ember cried. "Don't worry—the blade's not quite hot enough to cauterize."

Lanthe swallowed again. All the Pravus allies closed in on the scene, the promise of gore exciting them. Seeing them like this, she could almost understand why one species would feel the need to police them.

Unless someone swoops in to save the day, I'm about to lose my tongue. Though it'd grow back, tongues were supersensitive; mother of gold, this was going to hurt.

A toll I'll pay to get free.

She glanced over at Thronos. He was thrashing against the immovable stone. When she stuck out her tongue and Ember pinched the tip with her gauntlet claws, he grew crazed, ramming his horns into the rock until blood dripped down his face.

She tensed, readying for the pain.

Felix murmured, "Be over in a minute, Mel." Soothing words, even as he avidly watched—

Slice.

She screamed, blood spewing. Cheers and laughter broke out.

Agony assailed her; black dots swarmed her vision as she choked on blood. When her legs grew weak, Ember held her up by the collar. With her other hand, she raised Lanthe's severed tongue for all to see. Then she tossed it into the crowd.

Stay conscious, stay conscious.

Portia ran Fegley's hand over Lanthe's face before she used the thumb to remove the torque.

Freed, Lanthe dropped to her knees, digging into the ground. She spat up mouthful after mouthful of blood, crimson streams splattering over her gauntleted hands.

Colorful enough, you bitches?!

"The threshold, Lanthe," Portia said in a casual tone. "Directly to the centauri capital, if you please."

Lanthe gave them a shaky nod, as if she was about to get right on this. She began manifesting her sorcery, and the pleasure of it counteracted her pain. After her enforced hiatus, she was brimming with power!

When she caught Thronos's gaze once more, she smirked around pouring blood. Like him, these Sorceri continued to underestimate her.

She had a secret ability, one she'd been sure not to reveal in their cell. Because at heart, she was a sneaky, suspicious sorceress.

Even her new friend Carrow hadn't known Lanthe could communicate telepathically, a power stolen more than a century ago.

Lanthe's persuasive commands didn't have to be uttered by her; they merely had to be *heard* by her victims.

She raised her bloody gauntlets, iridescent blue light and heat blurring the air all around her. They'd think it was for the portal.

Wrong.

She would utilize the command that came in so handy whenever Auntie Lanthe babysat Cadeon and Holly's twins. She mentally ordered: *—Pravus, SLEEP.—* She watched as their legs grew unsteady, lids heavy, expressions baffled. *—SLEEP. And forget I was ever here.—* Bodies collapsed one by one. Portia and her platform of pebbles dropped to the ground, motionless.

Ember yelled, "Portia!"

—You are exhausted, must sleep NOW.—

Ember fell unconscious beside her lover's slumbering form.

All the Pravus were out.

The sorcery expenditure and continued blood loss had debilitated Lanthe, but she was in no way safe. Because for some inexplicable reason, she'd excluded Thronos from her commands.

Without Portia's force against the stone cage, he was able to lift the top slab. His scars and limp had always made Lanthe discount his strength. When he tossed the slab away like a piece of tile, she promised herself she never would again.

If he captured her once more, she'd be right back where she started from, minus a tongue. Just because she hadn't necessarily wanted him to be a Sorceri plaything didn't mean she wanted to be his!

So dizzy. Need a portal. She could crawl through it—away from him, from this treacherous island. She had a moment's worry for Carrow and Ruby, but they had been in the care of that lethal vemon. Surely, he'd protect them.

Lanthe spat more blood. Did she have the power to open a rift? She had just used her persuasion, and so many things could go wrong with a portal opening.

The last one she'd created had been to Oblivion, one of the demon hell planes. But she'd only had to reopen a portal that was already in place.

Easy as easy pie.

Now, in her exhaustion and haste, she might point a door back there. Or what if she portaled herself to somewhere even deadlier? Like a plane with mustard gas instead of oxygen, or a completely aquatic bubble realm?

Even worse than instant death, some planes could *change* a person forever.

Thronos limped toward her, his gray eyes intent, his expression determined. Behind him more centaurs galloped into the clearing, taking in their fallen comrades.

Double threat—no choice but to portal! Swallowing back blood, she began to open a rift, a small scalpel cut in this reality. She tried to concentrate on her home of Rothkalina, yet fears of all that could go wrong tangled in her thoughts.

Opening, opening. With a yell, Thronos started sprinting, snagging a sword from a sleeping demon on his way.

Opening . . .

When the centaurs charged behind him, Lanthe scuttled backward toward the threshold.

As he ran, Thronos kept his gaze locked on her, even as he made a sweeping downward cut with that sword. Why would he . . . ?

The blade came back bloody; Felix's head was rolling from his body.

Her jaw slackened, blood pouring from her mouth. *The Vrekener's crazed.* She twisted over to her hands and knees, now scrambling through the portal.

Night. Fog and murk. Definitely not Rothkalina.

The overcast day of the prison island flickered into this rainy world like a flashlight's beam. Before her eyes could adjust, she heard Thronos bellowing for her.

She commanded the portal to seal itself. Just as the seams were about to meet, he dove through them, crashing beside her.

As soon as the rift was no more, territorial growls and hisses sounded from all around them.

In the gloomy dark, Thronos grated, "Have you taken us to hell, sorceress?"

ELEVEN

Thronos struggled to get his bearings—while biting back his rage over what he'd just seen.

His female, maimed. By her own kind. He wished he'd had time to liberate *all* of their heads from their bodies.

Focus, Talos. He scented the air, surveying his new surroundings. They were on a small island of rock encircled by water that looked like mercury. Mist cloaked the night. Some kind of preternatural swamp?

Though he'd traveled to foreign planes in pursuit of his mate, he didn't recognize this one. She could've taken them anywhere. Thronos despised her portals; every time he'd seen one in the past had meant he was about to lose her yet again.

A massive red sea serpent crested above the water to their right, a razor-sharp fin slicing through waves. "Yes. We've gone to hell," he said, just as a green serpent surfaced to the left.

Melanthe would be creating another portal directly. But not to the Skye—he would never give her the directions to his hidden home, in case she somehow escaped him and decided to portal an enemy army there.

"Make another threshold back to the mortal realm," he ordered her.

"Somewhere in Europe." He knew she couldn't talk—blood still spilled from her lips. Yet all she had to do was nod, then get to work.

Once they were away from here, he would question her.

How did you make the Pravus sleep, and why not me? For what purpose would you ensorcel Omort? Do you grieve that sorcerer I beheaded?

"Be about it," he snapped, unused to repeating his orders. When Thronos led troops of his knights on Pravus raids, no one dared disobey him.

She shook her head, her braids bouncing over her slim shoulders.

Denying him? He crouched in front of her, baring his fangs. "Do—it—now."

—It'll take me five or six days to renew my threshold ability. I'm in a lag till then.—

He jerked away, grimacing from the feel of her words laid directly into his mind. So that was how she'd commanded them to sleep! Telepathy.

Now that he thought back, he could tell she'd had to feign hesitation under the threat of that blade. She'd had a plan, and she'd been desperate to get that torque removed.

He hated telepathy—a glaring reminder of what she was. But at least she could communicate with him until she regenerated. He knew he could reply the same way, thinking his words rather than uttering them, and she could pick them up with her mind-reading ability. But he refused to allow her entry into his thoughts, had developed mental shields specifically to block her. "How many other abilities do you possess?"

—Alas, only three.— Was she lying?

"If you have power enough for telepathy, then why can't you open a portal?"

—Just because I've walked for miles doesn't mean one of my eyelids is fatigued.—

"Your powers empty and regenerate independently?"

She shrugged. *—Telepathy is second nature. Cutting a rift into reality . . . not so much.—*

She'd said nothing about her most devastating ability. "And your persuasion?" Could she use it only every few days as well? Once she was strong enough for a threshold, she might be able to command him. A double-edged sword. He was in the same position as those Sorceri, could trust her just as little.

The loss of her collar was a grave one.

—Persuasion is unpredictable.— In the rain, she rubbed her chin over one pale shoulder, smearing blood there. Crimson ran down her arm, dripping from her elbow into a rivulet of runoff. *—It tends to come online when I'm in jeopardy, so you probably shouldn't frighten me again.—*

He shuddered to think of all the things she could persuade him to do. Could she truly make him forget her? Even as his rational mind thought, *Maybe that's exactly what should happen,* his instincts rebelled.

His body rebelled. Would it remember that Thronos was never to take another?

"There must be some way for you to shave days off your . . . lag." They couldn't be trapped here. Something about this realm put him even more on edge. Of course he perceived danger all around, yet his main sense was of *expectancy.*

Because he was with her?

—I have to wait several days, for me *to create* myself *a threshold for* me *to use. You're s.o.l.—*

So, unless they could find another portal or a Lorean who could teleport, they were stranded. "Where are we?"

—I don't know.— When the rain intensified, she started shaking even harder. With the amount of blood she'd lost she must be freezing in this weather. And regeneration was punishing on the body.

The wind picked up, bringing traces of scents. His muscles tensed when he smelled lava, corpse rot, and Lorean blood. Copious amounts of it. "Of all the realms, why did you pick this accursed land?"

She slitted her eyes at him, her own blood streaming from the corner of her lips. *—No one forced you to come with me! And hitchhikers don't get to complain about the destination!—*

"Answer me!"

—Sometimes I can't control what door I open! Especially not under pressure.—

He exhaled a breath. He'd best figure out how to keep them alive in this place. He squinted through the mist, spying what might be a pair of mountains in the far distance. He thought a high plateau stretched between them.

There were two other small islands between here and that coast, but each one was miles away, too far for even an immortal to leap. Without both of his wings, he had scant hope of crossing that span.

Another serpent swam by. Were they getting more numerous? This one flicked its forked tongue in the air directly beside their island. The tongue was as long as Thronos's leg. Rows of razor-sharp teeth glinted in the night.

When the skies opened up and rain thundered down, Melanthe shuddered beside him. The paler her skin grew, the more those bruises on her finely-boned face stood out.

Without thought, he started moving his good wing over her—but stopped himself, stifling any unwanted sympathy for her. "It seems you would want to work together with me, sorceress. You can't fly, so how will you escape this predicament? Or were you planning to remain here with the serpents for the better part of a week?"

She gave a marked glare at his injured wing.

"It will heal in hours." And then he'd find a secure shelter for them.

—You're acting like we're in a partnership, like I'm not your prisoner. We are NOT a team. I hate you! I plan to ESCAPE you, dumbass.—

"I expect nothing less. But until your next futile attempt, you're going to answer some questions for me. Who was that sorcerer to you?"

—An ex. Congratulations, you decapitated an old ex.—

"Do you grieve him?"

She rolled her eyes. *—I grieve that you didn't snatch his gold armor on the way out. He was no friend or ally of mine.—*

"Then *why* would you have slept with him?" Her sexual habits confounded him!

—Why not?—

Lose control, lose your mate. Biting back fury, he said, "Why did you ensorcel Omort?"

She jutted her chin mulishly.

"Answer or swim."

Her eyes darted as a purple fin sliced the water nearby. *—I commanded him to use no sorcery in the fight with Rydstrom.—*

Everyone in the Lore knew that Rydstrom the Good had slain Omort the Deathless, reclaiming his kingdom of Rothkalina; but Thronos *had* wondered how the rage demon king had circumvented Omort's vast powers. "Why would you favor Rydstrom, betraying your own brother and . . . lover?" he grated, scarcely able to utter the word.

Her face screwed up with revulsion. *—Lover??? He was everything vile! Not to mention that he was my BROTHER. Oh, that's just not—* The thought ended abruptly; she turned to throw up again, heaving, but only blood came out. *—I'd rather die!—*

Did he dare to believe her? Surely disgust that violent couldn't be contrived.

She swung a glare at Thronos, eyes sparking with rage. *—I will kill you in your sleep for saying things like that to me!—*

"Why should I, or anyone else, believe you weren't his concubine? It's common knowledge that Omort liked to mate his sisters, and you lived under his protection for centuries!"

—You want to know the truth about what life was like under his protection*? Horrifying. We lived with his insanity, saw it made manifest every day! He routinely threatened to kill me, came close so many times.—*

"Again, you lie. If you hated what was happening, then why wouldn't you abandon him? I know that you and Sabine were free to come and go. And why would he want his own sister dead?"

She turned away, her gauntlets balled into fists. *—Go to hell.—*

"You've already taken me here. Now answer me!"

Silence.

He grabbed her shoulders. "Feel the serpent's breath?"

She struggled in his arms, weak as a babe. *—He poisoned Sabine and me with the morsus.—*

"What is that? I'm not as versed in cowardly poisons as you Sorceri are." They loved deploying their poisons as much as they loved drinking and gambling, deeming themselves "toxinians."

—The morsus kills from withdrawal. If we left him for more than a few weeks, we'd die of pain. He had the only antidote, doling it out at intervals, so long as we didn't displease him.—

It sounded too strange to be true, which had Thronos leaning toward belief. Only a sorcerer would do that to his own family. "Why should I believe you?"

—A) I don't care if you believe me or not because you don't matter. *B) Your friend Nïx will verify everything I've told you.—*

He . . . believed Melanthe. Which meant Thronos's old friend wrath was placated a degree. The sorceress hadn't been a delighted participant in those atrocities.

Though she was lacking in so many other ways, Thronos decided then that she would suffice as a wife. "I do believe you in this, which means I will be marrying you. You'll be pleased to know that torture is now off the table."

Her eyes flickered. *—As if I'd* ever *accept you as my husband! You have no right to abduct me! You're no different from Omort. Taking away my choice, my life. And we killed Omort at the first opportunity.—*

"Threatening me again?"

—The only reason we went with him in the first place was that he promised to protect us from Vrekeners!—

"Not from *me.* I've seen you only a handful of times over these years. I dogged your heels, but always when I closed in, you escaped through sorcery. If there was a splinter group who targeted you, I had no knowledge of it."

—How could you not know what your own men were doing?—

He felt her probing his thoughts, trying to read his mind. He put up his shields within an instant, but apparently that was all she'd needed; she gasped.

—You truly didn't know! Allow me to fill you in. Not two years after the abbey,

your knights of good flew Sabine to a height and dropped her for fun. I saw her head crack open on the cobblestones. I barely pulled her back from the dead.—

Vrekeners were the curse of evildoers; they did not *commit* evil.

She read his expression. *—Don't believe me? Why do you think I grew to be so afraid of heights? Because I've seen what happens to a body when it lands! And then, not a year later, your kind were upon us again.—*

Her gaze went distant. *—We hid in a hayloft. But these huge winged males swept up after us, your knights. Laughing, the leader picked up a pitchfork and stabbed the hay.—* She flexed her right hand. *—Sabine jumped from the loft, running to distract them from me. They chased her into a river. She couldn't swim and drowned!—* Melanthe faced him once more, leaning in aggressively. *—I found her on a bank three towns away, and debilitated my power to bring her back.—*

"You expect me to believe that my own men tried to gore my mate to death when she was a helpless little girl? Ah, but it gets better. Only Sabine's selflessness saved you? How false that rings!" Melanthe was lying. She had to be.

Because Vrekeners didn't.

—I don't expect *you to believe that. Just like I don't expect you to believe that we weren't isolated cases. That your knights brutalized other Sorceri even worse.—*

"The enchantress spins her tales."

—The enchantress is DONE with Vrekener bullshit!— She spat blood in his face.

Thronos shot to his feet, lifting her with him. "You provoke me?"

—I wish I'd put you to sleep with the rest of those dicks!—

"Then why didn't you?"

She averted her eyes.

"Why, Melanthe?"

She frowned at something past him. He glanced over his shoulder, saw several serpents, in a prism's worth of colors. How many were there?

That was when he noticed that the shape of their little island had changed.

He bit out, "The water's rising," just as she said: *—I think they like my blood.—*

TWELVE

Naturally, Lanthe had spat in the face of the one person who could save her from being serpent chow. The rain was still washing red streams off his chiseled cheeks.

Of all her fears, being *food* was up there, just under Vrekener attack. Time to make nice with her hated tormentor.

Choking back the pain in her mouth, she faked a flirtatious demeanor. *—I seem to have gotten my blood on your face. Bad Lanthe! Hey, I have an idea. Let's team up!—*

He scowled at her as he tested his wings, the lines of his face growing tight with pain. The damaged wing was nowhere near ready to fly. He was like a plane that had lost one engine. When the water lapped at their feet, he said, "It'll have to be enough to get us to the coast I spied."

She turned, seeing nothing through the gloom. But the mercury water and rainbow serpents were giving her an idea of where they might be. If she was correct, then danger loomed everywhere. If they encountered rivers of fire and a perpetual demonic war, she'd know. . . .

Lanthe needed the Vrekener's help to survive this place—and she needed him bullish, convinced he could save her! How to get his adrenaline pumping?

She gazed at his chest. His shirt hung wide, revealing his scarred skin. His muscles were hard and generous. Attractive. No wonder Ember had desired him.

Reaching forward, Lanthe laid a shaking palm over his heart. He tensed, and at once its beat began to thunder. The second time she'd voluntarily touched him as an adult. She cleared her throat, then remembered she couldn't talk. —*Thronos, if you can get us out of this situation . . .* —

The water swept closer, the serpents growing bolder.

—*I'll let you touch me.*—

He narrowed his eyes down at her. "What you don't understand is that I'll be doing whatever I please to you."

Well. When had he gotten so cocky? Then she recalled that he had been as a boy as well.

He yanked her up into his brawny arms, against that unyielding chest. "You belong to me. By right of pain, I've earned you!" Lightning struck, punctuating his statement.

Like she'd belonged to Omort? She'd just been freed of that freak a year ago!

"But it doesn't surprise me that you'd bargain your body for safety," Thronos added. "Now, shut up, and put your legs around my waist."

When in trouble, leave. Seeing no other option, she did as he told her. With her short skirt riding up, he cupped her bare ass, holding her body high on his torso. His hands were rough and hot, like five-fingered brands on her damp skin. Electricity seemed to pass between them.

By the look on his face, she wasn't the only one who'd felt it.

How in the hell was he supposed to concentrate on getting her to safety when his palms were molded to her lush curves?

His only hope of protecting her was using the islands to reach the coast. He'd just been focusing his mind on the herculean task ahead when the sorceress started talking about him touching her!

He'd shot hard for her, diverting blood from his healing wing and, more importantly, his brain. He hadn't wanted her to know how easily she affected him, so he'd furtively adjusted his aching shaft.

How many other males had fallen for this enticing creature? For her lies? His old friend wrath erupted inside him. He would use it to fuel his escape from this swamp. "I suggest you hold on."

She laid her face against his chest, clutching him tighter.

With a yell, he leapt for the nearest island, working his good wing for loft as much as he could. He fell short, landing in the water up to his knees. He lunged to the center of the island just as teeth snapped closed behind them. When an angry hiss sounded, he felt the fetid air from the beast's mouth.

—*Too close, Thronos!*—

He focused his gaze on the next island, one even farther away than this one had been. He had his mate at last; all he had to do was keep her safe from dozens of giant swamp serpents.

Setting his jaw, he tensed, then lunged. Midleap he knew they would fall short of the island. A serpent surfaced beneath him; at the last instant, he alighted on its back, using it to vault to his target. They landed safely.

—*Serpents are not stepping stones!*—

He could do without her critiques. "You have no tongue, yet you won't *shut up*." He locked his gaze on his destination. As he'd spied before, there were two mountains bordering a plateau atop an enormous shelf of land. It ended in a sheer cliff face, as if a giant had cleaved its edges, halving the mountains in the process. Lava oozed down their sides, like glowing orange waterfalls.

The plateau was hundreds of feet above the swamp. If he missed, there'd be nothing to stop them from plunging into serpent-infested waters.

The storm was worsening. Wind gusted with the pounding rain. But this pile of rock had a little more room, so he could at least get a running start. Though the winds carried ill-omened scents from that plateau, he had no choice but to continue.

A horn rang out, echoing from one mountain to the other.

A battle call?

Bloodthirsty yells sounded, metal clanging against metal. Moments later, the night sky lit up, Lorean powers blasting.

He saw fire grenades, ice bombs, and swirling battle magics. Had to be demons. But how many factions of them could there be? "Well done, Melanthe. You took us from one war to another."

—I think I know where we are. Supposed to be a myth. The source of all demons.—

The source? Realization. "You brought us to bloody Pandemonia?" Plural of pandemonium. Because it was the fabled home plane of hundreds of demon species.

Another hiss sounded behind him. The water continued rising at an alarming rate. No other option but forward. He had to hope that they could skirt the edges of the conflict.

As he backed to the far end of the island, she wrapped her arms tighter around him, digging her gauntlets into his skin.

He took off in a sprint, waiting till the last second . . .

With a bellow, he lunged for his target. *Airborne.* Three heartbeats later, he knew he wouldn't make it in this headwind.

Too short, too short.

—We're going into the drink, Vrekener!—

When the green serpent crested, Thronos worked his wing as hard as he could to reach its back. Ha! Heading for a perfect serpent touchdown; he was getting handy at this.

He landed just as the beast thrashed. The momentum sent them hurtling toward one of those mountains as if they'd hit a thirty-ton springboard.

Thronos heaved his wing, fighting to right himself. The mountainside loomed, rushing at them.

He thought he spied a small cave opening between two lava flows. Could he hit that tiny target? Such a risk! He steered with his wing, down and left.

Down and left, down and left . . .

Left, left!

They bulleted through the opening. He dropped his legs, reversing his wing, touching his feet down.

The momentum had him barreling toward the back wall; he twisted to his side, leaning away, feet sliding sideways in the dust.

They stopped inches from the wall.

THIRTEEN

Lanthe had been certain of death, convinced their momentum would slam them into the side of a mountain, crushing them or giving them a lava bath.

Instead, Thronos had hit the bull's-eye, then slid home. She drew back to face him. —*Okay. That was a pretty cool move. Way to thread the needle.*—

She thought it took him a second longer than usual to scowl down at her. He set her to her feet, steadying her with a big palm over her shoulder.

—*Thanks.*—

He jerked his hand away, looking angry with himself. Then he turned to survey the area.

Thanks to the glow of the lava flows just beyond the cave mouth, there was enough ambient light for even Lanthe to see clearly. Each of the cave walls had been hewn smooth, as if to create a canvas for a multitude of etched hieroglyphs. There were pillars to support the ceiling, a raised rock shelf along the back wall, and layers of dust.

She'd been to ancient ruins before. This place seemed so old it made those other ones appear techno.

Thronos cased the perimeter, pausing at intervals to scent the air. What she wouldn't give for his heightened senses. *And his strength,* she added when he moved a fallen pillar out of his way, plucking it up as if it were a matchstick.

"You have no idea why we arrived here?" he asked.

She shook her head, trailing after him. In the back left corner of the cave, she perceived something that made the tiny hairs on her nape stand up. There was only one way her senses could trump Thronos's: recognizing the call of gold.

Yet the wall appeared solid. Looking for a door, she examined some glyphs, brushing away dust. She gave the marks a few pokes with a gauntlet claw, but found nothing.

Even as she walked away, she glanced over her shoulder longingly. Maybe there was a mother lode locked in the mountain, never to be discovered in this hell plane.

The idea left her deflated. Now that the adrenaline of their escape had waned, she was growing dizzy with fatigue and blood loss. Her regenerating tongue was sending waves of pain throughout her mouth and head.

"Do you recognize these markings, sorceress?"

She'd been learning Demonish in Rothkalina, was conversant at least, but she didn't recognize this. *—Proto-Pandemonian, maybe? Or some kind of primitive Demonish?—*

Thronos looked even more unsettled than before, shoving his fingers through his thick hair. Something about this cave was affecting him. "You expect me to believe your door to Pandemonia was random?"

—We could have gone anywhere, anyplace in existence. Believe me, it could've been worse.—

"Worse than Pandemonia?"

—Absolutely.— Foreign realms were often lethal to some degree, so dangerous that only an immortal could survive there.

Though many in the Lore believed immortals were quasi-deities, others thought they'd been forced to *evolve* in those foreign dimensions, to become ever more hardy, until one eon they became . . . undying. Then they'd traveled across realities to inhabit the mortal world, attracted to the relative ease of that plane.

So basically, Sorceri had evolved with senses only a little better than a human's, bodies that were weak compared to other Lore species, and life spans that could end from far more than just a beheading or mystical fire.

Her species sucked at evolution.

"What realm trumps this one, Melanthe?"

—At least there's rain here.— She started wringing out her hair. *—We could have gone to Oblivion, forced to fight other demons for water.—*

His wings twitched with irritation. "*Other* demons?"

—Would you rather we'd landed in Feveris?— Anyone who entered that plane was bespelled with unending, uncontrollable desire.

"Feveris, then?" Had his voice grown huskier? "The Land of Lusts?"

If she'd had more blood left in her body, she might have blushed at his tone.

"Have you been there?" he asked.

She *had,* just to dip a toe, to see if the rumors were true. Her servants had tied a rope around her waist to drag her back if she got bespelled, a precaution they'd been forced to use. Within minutes, Lanthe had begun stripping for a gnome.

—Maybe.— She'd never forget that perpetually sunny, coastal plane, redolent with the scent of Hawaiian Tropic, island flowers, and sex. Or its twinkling rays of sun . . .

"I'm sure you felt right at home there," he grated.

She was still smarting from his harlot comment on the prison island. *—Maybe YOU influenced me to open this door to Pandemonia, demon! All last night I was captive of a demon, so naturally I opened a threshold to YOUR home world.—*

He stalked up to her, yelling, "Do not call me *demon*!"

She forced herself to hold her ground, then repeated his earlier words: *—Sensitive about this, creature?—*

"Demons are savage. Vrekeners have grace and a sacred purpose. We are descended from gods!"

—How do you know this?—

"From the Tales of Troth—sanctified knowledge passed on from one Vrekener generation to the next for millennia."

—*I'm going to have to stop you, because you've already bored me. In any case, my brother-in-law Rydstrom is no savage. He's one of the best males I know.*—

"Enough of Rydstrom! You sound infatuated with him."

—*He* is *hot.*—

"That's what you like? Ever superficial, sorceress."

—*And you are ever pathologically jealous.*—

"It's much deeper than jealousy. The males you bedded stole from me. *You* stole from me."

—*What did I steal?*—

"Years and children. I would have killed any other for such a grievous loss."

—*That's what you've wanted from me all this time? Years and children? Even if those years would have been miserable?*—

"I accept that our existence together will be bleak. The most I hope for is that we can raise our offspring without killing each other."

Lanthe's biological clock—which had no idea Thronos was a kidnapping, judgmental prick—quickened at the words *our offspring.*

Being a doting auntie to the twins had jump-started Lanthe's clock. Caring for little Ruby in the prison had put it into overdrive.

That she was at the tail end of her fertile time probably wasn't helping matters.

But children with Thronos? *Never.* It would be bad enough if Lanthe was trapped in Skye Hell, being brainwashed; she'd be damned if her children shunned laughter, for gold's sake.

"You don't seem averse to the idea of young in general," he observed.

Not at all. And it wasn't like she hadn't been looking for a partner all these years.

Too bad each of her forays had ended poorly. She would either gain a creepy new admirer, have her powers stolen, or get the dreaded brush-off: males wincing at their watches, claiming, "Got a really early morning tomorrow, sweet." Then they'd blaze.

Hit it and quit it. Nail and bail. Yet never a conceive and leave, because she'd taken precautions whenever she'd been in season.

"How could you not have had children?" Thronos demanded. "Your opportunities for impregnation must have been legion."

She was making a note of all these slut-shaming comments, vowing to throw his demonic origins in his face at every opportunity. —*Each day, I'm going to give you two harlot cards to play. If you play more than your two, then I'm going to retaliate, and you won't enjoy it.*—

"Answer the question."

—*My wanting children is a recent development, one that has come to a screeching halt now that I'm your captive. Once I get free, I might investigate the possibility further.*—

"You'll never be free of me." The words sounded like a sentencing. Meeting her gaze, he said, "Every second we're together, I get under your skin as deeply as you've scarred mine."

This was like arguing with a wall. A demonic, flying wall. —*What's your plan now?*—

"Avoid the war on the plateau below." The sound of it filtered upward so unceasingly that already it had become a kind of white noise. "Which means we'll be staying in this cave until you can create a portal to the mortal realm. From there, I'll take you to the Skye."

—*You're not* hearing *me. Thronos, if you didn't know about the attacks, then your knights were acting outside your orders. What's to stop them from pitching me over the side up there?*—

"My knights would not have dared harm you." Had he sounded a touch less smug about that? Less confident?

She had to keep chipping away at his stubborn beliefs. —*This sorceress is predicting some big adjustments in your future. You're going to have to accept that Vrekeners break their word, and that your chivalrous and valiant knights laughed as they dropped a terrified girl to her death. You're going to have to accept that your men sought to murder your eleven-year-old mate with a pitchfork while she fought not to scream!*—

For a moment, Thronos looked almost *spooked.* As of today, she knew what it was like to have one's lifelong beliefs called into question. It felt a lot like Portia moving a mountain—in your brain. If Lanthe hadn't known him so well, she could almost have pitied him.

But she *did* know him well.

—As I said, you can verify everything with Nïx. For now, your bitterest necessity is too tired to keep arguing. You don't rate high enough anyway.— She turned from him, looking for a place to curl up for an hour or two. Right now the raised rock shelf in the back looked like the best bed ever.

"What do you mean I *don't rate*?" he asked. When she didn't answer, he started talking about that sanctified knowledge again, about being a "sword for right," so she tuned him out, heading toward the back.

"And you tell *me* I'm not hearing you?" he said from behind her.

He doesn't like to be ignored. Good to know. Ignoring him, she swept her arm over the surface. Though the air was warm inside this cave, the slab was freezing cold. *Beggars, choosers, blah.* She curled up, closing her eyes.

Was it only a day ago that she'd been coughing up grit in the tunnel? Since then, she'd suffered a fiery Vrekener crash, a log to the face, and tongue amputation.

And that was after weeks of captivity.

I'm not doing too good here. On top of all that, she was trapped in a cave with gold nearby, which left her antsy. She could *feel* it, could all but smell it, yet she couldn't reach it, to touch, to worship. Like an itch she couldn't scratch. No, worse than that—like a blade in the back she couldn't reach.

Think of something else. Shivering and miserable, she envisioned her lavish suite in Castle Tornin. Tonight, she'd be in her warm bed, watching movies—rom-coms and epic love stories. Or maybe she'd read a new self-help book.

Funny—before all this, she'd been chafing at Tornin. She often felt like a third wheel with Rydstrom and Sabine. Things improved when Rydstrom's sisters visited or when Cadeon and Holly brought the girls, but their visits weren't frequent enough to satisfy Lanthe.

Sharing a castle with Sabine and Rydstrom could be trying. Though Lanthe had her own tower in Tornin, she'd still see him kissing Sabine down in the courtyard, or holding her hand just to walk to dinner. Their obvious adoration for each other made Lanthe . . . jealous.

Not that her sister didn't deserve every happiness, but Sabine had never even wanted love for herself. Lanthe had dreamed of it for centuries, leaving no stone unturned to find it; yet she was the one alone, with no prospect of it.

The closest she could get to a lasting relationship was with a murderous Vrekener. *Ugh!*

She couldn't believe she'd had even a passing thought that Thronos's physique was attractive! Damn her Sorceri hormones.

If she could get back to Rothkalina, she vowed on all the gold in her private vault that she would never chafe again.

She squeezed her eyes more tightly closed. She was acting as if she'd see home again. If the male pacing this cave had anything to do with it, she'd live out her days in a floating hell.

Until she jumped.

FOURTEEN

At least one of us can sleep. After about half an hour, the sorceress had passed out—while he sat back against a wall of hieroglyphs, watching her.

She seemed to have blocked him out, ignoring him so totally that he might as well not be here. In a way, ignoring him was precisely what she'd been doing for the last several centuries.

Because he didn't *rate.* To her, he mattered not at all.

Positioned as she was, her ridiculous excuse for a skirt was riding up. Any higher and he'd be able to see the cleft of her ass. Recalling the feel of those shapely curves in his palms made his shaft stiffen with a swift heat.

Though he hadn't slept in weeks, he wouldn't with Melanthe near, for fear of what he might do to her. Over his adult life, every single one of his dreams had featured her—him *doing things* to her.

Sometimes he'd wake to find himself thrusting against the sheets, the pillow, his fist—anything to ease the pressure his body continued to struggle with.

Culminating like that was considered a disgrace for a mated male. Releasing anywhere outside his mate's sex was taboo, a waste of a precious resource.

Soon he wouldn't have to worry about such things. Once he wed her, he'd wake to find himself thrusting between her thighs.

In mere days, they'd be back in the Skye. Within his home, he'd take her to his bed—a Bed of Troth.

Craftsmen had begun carving it for him on the day of his birth, a practice that wasn't unusual among the more stable Lorean species. For Vrekeners, this lifelong bed was considered hallowed. By law, it was the one place he could claim her.

Just that act would marry him and Melanthe. They'd be officially bound, and—with the gods' favor—expecting.

But now he had another urgent reason to return to his home. If what she said was true and his knights had acted outside his specific orders not to hurt either sister, Thronos was going to rain down punishment.

Melanthe had once sent Thronos crashing to his doom. Years later, had they done the same to Sabine?

Not for justice. But for vengeance. *The master* I *now serve.*

Sabine had killed the sovereign of their species, his own father; Thronos could *almost* accept the idea of assassinating her, their vow notwithstanding.

But to target Melanthe?

It made no sense. In one thing she was correct: if he accepted Melanthe's version of events, then his beliefs would be turned inside out.

He would investigate thoroughly, keeping her under close guard. For her safety. *And ours.*

How was he going to control her powers without that collar . . . ?

Thronos rolled his head on his neck to loosen the knotted muscles there. Though he should be exhausted, he was wired. Yes, he was alert to danger, feeling less than secure in this place, but it was more.

That weird feeling of expectancy hit him then, along with an *easing* within him. Even as constant desire for Melanthe racked him, he was feeling more nonchalant about consequences. He found himself less concerned about missteps and offendments.

Which could prove ruinous with the temptation sleeping not ten feet from him.

Were these changes because of her or this place? Both?

So what would happen to him after six more days here with Melanthe? Perhaps he should head out tomorrow and scout for an alternative portal.

He heard her sigh in sleep. Without waking, she turned on her side to face him, displaying ample cleavage.

When he could drag his gaze from her breasts, his eyes followed the seam of her lithe thighs all the way up to the shadow beneath her skirt. He shifted uncomfortably as his length grew even harder.

Conclusion: the decision to wed her is sound.

He recalled that Feveris comment she'd made earlier. Thronos had been startled by his reaction. He'd imagined them bespelled with lust, and he'd longed for it.

In Feveris, he would be incapable of denying her, unable to follow the Vrekener law of marriage before touching, kissing, or claiming. They'd have no urge to leave that place, content just to mate . . . and mate . . . and mate . . .

He barely stopped himself from stroking his aching member. He knew better than to entertain these imaginings—because Vrekener law left him no recourse for his condition.

Not yet allowed to touch her body, or ever to pleasure his own.

Despite this, he wondered what would happen if he woke her with another forbidden kiss.

At the thought of her opening up to him—her red lips and smooth thighs parting—his shaft began to throb for relief.

Though inexperienced, he believed he could move her past any hesitations—because so many males had done so before him. And more, she'd admitted to a year of celibacy. For the duration of her imprisonment, he doubted she'd enjoyed any release whatsoever, just as he hadn't.

She'd likely melt for him.

Plus, if he wasn't mistaken, his mate was in season. At his earlier mention of children, he thought her eyes had briefly softened. Might his mate truly yearn for her own brood?

And thus his seed?

The idea of planting himself deep inside her sheath and breaking his seal put him into a lather. Especially now when she was fertile and needing. He had to bite back a groan.

Must get her to a Bed of Troth.

He turned from her to ram his horns against the wall. He grunted in pain; when had they become so sensitive? His vision briefly blurred, and he could swear he'd read words among the incomprehensible glyphs:

SACRIFICE THE PURE, WORSHIP THE MIGHTY, BEHOLD A TEMPLE UNEQUALED.

He jerked back. No, that wasn't possible. Though Thronos knew several languages, Demonish—especially primitive Demonish—was not among them.

There must be something in the air, making his vision play tricks on him. *This place is getting to me.* Even now the reasons he couldn't touch his mate grew dimmer.

He shook his head hard, attention easily returning to her. Her eyes darted behind her lids, her shoulders twitching. Was she always this fitful a sleeper? His first impulse was to take her into his wings. His second impulse was to take her into his arms, into his *hands.*

But he wouldn't. Though he now believed she was innocent of the worst of the crimes at Castle Tornin, she was still a liar and a thief who'd bedded scores of men. Already she had him doubting his own knights, who were epitomes of honor and forthrightness.

How could Thronos desire someone he'd long detested? He'd be damned if he valued her when she didn't value herself. He knew one thing that would cool his need like an ice storm, a memory that made his hatred seethe.

He'd been eighteen, closer to finding her than he'd been since the fall. Accompanied by his brother, Aristo, the new king of the Territories, Thronos had followed her sorcery to a hamlet, one sitting low between mountains, nearly hidden from the skies.

Though that night was centuries distant, he remembered each detail as if they'd been branded into his mind.

FIFTEEN

Lanthe woke, going from deep sleep to instant awareness.

How long had she been out? She tested her tongue . . . almost healed.

Even as weary as she'd been, she was surprised she'd slept. The siren call of gold still plagued her. Not to mention that a Vrekener hovered nearby.

He was presently limping/pacing. Had he rested at all?

Feigning sleep, she cracked her lids like the sneaky sorceress that she was.

His gaze was distant, eyes flickering silver. What was he thinking about? Perhaps he had lowered some of his blocks, and she could probe his thoughts.

Delving, delving—

In. His blocks were down!

Thronos was recollecting some distant memory from when he was a teenager. He'd been walking with another Vrekener, one around the same age who resembled him somewhat.

Oh, yes, she'd seen that male before, had a long and storied history with him.

She swallowed, spying as Thronos's memory played on. . . .

Anticipation burned inside him. After years of searching, he'd scented his mate the minute he and Aristo had arrived in this valley. Hastening down a winding lane, he glanced up at every window.

"I still don't understand your eagerness to reunite with her," Aristo said, following him. "Every limping step I took and every league flown in agony would fill me with rage. How can you forgive her?"

Because Thronos had put himself in her shoes to understand that night. "She was only a little girl. Her parents had just been decapitated, her beloved sister killed."

"As they should have been. The parents threatened Lore secrecy with their palpable sorcery outlays, and the sister murdered our father the king!"

Aristo thinks exactly like him.

"Why do you believe your mate will forgive you?"

"If I tell her how Father truly found out about the abbey, she'll know I was blameless." When they passed a tavern with a large window, Thronos spied his reflection, scowling at the scars.

Aristo caught his reaction. "She'd promised to be a little beauty, hadn't she?"

"Yes. So?" Thronos knew she would be the most comely female he'd ever seen. She had *already* been. He'd spent endless hours imagining what she would look like now.

"Sorceri are fickle creatures, brother. In addition to all the pain between you, it might be that she forsakes you for your looks. Have you thought of that?"

Of course. Every time he saw his reflection. "She's my mate; we're fated, and she felt it too." That last day, when she'd turned to him so sweetly and sighed—

"Mayhap you merely need to copulate?"

He did. With Melanthe. Gods, how he did! But Thronos had waited this long; somehow he'd wait the two more years until she turned eighteen and could be claimed. Twenty-four more months by Vrekener law. It seemed like an eternity, especially with the way his curiosity and lusts had been building.

He wondered if any other eighteen-year-old male could possibly think about intercourse as much as he did.

"I fear you set yourself up for disappointment," Aristo said.

"So you think I should give her up, without even trying? Just forget it. You wouldn't understand."

His brother hadn't found his mate, and likely wouldn't for decades, if not centuries. Thronos had been an anomaly to find his so young.

"Then explain it to me."

"Melanthe is"—*everything missing from my life*—"my ideal female." She wasn't thus because she was faultless, but because he adored even her faults. He didn't just want her; he needed her. They were each halves of a greater whole.

Why was that so difficult for others to understand? "She's mine," he said simply.

"We're at war with them," Aristo couldn't resist pointing out.

"Then mayhap we *shouldn't* be. . . ." He trailed off, homing in on her. "The building at the end of the lane," he said over his shoulder, already hurrying forward. "There's a dwelling above."

Heartbeat pounding, he alighted on the windowsill. Melanthe! She was in a bed asleep. Holding his breath, he crept inside.

A sharp exhalation left him. Melanthe was a woman now.

He greedily took in every new detail. He'd known she

would grow to be lovely, but she was beyond his wildest fantasies. Her lashes were thick against her pale face, her black hair a silken cloud around her head. The sheet gathered at her waist, allowing him to see the swells of her breasts beneath her filmy nightgown.

The *generous* swells.

Her nipples strained against the thin material.

To see her like this made his heart twist in his chest—and blood pool in his groin. He no longer felt his old injuries.

To see her like this, he could forgive her *anything.*

How am I to wait two years?

He'd had no idea what to say or do once he finally found her. Now the answer was startlingly clear: sit beside her on the bed, wake her with a caress, and explain the truth of that night to her.

He hated the pain he was about to bring her, knew she would feel guilt for her actions. But he had to clear the air between them—

An older vampire traced into the room, carrying bottles of wine. Thronos tensed to attack, to protect his mate.

"Lanthe, I'm back," the male said, unaware of him, gone motionless in the shadows.

She sat up, rubbing her eyes with a smile. "Marco."

The vampire *Marco* smelled of her. And she . . . of him.

Thronos was frozen, unable to comprehend what he was seeing. Melanthe was too young to be bedding anyone!

His senses were mistaken.

The vampire caught sight of him then, eyes going wide. Both males leapt for her, but the leech traced, reaching her first. He teleported Melanthe across the room.

She blinked in astonishment. "You?"

"Who the hell is this?" the vampire demanded.

Thronos found his voice. "Melanthe, I need to speak—"

"He's an enemy," she interrupted. "One I'd hoped never to see again."

"As you wish, sweet." The vampire traced them away.

"Nooo!" Thronos bellowed.

To be this close! Frenzied, he scanned the room for some clue to where she might have been taken. He would find her again!

He frowned at the bed—at the blood on the sheets.

Her virgin's blood? The room seemed to spin. *Can't . . . this cannot be . . .*

But it was. She'd given that male her virtue on this very night. *Despite belonging to me!*

Clawing at his chest, he threw back his head and roared like an animal. All the physical pain in his body flared, nearly putting him to his knees.

Aristo yelled for him, arriving seconds later. His narrowed gaze took in the scene. "Another male?" He didn't sound surprised.

The vampire's skin had been unmarked and smooth.

Blood on the sheets. *He claimed my Melanthe.* Thronos turned away and vomited.

Aristo snapped, "Will you forgive her now?"

Dazed, he let his brother lead him away. Before long, he was swilling the spirits Aristo offered. Not long after that, Aristo suggested they enter a forbidden house of flesh. Thronos deemed this an excellent idea.

Offendments be damned; he was determined to drink his sorrows away—and to bury himself in another woman.

But he *couldn't.* Any other female's scent was repellent to him. He knew of no Vrekener who could stray from a mate.

Thronos would claim Melanthe. Or none at all.

As the months passed, he'd convinced himself that she had to have been pressured by the older vampire to surrender her virtue. Once he found her again, Thronos would take her away, tearing her from the male's influence.

He'd been convinced—until he'd seen her the next year with a tall fey male. Laughing, the two had run through a portal rift. When the pair had kissed as they'd crossed, Melanthe had wounded Thronos far more than her command to jump ever had. . . .

Lanthe struggled to regulate her breathing after what she'd just witnessed: his memory of their first meeting after his fall.

She'd felt his devastation at finding her in Marco's bed. She'd experienced firsthand the sickness that had taken hold in him, the disbelief. She'd been scalded by his violent jealousy and rocked from the agony of his injuries.

He hadn't thought he could wait two years to claim her; he'd waited centuries.

Somehow she kept her lids half-closed, her breaths deep and even. The identity of his companion had shocked her as much as anything else she'd learned.

The male with the pitchfork, the one who'd dropped her sister upon cobblestones was . . . Aristo.

King of the Vrekeners. Thronos's older brother.

Obviously, Aristo hadn't given a damn that Lanthe was Thronos's mate. The king had wanted her and Sabine dead. If Thronos forced Lanthe to Skye Hall, would Aristo finish her once and for all? How the hell was she going to convince Thronos of this?

Well, Vrekener, I was scratching around inside your brain, and oops, I witnessed a memory that you would be humiliated for me to see. I realized the sadistic thug who reveled in my pain is your brother! Oh, and your king! He prolly helped raise you after my sis beheaded your dad.

She now understood why Thronos hadn't known about the attacks. Who would rat out their leader?

Looking as sick as he'd been that night, Thronos sank back against a column, then slipped to the ground to sit with bent knees. He tipped his head back, staring at the ceiling, his striking eyes lost. He was wondering if he'd ever be free of her hold. *Maybe in death,* he thought.

She stared at his face, then the skin of his chest, both scarred because of her. How fiercely he hated those marks!

And she'd mauled his mind even worse.

She'd known his seeing her with another would have to hurt, but she hadn't even plumbed the depths. Despite all the anguish she'd suffered at the hands of his kind, she ached for the young man he'd been.

At that age, he'd thought she was ideal. He'd planned to forgive her for his injuries.

Until she'd inadvertently dealt him a wound he'd never recovered from.

She still couldn't wrap her head around all she'd learned. Had someone else told his father about the abbey? And what was the "truth of that night"? Thronos had been so certain she would forgive him.

It frightened her how badly she wanted him to be blameless, even as the truth struck her: if he was, then he hadn't deserved any of the suffering she'd—purposely or unwittingly—caused.

I broke a little boy's body.

And a young man's heart.

SIXTEEN

When Lanthe woke again, night still clung to the realm, the battle ongoing. Perhaps both were endless here.

Thronos was gone, probably out sourcing food. Since she didn't eat meat, she had scant hope for her own breakfast. Would he remember the time he'd tried to hunt for her?

She was surprised he'd left her alone, not that she could escape. She rose, testing her tongue—all healed!—and stretched her stiff muscles. If she felt this rough sleeping on the cold stone, she could only imagine how he'd felt. *If* he'd slept.

Eager to wash the grit from her skin and hair, she crossed to the cave opening, removing her gauntlets and boots along the way. Rain poured, spattering the lava on either side of the entrance, producing steam tendrils. Sidling near the very edge, she commanded herself not to look down as she reached for warm rainwater.

Most Lore species were fastidious. Yet she hadn't had a shower in weeks, had been forced to bathe with freezing water from a sink.

She drank from her cupped hands, rinsing her mouth of residual blood, then removed her underwear and breastplate to clean them and as much of her body as she could. While she washed, she reflected on all she'd learned in the last two days and came to a startling realization: *I have nothing to hate Thronos for.*

At least from the past. He was innocent of the crimes she'd pegged him for. He hadn't had a direct hand in Sabine's deaths, had even taken pains to prevent them. She now believed he'd kept secret the location of the abbey.

Did she wish he'd given her a heads-up that his father was going to attack that night? Absolutely. And she wished Thronos had kept a better leash on his men—on his *brother*—but she couldn't have expected him to. In no universe would he *not* have trusted the word of another Vrekener.

After last night, her chronic anxiety over surprise attacks had begun to fade at last. She now knew who her enemy was: Aristo. And where their next encounter would be: Skye Hell, if Thronos got his way.

If Lanthe could be freed of that overriding anxiety, would her powers bloom?

After unbraiding her hair, she smoothed water over it. Once she'd rinsed it clean, she painstakingly plaited it into braids around her face. The rest she left to curl down her back.

She was glad of this time alone to digest everything that had happened—and to consider her burgeoning interest in Thronos. After she'd fallen back asleep, still heartsick at his memory, she'd had *vivid* dreams of him.

In one, he'd kissed her in the rain. He'd grasped her face between his palms, brushing his thumbs along her cheekbones; then he'd set in, his pained groans rumbling along her lips as he'd taken her mouth with furious need—until they were sharing breaths, until he'd stoked her own desperation.

Lanthe had never been kissed like that. Like the male would *die* if she didn't part her lips and return it.

In another, she'd traced her fingertips over every scar on his naked body, then followed her touches with her lips and tongue. He'd shuddered with sensitivity—but he'd bowed his rugged chest for more. . . .

She exhaled a breath, determined not to think about him like that—

or to even acknowledge that her nipples were stiffening in the sultry air. She arched her back, letting rain patter over her, cooling her breasts. She wished she could say these were the first sensual dreams she'd had of him. They weren't, and over the year since their last encounter, these reveries had grown more numerous.

She gazed out into the night. Surely Thronos would return soon. She dressed again, was reaching for her gauntlets—

A sound behind her. She whirled around.

The back wall of the cave was opening, directly where she'd sensed the gold. Thronos strode out, looking bored, while behind him was . . .

Heaven.

His mate had caught sight of the golden temple he'd found, and now looked like her legs were about to buckle. "Did I see correctly?"

Ah, her tongue was working again. Soon he'd be treated to more of her lies. But she wasn't a master deceiver, not like he'd expected. She had tells, and he was learning them.

In his absence, she'd cleaned herself. Her skin was scrubbed, looking rosier, highlighting the blue of her eyes. Her raven hair was drying into glossy braids and big curls.

He craved threading his fingers through that length.

To see it streaming over his chest as he held her close. . . .

Inward shake. Without those gauntlets, she appeared more delicate. Smaller somehow. He assessed the rest of her "garments" with a disapproving eye. When he got her to the Skye, he'd see to it that she dressed appropriately.

"Thronos, is there gold behind that stone?"

"Yes. A temple of it, built with gold bricks from floor to soaring ceiling. Even I found it wondrous to behold."

She sounded like she'd muffled a whimper.

When the heavy door began easing closed, she sprinted for it. The stone sealed shut before she could reach it. "Open this again!" Her tone was frantic. "Please!"

He didn't answer, dismissively striding to the cliff edge of the cave. Behind him, he could hear her digging around for an entry she'd never find.

For once, *he* would ignore *her.* He stared out at the horizon, taking in the storms over the swamplands—the slow fade of lightning strikes backlighting purple clouds. So different from his home in the heavens.

The Air Territories were a collection of floating islands, massive monoliths that hovered above the clouds. His realm was crowned forever by seamless skies—unbroken blue or star-filled black.

Skye Hall was the royal seat, but every island had its own city, each laid out with precision. All the buildings were angular and uniform, with sun-bleached walls. His home was a testament to order, an anchor for steadfast Vrekeners.

Unlike this plane.

The scene before Thronos was chaotic. Yet he found it surprisingly . . . arresting. Was there some kind of appeal to this entire domain?

His restlessness increased, that damned *expectancy* redoubling. He needed to get back to his anchor as soon as possible.

"How did you open this, Thronos?"

He'd read the instructions. Over this interminable night, Thronos had come to a conclusion: not reading the glyphs was cowardly; he was no coward.

This language might not even be demonic in nature. It could be some kind of mystical tongue that only certain Loreans could read. Perhaps only the worthy.

Like himself.

And, he'd reasoned, reading would help him learn about this plane. So he'd started at the outer cave wall, making his way in. Some sections had degraded with age, but he'd been able to glean that this cave was the entry to an ancient temple for dragon worship—and ritual sacrifice.

This hadn't alarmed him. Dragons weren't likely to roam war-torn Pandemonia; they'd gone extinct in most dimensions.

Then he'd come upon instructions to enter the temple, and had easily opened the door. He'd found a scene that would prove to be his mate's most fevered fantasy.

Everyone knew Sorceri loved gold. Thronos had firsthand knowledge of just how much.

He remembered a day when Melanthe hadn't come to the meadow. She hadn't felt well the day before, and he'd been worried. He'd flown to her home, stealing across the roof, trying to scent her room amidst the sorcery. He'd scrabbled down the side of the abbey to a window, peeking inside. . . .

A black-haired woman with an immense gold headpiece and crazed blue eyes was rubbing coins against her masked face, murmuring, "Gold is life! It is perfection!" She began to speak to each piece, as if she'd met it at the market to gossip.

Chills raced over him. He'd never seen a madwoman before, and he believed she was Melanthe's own mother.

Sorcery steeped the room as she chanted about gold: "Band it in armor over thy heart, and never will thy life's blood part. Gild your hair and face and skin, and no man breathes that you can't win. Never too much can a sorceress steal, those who defend she duly kills—"

Her eyes suddenly met his. He jolted back, but she cried, "I seeeee you. Come, hawkling. Visit a sorceress in her lair."

He swallowed, then eased over to crouch on the sill, ready for flight. Behind her were piles of gold coins and bars, more than anyone could spend in a lifetime. Melanthe's family had wealth; why would they let her go hungry?

"So you are the one who gives my Melanthe her new smiles," the woman said. "She raises her gaze forever to the sky and floats when she walks—as if she's still flying with you."

He was forever gazing earthward, as if he could watch over her.

"Earthward, then, Thronos Talos of Skye Hall?"

The sorceress was reading his mind!

"It won't last. Melanthe will never be what you need her to be. You can't break my daughter, and that's the only way she'd love you. . . ."

Thronos didn't *want* Melanthe's love, had no desire for it. He would break her—but only to make her become what he needed. And he'd start by using this temple against her, getting answers out of her.

From behind him, she cried, "Why would you keep me from such a place?"

He turned to her. The distress on her face was priceless. She was practically vibrating with eagerness. He repeated her words: "Why not?"

Must get in! Behind this door was more gold than Lanthe had ever witnessed in one place. Even the great Morgana, queen of the Sorceri, didn't have that much in her possession.

How could Thronos deny her?

Lanthe had already been on edge from his memory, then from her own dreams. She turned back to the stone, resting her body against it, raising her arms over her head—for more of her skin to touch the door that separated her from heaven. She remained like this, as if she could melt through.

He might as well be here blocking her way, her body pressed against his. He was the key! She had to convince him. *Think, Lanthe!* What did he want from her?

She faced him again. "Please, you can't keep me from it!"

He sat on the ground, one knee bent, a casual arm resting over it. "I found it. I claimed it. My temple, my gold—I make the rules."

There was something about his domineering tone that was weirdly arousing. Even though she was filled with turmoil, her nipples tightened again. She bit her bottom lip, wondering how far she'd go to sway him.

If she could just touch the gold, take its song into her . . .

She hastened over to kneel between his legs. He looked startled, but that didn't stop him from widening his legs to accommodate her—so she moved in closer.

That electricity sparking between them made her hyper-aware of his body, of his heat. His shirt was hanging on only by a low button, revealing his chest, which rose and fell with his shallowed breaths.

When his Adam's apple bobbed, she peeked down and found his shaft growing. It was only semihard, but already . . . generous. Demons were notorious for their size. *I hope this one's a show-er and not a grower, or I'm a dead woman.*

No, no! There would be no intercourse with a Vrekener! *So stop staring at his cock, Lanthe.* Dragging her gaze up, she cleared her throat. "Thronos, beyond that wall is nothing less than heaven for me. Why would you keep me from it?" she asked, noticing that he had gold dust on one side of his neck. Did the temple *rain* gold? The thought made her pant.

He frowned at her reaction. "I'll keep you from it because—"

He was cut short when she grabbed one of his horns and pulled his head to the side. "Gold dust," she murmured, unable to help herself. "Give me this first." His skin smelled as sublime as the gold. With a moan, she leaned in to rub her face against it, to get his gold on her. She rubbed her other cheek, then drew back.

A smattering remained right over his pulse point—which was palpitating along with his thundering heart.

Too much temptation! She dipped down to press her open mouth over his neck, feeling his pulse beneath her tongue, taking in the cool gold mixed with his own delectable taste. She shivered with delight. Once she'd licked him, she leaned in beside his ear to whisper, "I never knew you'd taste so good."

His big body shuddered, bringing her back to reality. Oh, gods, was she actually gripping his horn? Releasing him, she drew back to face him.

His expression was . . . dazed, his pupils blown, his eyes glazed with lust. He shifted where he sat, no doubt because his erection was paining him. His claws dug into his palms as he fought not to touch her.

In that moment an epiphany struck her, as bright and shining as the temple of gold just one door away from her.

She could enchant this male.

In their history, she'd befriended him, run from him, fought him, and spurned him. But she'd never tried to tempt him. She was descended from the enchantment caste of the mystical immortal species. She wasn't without innate skills.

Plus, she had centuries of sexual experience over this hard-up virgin novice. Though she'd never take it too far, she could tempt him up to a point. She'd run circles around him, wrapping him around her little finger.

If she didn't want him to take her to the Skye, then all she had to do was ask him very, *very* nicely.

When she slowly grinned, his gaze dipped to her lips, so she licked them. His brows drew together, and he swallowed thickly.

Your ass is mine, Vrekener.

SEVENTEEN

"Please take me back there, love." Melanthe's eyes were shimmering blue, her cheeks sparkling with gold.

Never in Thronos's imaginings had he thought, *She might lick my neck.*

The decision to wed this creature is very *sound.*

She kept touching him—with her hands, with her mouth—and each contact made pleasure explode through him. She might not like his appearance, but she'd liked his taste. All his earlier plans seemed to evaporate, his mind shuttling to fantasies best left buried.

I could coax her to taste other parts of me. Feeding his shaft between her red lips . . .

Or he could taste *her,* wringing a climax from her with his tongue. At the thought of licking between her thighs, he was seized by the urge to toss her to the ground and feast.

His claws dug into his palms, the bite of pain helping him focus. Somewhat. "Why should I take you back there? Why should I make any concession for you?"

"Because your mate needs to see it."

"Ah, so now you say you're my mate."

When she slinked even closer, her scent—a mix of home, sky, and *woman*—boggled his mind. "If that entitles me to fifty percent of your gold, then yes, I'm your mate."

Where was her hostility? He could handle himself when she was a typical hateful sorceress, but this was throwing him. "If you see it, you'll desire it. Then what? It's not as if we can take it with us."

"It would be enough just to touch it, to answer its call."

Like touching a talisman.

"What can I say to convince you? Thronos, you can't understand what the element is to me."

He spoke before he considered his words: "It's life to you."

Her eyes widened, and she nodded. "Yes! Gold is life. It's as beautiful as love, as divine as laughter." She took his hand, raising it. When she made him trail the backs of his fingers over the soft skin above her breastplate, he just stifled a growl.

"Gold is this"—she pressed his palm flat over her chest—"next"—he dipped a thumb into her cleavage—"heartbeat."

Her heart was racing; his must have stopped. *Don't squeeze her plump flesh, don't squeeze. . . .*

She laid her own hands on his thighs, shifting her weight to her straightened arms, which pushed his thumb deeper between her creamy breasts. "You want to show me your gold. You want my fingers wrapped around your gold, stroking it."

Trying to command him? With a scowl, he dragged his hand away. "Your power isn't working."

"I wasn't persuading you." She inched her hands higher, nearly to his groin. "I was seeing if I could get you to substitute a certain noun for the word *gold*." She pressed her thumbs in, indicating what she meant.

You want to show me your shaft. You want my fingers wrapped around your shaft, stroking it. When she gazed down at his erection, he almost rocked his hips. Yes, he *did* want to show it to her. So she could touch him, suck him. . . .

He hissed in a breath between his teeth. How much more of this could he be expected to resist? He needed to get space between them. "I have conditions before I agree."

"Name them."

"Tell me something that will ease my wrath a degree."

"Very well." She gazed up at the ceiling for a moment before facing him again. "I had sensual dreams about you earlier."

If true, this was at once encouraging and infuriating to him. "Once? I've had them of you every time I've slept!"

"I didn't say it was the first time we've been wicked together. In my dreams."

His lips parted. What wicked things did she dream of him doing to her?

"Clearly that eased your wrath a jot. Now, what's your next condition?"

"If I'm to show you my treasures—you're to show me yours," he said, shocked by his own words. He'd planned to get answers out of her; all of a sudden, he'd begun angling to see her unclothed!

Nudity in his culture was taboo. Even husbands and wives were expected to be clothed around each other at all times. When he took Melanthe in a Bed of Troth, there'd be a claiming sheet between them.

"You want me to strip for you?" she asked in a demure tone.

He'd started down this road. . . . Voice gone hoarse, he said, "Yes, if you enter that temple, you'll bare yourself inside it."

"Okay!" In a blur, she'd risen and was already at the door.

She'd acquiesced? Despite her Sorceri blood, he'd thought she would put up at least a show of resistance, and that they would negotiate: perhaps she'd only agree to revealing her breasts, et cetera.

Instead, the shameless sorceress had agreed to all. He felt like he was in a battle that had just gone sideways, like he should be jerking his head back and forth to understand his new position.

As he rose to join her, he wondered, *What else will she agree to?* And his mouth went dry.

She smiled up at him, her lips curling proudly. She was aware of her power over males, had lorded it over so many. She took his arm between both of hers, standing unaccountably close to him.

So the temptress was using her wiles on him? The thought should fill him with anger. *Not* excitement.

He must remember that this creature was descended from the greatest enchantresses ever to live. He had to be mindful of all her conquests, the ones who'd fallen before him.

"Is there a hidden lever, then? A combination to open it?"

"Yes. A combination." As per the instructions, he'd pressed in one hieroglyph, spun another, then ratcheted down a third. "Turn around while I open it."

Again, she went against his expectations by complying. "How did you figure it out?"

"Wasn't difficult," he said, unwilling to tell her, knowing she would attribute his comprehension to his alleged demon blood.

Press, spin, ratchet. The door opened once more.

She barreled past him, as if she feared he'd change his mind. Just inside, she drew up short. As her slim shoulders began to tremble, he tried to see the area through her eyes.

The temple was round, constructed of solid gold slabs and bricks that seemed to catch and magnify the weak light filtering in. A dais stood in the center, with gold benches fanning out from it, like arena seating.

The golden ceiling was divided into five wedges, each with different glyphs, like those in the cave. More had been carved into the floor-to-ceiling gold walls.

Still reeling from her assault on his senses, he decided to put space between him and temptation. Twenty feet above them was a shining shelf. He leapt up to it, crouching on one knee to watch his mate's love affair begin.

Slowly, she reached out her hand to one of the walls. . . .

Contact. She visibly shuddered, as if she'd touched a live wire. Would she react so sensually during intercourse?

With a look of wonder, she ran her fingers over a row of gold bricks, her eyes glimmering.

She was experiencing *joy.* The last time he'd experienced that for himself had been on their final day in the meadow. Rain had fallen, and he'd taken her under his wings. . . .

Now she hastened to the dais, spinning in place atop it, laughing with delight. When they'd been young, the sound of her laughter had made his heart swell. Now that sound affected a different part of his anatomy.

Perhaps he would approach joy once more when he saw his mate's body for the first time.

Lanthe hadn't caught her breath since she'd entered, her captivated gaze taking in every detail.

Happiness coursed through her veins. How had clever Thronos found this place?

Though she was in a room full of gold, her attention veered to him, crouched on that shelf. The muscles of his torso flexed with his movements. His stern, intense expression and that gargoyle-like position made him look very demonic.

She'd never bedded a demon before. Huh.

Yet as she strolled the temple, his constant scowl eased. Without that scowl, he was . . . gorgeous.

There was no more denying it—or her attraction to him.

Some females might consider his scars unsightly. Lanthe thought they made him look tough and warlord-y. Besides, who could care about them when those silver eyes were so compelling? When his warrior's body seemed to have been sculpted from granite?

He'd once believed that she was "everything missing" from his life. Could he still feel that way? And why was she contemplating these things—instead of how to transpo this gold to Rothkalina or calculating karats?

Why did she have the urge to peer up at him with equal captivation? She surrendered to her impulse, turning to him. He seemed surprised by her perusal but held her gaze.

They were—dare she say it?—having a moment.

"You face me when surrounded by gold? Perhaps I *rate* after all?" The scowl returned, as if he was hardening himself. She wanted to cry, *No, no, no, just a few more minutes!*

"We had a deal," he said. "I grow impatient."

She could imagine—he'd waited so long to see her. And now she knew he'd already been struggling with his lust and curiosity when he'd been a young man.

A deal was a deal. She would take the sight of this gold into her, a memory to last forever. *Unless I can return. . . .*

"Be about it, sorceress."

Since she'd planned to enthrall him, this would be a good start, but the way he was crouching forward, as if on the verge of pouncing, made her hesitate. "If I do this, how do I know you won't try to touch me? You're not supposed to, right?"

"I only intend to look," he said, though she could sense his aggression mounting.

"Uh-huh."

"Do it, then." When she still hesitated, he said, "Don't feign shyness—I know you've done this with a horde of males before me."

And just like that, her interest was checked. Though she was neither ashamed nor proud of the number of men she'd been with, his cruel jabs wounded her.

At least now she better understood his resentment. "I don't think it's a good idea to put myself in a sexual situation with you."

He growled at that. "After your purported year of celibacy, I would expect you to be climbing the walls for any male's attentions. And if I'm not mistaken, you're in season."

She flushed, lips thinning.

"I've heard tales of females like you." At her raised brows, he enunciated the words, "Easy quarry."

How could a maddened Vrekener hurt her so much?

Because he once looked at you with perfect acceptance, Lanthe. And she feared she'd been searching for that look ever since she'd lost it.

In order for her to be interested in a male, he needed to make her feel special—even if she knew it was a ruse. Despite Thronos's mind-blowing body and heartbreaking past, he stood no chance. "Even we 'easy quarry' girls have standards. And you, Thronos Talos, are leaving me cold."

He scoffed. "I could seduce you with ease. You've welcomed scores before me with only minuscule effort on their part. But I've no intention of taking you, nor even of touching you. Both are offendments. I only want to see my female."

"You think you can resist seeing your mate naked?"

"You think I can't?" A cunning light shone in his gaze. "You Sorceri like to gamble? To make bets? Then I'll enter into a wager with you—my first."

Dudley Do-Right makes a bet.

"If your body tempts me to touch it, then I'll tell you how I found this temple and opened the door."

"And if it doesn't tempt you?"

"The blow to your enchantress pride would be reward enough."

That is it! Now it was imperative to wipe that smirk off his face. "I'll take your bet." She thought she spied a flash of surprise in his expression. "No sex, though."

He glowered, as if she'd suggested something ludicrous. "I'll breed no bastards! Already my offspring will be half Sorceri. Do you think I'd allow the first to be illegitimate on top of that?"

Asshole! Only Thronos could ruin this: her, in a temple full of gold with a physically attractive male. He was like the anti-Sorceri—created to repel her.

Forget enchanting him! He didn't deserve her beguilement. "I'll remember this."

"What?"

"That you kill joy wherever you find it." She gave him her back as she unfastened the first of three clips on the side of her breastplate.

Had his breaths quickened?

She gazed over her shoulder, saw his claws digging into the gold shelf, his throat working. His voice dropped an octave when he commanded, "Off with it."

She unfastened the second clip.

"That's it," he murmured, his words dripping with pent-up lust.

As she was undoing the last clip, she heard something from beyond the main cave, and paused. The sound came again, growing in volume—movement down the mountainside. Something *big* was approaching. "Thronos, what was that?"

"Heard *nothing*. Continue."

"Come on, demon!" She began fastening the clips again.

"There's nothing to fear out there!"

When the entire temple rocked, she snapped, "Oh, really?"

He made a coarse sound of frustration; then she heard the swoop of his wings. She whirled around to find him charging toward her, that determined look on his grave face.

His eyes appeared to have darkened, and she could swear his horns were straightening—just like a demon's would when he became aroused.

In other words, *Thronos doesn't live here anymore.*

Reaching for her, he bit out, "To tide me over."

Till when?!

A roar sounded in the cave. Seeming to wake out of a daze, Thronos dropped his hands. And she could have sworn upstanding Dudley Do-Right grated, *"Fuck."*

EIGHTEEN

Thronos lunged for her, shoving her behind the stone door that led to the main cave. He pulled her close, then wrapped a protective wing around her.

"What is it?" she whispered.

"I smell a creature, but scarcely trust my senses. I thought they were going extinct across all worlds."

He couldn't be talking about a dragon? When she heard some great beast *breathing* at the outer cave entrance, she shuddered. Two bright lights blazed inside like a car's high beams.

Thronos craned his head around the door to catch a glimpse. His heart pounded at whatever he'd seen.

She delved into his thoughts . . . then sucked in a breath.

A dragon had its head in the cave opening, its brilliant yellow eyes glowing. Heated air blurred around its nose. Its scales were onyx and silver, glinting like metal.

She switched to telepathy. —*This place, the benches* . . . —

As if reciting something, he muttered, "Sacrifice the pure, worship the mighty, behold a temple unequaled."

So this place was dedicated to virgin sacrifice for mighty dragons? She wasn't surprised. Many demon cultures worshipped dragons. Rydstrom had the image of one tattooed on his side.

In Rothkalina's Grave Realm, the badlands of the kingdom, basilisks roamed wild. Lanthe had gone to visit them with Sabine a few times. Her sister had the power to communicate with animals, and had gotten to know one or two well.

But Lanthe wasn't Sabine. And this dragon looked hungry for a sacrifice.

If she weren't petrified, she might have laughed. Lanthe was no cherry-holder of yore; the dragon would probably spit her out like a pit.

The headlights shining into the cave shuttered off and on. Oh, gods, the dragon had *blinked.* Then the entire mountain rocked and claws skittered into the cave. Had the beast shoved its lethal paw inside?

The dragon sounded like it was blindly patting around the cave, reaching all the way to this door. It must have locked in on them!

Pat . . . pat . . . pat . . . pat.

Oh, yeah, the dragon knew they were in here, and it wanted its treat.

Thronos whispered, "Easy, Melanthe. Stay quiet."

Quiet? Did he think she'd cry out in hysterics? Galling!

—*Quiet, yourself! I have some experience with such situations. For instance, in that haystack, I never made a sound, even when pitchfork tines stabbed me.*— She held up her hand, showing him the two puncture scars on the back. Granted, you had to *really* look for them, and she usually wore gauntlets. . . .

He clasped her hand in his, turning it this way and that. She sensed his anger and confusion, but he made no comment.

When the dragon snorted with impatience, Thronos drew her hand to his side and wrapped his wing tighter. She frowned down at it.

Metallic onyx and silver scales. Just like this dragon had. In Rothkalina, the basilisks' scales were red-toned.

Curiosity made her brave, and she darted a glance around the door, before Thronos dragged her back. This dragon differed from its cousins in Rothkalina in one other way.

It had four horns instead of two. Just as Vrekeners had four instead of a customary pair.

As if with annoyance, the dragon pummeled its wings against the mountainside, causing a shower of grit and dust even deeper within the cave. Finally it gave a blood-curdling roar, then flew away.

"Thronos," she murmured, "you come from this place."

"Are you mad? I do *not* come from this place," Thronos snapped the moment they were in the clear, releasing her from his wing. "One more time, sorceress: I am not a demon! Vrekeners are descended from gods. We have *purpose.*" His tone was harsher than he'd intended, because . . . because he *had* felt an affinity for the beast.

There was no mistaking the similarity of their scales, their horns. Some said demons sprang from the same tainted well as dragons, that they lived and evolved on the same types of hell planes.

Such as Pandemonia.

"I thought Vrekener horns were only for show," Melanthe said with obvious glee. "Yours *straightened* when I began to undress."

"I'm to take your word on that?" But how they'd ached!

"I'll bet you have a demon seal. You won't release seed until you're inside your mate."

Only this sorceress could make that sound like a huge failing. A Vrekener male could orgasm, but could never ejaculate until he first claimed his female. Thronos racked his brain for another species besides demons that shared this singular trait.

"So I have a couple of things in common with demons." He ran his fingers through his hair. "I also have fangs—does that make me a vampire? My eyes turn silver, so I must be a Valkyrie."

"Deny, deny, deny. Look at you, struggling to keep your head above water with this. Returning to this realm is crumbling your stuffy Vrekener façade, exposing your true demon nature."

When he'd viewed Melanthe's scars—puncture wounds that had pierced her hand clean through—his eyes had felt like they were *on fire.*

When he'd imagined the pain she would've felt, his fangs had elongated to rip out someone's throat.

As a demon's might.

No, he was not a bloody demon!

So why had he behaved like one earlier? He'd told himself he would only look at his mate. But when he'd realized she was actually going to bare her body, he'd known he would be helpless not to touch it.

He'd imagined kneading her breasts, *suckling* them, licking her nipples until she couldn't stand it anymore. By the time she'd started to remove her top, he was already envisioning even more forbidden taboos.

Placing her hand into the heat of his pants and guiding her to fondle his length. Reaching beneath her skirt and exploring her sex with seeking fingers.

Claiming her. Breaking his seal and spending his seed at long last.

The dragon was gone; what was to stop Thronos now? He raked his gaze over her, his thoughts darkening once more.

"Thronos, it's not *bad* to be a demon," she said, her tone softening a touch. "Some things just *are,* okay?"

At her words, he lifted his eyes to hers, felt like he couldn't get enough air. He'd been about to start the madness all over!

Must leave this place. He needed to get back to the Skye. To sanity and reason and order.

She was making him doubt everything—just as she had when they were children! "If you can create portals, can you sense other ones? Feel their energy?"

She hesitated, then nodded.

"We could find Pandemonia's portal." Thresholds like that were valuable—and vulnerable. They were often hidden. "You'll direct me, and I'll protect you."

"Ha! I will never leave a place like this to slog through a war-torn demon plane. You can close the stone door against the dragon, and we'll wait out our time."

"You and I could skirt the fray." Her speed was considerable, a fact that he used to curse. "I'll keep you safe."

She crossed her arms over her chest. "Not even going to discuss this. I'm going to stay in my gold house and sleep on my gold bed and ski down my piles of gold like Scrooge McDuck."

Whatever that meant. Another *TV* reference? "We can't stay here. Sooner or later that beast will get frustrated enough to dig through stone."

She pursed her lips. "Out there, we'll face nothing but danger, even more than the homicidal demon armies. This place is rumored to be littered with traps."

"What kind of traps?"

"You know how the humans have certain ideas of hell? Well, all those ideas are supposed to be based on the realities of Pandemonia. Torments of fire. Hell beasts of legend. Unearthly pleasures followed by punishments. The condemned cursed to repeat labors."

"Like Sisyphus having to roll a stone up a hill for eternity?"

"Bingo."

Thronos was undaunted. "Then we'd best find that portal as soon as possible."

"Nope. You will *never* convince me to leave this temple—"

Whirring gears sounded from above. The circular ceiling started to rotate. "What's happening, Thronos?"

Gold dust rained down as the ceiling shifted to reveal a pie-shaped opening.

A meaty, scaled arm shot through it, black dragon claws grappling over the floor beside them.

NINETEEN

Thronos snatched her hand, sprinting for the main cave—then skidded to a stop just beyond the door. The outside opening was blocked by another dragon, apparently the same one from earlier! Had it returned with reinforcements?

Back to the temple. "They're getting angrier," she cried. "Fire comes next!"

The dragon perched at the ceiling opening sucked in such a deep breath that Lanthe's braids rose. She heard a hiss like a punctured oxygen tank. *That sound must be its fuel.*

Just as fire erupted, Thronos hunched over her against the wall, covering her with his wings, two mighty shields. The force of the flames was like a boot kick to his back; he lurched forward against Lanthe.

"Ah, gods, are you okay?"

He bit out, "Why *wouldn't* I be?"

Had he just made a joke? Now?

"Ready to leave?" Sweat beaded his strained face.

"How?" She could swear she scented . . . melting gold. Was the dragon fire burning it to liquid?

When the flames receded, Thronos lowered his wing, glancing out. "The temple has another secret doorway."

She peeked out through two folds of his wings. "But the dragon's still above." She spotted something that couldn't be right. Amid a piping hot puddle of molten gold was a red medallion on a matching chain.

Red gold. It *had* to be silisk gold—a.k.a. dragon's gold.

"Down!" Thronos covered her again, and once more a blast of flames battered them. "We're going to run when he draws his next breath."

"I-I need to collect something."

"Your gauntlets? You don't need those!"

"First of all, yes, I do. Second, I'm talking about a medallion, behind you. Three o'clock."

He glanced in that direction. "Forget it, sorceress." Gritting his teeth, he said, "Past the benches is a second door. We run as soon as these flames end. *Now.*" He shoved her in front of him, wings cloaking her as they rushed to the wall across the temple.

When Thronos's eyes darted over the markings, hers went wide. "You're reading them! That's how you found this place!"

He started manipulating sections of gold. "What of it!"

Just as the gold door began to inch open, the dragon drew another breath. She heard that hissing sound.

The door was too slow . . . too slow! Through the opening crack, she spied a shadowy corridor with stone steps leading down.

"Go!" Thronos propelled her inside.

She was several flights down before he closed in behind her. Flames followed them.

He blocked them with his wings. Once they were out of range of the fire, he said, "Get behind me! We've no idea what we're heading into."

She nodded, shifting aside to let him lead as they raced farther down. A narrow passageway like this would prevent him from using his wings to strike. Now that she was working with him—somewhat—his vulnerabilities were hers as well. If they'd encountered those ghouls in this tight an area, she and Thronos would be dead, or worse.

The air grew hazy. Steam and smoke choked the corridor. Ahead, a rectangular opening seemed to glow. An exit! She stumbled. He glanced back.

"I'm fine!"

He sped through the exit onto a pathway—

A pathway that was bordered by a sheer cliff dropping into a river of lava. He was pinwheeling at the edge! She didn't think; her hand shot out, grasping the back of his breeches to reel him back in.

He gave her an irritated look over his shoulder. "I *can* fly, you know." Lava erupted from below in a geyser inches from his face. "Run!" As they sprinted down the winding path, he positioned his wings over them.

They barely evaded the deluge of lava. Glancing back, she said, "If you'd fallen and tried to fly, that lava would have engulfed you."

He couldn't deny it.

"I think the words you're searching for are 'Thank you, oh great and wonderful sorceress.' "

He narrowed his eyes. "You saved me from falling now. If only you'd shown me the same consideration when I was a boy."

"If only you'd warned my family that yours was coming over for tea and decapitation! What else have you got? I can do this all day!" She heard rock crunching behind them. The dragons were scaling the mountainside in pursuit!

Four lights blazed on the other side of the peak—from the dragons' eyes. Like movie-premiere spotlights directed straight up into the sky, they cut through the steam and murk.

"When they crest, we'll have to hide," Thronos said. "For now, get as far down the path as you can."

As she ran, she could see that the mountains on each side of the plateau below were actually the beginnings of two jagged ranges. More peaks lined the ongoing plateau and distant valleys—like teeth.

Farther down, she came upon a wooden handrail. She reached for it, nearly stumbling when it disintegrated into ash.

"Careful, Melanthe!"

Like a domino chain, the rail began collapsing into ash, foot by foot for what looked like leagues. "I'm sick of heights!"

As they raced forward, Thronos kept her between him and the mountain. The lower they got on the path, the more lava spurted in their way, forcing them to leap and dodge.

Molten silver ore spilled from the charred mountainside, flashing in the firelight—distracting her.

"Eyes forward, sorceress!"

When they had to vault over a burned-out section of the ledge and she nearly fell short, he snapped, "Come to me."

Without a word, she turned to hop into his arms, locking her legs around his waist, her arms around his neck. When he squeezed her against him, she said, "I'm getting used to jumping you."

He did a double take as he set off once more. "Are you, then?"

"Easy, tiger. I meant that we keep having to run for our lives."

"Just watch our back." As he lunged across another gulley, he said, "I couldn't have warned you about my father."

"What?"

"I had no idea of his plans until *after* he and his men had left. I dove for the abbey, but by the time I got there, he'd already killed your parents."

The truth of that night. "How'd he find out?"

"My tutor saw me sneaking out and followed me." Thronos slowed to meet her eyes. "I never betrayed you, Melanthe. I'd been tempted to tell my parents about you—I knew the Hall would move soon—but I would've talked to you about it first."

To his clear surprise, she said, "I believe you." Then her gaze drifted past him. "They're cresting! We have to hide." Thronos's wings would perfectly match this blackened rock face and the silver ore that drizzled from the stone. "Good thing you blend."

"I do not *blend*."

"Face it, demon, you blend like a native of hell. Luckily for us, the fire-breathing dragon breeds don't scent so well."

"How would you know?"

"I've hung out with a pack of them in Rothkalina. My sister can talk to them. They're really nice once you get to know them, only attacking trespassers and such. . . ." She trailed off when Thronos froze in place, craning his head up. She followed his gaze.

At least a dozen dragons swarmed the side of the mountain like bats coating a cave ceiling.

TWENTY

"We *are* trespassers." Thronos crouched down, pressing her back against the mountain. He spread his wings, enclosing them completely, and—damn her—*blending.*

When Melanthe shook against him, he muttered, "They haven't seen us. We're hidden here. Just think of something else."

For long moments, the sounds of their heartbeats were loud drums in the insulated hush beneath his wings.

"You used to enclose us like this when we were young," she finally said in a low voice. "I always felt I should whisper, as if we were under a sheet, staying up too late."

"We told each other secrets."

"So you do recall our months together?" she asked, looking pleased by this.

Some minutes less than others. He shrugged.

"How long do you think we'll have to wait here?"

"We can stay for as long as we need to." He'd no sooner said the words than he sensed a section of path disintegrating to his left. The dragons above roared in reaction. Then another section to his right collapsed, leaving him and Melanthe on a precarious island of rock.

"More heights." She bit her bottom lip until he thought she would split it.

He wanted to talk to her, distracting her mind from their situation. What to say?

She took care of the problem. "If we live through this, I'm going back for the medallion."

"The hell you are." Besides, she wouldn't find it if she returned.

"That wasn't regular gold. It's red silisk gold, also known as dragon's gold, the rarest and most valuable in all the known realms. I must have it, Thronos."

"Your timing is *poor*. I can't believe you're still thinking about it, considering our current circumstances." He was one to talk. He'd just glanced down, glimpsing Lanthe's thighs spread around his waist, her skirt worked up perilously high—and his thoughts had boomeranged back to the temple, to the treasures he'd almost seen. Even in this situation, his shaft hardened for his mate.

As if that weren't uncomfortable enough, the temperature continued to escalate. Like metal, his wings were still emanating heat from those direct flame hits. The river of lava below didn't help matters.

While Melanthe's skin grew flushed, he began to sweat. A drop slipped from his forehead onto her leg, high on her inner thigh. His eyes locked on the drop as it clung to her pale flesh, poised . . . before it slid down like a lazy touch.

He wanted to follow that trail with his tongue—then tug her little panties aside and discover what made her moan. . . .

"Um, Thronos, maybe we should change positions?" When her thighs flexed around his waist, he jerked his gaze up.

There was an unexpected metallic gleam in her blue eyes. Was that *interest*?

The urge to investigate this, to test boundaries, was overwhelming. *Wrong place, wrong time, Talos.* "Good idea. Yes." They shifted limbs, until she was seated with her legs together, perched across his own.

"Interesting that you can read those glyphs," she remarked casually.

"The language might not be demonic in nature."

"Uh-huh." Her way of saying *untruth.*

No one got his wings up like this sorceress! "You have much invested in convincing me I'm a demon. You want this to be true, solely to make you feel better about yourself."

"You're changing, and you know it. You lied earlier when you said you heard nothing, even though a dragon was approaching. You told an untruth to get what you wanted: a look at my body. But a Vrekener never lies, right?"

"How would you know if I've acted demonic? How many of their kind have fallen prey to your charms?"

Instead of answering, she said, "Forget it. If we're about to die, I don't want to fight with you." She wiped moisture from her own forehead. "This is like a sauna in here." Her gaze dipped to his chest, to the scars visible between the sides of what remained of his shirt.

Now it was her turn to follow drops trailing along his body. She watched them as they meandered over the rises and falls of his scars.

She'd mentioned them more than once yesterday. How foul did she think them?

He should be used to his appearance after so long; instead he was often dumbstruck by his reflection, hating each slashing scar, each raised welt. He would absently trace them when lying in bed.

Did she feel any guilt for them? Was she even capable of it? "Go on, then." He grasped her wrist, forcing her hand to his chest to explore the damage she'd done. "Feel the marks you gave me." He peered down at her, assessing her reaction.

To his surprise, she slowly ran the pad of her forefinger over one, a line below his collarbone. She continued on to another one, her expression contemplative.

Though he'd wanted Melanthe to acknowledge his pain—to *comprehend* it—he grew uncomfortable with her appraisal. He was about to stop her when she traced the worst one, the one that had nearly taken his life.

That shard of glass had pierced him deepest. He had hazy memories of each heartbeat causing him agony. And of his mother, reeling from her mate's death, sobbing over Thronos's hand, begging all the gods to spare her youngest son.

Wrath. He grasped Melanthe's wrists.

She blinked up at him, as if waking from a trance. "What?"

"Do you ever regret what you did to me?" He released her.

She leaned away, until her back was against his wing. "Sorceri disdain regret. We consider it the equivalent of an offendment. So no, I don't."

Yes, he was learning her tells. Whenever she lied, something in the timbre of her voice made his wings twitch. Plus, she always leaned back from him, as if she wanted to put distance between them, and she blinked for much longer. "Untruth, Melanthe."

"Is that a Vrekener way of saying *bullshit*?"

"So you do feel guilt." She *was* capable of it. "You must have heard I feel pain when I fly. It seems everyone in the Lore has. I always wondered if you were gladdened."

She crossed her arms over her chest. "Do Vrekeners not have healers for their young?"

"Of course we do! My bones were set true, and healed strong."

"Then what happened?"

"I pushed the torn muscles before they were ready, continually reinjuring my wings and leg." *As well as my back and my other leg. My neck and shoulders.* "I did this up to the point when I froze into my immortality—never stopping."

"You had to know the pain you were courting."

"What do you think would make me do that, Melanthe? I was on your trail before I was thirteen."

"So you overused your wings, and I overused my power because of your knights, and now we're both screwed. Blame me, and I'll blame you. Again, I can do this all day, demon."

His brows drew together. For all these years, he'd never imagined that she might have a legitimate cause to hate *him.*

"Maybe I would feel guilt if you stopped treating me like a slave and insulting me at every turn." She leaned forward aggressively. "And for gold's sake, enough with trying to shame me about my sexual past—just because you've never been with anyone."

As much as he hated that fact, it couldn't be changed.

"So you haven't been," she said in a quieter tone.

He couldn't read her expression, and that frustrated the hell out of him. Probably inwardly mocking him! "Unlike your kind, Vrekeners mate for life. So, no, I haven't enjoyed a horde of other lovers, as you've done."

Another flashing blue glare.

"It seemed you were with every male but the one fate intended for you. From me, you ran."

"What did you expect me to do whenever I saw you? Skip into your arms and hope you weren't bearing a pitchfork? I didn't have any reason whatsoever *not* to run from you."

He had no answer for that. He wasn't *her* mate. She'd told him that she had just lived her life.

Without me. As if he'd never existed for her.

Maybe that was what angered him the most—how easily she'd forgotten him, when his every waking moment was filled with thoughts of her.

TWENTY-ONE

Lanthe actually did feel the seeds of guilt.

Seeing that memory of his had softened her toward him. And now that she'd acquitted him of all the things she'd once blamed him for, she found it difficult to hold on to the worst of her hatred.

In fact, she could almost see herself and Thronos coming to an understanding, except for four things.

He now hated her for his injuries. He hated her for the loss of "years and children." He treated her like a war prize. And he had a pathological level of jealousy and distrust.

She would never convince him that his own brother had tried to kill her as a girl. She'd never convince him that she was more than a lightskirt, and she had zero tolerance for his slut-shaming.

Yes, she understood his jealousy and anger better; didn't mean she could accept his disgust.

So why was she feeling an intense attraction to Thronos? Like right now, with his face set with determination, his wings enclosing her, and his scarred skin sheening with sweat.

Those scars made him look hardened, as dangerous as he'd become. Which she found . . . sexy.

And when she'd explored the marks, she'd noticed things about his body she hadn't before.

How smooth the unmarked areas of his tanned skin were. How sensitive his flesh was to her touch. How his muscles leapt to her fingers.

His breeches had ridden low on his hips, and she'd realized he didn't have a tan line. She'd always heard that Vrekeners frowned on nudity in any circumstances. Yet sometime when he'd been transitioning to immortality, he must have lazed naked in the sun.

How *intriguing.*

He'd said he'd had dreams about her every night. Had he thought of her as the sun kissed his rugged body? Her breaths shallowed as she imagined Thronos touching himself to fantasies of her.

When she adjusted her position on his legs, he grated, "Melanthe, we need to make haste to find a portal." He looked like he was struggling not to stare at her damp cleavage—and failing.

She glanced down, saw him stiffening. If she scooched a couple of inches closer, she'd be able to feel his swelling erection against her hip. "I'm on board with the idea now." Because the only thing she feared more than dragons and demonic hordes was getting pregnant by a Vrekener. Thronos was clever and unexpectedly sexy. If he ever managed to cut the insults . . .

She couldn't give this male several days to figure out her weaknesses.

So she attempted to concentrate, to sense a portal amidst all this confusion on the mountain. Hunger and thirst made it even more difficult to focus. Plus her gold senses were pinging like crazy. She swiped her palm over her cheeks, but the gold dust was gone. Could she still be sensing that temple?

"Anything?"

She did feel the tiniest vibration of portal power, like an echo. "Maybe. I don't know."

"Try—harder."

She glared at him. "Back—off," she snapped, then regretted it immediately. Why was she being so adversarial with him? She wasn't the type of female who always kept her cool, but she also didn't go around provoking male anger, not with her history with men.

So what if Thronos continued being a dick? It wasn't like she was going to keep him; they didn't need to hash out their problems and come to a grand understanding. She just needed to beguile him so she could get back to Rothkalina. If she beguiled him hard enough, he'd take her directly there!

Back to enchanting. She leaned into him, inching closer to his erection. "Tell me a secret."

"What?"

"Whenever you've enclosed me like this, I've received a secret from you."

"I don't . . . why are you acting differently?" he asked, voice hoarse.

Uncomfortable, Thronos? "You haven't been around many females, have you?" He would have no clue how to find his footing with her—making her plan all the easier.

It wasn't even fair. Which was okay, since Sorceri only cared about fair play when it benefited them. Otherwise, they were *not* fans.

"Females don't belong on a battlefront, and I spend most of my time there, so no."

Don't belong? She and Sabine had been in the Pravus front line against an army of rebel vampires. *Bite your new tongue, Lanthe, bite it!* "But you're with a female now, and she's instituting a new rule. Under these wings, you have to tell me your secrets," she said softly. "Consider this our confessional, the wing sauna of truth."

A raised brow. "Wing sauna of truth? Peculiar sorceress. You always did have a fertile imagination."

"I know something you could tell me." She trailed her finger down the slickened skin of his chest, dipping it just inside the waist of his breeches.

He released a sharp breath. *Puh.*

"Why does an angel like you have no tan line?"

He coughed into a fist. "We don't have roofs in the Air Territories, have no need of them because we're above the clouds. As I told you, in the months of my transition, I was searching for you. Often I'd come home, shower, then pass out in bed before dressing again."

"I would have liked to see that," she said in all honesty.

"What is this, Melanthe?"

"This is me realizing we could die at any moment. It's my responsibility as a sorceress to play out my best hand all the way up to the end."

"Is that what I am to you? Another hand of cards you've been dealt?"

Well, yes. "You know what I think? I think you're surly because you didn't get your peek earlier. Get me to safety, and I'll show you *anything* you want to see." She eased her thighs open a touch.

He sounded like he'd bitten back a groan. He shifted his position again, probably because his breeches were cutting off his circulation down there.

"Don't you have a private question for me?" she asked.

"You told me you had sensual dreams about me when you slept." He narrowed his eyes. "Tell me, sorceress, was I scarred in those dreams?"

He was reaching for his anger because it was familiar to him. *Hating me is what he knows best.*

She'd chip away at that as well. "Yes, you were scarred. And I was kissing every one of them from top to bottom. You were so sensitive, but you craved more, your big body shuddering."

He frowned at her. "You're not . . . you're *not* lying."

"No."

In a gruff tone, he said, "I would've thought a fickle Sorceri would find the marks distasteful."

"Thronos, we have problems between us—gods, I know that—but lack of physical attraction is not one of them." A regrettable truth.

The hope in his eyes almost made Lanthe lose her nerve with her plan.

"You must have noticed our crackling sexual chemistry?" she asked.

"I thought that was just the way one felt around a mate," he admitted.

"Yet you feel it for me as well." His brows drew together. "So why did you tell me I left you cold?"

"I said I felt physical attraction. But I find it difficult to desire a male who insults and hurts me."

Instead of addressing this, he said, "How many have you felt this chemistry with?"

And here we go.

"How many males have there been, Melanthe?" he asked in a quiet voice, as if he were bracing for her answer.

"You'll never get a number out of me."

"Then it must be huge."

"I'm more than just a number," she pointed out. "Besides, it's not only the number that's bothering you; it's the fact that I was with others after we'd met, and you couldn't bed just as many." *Bite your tongue!*

"Why couldn't you have settled down with one? I know that some Sorceri wed for life."

"Would you have preferred to find me in love with another male, happy, with ten children? Why, that would make me a virtuous woman! Would you kidnap a virtuous female for your own selfish needs? Would you separate her from her beloved husband and children?"

He bit out a sound of frustration.

"If our sexes were reversed, everyone would've *expected* me to take lovers. I would have been applauded for it. You would have been revered for your purity. And if I were a demon male *like you,* I would have bedded thousands, searching for my mate. You know"—she made air quotes—"attempting."

That's what demons called it when they had sex just to see if a female would break their demon seal. Though a demon could usually scent a female and know she was his mate, the only way to be a hundred percent sure was through intercourse.

Baring his fangs, Thronos grated, "Have you been *attempted* by many demons, then?"

"I've never been with one." He parted his lips, no doubt to call "untruth," so she explained, "Like Vrekeners, the Sorceri stupidly think demons are savage. I didn't know better until Sabine fell for Rydstrom. By the time I realized demons could be wildly attractive, I was locked into celibacy for a year."

"You find demons wildly attractive? I thought you were drawn to the more polished, slick liar sort."

Right now she was drawn to seven-foot-tall males who simmered with pent-up lust and untapped carnality. "Hmm. Physically, I like—"

"Straddle me," he bit out.

Her brows shot up.

"I'm about to need my hands."

Without question, she wrapped her legs around his waist and her arms around his neck yet again. He'd just latched onto the side of the mountain when the path disintegrated beneath them, rousing the dragons once more.

TWENTY-TWO

Behind the crumbled stone was . . . an opening. A tunnel no more than five feet in height had been revealed.

Despite his claustrophobia, Thronos clutched Melanthe with one arm, then swung his legs in, scrambling to get as far inside as possible. His horns hit the low ceiling, the jagged rock abrading the tops of his wings.

"How are you doing with this tight spot?" she asked.

"Not my favorite environment."

He thought she muttered, "I figured swaying trees were." Meaning that night on the Order's island.

He winced to recall his behavior. But he'd believed she was different then—

A dragon shoved its snout into the opening, its breath stirring up grit, making it difficult to see. Effectively trapping them.

No other choice but forward! Red light spilled from some opening farther in; he made for it with haste, fearing the beast would fire on them.

It reached in, pawing, disturbing rocks. Thronos covered Melanthe with his wings as the ceiling began to rain stone and sand. Piles of it heaped around Thronos's legs as if from an upended hourglass.

Panic threatened to take hold, but he fought it. They had to get out before the tunnel was choked, burying them alive. As Thronos slogged onward, his throat felt just as choked.

The farther inside, the hotter the air was. That red glare grew as they neared. When he reached it at last and paused in the arched opening, he saw a larger cavern, filled with bubbling lava. A sole raised path bisected it, one that appeared to lead straight into hell.

Kicking free of the piles of stone weighted around his legs, he launched himself off the edge. He glided down to the path, then set Melanthe on her feet.

As he shook sand from his hair, he gazed back at the tunnel.

Completely caved. Only one way to go.

He turned back to the path. Ahead, more streams of lava wound along it. A metal bridge in the distance glowed red hot. "I think we're in one of the armies' lairs."

"Then we need to find a way out, before anyone sees us."

"I scent food cooking from one direction," he said, "and corpse rot from the other."

"So there's a camp and a burial area? Let's head toward the latter. It'd be less populated, less guarded."

As they walked in silence, he kept his hand on her arm, in case he needed to shield her in a hurry. With each step away from that cave-in, his unease faded.

"When you find yourself going through hell, keep going, right?" she asked, casting him a look from under her lashes. Again, he didn't recognize the look, but he thought it was . . . flirtatious.

He tried to focus, lest he get them captured or killed, but he couldn't stop replaying their interaction under his wings—and how she'd run her finger down to his breeches. He'd been a heartbeat away from taking her hand and making her feel what she was doing to him. He'd imagined how he would groan her name as she outlined his shaft through the leather. He'd barely defeated the urge to lick sweat from her neck.

Finding this realm's portal had become even more important, because his sense of right and wrong seemed to be eroding. He could no longer trust himself to heed the laws of his people.

He was the prince of the Vrekeners, a general of knights. Yet how easily she had him falling under her spell! He'd known she was using her wiles on him, but that hadn't lessened the effect of her charms.

Until he could return home, he needed to steel himself against her, a task that would be even more difficult after his discovery today.

Sexual chemistry is addictive.

Whenever he'd felt that electricity sparking between them, the pain from his old injuries had ebbed under the heat of excitement. . . .

She cast him a quizzical look. "What are you thinking about?"

"Chemistry," he answered.

Her lips curled, and she left him to his thoughts.

All his life, he'd speculated how she would react to his scars. He'd been astonished to learn that she had no issues with him physically—merely issues with, well, everything else.

Even she admitted that their chemistry *crackled.*

From thousands of lofty perches, he'd gazed down upon Lorean wickedness. Watching an offendment was almost as bad as committing one, so he'd always turned away, but those glimpses had taught him much. He'd seen immortals addicted to intoxispells, begging to do anything for more.

Thronos had never understood addiction before. Now he wondered what he wouldn't do for more of this sizzling interplay with his mate.

Might he stop insulting her?

Perhaps he should go even further and court her. As a boy, he'd done so and found success. She'd liked to be given presents. Good thing he'd snagged that medallion from the temple.

When they'd run from the dragon, Thronos had stretched out his talon for it. Now he had it hidden in his pocket.

A stray thought flitted through his brain. *How many gifts of jewelry have other males given her? To reward her for sex?* His grip tightened around her arm, his horns aching to mark her again.

Just because he had a goal of treating her better didn't mean he could achieve it. Wrath still lived within him. . . .

"Strange that we haven't seen a soul," she said, frowning at his grip.

He eventually eased it. "There's nothing of value to guard. Plus, they're probably still on the battlefield."

After what felt like leagues, the trail forked, the two branches heading in opposite directions.

"Which way to the corpse rot?" she asked him.

He waved to the right, and they kept moving.

As they neared the burial area, the stench became overwhelming. Another cavern opened up, larger than the initial one. It'd likely been chosen for its size because it was filled to the ceiling with a mountain of bones, decapitated bodies, and horned skulls.

The mound had a creeping, rippling coat of rats. The skittering mass darted in and out of the remains, as if along paths.

When Melanthe's eyes went wide at the gruesome sight, he tugged her back. "There's no exit. Let's head the other way."

"Are you trying to protect my innocent eyes?" This seemed to amuse her. "I was just nine when my parents' heads dropped off their bed and rolled toward me like wayward toys. When I was eleven, I used a shard of my sister's skull to scoop up her brain matter and put her back together again. I haven't been innocent since my life became entangled with Vrekeners."

If his knights truly had hunted the two Sorceri girls, the attacks would have been unending. A living hell.

Vrekeners never abandon their hunt.

"Not to mention Omort's court," she said. "I can never unsee the things I witnessed there."

"I wish that I could have spared you that," he said honestly.

"You *could* have spared me some. Last year when you set that trap for me, I'd been in Louisiana to retrieve my sister, so she could take her dose of morsus. She was *dying*. Because of you, I had to flee, getting completely turned around in a strange city. I was lost and frantic. Because of you, I couldn't rescue Sabine. When the portal door shut on your leg, I'm sure you were suitably pissed on your side. On my side, I kicked your leg around, cursing it. Until I heard Omort from the shadows—*in my room*—grating, 'And you dare return without her.' " She visibly shuddered. "I've never been closer to death than I was then. Never. So thanks, Thronos."

"I couldn't have known that." One year ago, she'd almost been murdered by her brother. The idea of Melanthe dying while Thronos was helpless to protect her . . .

Would he have sensed the loss, even across worlds?

She regarded his face. "I've tried to live my life. And you jeopardized it. It's a miracle that I've survived this long. Speaking of which . . ." She crossed to the burial mound, reaching for something. She hauled a battered sword out from the bottom. A few bones and skulls tumbled down like a mini rock slide.

She laid the sword flat over one of her shoulders. "You ready?"

He nodded, and they set out once more, his thoughts in turmoil. *Never been closer to death.*

Because of him. No, he couldn't have predicted what his actions might bring about—because it'd never occurred to him that Melanthe was a prisoner of Omort.

Had he assumed the worst about her in every instance?

Back at the fork, they chose the other direction. The path began dividing regularly, some routes leading down, some up, connecting to landings or more caverns. Along the landings were recesses of differing sizes.

"I can't believe we're in a subterranean demon den," she murmured. She didn't sound unnerved by this, more intrigued—as if the two of them were on a hell safari.

His instinct continually urged him to take the higher path, but he didn't think there'd be an entry point at the top of this lair, so he tried to keep them on one level.

The noise and scents grew into a tumult as they neared the demon encampment, situated in one of those larger caverns. Cautiously they found a vantage on a raised landing, where he and Melanthe could take stock of most of the camp. It was occupied by dozens of different types of demons: fire, ice, pus, storm, shadow, pathos, and more. All appeared to be returning from that battle.

Thronos found it strange that members of such varied demonarchies were working together. Was the other army as diverse?

Here, warriors regenerated from injuries, some regrowing flesh, some entire limbs. Others ate, drank, or whored. Thirty or so harried demonesses serviced the males, with lines forming.

And my mate thinks me related to these brutes? He ground his teeth at the thought, turning away from the iniquitous scenes.

Melanthe, however, appeared quite comfortable with what she was witnessing. And she seemed to be listening for something.

"Come, sorceress," he muttered. "I scent an exit nearby." At last, a way out of this literal hellhole.

She didn't follow him. "Just a minute. I've been reading their minds, getting the lay of the land."

He hesitated. "And?"

"This war has been going on since before even the oldest demons were born, so thousands of years. Each night, the armies march out to do battle. They break each morning because the dragons fly from their hive to come scavenge the plateau. If the demons are returning now, I guess dawn happened while we were down here?"

"It must have. Those dragons on the mount were probably waiting to feed on the fallen." As if they'd been trained. Crafty beasts. It was a wonder there were any bodies in that burial mound at all.

"The dragons have been abnormally hostile of late," Melanthe continued. "The demons fear the last female has died, leaving a pack of aggressive killer males. It's only a matter of time before they attack the demons. Oh, oh, this just in . . . We're in a lair called Inferno. It's protected by that moat of lava outside and is home to the *Infernals.* They fight the Deep Place warriors, also known as the *Abysmals.* Deep Place is equally difficult to breach. There's only one entrance, and you have to navigate a maze of ruins to reach it."

"What are they fighting over?"

"Portals. The Infernals have the First Gate of Hell and the Second Key. But the Abysmals have the Second Gate and the First Key. In other words, they each have a gate of hell and a key that doesn't work on their own portal. Each side fights to protect its portal and to seize the other's key. Both armies are desperate to leave, but none can teleport here. They have no idea how the keys and portals got mixed up. Some believe the eternal war is a punishment for something."

"A portal is within this lair? With your power, could you use it without a key?"

She shook her head. "If it's locked, it's been barred for a reason. Against anyone."

"So we could take a key from here to use with the Abysmals' portal?" And if they managed to make it out of Inferno alive, would he drag her into Deep Place as well?

He didn't know enough about the dangers in Pandemonia to leave Melanthe in hiding, which meant she would have to accompany him to yet another demon lair—without any advance scouting. Who knew what he could be leading her into?

The only other option would be to spend several more days in hell. Away from his home, his anchor. *Will I even recognize myself?*

Not to mention that he could never wait that long to claim Melanthe. "We search for the key, then. We'll find it. I'll kill any demon that gets in our way."

"Hold on there, tiger. When was the last time you ate? Or slept? We're coming off a prison stay, remember. We should at least find food and water. Maybe spend the day recuperating. We can return when they go back to the battlefield."

He couldn't argue with her logic. "Very well." He steered her toward the exit he'd scented.

Across a narrow rock bridge, he spied the opening. Murky rays of sunlight wavered through it.

They were just about to traverse the bridge when a Volar demon swooped into the area directly below, beginning to remove pieces of his armor. Thronos and Melanthe flattened themselves against the wall of an alcove.

They wouldn't be able to reach the exit without being seen by that Volar. Thronos could take him, but not before the male raised the alarm.

—Look, Thronos, your long-lost brother.—

More telepathy? Yet she'd sounded almost impish, so he could forgive the intrusion, as well as the slight.

When she found a flat length of stone in the dim alcove and took a seat, he cautiously joined her. From the shadows, he surveyed the Volar. Its kind had features in common with Vrekeners, he supposed. Their wings were similarly shaped with glowing pulselines, and their claws were the same. But the Volar only had two horns, and its wings were all black.

The demon paced the area, seeming to await someone. Moments later, a small demoness of indeterminate subspecies rushed in. They ran to each other and began kissing.

Thronos turned his head away, but Melanthe leaned forward with eagerness. *—An assignation! Oh, darn, Thronos. We're stuck here until they get finished.—*

"They aren't about to . . . here?"

She grinned.

"Turn from them, Melanthe." Watching an offendment . . .

—You've never watched?—

"It isn't done!"

At Thronos's low words, the Volar turned sharply, scanning the shadows. Thronos held his breath until the Volar's mate drew the male's attention back to her.

—I might as well read his mind too.—

Thronos wanted to tell her to ignore them, to think of something else, but he couldn't risk the sound.

—This Volar is the leader *of the Infernals and is fresh from the battlefield. He*

thanks the gods for his mate, stolen during a raid on the Abysmals. If not for her, he'd meet a dragon's fire.—

Though that was all well and good, Thronos needed pertinent information. He couldn't believe he was about to do this, but . . . he lowered his shields against Melanthe, which drew her attention. Then he thought the words: *—Can you hear me?—*

She smiled softly. *—I like talking to you this way.—*

—Can you find out from him where the key is?—

—That's pretty much the last thing he's thinking about right now!— She fanned herself.

The Volar and the demoness began to kiss even more passionately, making Melanthe sigh. When the male murmured in Demonish, she translated. *—He told her that he loves her, and he couldn't withstand this hell without her. And she says she feels the same way! They're desperate for each other.—*

—She's no warrior. She must have been a camp follower.— A prostitute.

—So? She's with him now.—

—But he knows many others have seen his mate. They've touched her and pleasured her.—

—Do you think that matters to him?—

Thronos knew this was dangerous ground, but answered honestly. *—I can't see how it wouldn't.—*

—It wouldn't because he obviously knows a very real truth. The honor doesn't go to the first male she bedded; it goes to the last male, the one she'll spend eternity with. Him. He probably walks around this place feeling ten feet tall, superior to all.—

Thronos had never thought of it that way. *—I'll be the last male you ever bed.—*

—That remains to be seen.— She turned to him with a frown. *—You know, up in heaven, I'm sure things make sense and everyone acts as they're expected to and surprises are few. But outside of heaven, life can be confusing and heartbreaking and dire. So most of us take pleasure where we can find it.—* She pinned him with her gaze. *—And we don't judge anyone who does the same.—*

Could Thronos ever take pleasure where he found it? For a moment, he considered how easy life would be if he were a mere demon. That

Volar could mate his female whenever he felt the urge for release. He didn't have to worry about laws or expectations or the Tales of Troth.

As a demon, Thronos would be able to forgive Melanthe her profligacy, because he would be in no position to judge. As soon as he led her from Inferno, he could find a place to take his demon's due. The idea of claiming her this very day, without repercussions, was so seductive that he nearly groaned with want.

His shaft ached for her, his horns as well. Part of him wondered, *Why fight something I need so badly?* His mate was in need too. Her season was upon her, and he had a driving instinct to pleasure her.

A groan drew her attention back to the pair. He kept his eyes on her.

—*They're so in love.*— Yearning emanated from her.

She'd said gold was "as beautiful as love." Did she want love for herself?

His mate was such a contradiction. She was hardened to violence and death. But he'd also seen her joy in the temple and now her longing.

As a girl, she'd been thoughtful and gentle. Her eyes had usually been lit with merriment, especially when she'd teased him, making him laugh despite himself. Each day, he'd gone from the dour Skye to that meadow, to levity and play. They'd settled in so easily together.

Merry, gentle, thoughtful. Could she possibly have retained those traits after all she'd been through?

Before he considered his words, he asked: —*Have you been in love?*—

—*I've never known romantic love.*—

This surprised him. With not a single one of the males she'd been with? —*Why?*—

With a raised brow, she replied: —*I haven't found my future husband yet.*—

—*You do not know how wrong you are about that.*—

—*Hmm.*—

What kind of answer was that? Vexing female!

The two below began making unrestrained sounds of passion. This too struck him as odd since Vrekeners were . . . discreet when mating.

As Melanthe watched, her lids grew heavier. What was affecting her like this? Cursing his weakness, he stole a glance.

The demoness had her legs and arms wrapped around the Volar, while he kneaded her ass beneath her long skirts. This was the same position Thronos and Melanthe had repeatedly taken! Was she imagining Thronos cupping and kneading her?

The Volar took his female's lips with a deep kiss, then eased them to the ground so that she was astride him. *As Lanthe had been astride me, her sleek thighs flexing around my waist.* The Volar fumbled with something beneath the demoness's skirt, then with his own breeches. Lifting the female up, he slowly lowered her, growling with pleasure.

At that, Melanthe inched forward even more, placing her hand flat on the bench of rock. It was small-boned and pale. Not the one that bore scars.

He moved his own hand closer. *—Tell me how many you've done this with.—* Ever since she'd refused to say a number earlier, his imagination had gone wild.

—This? They're making love, so my answer is never.— Before he could argue, she said: *—There's a difference between sex and making love.—*

He'd heard this said, of course. But he had experience with neither. Though he was desperately curious as to what she considered the difference to be, he didn't want to highlight his own ignorance of such matters.

When the Volar spoke, Melanthe translated again. *—He said he's been thinking about her all night, wanting only to return to her.—* With a grin, she added: *—He said he'll be tender with her for as long as he can.—*

And then what? Thronos refused to ask her, just said: *—Females like tender.—* Not an embarrassing question; merely an observation.

—Hmm. Sometimes.—

Enigmatic sorceress!

She arched her brows at him. *—I would let my partner know exactly what I desired every step of the way. He'd never have to worry on that score.—*

Did she mean *him* or males in general? One of the reasons he hated her past was that he had no experience of his own. If she compared him to other lovers, how could he acquit himself well?

Yet if she told him exactly what she wanted . . . —*When you tell me what you desire, I'll give it to you. Anything.*—

Had she inched her hand closer to his? —*What about offendments? Some of the acts I might crave have nothing to do with procreation.*—

With comments like this, she set his mind afire! —*I will hear of these acts now.*—

She slid him a mysterious smile that put him into a lather as much as her words had.

Since Thronos had captured her, Lanthe had seen entirely new facets of him—and each one confused her more.

The warlord in pain, roaring in a lightning storm.

The domineering demon in the temple.

The protector who'd saved her from dragons.

Now she could sense the conflict within him. His sexual curiosity and long-denied urges goaded him to learn about her own desires—and to watch others', though he believed it forbidden.

How shocking these sights must be to him! —*I think my angel's a budding voyeur.*—

—*You lead me down a dark path, sorceress.*— Thronos looked astounded that he was actually watching, but helplessly intrigued.

—*You've really never seen others in the throes?*— Their hands on the bench were inching closer together.

—*Never. I've turned away every time.*— His little finger brushed hers, and even that small contact shot currents into her skin.

—*Then why look now?*—

—*Because I see myself as him and you as her. Because I ache for what I almost took in that temple.*—

The demoness moaned loudly. The Volar's claws dug into the rocky ground.

Lanthe swallowed. *—What had you planned to do to me?—*

—For the first time in my adult life, there was no plan, only impulses.— Thronos's hand suddenly covered hers. His was hot, rough with callouses.

She glanced up at him. Thick dark hair tumbled over his forehead, almost reaching his vivid eyes. Their color was the same as the ore that had spilled from the mountain.

Molten silver lit by fire.

His shirt clung to his broad shoulders and brawny chest. His normally clenched jaw was relaxed, the grim line of his lips softened, allowing her a glimpse of his true mien: masculine, compelling, sigh-worthy.

Her heart thudded. Irresistible warlord.

His face was flushed with excitement, as if he'd just discovered flirting.

Oh, wait. He probably *had.*

—What would you have allowed me in the temple, Melanthe?—

She felt like she was punch-drunk, losing any inhibitions she might have had with this male. By the way he stared at her eyes, she knew they were metallic, colored with her desire. *—I honestly don't know.—*

He scowled when she pulled her hand away.

—If I based my decision on physical attraction alone, then . . . — She turned her hand palm up and parted her fingers for his.

A breath left him. His hand shot to hers, fingers entwining.

They fit . . . perfectly.

—You would have received me? Parted your thighs for me?— He pressed the heel of his palm into hers, tightening his grip so sensually.

She bit her bottom lip. *—It's not based just on physical attraction, is it?—* How could the mere contact of their hands make her this aroused? Her nipples stiffened, her sex growing wet.

Averting her gaze from his, she turned toward the couple. The Volar cast his demoness a look of open adoration. Gripping her breasts, he bucked his hips, bouncing the thrilled female.

Did Thronos realize he'd begun rubbing the palm of his hand against Lanthe's in time with the Volar's thrusts? Their palms were hot with friction, and Thronos's every movement sent pleasure rippling through her body.

She exhaled a tremulous breath. Could he make her come like this? A completely new meaning for the term *hand job*. . . .

She would catch him staring at her as she watched; then she'd gaze up at him as his flickering eyes took in the scene. Since they were communicating telepathically, it was easy to slip into his thoughts.

He was reluctantly enjoying this spying because she obviously did, but also because it was a wicked secret between them—something *they* were doing together. He wanted more secrets between them. She hid a grin when she caught another of his thoughts. He was wondering how much more his swollen shaft could pain him: *There has to be a limit.*

Oh, there was! Would they discover it together?

When the demoness took the Volar's horns in hand, Thronos sounded like he'd stifled a groan. —*You did that to me earlier.*—

—*Would you like me to do it again?*—

Hesitation. Then: —*I can't lie. I'd want that very much. Your soft palms on me, handling me.*—

Even out of the corner of her eye, she saw his engorged member pulse in his breeches. Her sex clenched in reaction.

When the Volar ripped down the demoness's peasant blouse to suckle a breast, Lanthe's lids went heavy, her own breasts swelling in the molded cups of her top.

Thronos moved his hand on hers faster. —*I would do that to you at every opportunity. I'd kill to do it now.*—

She turned to him, found his spellbinding eyes filled with promise. Somehow he was beguiling *her*. The virgin was seducing the seductress!

If he had this power over her and made a move to claim her, how could she resist him? During this time, that could spell disaster!

Pregnant with Thronos Talos's babe? The idea was too insane even to contemplate.

When the demoness cried out, she and Thronos both turned to the couple.

The Volar had positioned his female on her hands and knees, lifting her skirts. He'd taken her tenderly for as long as he'd been able to, but now his demon nature was clearly at the fore. With one animalistic shove, he entered her from behind, eliciting a lusty moan. After each thrust, he used his wings to draw his body back so he could plunge forward again. And again.

—I could take you thus.—

She barely bit back a whimper. *—If you ever looked at me like he looks at her, I'd consider it.—*

Though the two below were groaning and moaning in abandon, their pace hitting its crescendo, Lanthe faced Thronos.

She felt light-headed with arousal, desiring him more than she'd ever thought possible.

—I've got to kiss you, Melanthe.—

Irresistible. Was she nodding?

At least here, they couldn't do anything more than kiss. Things couldn't get out of hand.

Our first real kiss. His lips were inches from hers. . . .

A yell in Demonish sounded. She gasped. A pair of armored sentries had spotted them.

TWENTY-THREE

"Come on!" Thronos snatched Melanthe into his arms, charging toward the rock bridge and the exit he'd scented.

"My sword!" She was reaching back for it.

"No time," he snapped as he ran, bursting outside. Was this a continuation of the same mountainside path they'd hidden upon earlier? With more scavenging dragons? *Can't take to the air till I'm sure.*

A bower of black and silver foliage grew over the trail here, providing cover from above, from the hazy sun that had finally risen.

As he sprinted headlong down the mountain, Melanthe peeked over his shoulder. "More are coming!"

He glanced back. Two had become half a dozen. They were burly pathos demons, a vicious breed. Their armor could deflect his talons.

"Where are we going?"

The trail led toward a wooded valley between those two jagged ranges. "That's a forest down there. We could lose them among the trees."

"You're heading *toward* a Pandemonian forest?"

"You have a better idea?" The lower they got, the closer they were to the river of lava. Sweat poured from him, ash drying out his mouth. The demons stayed right on his heels.

"I feel like I'm cooking!"

"We're almost there." The path finally veered away from the lava, leading straight to the forest.

As he and Melanthe neared the edge of it, she said, "They're too close! We can't lose them."

"Then I fight." He set her down, readying to combat the sentries. "Stay behind me. But remain close." He faced off against the pursuing warriors, positioning his wings to strike.

Out of the corner of his eye, he spied two marble markers flanking the path. But he couldn't divert his focus to read the glyphs.

Swords drawn, the sentries charged as one—

They stopped before him, just out of range. Right at the line of those markers.

"Come on, then!" He flared his wings, antagonizing them. "Fight me!" But they wouldn't cross that line, shifting and muttering.

So there was something in these woods that even a cadre of demons feared?

A heartbeat later, he heard an earsplitting buzzing sound above them—hair-raising in its intensity! Melanthe shrieked. Was she running from him?

He whirled around, saw a black swarm oozing through the tree canopy as if it'd been poured.

"Wait, Lanthe!" he yelled as he sped for her deeper into the brush. The swarm was already between them, a multitude of solid black wasps with dripping stingers.

Their buzzing seemed to make the entire world vibrate, like his brain would be jostled to mush.

BUZZZZZZZZZZ

Melanthe had clapped her hands over her ears, still careening along that path. "I can't take that sound!"

BUZZZZZZZZZZ

Using his wings to fan and bat the wasps, he fought through the cloud to reach her, biting back yells with each sting—like icepicks stabbing his skin!

And that sound was about to drive him *insane.*

Closing in on her, he nearly tripped over one of another pair of engraved marble markers along the path. They read:

The pest that WAS . . .

What did that mean? *Confusing bloody place!* He lunged for Melanthe, enclosing her in his wings as they hit the ground.

BUZZZZZZZZZZ

Even with his wings shielding them, the sound was deafening.

"Thronos, I-I can't! It's too loud. My head!"

BUZZZZZZZZZZ

He wrapped his arms around her trembling body. "Shh, shh, I know . . ." How the hell was he going to get her away? When he could barely think past that sound?

Yet then it . . . dimmed.

Were they no longer swarmed? He poked his head up to glance out.

The towering black mass had stopped before those stones, hovering in the air—as if there was an imaginary line that couldn't be crossed.

Then they began dissipating, their buzz receding.

He squinted at the stones. On this side, both read:

The pest that IS . . .

He rose above her. "Melanthe? Are you okay?"

Between breaths, she said, "My head still feels like a jackhammer was in it."

He levered himself to his feet, helping her stand. "Were you stung?" As he looked her over, he rasped his palms over his skin, scraping stingers away.

"Only a few times before you covered me." She plucked stingers from her arms, leaving angry red welts. "Why'd they stop?"

"I think you were right about there being traps all over this realm. I'm beginning to believe there's a patchwork of danger zones, and we reached the edge of one." What he wouldn't give for a map!

"What do those markers say?"

"On the other side, they read: *The pest that* was. On this side: *The pest that* is."

She brushed hair from her eyes. "They sound like demonic road signs. Like if we were heading back into the swarm zone, the signs would be saying: *Entering hazardous area.*"

"Does *The pest that was* mean we left the hazardous area?"

"Only to enter another one?" she asked, her face wan.

He noticed she wasn't sweating. In this heat? Not good. Wasn't that a symptom of heat stroke?

He scented water, but it was far in the distance, several leagues away. Though most immortals could go without water for days, she wasn't like most immortals. Reminded of how fragile a creature she was, he reached for her. "Come here, Melanthe."

"I'm fine."

Ignoring her protests, he took her in his arms and cradled her slight weight. He started along the trail, working to minimize the jostle of his limp. With each step, she relaxed a degree more in his arms. Every now and then, she'd grumble about walking on her own.

"Why don't you rest? We've got a long way between us and water." Maybe there'd even be fruit growing nearby that the little sorceress would actually eat. She'd thrown up her last meal.

Had that been two nights ago?

In that short time, she'd gotten to him—until his thoughts and emotions were in chaos. "Try to sleep, Melanthe."

"While you carry me? When we're in a place chock-full of swamp serpents, demons, dragons, and pests?"

"I'll watch over you."

"Ha. Never'll happen . . ."

Ten minutes later, she was out, her head turned toward his chest, her hands curled against him. She'd fallen asleep in his arms—and it felt like one of his greatest accomplishments.

Surely this meant she trusted him? He squared his shoulders. She believed he would keep her safe against all the dangers they kept encountering.

He frowned. Or else she had heat exhaustion.

Inwardly waving away that thought, he regarded her relaxed face, her lips parted in slumber. This wasn't the first time he'd held her sleeping. When they'd been young, they would lie in the meadow together, peering up at clouds to identify shapes. Sometimes, she would doze in his arms as he lifted her raven locks to the sun, just to watch them shine.

Their cloud pastime always made him grin because she thought every single one resembled some small befurred creature or another. "That one looks like a tree," he'd say. She'd answer, "Or a squirrel on its hind legs with a mouthful of acorns." He'd offer, "That one's like a cottage with a chimney." She'd sigh, "Or a very fat rabbit. With short ears."

One time she'd woken from a nap, lifting her head from his chest to sleepily ask him, "When we're apart, do you ever gaze down at clouds as I gaze up? Do you ever miss me as I miss you?"

More, Melanthe. So much more.

And that left him conflicted. Thronos had heard of the mate effect, that the mere presence of one's mate would be a balm on all woes. His mate was as soothing as a cyclone.

After Inferno, his customary sexual frustration had been ratcheted up to a painful degree. But he was also experiencing this new . . . fascination for the female in his arms. She was a woman with her own desires. He wanted to learn them—so he could tease her and make her crazed for him.

He'd been committing offendments left and right, but he couldn't muster much regret. Holding her hand like that had been the most sensual act he'd ever enjoyed.

He still burned for the kiss he'd almost taken. At the time, he'd thought she'd wanted it just as dearly.

And after that kiss? Even more delights awaited him! *If you ever looked at me like he looks at her, I'd consider it.*

Thronos had predicted a bleak future for them. But what if they could share pleasure, building on that?

Melanthe is misery. Had he really thought that only yesterday? Now he realized, *Melanthe is doubt.*

She'd always made him doubt his beliefs. He remembered a time when he'd tried to explain what she was to him. She'd been only nine, yet she'd questioned something he'd thought was absolute.

"Lanthe, when we get older, you're going to be mine."

She blinked up at him from a garland she'd been braiding. "How can I be yours when I'm my own?"

"You're my mate. Do you know what that means?"

"Sorceri don't have mates," she pointed out.

"But you'll belong to me."

"That doesn't sound very fair."

"It . . . doesn't?"

"Let's just stay best friends. That sounds fairer."

Now they'd been together for less than three days, and she'd already made him doubt the word of Vrekeners. He . . . believed her about the attacks.

He gazed down at her pale hand, curled so delicately on her torso. Those faint scars still filled him with rage. She'd said she had to bite back her screams. He didn't understand how she could have at her young age. Was it because she'd already grown so used to pain? Or because she'd been that terrified of being discovered?

For centuries, he'd believed her existence had been filled with wanton revelry, a sorceress's dream. He now knew those years with Omort and his poisons had been hellish for her. Running from Vrekener attacks? Hellish.

As a girl, Melanthe had wept over the death of a single rabbit.

Yet she'd had to scoop up her sister's brain.

Perhaps Thronos should consider himself fortunate that she hadn't grown to be evil like every other Sorceri he'd met outside of the Territories.

But evil or not, once she regained her persuasion, she would use it against him. Every day, every hour, her sorcery was replenishing itself, and he was defenseless against it.

If he could get her to the Skye before then, he could harvest the ability with one of his people's four fire scythes.

She would have even more reason to hate him—but he would *never* lose her again.

As soon as the thought arose, so did his guilt. Though Vrekeners didn't believe a power could be a soul, Melanthe did. He could never do that to her. Which made him the biggest hypocrite. He was the one who'd pressed for his kind to collect sorcery, in order to spare lives.

Short of separating her from her persuasion, his only hope of keeping her was to convince her not to use it on him. He exhaled. In other words, she'd be gone at her first opportunity.

How to get her to go with him to his home, and stay there?

His heart stuttered when he realized the answer: she would bond to the father of her offspring.

She was in season—*now.* Who knew for how much longer?

Yes, impregnating her would be a grave offendment, but desperate times . . .

Even if she managed to escape to Rothkalina, Thronos still had more hope of seeing her. Though Rydstrom the Good was a demon, even he would never bar the doors of his kingdom to a father seeking contact with his child.

Thronos could be inside Melanthe. Tonight. The portal key could wait—until he'd made her his.

Was he succumbing to this reasoning because it was sound? Or because he wanted her so badly he'd commit any wrong to have her?

TWENTY-FOUR

Lanthe cracked open her lids to find Thronos staring down at her, a curious expression on his face. She couldn't believe she'd passed out. The rhythm of his breaths had lulled her, just as flying with him on the island had done.

"How long was I out?" Though still thirsty and hungry, she felt rested.

"A couple of hours."

"I'm better now." Her welts had faded to nothing. "I can walk."

With clear reluctance, he set her on her feet, steadying her with his big hand covering her shoulder. She glanced around. They were in a dense forest, surrounded by trees so massive, they made redwoods look like saplings. They had to be moonrakers, a type often found on demon planes.

Not only was the stone of this realm black, most of the foliage was onyx and silver. Even the smooth bark of the moonrakers was black.

Though there was little sunlight—just a few rays stole through the canopy—enormous flowers grew in profusion, subtly scenting the air.

She inspected one bloom. Its large dark petals were shiny and open. In the center was a silver pistil the size of a baseball bat. Its pollen sparkled like white-gold dust.

Other weeping-willow-type plants swayed above them, their silver leaves glinting in the scattered spears of sun, like Thronos's wing mosaics did. As a sorceress obsessed with metal, Lanthe found all these sights mesmerizing, yet her attention couldn't stray from him for long.

As in the temple, she turned from infinite wonders to face him, a towering Vrekener warlord—who couldn't intrigue her more. "So, any new threats I should be concerned about?"

He shook his head. "When was the last time you slept for more than an hour or two?"

"Before I was captured three weeks ago. You?"

He shrugged. "Weeks."

"So what do we do now?"

"I've been following this overgrown path deeper into the woods, toward the scent of water," he told her. "There's prey all around us. I could catch something, but I doubt you'd eat it."

"Like the first time you tried to provide for me?"

All these years later, he deadpanned, "The rabbit had it coming."

A burst of laughter escaped her lips so quickly, so unexpectedly, she almost slapped her hands over her mouth.

"Too soon?"

Another joke! And more . . . "You do remember!"

"Everything." He reached forward, tucking one of her braids behind her ear.

Why was he being so nice to her? Had she beguiled him so swiftly? She'd been unconscious for part of the time!

He canted his head at her, then continued walking, seeming deep in thought.

Her brows drew together when her gold senses pinged again. They had outside of Inferno, but she'd thought the temple's proximity had continued to set them off. Now she glanced all around for the source. Her gaze kept returning to Thronos.

She'd bet her best headpiece that this Vrekener had gold on him. But how?

Her eyes went wide. Could he have collected that medallion? If so, and if he gave it to her tonight . . .

The Vrekener would get laid.

No, no! No sex with Thronos. *Bad Lanthe!* Clearing her throat, she said, "Karat for your thoughts." When he hesitated, she asked, "Are you beating yourself up for what we saw?"

"Not as much as I should be."

"Question: Are people like you and me called *offendmenters*?"

"Have your fun, sorceress," he said without heat.

"Always. So tonight, we steal a key and use a portal?"

"That's what we'd discussed."

"But won't angelic Thronos balk at thievery?" she asked in a playful tone. "I remember when I once asked you to steal for me. You were embarrassed for me, putting up your nose as you said, 'I will *never* take what doesn't belong to me.' "

"You asked me to empty the coffers of Skye Hall!"

"What's your point?"

He opened his mouth to explain, then must've realized she was kidding.

Sort of. "If we unlock a portal, how can you trust me not to direct it to Rothkalina?"

"You tried for Rothkalina last time and brought us to Pandemonia. I believe you'll aim for the mortal plane. It's a vastly bigger target. From there I can fly to the Skye."

"Still bent on getting me to heaven? Look, I'm not saying I'd never go to your home. Of course, I'm not *not* saying that either."

He raised his brows. "We can wed only there. I must claim you in a Bed of Troth, my lifelong bed."

She knew of some factions that had the same tradition—basically the ones that weren't forever scrambling for their very survival. When a male was born, a bed would be created that he would sleep in his entire life, eventually bringing his mate to it. "What does the bed have to do with marriage?"

"That's *how* Vrekeners marry. When I claim you in a Bed of Troth, we'll be bound."

"No ceremony with tons of people? No fabulous dress and gifts of gold? No celebrating with far too much sweet wine?"

"We've no need for ceremony. In any case, my home is the only place where I know I can keep you safe."

Har. "What would someone like me eat up there?" Vrekeners were omnivores, but they preferred meat.

"We have an entire island dedicated to growing crops. It's the sole one that hovers below the clouds."

"I've heard it's austere up there. In Castle Tornin, I live in utter luxury, with all the mod-cons."

"Don't know what a mod-con is, Melanthe."

She sighed. Of course he didn't. "They're things I couldn't live without." Lanthe and Sabine had endured some *lean* early years and felt like they deserved to be spoiled. Now that Lanthe had gone from her castle tower, to Order prison, to roughing it—in hell—the greedy sorceress in her demanded a return to pampering. "If your realm is above the clouds, wouldn't that put it higher than the tallest mortal mountain? Vrekeners might be used to altitude and temperature changes, but I would suffer. Other Sorceri must suffer."

"Not at all. The same forces and wards that conceal the Territories and bind the islands together provide breathable air and warmth."

"Forces and wards? Sounds like sorcery to me. I'll bet sometime in your history, a Vrekener was chummy with one of us."

"It's possible," he conceded. "We have machines in place to move and shape the islands, and engineers to run the machines, but we don't know what the source of the power is."

Interesting. She pictured sorcery-fueled steampunk contraptions. In another lifetime, she might have liked to see such a sight. But in this lifetime . . . "Just because I don't want to go to the Skye doesn't mean we couldn't date each other. If you accompany me to Rothkalina, I could introduce you to nice dragons."

"If I even consider it, then I'll *know* you're enchanting me," he said. "Your sister would plot to murder me the second I stepped into that kingdom. You forget I've witnessed the manifestation of her powers."

When Sabine had forced Thronos's father to see his worst nightmare. Whatever she'd shown him had made the male claw at his eyes.

"Your sister doesn't seem to bear ill effects from her . . . deaths."

"Not surprisingly, they left her deadened, blasé about tragedy."

When Lanthe had accused her of not caring about anything, Sabine had replied, "That's not true. I care about nothing very much."

Lanthe added, "At least, she was blasé before Rydstrom came along. But she weaves illusions over her face, so you rarely know what she's feeling anyway."

"How many times has she died?"

"Over a dozen. Not all by Vrekeners." When he raised his brows, she admitted, "Sorceri plotted against her. Humans executed her for being a witch. And so on." She paused a moment, then said, "What about your own sibling? Will your brother not plot to murder me?" *Might as well dip a toe.*

"Aristo? I grant that he hates Sorceri. It's the cause of much strife between us."

"So he's like your father, then?"

"Yes. But if Aristo harmed you, his brother's sole fated female, it would be like harming me. It would be like killing my future offspring." He held her gaze. "We hold mates sacred."

Thronos will never believe me. Lanthe remembered Sabine lamenting that she couldn't get Vertas warrior Rydstrom to trust her—just because she'd been a Pravus player who'd lied to him and tricked him into a dungeon imprisonment. Sabine had sighed, "How was I supposed to know to act like my word was good?" *I hear you, sister.*

"Would Uncle Aristo accept those future offspring of yours?" Lanthe asked. "You made it clear that Sorceri blood would be a detriment to any child we had."

"I was angry when I said that. I would not love a halfling any less."

"But others might look down on them."

Thronos's face turned cold and intent. "I will not tolerate the *slightest* disrespect to our children."

Our children. "Aren't you worried about the insanity tainting my line?"

He scrubbed his hand over his face. "Again, I was angry when I mentioned that."

"It was true. My mother wasn't well. With me, you risk having crazed offspring."

"I met her once."

"What? When?"

He told her of a brief encounter, when he'd seen Mother worshipping her gold. She'd called him hawkling.

"Wait, Elisabet had known I was seeing you?"

He nodded. "Your mother was harmless, Melanthe. Yet my father murdered the parents of my mate." Thronos's eyes grew matte gray. "I looked up at him that night in the abbey and saw a stranger. I grieved his death, but gods I blamed him. I lost you because of him." He glanced up sharply, as if he hadn't meant to say that much.

"Why didn't you tell me about my mother?"

Clearing his throat, he said, "I wanted to. Never seemed like a good time."

She could scarcely believe her mother had known that secret. Why hadn't Elisabet feared an attack? Lanthe would have to get Sabine's take on that.

"Do halfling Sorceri have powers?" Thronos asked.

"Usually, but Vrekeners have stolen so many powers that they're not being reincarnated. Children are born without souls."

His lips thinned, but the wheels were obviously turning. "How old were you when you discovered your persuasion?"

"Really young. I told Sabine to close her mouth. She couldn't open it for a week, not even to eat. She was starving but no one could figure out what had happened to her. You should know, these kinds of things happen with Sorceri kids."

Instead of appearing horrified by the prospect, he confidently said, "We can handle it."

It was then that she noticed how much steadier and calmer he'd grown since the island. She would bet *steady* was his default setting—unless he suspected that his mate had slept with her brother among her string of other men.

Didn't mean she wouldn't call him on his bullshit. "Oh, come on, Thronos. What would you do with Sorceri young? If we had a teenage daughter and her skirt was short, I'd think it'd be even cuter if shorter. How would you react to that? And if she hadn't stolen gold by the time she was twelve, I'd put her in counseling."

"You're exaggerating."

"Not at all. We'd have you not knowing up from down." But this didn't even bear discussion, because if she and Thronos ever did end up together and she got pregnant, the reality would prove far different: She'd happily go to tell him the good news, all *fa la la*. He'd ask her if he was the father. She'd behead him in a maniacal rage. . . .

"While we're on the subject, Vrekener, would you expect *me* to dress differently up there?"

He raked his gaze over her. "Not behind closed doors." He must have realized how objectionable she found his words, because he added, "I'm sure you wouldn't want to stand out as the least dressed female in the Territories."

"You've just given me a title to aspire to. And besides, behind closed doors, I wouldn't dress at all."

His brows shot up.

She tapped her chin. "Unless I was in the mood for leather or lace."

"Leather." He swallowed. "Or lace."

Then she frowned. "What's this talk about having no roofs?"

Seeming occupied with his own imaginings, he took a moment to answer. "We feel more comfortable with nothing except sky above us."

"Yes, but can't you hear couples having sex all the time?"

He rubbed the back of his neck, as if the skin there had just heated. "We are quiet in matters like that."

She stopped in her tracks. "What does that mean? Sometimes it can't be controlled."

"Vrekeners take pains not to get . . . overly excited."

"I don't understand. What about horny young newlyweds? And what about *you,* Thronos? I've discovered you hardly have ice in your veins."

"Avoiding the truly licentious acts is supposed to help." Gazing to one side of her, he said, "I've seen males with bite marks on their arms, from where they'd muffled their reactions. That's a common enough practice."

She knew she looked gobsmacked, but this was just too *wrong.* "What's the point if you're not getting overly excited? I guess you've never heard the phrase 'bellow to the rafters'?" Especially since they didn't have rafters.

At his blank look, she said, "When you throw back your head and roar with pleasure? Come on, roaring isn't just for battle." Or for unleashing fury in a tempest.

"In a sexual situation, that would indicate . . . a *significant* loss of control."

She'd begun to recognize the expression he wore now, the one that said, *This goes against everything I know. But, gods, tell me more.*

"If *we* had sex, 'overly excited' would only be the beginning," she explained. "Next would come the point of no turning back, when we're angry at our clothes for getting in the way and our hips move on their own and we can't seem to kiss deeply enough and your fingers grip the curves of my ass and my nails dig into the muscles of yours."

"And then?" he said hoarsely.

"Then comes the really fun part of the program." She was getting caught up in this, savoring her virginal Vrekener's reaction: utter enthrallment. "The panting, licking, rutting, keening, sucking, mindless, animalistic, about to explode/erupt/die with ecstasy part."

A sharp breath escaped his lips. She loved the *puh* sound he made. "Next?"

"The last part's difficult to put into words. Better explained by example. Let's just say that we would be anything but quiet."

When he tried to speak, his roughened voice dropped an octave. He coughed into his fist, then finally managed: "I see."

She expected him to make some comment about her sexual past, something along the lines of "How many men have you been *rutting* with? Did they all make you *erupt* with pleasure?" But he didn't, so she asked, "What about flyovers?"

"Huh? Oh. It's bad etiquette to fly over another's home."

"I've heard that all the buildings look the same and all the walls are white, with no color to be seen."

"They are uniform."

"And there's not a drop of wine in your realm? No gambling or carousing?"

"Correct." He was describing a floating, whitewashed, sterilized, stifled, mirthless hell.

She was surprised he'd acknowledged these things about his home, even as he knew how much she would dislike it. "What would you expect me to do all day?"

"Perhaps selfless acts, helping others. Or even studious contemplation." He seemed to have found his footing again. "You could read about our culture, studying Vrekener history."

She'd used to enjoy reading about history, but only if it wasn't *lame.*

"Would those pursuits be so bad?"

Yes, yes, a thousand times yes. Which begged the question: How exactly did he plan to get her to stay there? Once her power was replenished, no one could hold her.

She skated away from that subject. "Thronos, if there's a splinter group up there with its own agenda, then what's to prevent someone"—*your brother*—"from attacking me now?" She expected him to deny, to bluster.

Instead, he said, "If someone disobeyed my order and tried to hurt you, or your sister, he will pay."

"Anyone? Absolutely anyone?"

Curt nod. "I give you my vow," he said, having no idea of the bind he'd just gotten himself into.

And this was why Lanthe rarely kept her promises. "You're starting to believe me?"

"I've learned your tells. I know when you speak untruthfully."

Her eyes darted. That could prove disastrous! Damn it, what were her tells?

If he noticed her distress, he let it go. "There's water ahead. But I also scent resin pits." Seconds later, he pointed out a shallow depression filled with some kind of amber-colored gel. "Resin will trap you like an immortal-strength tar. Step where I step."

In a pit farther ahead was a dead animal, an unidentifiable reptilian beast that had gotten its legs caught. Predators had eaten its guts.

Lanthe shivered. What if an immortal like her got trapped? Those predators would chomp on her, but she might live through the ordeal—only to regenerate for subsequent feedings.

Potentially for eternity.

Being an immortal had its downsides.

"I've been pondering something," Thronos said. "How did Rydstrom forgive Sabine?"

Ah, so the Vrekener was moving his mind toward a pardon for Lanthe? With his new tenuous trust of her, he was starting to look for more between them. He probably figured he could shed some of his anger if he absolved her.

One problem: Lanthe didn't see her sexual history as something that needed absolution.

Especially not from him.

Did she wish Thronos hadn't found her with Marco? Sure. Did she want Thronos's forgiveness for sleeping with that vampire?

Hell. No. "Why do you ask?"

"Rumor holds that Sabine trapped him to use as a sex slave, tormenting him until he agreed to wed her. Then he made a slave of her."

She blinked at him. "Like those are bad things?" At his look of astonishment, she said, "They enjoyed tons of bondage, some master/sub stuff, a real-live dungeon with shackles, role and cosplay. Spankings and repeated orgasm denial. You know, typical BDSM. But don't worry, they were doing it before it became cool."

"BD what?" Thronos's expression was priceless—part confusion over the lingo, part horror, part helpless fascination. She'd bet this angel had an untapped wicked streak.

"Look, it's not for us to understand. It worked for them." The whole truth was much more involved. Sabine had wanted to overthrow Omort, seizing the kingdom for her and Lanthe to rule, while gaining control of the mysterious, demonic Well of Souls in Castle Tornin. No one had ever expected Sabine to fall for Rydstrom—least of all Sabine.

Thronos helped Lanthe over a resin pit. "Answer the question."

"Fine. Rydstrom was able to forgive her because he got a like revenge. Everything she did to him, he did to her."

"The parallel would be for me to bed scores of other women. Which is impossible."

"Then lucky for me I'm not looking for your forgiveness. I'm happy to have experience and to know my own mind."

He appeared to be grinding his molars to dust, but he didn't make any slut-shaming comments.

"Look, my sister went to Rydstrom a virgin. In a hundred years or so, do you think she'll imagine what it's like to know another male? Maybe she will, maybe she won't. But do you think *Rydstrom* will worry that she's imagining it?" She continued, "All those virgin females out there will always have to wonder. I *won't.* I am *informed.* I've done my due diligence, and now I'm ready to settle in for the long haul of eternity."

"That is something to consider, I suppose." Then his brows drew together. "By that logic, in a hundred years you'll wonder if I'm thinking about other females."

In a throaty voice, she said, "Thronos, understand me: if I ever decided to bed you, there would be no doubt. You'd be completely undone, absolutely taken, forever *mine.* If you were ever inside me, you would be broken down at a molecular level—altered irretrievably."

His expression told her he very much wanted to be altered irretrievably. "You guarantee this because of your . . . experience?"

When she merely shrugged, she expected him to launch into a tirade about her past. Again, he held off.

Yet she didn't think this was because he'd had a change of heart. He might not be calling her a harlot, but he still had to think of her as one.

Lanthe had a theory about his turnaround. Before, he'd seen her as a sexual object for other males; after Inferno, he now viewed her as a sexual object for himself to enjoy—and, sadly, she believed he'd learned his first lesson as a potential sexual partner: *Act like an asshole and you won't get any.*

Which meant he was biding his time and biting his tongue until he could get what he wanted.

Just like every other male she'd been with.

TWENTY-FIVE

"Oh, look! Pitha fruit." Melanthe stretched for a black gourd above her, just out of her reach. She scratched at the bottom of it like a little kitten.

He pulled the fruit down for her, scenting it. "This could be poisonous."

"It grows in Rothkalina."

He cracked open the gourd for her. The inside was succulent and smelled sweet.

When he handed the halves to her, she scooped some into her mouth, then rolled her eyes with delight.

"You're certain of that?" he asked. "Though Sorceri are vulnerable to poisons?"

She was already finished with one half. "Poisons *and* venoms." Between chews, she said, "But I'm sure of this."

"How did you get cured of that morsus anyway?"

"When Omort died, his poisoner—a fey female dubbed the Hag in the Basement—delivered the antidotes to us. Otherwise we would've died."

Yet another time Melanthe might've perished when she'd been outside his protection. "This hag did so despite the fact that you called her that?"

Melanthe shrugged, taking another bite, chewing happily.

Dragging his gaze from her, Thronos surveyed their surroundings. Though he'd scented water nearby, he still hadn't found the source, and it was growing darker. Dusk was abnormally long here—and as the sun had begun its lazy descent, the dragons had retreated from the field, their enormous shadows wavering over the treetops.

He and Melanthe had decided to return to the demon valley tonight, but they remained without water. And he hadn't recuperated whatsoever.

Plus, he had plans for them. . . .

When a breeze blew, rustling all the flowers, she set down her finished fruit. "It's beautiful here."

Her black, black hair matched the petals of those flowers. Gaze still on her, he muttered, "Yes. Beautiful."

Since Melanthe had described what copulation between them would be like, he'd found it difficult to look at anything except her. When he took her home to his Bed of Troth, would he not *want* to hear her keen with ecstasy? Would Thronos not *want* to empty his lungs as he emptied his seed inside her?

He'd been vacillating over his decision to claim her tonight—up until the time she'd said those blood-heating words to him. After that, he knew nothing could stop him. All he needed was a secure place to commence his plans.

But how to get her naked and in his arms? His skin flushed when he realized that would mean he too would have to be unclothed.

Naked. In front of her.

He'd figure it out.

Finding another pitha, he used his claw to stab a hole in the bottom to drink from. Its juice was sugary, but welcome. He handed her another pierced gourd to drink.

When some juice ran down her chin, she grinned mischievously—as she used to do when a girl.

That grin affected him differently, yet just as strongly. He wanted the kiss he'd almost taken.

Whatever she saw in his expression made her murmur, "Thronos?"

Before he could stop himself, he took her face in both of his hands, leaning in closer to her.

"Whoa, tiger!" She pushed against him. "You promised me water. Even I can smell some nearby."

He surprised himself by letting her go. As he bit back his disappointment, he caught movement out of the corner of his eye.

A bubble filled with water was floating through the air between them. He and Melanthe silently watched it bobbing along. Without a word, they both hastened in the direction it'd come from.

He lunged in front of her. "I lead the way." He pushed past some brush into a clearing, bordered by moonraker trees. The massive roots encircled the area like walls, while tightly woven branches made a ceiling above them. Countless water-filled bubbles floated up like helium balloons, bursting against the impenetrable canopy.

Drops fell over this glade like a cool summer rain, then rose up to coalesce again.

Not a peek of sky could be seen, making this literal *rain forest* feel like a pocket of muted light and sound.

With his and Melanthe's every step, more drops pattered up from a mat of silver grass. Bubbles were even released by flowers fringing the tree roots.

"This is wild!" Melanthe cried. "Like a fairy ring, or an enchanted glade. Let's name this place . . . Zero-G Glade!" She popped a bubble into her cupped hand to drink.

"Let me test the water first." When she offered her hand, he leaned down to scent and taste it. "Clean."

After they'd both had their fill, he pierced a large bubble over his head. Water poured as if a bucket had been tipped over him, a cool splash over his ash-covered skin. He tossed his sopping shirt onto a root, then scrubbed at his face and hair, his chest and arms.

Another bubble burst over Melanthe's shoulder, making her shiver. Thronos watched, riveted, as each drop slowly trailed down her body—only to be sucked back up to fuse again.

When she let loose a peal of laughter, he asked, "What?"

"It tickles!"

Earlier, she'd laughed in the temple. Then he'd made her laugh on their march. The only thing that could make that sensual sound better? Being the cause of it.

His brows drew together when he realized she'd already laughed more today than he and all his grim knights had in centuries.

"Ah! Drops are going up my skirt!"

"Lucky drops." Had he said that aloud?

Yes, because she faced him with an inquisitive look, as if she were taking his measure. Or making a decision.

Go to her, kiss her.

Yet when he heard bugle calls in the distance, he was reminded of all the perils of this realm. This strange glade might be the only source of water around, which made it a target.

Thronos leapt to a moonraker tree to keep watch.

Cold water seeped along Lanthe's back, wetting her hair and cooling her heated skin.

She'd never seen a place like this glade and was determined to relish it—even if Thronos had deserted her.

After drinking her fill, she sat on the silver grass, removing her boots. "Just because you don't have a skirt doesn't mean you can't enjoy this."

He crouched on a limb, scanning the woods, looking both sexy—and demonic.

She didn't know how he could continue to deny his demon blood when evidence kept mounting. Aside from his similarities to those dragons and his seamless adaptation to this place, he could read the demonic writing!

Maybe that was due to a genetic memory, passed down through the blood—a memory formed here.

By his ancestors.

Now that Thronos had returned to his "realm of origin," his very behavior was changing. There'd been an overall mellowing of rage, and he'd actually cracked jokes. In the last twenty-four hours, he'd probably committed more offendments than in his entire lifetime. She could take some of the blame for those, but not for other changes.

His voice, already a baritone rumble, had grown even deeper, raspier. And his language was deteriorating rapidly. Over the day, he'd begun carrying his seven-foot-tall frame differently, with not quite so much tension in his shoulders, not so much stiffness in the spine. Even his horns seemed prouder somehow.

He not only sounded like a demon, he looked like one. Which she was discovering she might have a weakness for.

Sabine adored having a demon lover. Would Lanthe?

Maybe the realm of Feveris was precisely where she and Thronos needed to go. In the Land of Lusts, she'd feel no guilt for bedding an enemy Vrekener. No fear of the future.

Wait. What was she thinking? She was a daughter of the Sorceri, a born hedonist. She'd take pleasure where she found it, and laugh in the face of guilt.

Well, as long as she didn't get knocked up.

Thronos could be an endless source of pleasure. She'd enjoyed teasing him earlier, wanted to some more. "Come back down here"—she crooked her finger at him—"with all the other offendmenters."

Though he looked like he wanted nothing more than to join her, he remained where he was. "I'll keep watch. It's my job to protect you."

Because his instinct told him so. She sighed. She appreciated the protection, but she wished he was doing it because he *wanted* to, not because he was *compelled* to.

For once, she'd love to hear a male say, "I'm going to do you a solid—not because of what you can do for me in return or what you can give me—but simply because I like you."

Was Thronos so different from Felix? Thronos wanted offspring. Felix had hungered for power.

Both of them sought something from her; yet neither truly cared about her. They only saw what she could give them, how they could use her.

Which she didn't care about, because she had a plan to get her back to Rothkalina: *beguile Vrekener.* Afterward, she'd never have to see Thronos again. "Come on, don't be a killjoy. You'll scent anything that comes near." When he made no move, she said, "I think you don't know how to have fun."

"Why would I be versed in something I haven't experienced since our last day together?"

She frowned at that. How . . . sad.

But she wouldn't dwell on it when fun was here to be had now. "Thronos, we might not make it out of Pandemonia alive. We *should* have died multiple times over the last few days. These things remind me . . ."

"Of what?"

"You're bound by your sacred duties—and I'm bound by mine."

"This I must hear."

"I'm bound to show gratitude for every second of life I'm given by enjoying it to the fullest. Why should the gods—or fate or whatever—grant you more of these precious seconds if you waste the ones they've already provided? It's exactly like—are you ready for this?—GOLD. There's only so much of it to be had. Sorceri believe The End of the Ore will come one day. But life can be shiny and savored and glorious until then."

He raised his brows. "Shiny."

"You squander the coins you've been given. In my eyes, you're more of an offendmenter than I am."

"How do I squander them, then?"

"Your mind is always in the past."

He scowled. "You're as mired in the past as I am."

"Maybe, but I usually recall good memories. Like how much fun we used to have playing in that meadow together."

Thronos rose to pace that limb. What was he contemplating?

She probed, but found his shields up. Fine. She turned from him, determined to enjoy Zero-G, and its upskirt rain, all by herself.

She spied a leafy branch that arched down beside a smooth trunk, heavier streams of water following it, making a shower head of sorts. She wished she could shuck off all of her clothes and finally take the shower she'd been longing for—

A bubble burst against the back of her head.

With a gasp, she whirled around—and caught another bubble against her arm.

"Thronos!"

He was using a wing to wave them over to her, because he was playing with her, having *fun.*

She gave a cry when another hit her chest, cool water trickling behind her breastplate. And once those delicious drops trickled down, they traveled right back up her body.

She opened her arms wide. "Give it your best shot. I'll bet you can't hit me"—she pointed to her navel—"here. Oh, wait, I forgot, Vrekeners don't gamble."

"I'll enter into another wager with you. If I hit your target, then you have to remove your breastplate."

He was certainly getting the hang of flirting. "And if you don't?"

"You have to remove your breastplate."

Her lips curled. "I think I'm going to have to teach you the finer points of wagers, demon." For once, the word didn't seem to bother him; of course, she'd all but purred it. "Honestly, I would love to take it off, would kill to bathe under that tree limb's cascade." She hiked a thumb in that direction. "But we're back in the same boat as before. How can I be sure you won't lose control?"

"Melanthe, you *want* to be naked for me."

This authoritative side of him was kind of *hot.* "Do I?" She sounded completely unsure, even to her own ears. Maybe they could just play tonight—taking the edge off their need. They didn't have to go further.

Surely premarital sex was an offendment Thronos would never commit, no matter how worked up they got. *I'll breed no bastards.*

"You told me that if I got you to safety, you would show me anything I wanted to see," he said. "I got you to safety, and I want to see *everything.*"

She arched her brows. Sexy Thronos. And a promise was a promise, right?

Lanthe shouldn't want to take off her clothes for him, but he was right; she *did.* She wanted him to see her and desire her. She wanted to experience his reaction as he beheld his mate for the first time.

If simply holding hands with this male had nearly brought her to the edge . . .

At that thought, she reached for her breastplate, eager to have it gone. As she had in the temple, she gave him her back while she unbuckled the piece. Tugging it off, she tossed it away, then started on her skirt, unfastening the hidden hooks. With a swish of her hips, the garment dropped, pooling at her feet.

Leaving her in a black thong.

She grinned when she heard his wings shoot open with a snap.

Draping an arm across her breasts, she craned her head around to find him crouched, body tensed. His horns had straightened. There was no mistaking it.

Just as unmistakable? Her response. As her gaze followed those proud lengths, her nipples hardened and the folds of her sex grew slick.

"Your panties too," he rasped. The pulselines on his wings were glowing brighter and moving faster than she'd ever seen them.

Keeping her back to him, she hooked her thumbs around the frayed lace, pulling them down her legs. As she kicked the thong away, she thought she heard him swallow thickly.

"Ready?" she asked.

"Very." The word was a harsh grate.

"You sure?"

"Melanthe," he growled in warning.

She dropped her arm and turned with her shoulders back. She caught one of his thoughts, and it sent a ripple of satisfaction through her.

—Mother. Of. Gods.—

TWENTY-SIX

Thronos had barely recovered from the vision of her flawless ass when she turned to him, unleashing the full force of her beauty. At the sight, three things happened:

He almost fell out of the tree.

His shaft shot so hard so fast that he grew dizzy.

And he decided he'd deal with any danger as it came along.

He'd known her breasts were generous. Now he saw they were perfection. Milk-white, a touch fuller at the bottom, topped with cherry-red nipples.

If he were a fanciful male, he'd swear those peaks were stiffening under his avid gaze. His member began to *throb*.

Her narrow waist flared to shapely hips. The black thatch of hair on her mons was a small, trimmed V. Her legs were long and lithe. He imagined them bent beside his hips as she rode his shaft—or kneeling over his head as she straddled his tongue.

"I'll just wash off, then," she said in a casual tone. Seeming unaware of her earth-shattering effect on him, she stepped under the cascade, tipping her face to the water, and started to bathe.

She must be confident that he could control himself; she was mistaken.

But considering the way his erection ached, intercourse would be short-lived. He decided to get his first release behind him, then seduce her slowly.

He had a last brief thought about dangers and being alert, but then she rubbed water over her breasts—the most breathtaking sight he'd ever witnessed.

Conclusion: the plan to mate her as soon as possible is sound.

Never taking his eyes off her, he was only dimly aware that his shaking hands had begun removing his boots.

As she rinsed her hair, she noticed him removing his second boot. "You didn't say anything about *your* getting naked."

"I plan to touch you."

"Hmm. Wouldn't that be an offendment?"

He nodded ominously.

"Do I have any say in this?" She drew her hair behind her shoulders.

"You told me that if I saved you from the swamp serpents, you would let me touch you."

"Oh. That. I didn't say you could while I was naked."

In answer, he dropped to the ground, striding toward her.

Lanthe was in a precarious position. She desired Thronos. If she was honest with herself, she'd admit that her attraction to him was already greater than to any other male.

But touching led to claiming.

She was going to have to trust Thronos not to follow his most primal instincts. In general, males had never given her much reason to trust them. And this one was already rock hard, his cock straining against the leather of his breeches.

Thronos started on his pants as he closed in, his scarred fingers unlacing them, his stomach muscles flexing. Once the fly gaped, she followed his dark goody trail from his navel—

Down went his pants. Her jaw dropped in time. Well. *Thronos is all growed up.*

He planned to claim her. With *that*?

She could tell he was uncomfortable, obviously unused to being naked around another. But apparently his need was burning away his instilled modesty.

When he pressed closer, she stepped back against the smooth tree trunk, putting the curtain of water between them. With a second's reprieve, she resolved again to go only up to a point with him. She could control herself, despite her hormones, despite the body he'd just revealed!

He continued forward, letting the water run over his back and wings. He shook his dark hair out, wet locks whipping over his broad cheekbones. Between his narrow hips, his erection jutted hungrily.

She waved to it. "You still deny your demon blood? Exhibit A. Case dismissed."

Aside from his nearly dismaying size, his cock was gorgeous. The shaft was straight and thick, with a dominant vein visibly pulsing. The crown bulged so much that the slit was almost hidden. His testicles were large, and looked in need of cupping and kissing.

When she could drag her gaze up, she was treated to his entire body in all its naked glory. His rugged muscles were ideally proportioned for his seven feet of height. The width of his shoulders only highlighted the leanness of his hips.

Above the sculpted planes of his torso, his pecs were rigid slabs of masculinity. Were those flat, dusky nipples of his sensitive? The thought had her twirling her tongue in her mouth.

Scars crisscrossed his chest, one curling around his hip, another deep one slashing up his left thigh. But they didn't blunt her attraction whatsoever.

He was indeed tan all over. The sun had kissed him from the top of his head to that mouthwatering shaft to his feet. One of his lower legs looked swollen, as if the tendons were knotted there, and his foot curved inward. The cause of his limp. She thought he was fighting to keep his foot straight for this perusal.

She wished he wouldn't bother, but males were funny like that. *Show no weakness, grrr.*

He'd seen all of her; she wanted a similar viewing of him, so she emerged from the water, sauntering around him. When he realized what she was doing, he lifted his chin, as if steeling himself against her reaction. But he didn't move out from under the cascade.

Revealed between two glimmering wing tapers, his ass was a purr-inducing work of art. Streams coursed over the smooth skin there, over the tight muscles framed by shaded hollows. The cleft of his ass was so taut, she wondered if she could even nip it with her teeth.

As she continued around, he remained still, allowing her to ogle him. Now that she knew how he felt about his looks, she found this tremendously brave.

Sometimes Lanthe wasn't as brave as she could be—certainly not like everyone else who lived in or even visited Tornin—so she applauded anyone who demonstrated the trait.

Shouldn't Thronos's bravery be rewarded?

When she stood before him once more, he scanned her face. Searching for some hint of her thoughts?

"Thronos, if I honestly tell you what I think of your body, will you tell me what you think of mine?" He hadn't said anything aloud.

"Peculiar sorceress. Yes, I will." And then he held his breath.

"You're so *big*. And hard. When I look at your body . . . I get wet for it."

His lips parted around an exhalation. *Puh.*

Thronos was still reeling from her words. His body aroused hers? Only fair since she made him hard as stone.

Yet then her gaze dipped to his chest. To his scars. He stood unclothed before her, and she focused on the most hated parts of his body.

She leaned forward. She kissed a scar.

His head fell back. Was this her way of apologizing? Of showing her regret? Another feather-light graze of her lips followed.

If this was the way she expressed remorse, he might be helpless not to forgive her!

"And now, what do you think of mine?" she asked against his skin.

I almost come just from looking at you. I need to lick every inch of your flesh. I want to pin you down and suckle you—for hours. "You're exquisite," he finally bit out, laying his palms against the tree trunk above her head. His wings closed in on her. Trapping her.

Her gaze darted from one to the other, but she didn't say anything.

"*Impossibly* exquisite." He leaned his head down to her neck, drawing deep of her scent, letting her feel his exhalations. Gods, she smelled so inconceivably right to him. He couldn't stop himself from nuzzling her neck. It made her shiver, so he did it again. Then he ran his lips beside her ear, rasping, "I'll likely wake to discover this isn't real—just another dream of you."

"What happens when you have those dreams? I'm sure you have a law against masturbation."

He nodded, then confessed, "I wake up thrashing, thrusting at anything, already culminating."

She released a shaky breath of her own.

"I've fantasized about you, about all the forbidden things I want to do to you, for hundreds of thousands of nights. And now you're here with me," he said, voice laden with disbelief. "If just one of my dreams would come true."

"What would you like to happen?"

Need to be buried inside you! But . . . "Melanthe, let's begin with a kiss." In Inferno, he'd decided that their first real kiss would be vastly different from the frenzied taking when he'd first captured her. He could be tender.

When he curled his finger under her chin, tilting her head up, she asked, "Have you ever done this before?"

He shook his head.

"Do you remember when you taught me to swim?"

In the lake by their meadow. "I remember." She'd been terrified at first, clinging to him, but by the end of that afternoon, she'd taken to the water like a selkie pup.

"You taught me the basics, and then instinct took over. Maybe I could teach you the basics of kissing?"

"I want that."

"You could brush your lips against mine a couple of times, to get used to the feeling. Then when you're ready you could slip your tongue in to find mine."

He raised his knee beside her, boxing her in, as if he subconsciously feared she'd escape him yet again. "And then?"

"You'd slowly and sensuously lick the tip of my tongue."

"Yes." His swollen length shot even harder.

"Hopefully we'll drive each other crazy. When that happens you can take my mouth deeper. Just do what feels good for you, and it'll likely feel good for me."

With a nod, he leaned down to graze his lips over hers and back. Again. Hers were so plump, giving. When her breaths shallowed, he slanted his mouth to deepen the kiss.

As he slowly dipped between her sweet lips, she clung to his shoulders, gripping his muscles when the tip of his tongue found hers. The contact was electric! He groaned into her mouth, wondering if he would instantaneously spend.

Considering the pressure in his shaft, this seemed probable.

Though he'd wanted to get his first release out of the way, now he realized that would be squandering the experience.

Thronos would endeavor to last—

She began licking back, with light laps of her tongue that made his head swim. Still, he kept the pace slow, lazily teasing her, as if he had all the time in the world. He was rewarded with her seductive moan.

When he grew more aggressive, she murmured against his lips, "Yes, yes." She laid one palm on his chest, turning it until her fingers were pointed down. Inch by inch, she lowered her hand.

Between the kiss and her touch, he was awash in stimulation. Too much! His member jerked as if to meet her halfway. By the time she reached it, he would release in her palm.

Breaking from the kiss, he collected her wrists, pinning them above her head. Her eyes were glittering, her body trembling—because of him. *Him.*

In a breathy voice, she said, "Well. You certainly have the hang of it. But don't you want us to touch each other?"

He bit out an anguished sound. "You have no idea." He recalled how that Volar had used his wings to stroke the demoness. Gaze locked on Melanthe's, Thronos began tracing his talon over her collarbone.

Her eyes went wide. "Oh! You're touching me with your wings?"

"If I put my hands on you . . ."

She seemed to realize his quandary.

"Trust me not to hurt you, Melanthe."

Gradually, he felt her body relaxing under his exploration.

As he trailed the talon between her breasts, his need to cup them was overwhelming. He made fists, claws digging into the palms of his hands until blood dripped.

His talon smoothed along the undersides of her breasts, those perfect, pale globes. They would be a heaven of softness beneath his rough palms.

As he finally skimmed toward one of her nipples, she shook, arching to him.

Then he scented her arousal. *Dear gods.* The luscious scent of her sex readying for his length . . .

Nearly put him to his knees.

How much more could he withstand?

TWENTY-SEVEN

Oh, my gold. Just as she'd feared, Thronos had turned irresistible.

His kiss had made her toes curl. He was a natural, which made her wonder what else he'd be a natural at.

Even his exploration of her—weird as it was—was turning her on. The idea of that lethal talon caressing her so gently messed with her mind.

His wings had once been a symbol of her fear. How perverse was she if she got off on this? Maybe she liked perverse?

Her nipples were pouting for attention—which he seemed determined not to give. Was he never going to put his hands on her? She understood his predicament; he feared coming too quickly. After such a long wait, who could blame him?

Eyes ablaze with lust—and intent—he lowered his wing, circling her navel.

Surely he wouldn't go lower. "Thronos, wait." He couldn't. And, gods, she couldn't desire him to. . . .

The smooth curve of his talon dipped between her legs.

She might've tried to get away, but he had her wrists trapped, her body boxed in.

He began stroking her sex, and it was . . . pleasurable. The talon was firm against her as he eased it back and forth over her needy clitoris.

Back. And forth.

This is so weird. And pervy. And I like it so much!

She squeezed her eyes closed, disturbed that she wasn't more disturbed by this. She had a sinking suspicion: Thronos could do just about anything to her and she'd like it.

Because he *was* her mate? Was she fighting fate?

Sorceri don't believe in fate!

Seeming to lose his inner battle, he gave a groan of frustration, releasing her wrists.

Her eyes flashed open when his palms landed on her shoulders. He was bleeding—from digging his claws into his hands? Hot crimson mixed with the cool water in streams.

If she'd thought something was wrong with her before, now she was convinced, because she found his searing blood on her skin arousing—as if he was marking her, like he'd done in that tunnel when he'd painted her lips.

And though his blood was washing away, she could swear she'd perceived the heat of it streaking across her aching breasts and over her stiffened nipples. Over her hips and ass. Between his blood and the weird talon caresses, she was shaking with need.

She sucked in a breath, holding herself motionless as his hands roamed, starting to descend. And all the while his talon petted her clitoris.

His transfixed gaze followed his hands. "None lovelier." His tone was awed.

Why did it feel so unbelievably good with him? He seemed just as lost, overwhelmed by this pleasure, starved for it.

Because he *had* been. So how would he react the first time they had sex? *If* they did. How would that magnificent cock feel plunging inside her? Imagining it made her moan.

To her surprise, she felt a glimmer of welling power, then another. Sorcery began whirling within her, as if she'd been an empty vessel waiting to be filled. Her lips curled with delight.

Wait . . . had his hands just bypassed her chest? He molded them over her waist, then rested them on her hips. He drew his wing back from her sex, leaving her yearning for release. *Pervy, girl.*

Without warning, he pressed a muscled thigh between her legs. She couldn't stifle a cry. Positioned like this, his rampant cock prodded against her, the bulbous head rubbing along her damp torso.

Taunting her.

She craved that thick length, craved all of his throbbing heat filling her. Of their own accord, her hips rocked in invitation as she slowly rode his leg.

"I feel your arousal, your wetness. I scent it." Against her neck, he murmured, "Before this night is out, I want to know your taste, take it into me."

"Oh! *Ohhh.* We can definitely work something out."

"Ask your male to kiss you there. Though forbidden, I'd do it to you." What *wasn't* forbidden in his mind? "I'd do it till you came for me."

I have to ask for it? With a mental shrug, she parted her lips . . . only to close them as doubts arose. *What must he think of me now?* As easy as he'd predicted?

Yet when he moved his thigh against her sex, those qualms faded into the ether.

At last, he covered her breasts with his rough palms! He shuddered to feel her. She gave a low cry as her head lolled.

He took several breaths, nostrils flaring, as if he were just preventing himself from coming. With a growling sound, he began to knead her. "Tantalizing female." Holding one breast poised—to receive his mouth?—he dipped his head. "Need to suckle you."

She cried, "By all means!"

Lower, lower. She watched him lash a wet lick over one of her pebbled nipples. "Yes, Thronos!" Dimly she realized, *His tongue is pointed.*

Wicked demon.

Groaning, he wrapped his lips around her nipple, sucking it with greedy pulls.

She started panting. "You're making me feel so good." Tunneling her fingers through his hair, she held him close.

Against her breast, he rasped, "Your nipples are so sweet. As sweet as your lips. How I've hungered for this! Hungered for you."

The disbelief and awe in his voice made her melt for him. His unshielded thoughts too: —*This is real, Talos. You are* with *her. This is happening. Had no idea what pleasure was. . . .* —

Thronos was never supposed to be like this.

She would've hungered for him too—if she'd known this was in store.

Giving the peak a loud suck, he moved to her other nipple, growling around it. His thigh kept rocking, his cock sliding up and down her belly. His pointed tongue was making her forget why she would ever resist him. She was in a heaven of sensation. Add to that his masculine scent and barely harnessed lust . . .

When he took his kisses away to stand fully, she gave a frustrated cry.

"Have to get closer to you."

Closer?

One of his arms coiled around her shoulders, his other around her neck. As he continued to thrust, he wrapped her tighter in his wings, tighter still—until their slippery bodies were mashed together, his cock trapped between them.

Was this a Vrekener thing?

With each of his ragged breaths, his chest heaved against her breasts, against her achy nipples. She could feel his heart thundering.

Her arms were pinned by her sides; she should be panicked. He was a Vrekener—but she'd never felt this safe. Their bodies were so close, she couldn't tell where he ended and she began. And at that moment, she didn't want to be anywhere else in any world.

Would he enfold her like this for sex? *Pervy Lanthe is on board.*

She'd planned to wrap him around her little finger; instead, he'd wrapped his wings around her! He'd made her nearly mindless with desire. Hot, slick, swollen desire.

With each degree he constricted those wings, his groans deepened. He was going to come like this.

She would too, right upon his muscular thigh.

"I've waited so long for you." Pressing openmouthed kisses to her neck, he pumped his hips faster, rutting against her body. Her nipples raked his chest with each of his jostling movements.

When she undulated against his leg to grind her clitoris, he gave a brutal growl. "You like my wings around you? Trapping you to me?"

"Yes!"

"And if I never let you go, sorceress?"

She moaned in reply. The pressure kept mounting, until she was on the verge of coming. "Don't stop, Thronos!"

"The *pleasure* . . ." he bit out in a tone of wonder as he rocked her. "It's almost agony." His biceps bulged as he squeezed her. "I grow nigh!"

Her head shot forward, her mouth on his neck. She was losing control, as she hadn't in memory. Tongue flicking, she sucked on his skin as wanton urges suffused her.

Snaring his thick cock and working it inside me. Or tonguing his throbbing, veined length.

What would he think of her if she dropped to her knees before him—with her lips parted to be fed . . . ?

"Ah, gods, woman!" His shaft jerked in the tight sleeve they'd created as he rocked faster and harder. "Never knew . . ." Faster. *Harder*—

Massive body quaking, he threw his head back, tendons taut as bowstrings. Then he *roared.*

Just as he wasn't supposed to do.

Through her lips, she felt the reverberations in his throat. She was about to go over the edge with him, moaning with abandon.

Though she didn't feel seed, his wings rippled around her each time his mighty shaft pulsated. Another bellow shook the night. And another, over . . . and over . . . and over . . .

How badly he must have needed that!

As those dry spasms finally eased, he gave one last shudder, leaving her right on the brink.

"You came?" she murmured. *No seed means demon.*

Catching his breath, he rested his forehead against hers. "Harder than I could ever have imagined. You made me bellow to the rafters." Unguarded, he rasped, "And now I feel no pain in my body."

He raised his face, meeting her eyes. His pupils were blown from his recent pleasure, his irises . . . darker?

What was he thinking about his first orgasm with another? And just like that, those damned doubts returned. *What is he thinking about me?*

"Now it's your turn." He released some of the constriction around her. When he trailed the backs of his fingers across one of her breasts, then lower, her lids grew heavy. "How does my mate like to be petted?" He sifted his fingers through the curls on her sex.

If he touched her clitoris, she was going to lose it. And if she totally let go, she'd be confirming everything he'd said about her. "Wait." This very day he'd called her "easy quarry," and she was proving him right! At the thought, she tensed, her impending orgasm dissipating. "I can't do this."

"No, sweet, you don't want to stop. I scent how badly you need release."

Desperately!

The sorceress in her was clamoring, *Pleasure's there for the taking!*

The vulnerable woman within murmured, *If he shames you after this, it will hurt forever.*

"Let me tend to you, Melanthe. You must be aching."

"I . . . can't." She turned her head away.

TWENTY-EIGHT

She'd let other males pleasure her—just not him!

Thronos punched the tree, cracking the trunk, but Melanthe never faced him.

Before he said something he regretted, he drew back his wings, striding away from her. He found his breeches, nearly ripping them apart in frustration.

Touching her had surpassed all of his fantasies. He'd never known a female could be so soft, so sensual. But she'd denied him. He'd failed to overcome her resistance—he'd . . . failed.

And he'd been unable to hold out against the feel of her. His legs were still unsteady from that mind-blowing release. His shaft had liked its culmination so well, it'd been primed for the next one immediately.

He would *never* get enough of her! Yanking his breeches up his damp legs, he fastened them over his still raging member, then collected his shirt. By the time he was dressed, she'd donned her skirt and was fastening her breastplate.

Yet again things had gone sideways. Yet again Thronos didn't understand his current position. She'd described Pandemonia's traps; was this an unearthly pleasure followed by punishment?

Or merely a foiled plan to get her pregnant? "Why would you let other males give you pleasure but not me?"

She met his gaze. "Because none of them would ridicule me if I let go. And none of them deemed me a harlot. There were things I wanted to do to you, with you, but I heard your voice in my head, sneering that I was easy quarry."

He wanted them to get past this, to start over. So he could touch her again, wrap her close to him. Gods, how erotic it had been, with the skin of his wings molding over the curves of her womanly little body. Enfolding her had fulfilled some primal need in him, had made him feel like he was taking her into him. "I won't insult you like that again."

"No, you'll just think it. Thronos, I want to be with a male who likes me. Not one who hates me but is forced by his instinct to be with me anyway."

"I don't hate you, Melanthe."

"Three nights ago, you compared me to a broken bone!"

"I thought you were different then."

"Ah, yes, you assumed that I was sleeping with my brother. Yet after we resolved that little misunderstanding, you've been *trying* to shame me. You expect me to lose control with you—when you scorn that very behavior? How can I just snap my fingers and get over that?"

"Why did these thoughts arise in the middle of what we were doing? If *I* could temporarily clear my mind of all the males who'd come before me—"

She gasped.

He rubbed his hand over his face. "That came out worse than I intended."

"And proved my point utterly!"

"Though I'd once wanted to hurt you, I no longer do."

"Why this turnaround?"

"I was cruel before because I thought you were evil. For centuries, I believed that. This anger inside me grew and grew. It's been seething there so long, and I felt like I'd explode if I didn't vent it."

"Thronos, you haven't been venting it—you've been giving it *to me* to keep. You might have eased your ill will, but you've kindled mine."

"Do you want me to just forget how many males have bedded you? Every time you and your sister left Rothkalina, I knew it was because you were on the hunt for a power. I knew you'd bedded yet another sorcerer who'd stolen one of your abilities." He paced, his leg beginning to ache once more, a stark contrast to those moments when all he'd felt was her lush body against him and the residual heat of pleasure. The pain was all the worse after its temporary absence. "I was left so damned conflicted. Even as I was enraged because someone hurt my mate, I'd be racked with jealousy. Whenever you let another take you . . ." He stopped to face her. "Melanthe, there is no word to describe that pain."

She lifted her chin. "I can't change my past. I wouldn't even if I could."

"Why? I suppose those lovers were so amazing that you couldn't stand to miss a single one?" And yet his first sexual encounter with Melanthe had resulted in no orgasm for her, and him releasing against her belly.

How excellent, Talos.

"I wouldn't take back my past, because then I wouldn't be *me*. I've done these things, and I've had these experiences. Which means I'll only fall for someone who can accept me—as is. There's nothing worse than when a male looks at a female and thinks, 'She would be perfect, if only . . .' "

"You believe I think that?"

"I know you do! Melanthe would be perfect if only she were a convent-raised virgin, innocent in the ways of men. If only she could fly, tell the truth, and go without stealing/drinking/gambling. If only she were a Vrekener."

He couldn't deny these things. "And have you reasoned so about me?"

"If only you laughed. If only you valued gold—and each minute alive. If only you could comprehend that I'm more than a number."

He bit out a sound of frustration. "I don't want to think of you like this! But it *guts* me to know you've been with others, and I can't stop imagining you with them! Jealousy claws at me from the inside!"

"I need to know: Can you ever get over my past?"

"I will not hurt you again, not as I have."

"That's not what I asked. Can you get over it?"

He didn't want to lie to her, but he didn't see how he could ignore what she'd been doing for five centuries. "You have to give me time to wrap my head around all this. For very, very many years, my life was simple. I had one job to do, one thing on which to focus. Now? I'm always conflicted. I just need time."

"How much time were you planning to give me to get used to life at Skye Hall? To dress differently, to act differently. Even to make love differently. How much time would I be allotted to become someone other than myself?"

He stabbed his hands through his hair. "Then tell me something to change my mind. You've always made me rethink things. Do it now!"

"I can't—not when you boil my past down to an imaginary number of males. Know that you're about to join their ranks."

"What does that mean?"

"Just like you, they *all* failed to win me. When I finally find the one I'm supposed to be with, I'll give him something no other has claimed."

"Which is?"

She pinned his gaze with her own. "My heart."

Something of hers he could possess that no other had before.

"You're no different from Felix. Both of you *wanting* something from me. But neither of you ever *liked* me."

"I am nothing like that sorcerer! I'd give my life for yours. You know that."

"Because of your instinct. Remember when you yelled at me, railing that it compelled you to pursue me—otherwise you would have taken my head yourself? If instinct is what's driving you to be with me, then you might as well be ensorcelled against your will."

Guilt flared—he had even *fought* his instinct when it urged him to bestow a kindness on her. He'd had numerous opportunities to limit her suffering, and each time he'd opted for her misery.

"We're kidding ourselves, Thronos. With our history, these last three days have just been a recap. The damage has long since been done."

"You're the one who's trying to get me to forget the past."

"Not to forget it! To see it differently." She pinched the bridge of her nose. "Why am I even trying? It's like arguing with a flying, demonic wall. I just can't do this with you!" She sat to put on her boots, refusing to look at him.

Ignoring me once again. Keeping her within his sight, he paced the glade.

Yet as his ire cooled, he began to feel like the worst hypocrite. Who was he to judge her? He'd planned to commit an offendment to impregnate her, to *trap* her, though they weren't wed.

I dare to judge?

Why couldn't he get over the past? He was going to destroy her before it was all over.

She'd been hunted, attacked, and poisoned most of her life. It was a wonder she had any goodness in her at all! She could have done truly unforgivable deeds. Instead, she'd lived her life.

Without him.

And that's really what you can't forgive.

For ages, he'd told himself that her actions had forever changed him—a stream carving a groove through rock—ensuring he would always despise her.

But deep down, hadn't he feared the opposite was true? That *no force in the universe* could change his feelings for her?

He recalled his conversation with Nïx, when she'd told him how to find Melanthe. He'd been choking back frustration that he would have to wait an entire year to capture his mate, predicting he'd go mad in the interim, when the Valkyrie had said, "I'll give you a piece of advice, Thronos Talos. Before Melanthe became this, she was that. . . ."

He hadn't known what the Valkyrie was talking about. Now, as he gazed over at his mate, the answer came to him.

Before Melanthe became my enemy, she was my best friend.

TWENTY-NINE

When Lanthe stood, dressed once more, she realized she was overflowing with power.

Which meant she was done beguiling Thronos. She turned a mean smile in his direction. *I'll go wherever my happy ass feels like.*

He stopped his pacing. "Melanthe, we don't have to figure this out all at once. We can't expect to wade through everything so soon. It will take time, which we will have once we get home."

For a crazy moment, she thought, *Maybe I should just go with him.* It was rumored that the Vrekeners stored all the sorcery they harvested in a vault in Skye Hall; Thronos was planning to take her straight there.

As charged up as she felt right now, she could command Aristo to kiss Sorceri ass and order him to release all the abilities his kind had stolen (maybe taking one or two or ten for herself and Sabine).

Lanthe would be a Sorceri superstar, no longer preyed upon by the likes of Portia and Ember!

Wait a minute. Surely Thronos had to worry about the havoc she could wreak up there? "I don't get it, Thronos. How do you think you're going to keep me captive? You don't have a collar, and my persuasion is recharging with a vengeance. . . ." She trailed off, comprehension dawning. "Oh, dear gods. Y-you planned to take my power."

For the briefest instant, had he winced?

She fought for breath, feeling like he'd punched her in the chest. His face blurred as her eyes watered. "You'd steal my soul? Turn me into a mindless breeder for you?"

"I would not do that to you!"

"And you wonder why I don't want to have children with you! Would you take their souls, too?" She made a fist above her heart. "Press a fire scythe to their chests?" As she began backing away from him, sorcery whorled around her.

"No!" He looked like the idea appalled him. "I did consider doing that to you, but immediately decided against it."

Her voice shook with fury when she said, "I'm done with this. With you. *Done.*"

When he strode toward her, she commanded him, "Freeze in place." She was astonished at how easily she wielded her persuasion, her sorcery flowing unhampered. Maybe her nervousness *had* affected it.

After all, every time she'd used it in the past, she might have been calling Vrekeners down upon herself and Sabine. No chance of that now.

Though Thronos fought the command, he was forced to obey it. "Gods damn it, Melanthe, don't use your sorcery on me! You can't comprehend what it's like for me to lose control of my body and mind." When she merely raised her brows, he said, "Don't do this now. We've been moving in the right direction. You can't deny the change between us."

"Because I didn't know what you were plotting! I command you to remain in this glade for twenty-four hours. That ought to give you some time for *contemplation.*"

Incredulous, he bit out, "You don't believe I've done enough of that? And where will you go? To steal a key by yourself?"

"Precisely." If she reached both demon lairs before dawn, the armies would still be locked in conflict. Not only could she follow the sounds of their skirmishes, she would encounter few demons within their respective dens.

Of course, with her sense of direction, she should be lost directly.

Even if she somehow made it to the Abysmals' stronghold, it was fronted by a maze of ruins. Yet she expected to find her way into and out of them? She couldn't find her way out of a human mini-mart.

As if he read her mind, Thronos said, "How will you know where to go? If you follow that path back toward Inferno, you'll have to cross the pest zone."

Or she could follow the path *away* from Inferno for a time, then cut north (or south, or whatever) to reach the plateau. Inferno would be on one side, Deep Place on the other.

She'd thread the needle, get the lay of the land, and decide her strategy. "I have a plan."

He shook his head hard. "You're going to get yourself killed."

"I'll be fine. I've managed all these years without you." Of course, she'd always had Sabine to protect her.

"You've managed, but you've never been in hell."

"Debatable." Perhaps Lanthe could finally protect herself, take off the training wheels to become a badass like her sister.

Lanthe remembered a time centuries ago, when she'd asked Sabine, "Why are you so much bolder and braver than I am?"

Sabine had told her, "Illusion is reality, Lanthe. If you look or act all-powerful for long enough, guess what you'll become."

Lanthe squared her shoulders. "One last thing. I'm sorry to have to tell you this—actually, I'm not sorry at all—but your brother is the one who stabbed me with a pitchfork and brained Sabine. He and his men are the ones who hunted us."

"Aristo? What are you talking about? You've never encountered my brother."

"I peeked into your head and saw your recollection of our first meeting after your fall. I saw your brother's face, but it certainly wasn't the first time."

While Thronos gaped at her words, she said, "Now, hand over that medallion." She couldn't believe she'd been so wrapped up in him that she'd all but forgotten about it.

He reluctantly removed the piece from his pocket, handing it over as ordered. "How did you know?"

"Did you think I wouldn't sense this gold?" She ran the pads of her fingers over the gleaming smoothness. Red gold. In her hands.

It was the size of a pocket watch, with the finest engravings across the surface, depicting . . . flames. Seeing it reminded her of her dream on the island, of a woman saying, *Set worlds aflame.*

Lanthe looped the chain around her neck, telling Thronos, "I kept waiting for you to make a gift of this. Now I realize you probably meant to use it against me."

"That isn't true. I did intend to give it to you."

"What do you think my reaction would've been like? How might I have expressed my gratitude? Maybe you've learned a Sorceri lesson: never put off till tomorrow what you can revel in today."

"If you leave me here like this, I won't be able to protect myself."

"Then I command you to remain in this glade for twenty-four hours unless there is a threat to your life."

"Damn it, Melanthe! Can you not imagine what this is like for me, to feel the force of your sorcery again? It makes my skin crawl!" His muscles swelled as he strained against her commands. "There is no more horrific feeling. When I jumped through that window . . . and I couldn't fly . . ." His voice grew hoarse. "To see the ground rushing closer, and I couldn't move my wings. I just wanted . . . to move my wings. Look into my thoughts right now—see *that* memory!"

To do so would be like looking back over her shoulder—when she should be running away. She'd done that twice with him, and rued both times.

With an inward curse, she gave a light probe into his mind.

She saw the ground rushing closer. She heard his instinct screaming inside him to save himself. She felt his roiling emotions when his body refused to obey—when he realized he was about to die.

A stranglehold of shock. Raw terror.

In such a young boy.

"Do you know why I never yelled on the way down?" he asked quietly. "Because fear had robbed me of breath."

She withdrew from his thoughts as swiftly as she'd entered them. Tears pricked her eyes, but she willed herself not to cry.

"Now you understand what it feels like, to act in opposition to instinct—to the very will to survive! But I'd relive that night again if it would make you stay here with me."

She reminded herself that he still planned to kidnap her. He'd considered stealing her soul! He was going to serve her up on a platter to his brother. She replayed how he'd tossed her into that tree and lifted her by her jaw. And his comments.

Someone like you. I'd take your head myself. I should drop you.

If she allowed him to treat her this shittily, then she was no better than he was. *When in trouble* . . . She turned from him and walked away.

"Melanthe leaving me—not exactly new! I'm sick of pursuing you! All my life you've turned from me again and again. Begone, then. Good riddance!"

As she strode off, she heard him cursing her, but hardened herself against him. The sooner she got to the lairs, the sooner she could be back in Rothkalina. She might make it to the castle in time for dinner!

She found the overgrown path they'd traveled upon, then headed away from Inferno. In theory.

For the next hour, she followed the trail, the forest brush growing sparser. Each time thoughts of Thronos flickered into her mind, she told herself: *Don't think about his fall, Lanthe.*

She came upon a fork in the trail, with another inscribed rock marker that she couldn't read. She could go straight or turn left. Imagining the marker read *Go left to thread the needle,* she turned in that direction, readying for danger.

When nothing happened, she trudged on.

And on and on—for what felt like eternity. Surely day would soon break. She was beginning to think time moved differently on this plane—not uncommon for demon realms. At last, the skirmishes grew louder.

Don't think about his fall.

Oh, who was she kidding? Thronos hadn't *fallen.* She'd lashed out and hurt the one innocent Vrekener among that group. Yes, she'd been a traumatized girl, but he hadn't deserved the horror she'd meted out.

She'd just admitted to herself that she'd been . . . wrong, when she emerged into a large field, the underbrush giving way to craggy terrain.

For a moment she thought the sun was rising, then realized she was seeing displays of demon power over the plateau. Fire missiles soared. Ice splintered from frozen bombs, hail arcing across the night. Battle magics cascaded like Disney fireworks.

She'd threaded the needle! On one side of her were rivers of lava. Miles across from them were ruins. Both lairs had sentries fronting them, or as Lanthe liked to call them *guides.*

So which should she enter first? *Eeny, meeny, miny* . . . She headed toward Inferno.

Sabine would never believe her little sister had found her way here—well, anywhere. Lanthe couldn't wait to tell her, to talk to her about all the things she'd learned and felt.

She'd also have to come clean about how close she and Thronos had been.

Thronos. With his heartbreaking eyes and tragic memories. With his determined expression.

With his toe-curling kiss and stubborn jealousy.

None of which she cared about because she was going home. No more dwelling on Thronos—just because she'd hurt him didn't give him the right to damn her to the Skye!

By the time she felt the heat of the lava, her guilt had waned under the weight of resentment. Sorcery began sparking from her skin. Thronos had abducted her, expecting her to give up her entire life for his. She was done being captured, done enduring mistreatment, done muzzling her sexuality.

Melanthe of the Deie Sorceri was an empowered sorceress on the prowl. Even hell should tremble!

When those sentries approached with swords drawn, she smiled. "Well, hello, boys." With a wave of her hand, she mesmerized the pair, commanding them to lead her into the cavern, protect her with their lives, and tell others that she was their leader's female.

Then she bade them to take her to the key.

Easy as easy pie.

THIRTY

For most of the night, Thronos had grappled against her sorcery.

He didn't know what shocked him more: the revelation about his brother, or that Melanthe had bespelled him—without hesitation.

But her persuasion would be useless against demons, or the pest! If she perished, he would . . .

He would what? Vrekeners simply didn't go on without their mates.

Ages ago, after he'd healed from the worst of his injuries, his own mother had found solace in suicide, unable to live without his father.

Thronos's brows drew tight. By that reasoning, so long as Melanthe's life was in danger, then so too was his.

At once, he felt her command fading. In minutes, he'd freed himself from her invisible bonds.

His head swung upward. If he took to the air, he couldn't see markers warning of danger zones. *Chance I'll have to take.* He swooped his wings, shooting into the sky with his usual grinding pain. He hovered over the canopy, tracking her by her sorcery and her entrancing scent.

While he trailed her, he replayed all the things she'd told him about Aristo. Over the centuries, Thronos and Aristo had grown apart, seeing little eye to eye. There wasn't a Vrekener alive who reviled Sorceri more than Aristo. His brother's voice echoed in his head: *"They murdered my father and crippled my younger brother. Death to every last one of them!"* Aristo had even threatened the Sorceri wards within the Air Territories, until he'd seen how unpopular a move that would be.

Melanthe's accusation was possible, logistically speaking. It'd taken Thronos years to heal, to learn how to walk and fly again. He'd been in his teens before he'd been able to travel long distances. Consumed with locating her, he'd had no interest in politics.

Had he suspected things were amiss? In the last century or so, worrying accounts had made their way to him, but his mind had remained focused on the search, and he'd easily discounted them.

Because they'd all concerned the King of the Skye.

And now his mate had added her own account. Yes, Thronos had learned her tells. When she'd told him about Aristo, she'd been leaning forward aggressively, eyes wide. His wings hadn't twitched.

No wonder she was desperate to avoid his home. He had to convince her that he could keep her safe. He had no doubt of it; a Vrekener protecting his mate was stronger than any others of his kind.

And no male would fight more savagely for his female.

But once Thronos caught up to her tonight, what would stop her from commanding him again? What if she ordered him to forget her, as she'd threatened on the island? Before, he'd questioned if that mightn't be a boon.

Now the idea made his heart pound with dread, sweat beading on his forehead.

The closer he got to the demon strongholds, the louder the skirmishes grew. In the sky over the plateau, Thronos saw more Volar demons locked in combat. So members of the same demonarchy had become enemies?

If what Melanthe said was true, then those creatures were his demon brothers. Of course, if what she said was true, then the Volars would be preferable to Aristo.

Thronos breathed deeply for her scent, seeking her sorcery. Her trail was confusing, seeming to lead to both encampments.

The freshest was to Deep Place. With its maze.

Thronos could fly over it, but would those Volars spot him? And if the maze was meant to keep out enemies, there would likely be air mines planted above it.

He descended, hastening by foot to the labyrinth. The ruins were a riot of shapes—pillars, disks, remnants of arches and walls—creating misleading plays of light and an infinite number of hiding places.

Threats could be anywhere. Everywhere. Would he find her mauled body in these ruins? Hear her screams as she was attacked by demons?

His lungs burned; he increased his pace even more.

At the entrance to the maze was a sign inscribed with those foreign glyphs. The markings seemed to vibrate, before growing legible to him.

Behold Deep Place, lair of the Abysmals, possessors of the First Key, guardians of the Second Gate of Hell. Woe to all who enter the bowels of this realm.

Exactly *how* deep was this den? Vrekeners hated all things deep. He charged forward anyway—

His eyes widened. Melanthe!

Apparently, she was just leaving, looking bored as she strolled from the labyrinth.

Great. Killjoy had freed himself. He was dripping sweat, looking like he'd run or flown marathons to get to her.

The unbidden thrill she felt to see him only worsened her already bad mood.

He hurried toward her, but she kept walking, her portal plans on hold for tonight. Escaping hell wouldn't be as simple as she'd envisioned.

"Melanthe, wait!"

Sadly, she wouldn't be able to command him so easily after her sorcery outlays. She'd drained much of her power, though she hoped not in vain.

Thronos caught up to her and reached for her arm, but her withering look made him drop his hand.

"Are you safe?" he asked between breaths.

"How did you get free? Did something attack you?" She was already looking past him, debating her next move.

"Not in the strictest sense. What were you doing in there? Have you lost your mind, going into that lair alone?"

She shrugged.

"You just walked in?" He frowned. "Wait. You've got two keys. My gods, you've been to Deep Place *and* Inferno!"

Around her neck, on either side of her priceless medallion, she'd strung two ancient-looking keys to a gate of hell—because she'd already stolen both treasures.

Nearly identical, each key was the length of her little finger. At one end was a filigree bow; the other end was flat, notched, and engraved. Overall, they were as dainty and elegant as Pandemonia *wasn't.*

Bonus: they too were made of dragon gold. She now wore three pieces of priceless silisk gold.

Lifting the keys had been the easy part. Hidden within each stronghold was its portal. Beside it? A key. She'd thought she would have to go all *Italian Job* for her mission, but the only security had been manual: hulking guards.

Hulking guards who were now sleeping like little babies.

With her talents, the keys might as well have been under the front doormat. "I stole these with ease," she told Thronos. "Your 'lacking' mate is still a thieving sorceress, remember?"

"So all these brutal demons have been locked in endless warfare, and you managed to do what armies couldn't over an eternity?" He looked a little . . . awestruck.

She brushed off one shoulder, then the other. "Just let me do like I do."

Unfortunately, the portals had turned out to be trickier than she'd suspected. Each one was ensconced in stone, with etchings all around the opening. In Deep Place, clouds and vines were depicted, indicating a heaven plane. The one in Inferno was surrounded by dripping fangs, as if the opening were a ravenous mouth.

Should be a no-brainer—*I'll take the heaven plane, Alex*—but then, this *was* Pandemonia. Could be a trick or a test.

Worse, they were old-school portals, basically huge vacuums, which meant she couldn't dip a toe and then return.

Worse still, she couldn't steer them. Even though she had the keys, those portals were permanently pointed in one direction like subway tubes—and she had no idea where they led.

"I can't believe you've seized these." Thronos reached for her chain, raising the keys. He inspected the engraved ends, one depicting dripping fangs and one those vines. "Why do you remain here? Were you . . . had you been coming back for me?" The hopefulness in his tone tugged at something inside her.

She snatched her keys back. "Nope."

Scowl. "Then why are you still here?"

"Because the portals are more complicated than I expected." *Not* because she hesitated to abandon Thronos on a hell plane.

Not at all.

"I don't want to rush anything." She might be better off in the Zero-G Glade for another day. She might be better off waiting to create her own portal.

She gazed past him. Dawn was finally breaking. Her crime-playtime was over for the day. In any case, before she made another foray into either camp, she should probably recharge. Remarkably, she hadn't tapped out her persuasion, but a top-off wouldn't go amiss.

Without a word, she headed back toward the glade.

"Where are we going?" he asked as they neared the brush.

We? *Optimist.* "I just burgled the two most valuable possessions in this realm." She cast a wary glance over her shoulder. "Eventually those demons are going to want them back. I'm returning to the glade."

"I'd fly you there, but the dragons will be out foraging soon," he said. "I'll guide you back."

"Clearly, I don't need your help." No sooner had she said that than they reached a junction where the path forked out three ways, engraved stones marking each. She didn't remember this from before.

Mental shrug. *Eeny, meeny, miny* . . . She turned toward the one all the way to the right.

"You don't want that one."

She faced him with pursed lips. "Why not?"

"The marker reads: **The Long Way.** Which doesn't sound very promising."

"And the other ones?"

"One reads: **To the Frozen Lake.** The other: **Hell Beast Trail.**"

She headed toward the frozen lake, intending to step off the path as soon as things got close to chilly.

He remained by her side. "Melanthe, I need to talk to you about what you told me. About my brother."

"You'll find out the truth for yourself soon enough. Everything I've told you can be verified."

"You were young, and it was so long ago. Perhaps you mistook him? Aristo's talons are silvered—his wings would be like any other knight's."

"He used to swig from a golden flask." When Thronos paled, she said, "Oh, so you remember it? Even if I could forget his face, I'd never forget his gold."

Thronos swallowed. "Maybe he didn't mean to hurt you in that haystack."

"After my hand got stabbed, the next pitchfork jab nicked my ear. Before another one could land, Sabine ran to distract them. If not for her, your brother would have gored me to death. Look, I don't care if you believe me—"

"I . . . believe you."

"You do?" In spite of how gut-wrenching that must be. "Then do something about it. You should go to the Skye—and clean house."

"I intend to. I will make my brother see reason when we return."

She stutter-stepped. She didn't know which part of his statement mystified her more—the fact that he still intended her to go with him, or that he planned to rehab Aristo. "I hate to tell you this, but your brother is evil. EVIL. The kind you can't rehabilitate. Face it, Thronos—in the brother department, we both lost out."

"Do you expect me to kill Aristo without trying to reach him? I also thought you were evil, but decided not to harm you."

"He's not going to turn out like me. You're setting yourself up for disappointment. Which is *your* business. I just want to return to *my* home." She started forward again. The brush began to thin. In the distance, she could see a field.

He walked backward to keep his gaze locked on hers. "I can't allow that. We will not be parted. After this long without you, how could I release you now?"

She waved a hand shining with blue energy in front of his face. "You won't have any choice."

He glowered at her hand. "Melanthe, just stop and discuss this with me."

"The same problems as before apply. When you can see past my number, then maybe we'll talk."

"So if I could see past it, you'd come with me to the Skye? Then use your power to make me forget the men you've been with," he said, as if he'd just lit on the idea and found it excellent. "If that's what it takes, then I'll subject myself to your sorcery once more."

She clenched her blue fists, hating him for hurting her yet again, hating that he didn't even understand *how* he was hurting her. "Should I make you think I'm totally a virgin, or maybe that I only had a couple of fuck buddies? How about one conquest per century?" Voice rising with each word, she yelled, "I hate the way you make me feel!"

"I don't want to! But I don't know how to handle this. I can't just act like I haven't felt wrath. Like I haven't been brought to my knees with jealousy. . . ." He trailed off, frowning at a pair of marble markers that bordered the path. Only two lines had been carved on them.

Thronos had already gone across their border.

"What do they say?" she asked, backing away.

He read them, gazing up with bafflement. And then things really got weird.

THIRTY-ONE

The markers read:

Pain confesses all.
And Time cares naught.

What did that *mean*? Enough with this bloody place! What would this zone have in store? The mention of pain didn't worry him; he knew pain, could handle any physical agony. But what about Melanthe?

The sun was beginning to rise, purple clouds in the background like a halo over her black hair. He'd just taken a step in her direction when he spied movement.

He disbelieved his sight—not far behind her was a tank-sized beast with bloodred eyes, dripping fangs, and bony spikes protruding from its spine.

A hellhound.

"Freeze, Melanthe."

She did. Eyes wide, she whispered, "Something's behind me, isn't it?"

He gave a shallow nod.

The beast's soot-colored pelt was said to be dense enough to repel swords. *And talons.*

But if Thronos could reach her and get them into the air . . .

The hound lifted its snout. Catching their scent, it let out a chilling howl. When it charged them, Thronos lunged for her.

He never reached Melanthe. Another beast collided with him from the side, a locomotive of force that nearly knocked him out of his boots.

A second hound.

Thronos crashed to the ground. When his vision cleared, he found one mammoth paw pinning him by the waist. He cast his wing up, talon slashing.

The strike didn't even disturb the beast's dense fur.

"Run, Lanthe!"

She was already sprinting in his direction, as if a hound of hell pursued her—because it did. She ran with a feylike quickness.

Melanthe was fast. It was faster.

Thronos launched another strike of his wings, and another, buying time to glance over his shoulder, taking in every detail of their possible escape route.

Behind him was an open field fringed with moonraker trees. To the west, a charred mountain peak loomed over the field. Atop it were dozens of dragons, jostling for territory. Their hive? They clawed the black stone for purchase and loosed great streams of fire. Rocks plummeted.

A pair of dragons took off from that height, heading in the direction of the demon valley. Sparring in the air, they tore chunks of flesh from each other, scales raining down.

Sunrise; feed on fallen. More dragons would follow.

As Melanthe high-stepped past Thronos, she cried, "Stop playing with yours and kill it!"

"Why didn't I"—he jerked his body left to right to avoid snapping fangs—"think of that?!"

If the beast's pelt was impervious, it'd have only a few vulnerabilities. As swiftly as he could, Thronos whipped his wings up, talons crossing over the creature's face. Before the hound could bite down on them, he gave a yell, dug in, then ripped his wings to the sides.

His talons raked across the beast's eyes, slicing through to the very bone of its eye sockets.

Blood spurted. The beast yelped in pain, blindly stumbling toward the brush. A mistake. Dozens of huge reptilian-looking predators snatched the defenseless hound into the shadows.

With a haphazard swoop of his wings, Thronos half-lunged to his feet, stumbling after Melanthe, pain coursing through his bad leg. He craned his head around. Where was she—

He caught sight of her, eluding the hound on her tail. He stepped forward, nearly planting his foot in resin. "Watch for resin!" This pit was covered with silver reeds, almost indistinguishable from the rest of the ground.

Risking the dragons, Thronos bounded into the air. He wouldn't be able to reach her before the hound did. So he pulled his wings tight and dove, aiming for the beast itself. At the last second, he rolled to launch a shoulder into the hound's flank, knocking it off its feet.

While it shook away confusion, Thronos snared its meaty tail, pinning it between his arm and torso, digging his claws in. Gnashing his teeth, using all the strength he possessed, he hauled on the tail as he began to rotate. As if throwing a discus, he spun the beast. Again. And again. With a bellow, he released the thing, sending it flying through the air.

When it landed against the mountain, stone fractured. Its limp body collapsed.

Hounds dispatched, Thronos tensed to run for her; almost fell flat on his face. His feet were caught in mere inches of resin! He pulled with all his might.

More of the dragons launched themselves from the peak, heading toward the plateau. The mountain shook with an earthquake's force, boulders falling.

Melanthe was about to run through a narrow ravine. From this distance, he could see a rockslide crashing toward her.

"The rocks, Lanthe!"

She spotted them herself, skidding to a stop. Whirling around, she headed back toward the field.

Toward him. *"Hurry!"*

The sky rained boulders. They pocked the clearing, shaking the ground with each impact. *Thunk, thunk, thunk.*

She sidestepped, dodging an arrow-shaped boulder of charred stone. If it'd hit her . . .

Her body would've been pulverized. He strained harder, working his wings to free his legs. She would have *died.*

A real death. He'd heard of Sorceri ended by illness and by stab wounds, for gods' sakes.

She was almost back to this clearing. She ran under one of those gigantic trees for cover, nimbly skipping over its roots.

Then she—stopped. Her upper body jolted forward before she righted her balance.

Their eyes met. "Melanthe?"

She peered down, frowned.

She . . . *no.* She couldn't be caught in a pit. "I'm coming for you!" Every muscle in his body strained. Though the quakes had stopped, the onrush of boulders continued. He could hear their deafening descent down the side of the mountain.

A monolith the size of a garbage truck was heading for Melanthe's tree. She gazed up in horror, hunching down.

"No, no!" He thrashed, kicking, sweat pouring into his eyes, wings heaving. Damn it! The backdraft was cooling the resin, only solidifying its hold.

High in the tree, a giant limb caught the boulder. He and Melanthe shared a look of relief.

Until they heard the first crack of wood above her. The limb was about to give way. She started struggling in a frenzy.

He'd never get to her in time! He flared his claws to sever his legs, slashing at his skin. When the top tree limb snapped, the boulder landed on the next one down. It was already bowing . . .

He bit back yells as he cut, hacking through his calf muscle, baring the bone. Gripping his bloody leg in two fists, he wrenched his hands in different directions. The bone wouldn't break!

She murmured, "Thronos?" Across this distance, he heard her distinctly, felt the timbre of pure fear in her voice. She had to know a boulder that big would kill her.

"I'm coming!" Even as his talon gouged chunks of flesh from his other leg, the process was taking too much time, too much! Three failed tries to break one leg!

Craaaack. His bone snapped just as a tree limb did. A leg free! But the boulder was plummeting like a juggernaut, crushing one limb after another until it caught on the one directly over Lanthe, not twenty feet above her head.

A final defense. Could he reach her in time, and have the strength to pull her from her own pit?

She'd gone still, as if she feared making too much movement.

"Start cutting!" he yelled as he set to his other leg, balancing even as he swung his razor-sharp claws.

She didn't answer. Never slowing his gruesome task, he glanced at her. She was holding up her bare hands, with their tiny pink fingernails. No gauntlets. Tears began trailing down her cheeks.

The last tree limb was about to go; splinters fluttered over her, dusting her braids. "Tell my sister I love her"—she swiped at her eyes—"and f-for what it's worth, those months in the meadow . . . I was happy. Happiest."

"No, NO!" He was free of the pit! Using wings, hands, and what was left of his legs, he sped toward her.

Their eyes met again, tears pouring from hers. She raised her chin and gave him a pilot's salute.

The wood broke. The boulder crashed down.

One second Melanthe was standing there. The next she'd disappeared, crushed.

Dead.

He bellowed, *"NOOOOOOO!"* She couldn't be gone!

When he reached the boulder, he thought he could scent blood and . . . ground bone. Because there was nothing left of her.

With a strangled yell, he dug his claws into the stone; using his wings for propulsion, he shoved with all the strength he had left.

Moved it not one inch. *She's dead.*

Another desperate shove. Not a godsdamned inch.

She was dead. He *felt* it. *Knew* it.

He roared with agony. He had five centuries' worth of hate to give that stone—his new enemy. Another shove. Another. And another. And another. He rammed his horns into it until blood poured down into his eyes.

In the midst of this frenzy, memories of her flashed through his mind.

Of him telling her they would be wed when they grew older . . .

"Would that make me a princess of heaven?" she asked with a chuckle. "Would we have much gold up there?"

"You'll have me*—and you like me far better than gold!" He tickled her, chasing her around the meadow while she squealed with laughter.*

Of the first time he'd taken her flying . . .

She peeked up from his chest, her eyes wide, as blue as the sky they crossed. "Thronos, this . . . this . . . let's never go back down!"

Of them as children caught in the rain, on the very day his father had later raided the abbey.

Thronos took her in his arms, and she leaned against him.

When the drops grew heavier, he spread his wings over his head, creating a shelter. "I've always room for you too."

She nestled against him. As they watched the rain fall, she sighed, "I love you, Thronos."

His heart felt too big for his chest, and he had to swallow past the lump in his throat to answer her.

He'd squandered the treasure he'd been given.

His claws and horns were gone, but he hadn't budged the stone. Blood from his hands and head painted his enemy.

That stone . . . not a godsdamned inch.

Unmovable. So too would he be.

Tears blinded him when he realized the stone would be her grave marker. Thronos closed his eyes and took comfort in knowing that they would share it.

THIRTY-TWO

Melanthe whispered, "Something's behind me, isn't it?"

Thronos's eyes shot wide open. She stood before him on the path, frozen, her black hair haloed by purple clouds.

With not a mark upon her. He was unwounded as well.

"What is this, sorceress?" he rasped. "Real?" Of course not; he must be delirious, still sitting in his own blood, his back against the gravestone, dreaming this. But what if . . . "Do you have no memory of what's just occurred?"

"We were fighting, *as usual,*" Melanthe snapped under her breath. "Focus, Thronos—what's behind me?!"

That same hound howled and charged; with a screech, she took off past Thronos.

"Melanthe, watch for resin!" *What the hell is happening? I* am *in hell.*

No, maybe a benevolent god was giving him a second chance to save her!

On that thought, he did a swift about-face, readying for the side attack. He knew what was coming.

The second hound leapt; Thronos evaded as his wings lashed out, blinding the beast.

One down.

He'd taken the hound out earlier this time. The events would be different; he could snag Melanthe before the other beast got too close. He took to the sky, planning to scoop her into his arms.

The hound pursuing Melanthe must have heard Thronos's wings swooping; it veered from him—

Suddenly its body crumpled. Its front paw was stuck in resin!

See how you like it, beast!

The pair of sparring dragons launched from the peak then, sending the mountain quaking. As Thronos closed in on Melanthe, the two creatures spotted him in the air and plunged for him.

New threats. If hell conspired to keep him from saving his mate . . . *I'll defeat hell.*

The dragons spewed fire, but he evaded the crisscrossing streams. He dove under them, heading for the camouflage of the ground.

Thronos landed, dropping to his hands and one knee, beginning to sprint as if from a starting line. He chanced a glance behind him. As he'd hoped, the pair had abandoned their hunt, continuing on to the plateau for a guaranteed meal. But more followed, so he stayed on the ground. With the hound taken care of, he had more time—

His third stride was his last.

His feet were caught again. Another godsdamned pit! He'd done exactly as the hound had! "Oh, come on!" he yelled, grappling to free himself. "Melanthe! Don't run, if you move another inch, you will die!"

She couldn't hear him, was about to enter that ravine. With the boulders falling! She skidded to a stop, then whirled around to sprint for the field.

"Don't go under that tree!" He gritted his teeth, pulling with all his might.

She sidestepped, dodging that first arrow-shaped boulder, the charred one from before.

"Don't head for the tree!" She was heading for the tree! "There's a pit between the roots!"

Still not hearing him, she skipped over the roots. Then . . . too late. Her upper body jolted forward before she righted her balance.

She murmured, "Thronos?" Even from this distance, he could hear her distinctly, felt the timbre of pure fear in her voice.

Their eyes didn't meet this time; he was too busy hacking at his legs. *Break the bones in one go or she dies.* "Just hold on! I'm coming for you!"

Every muscle in his body strained. He could already hear the gravestone's descent.

Thrashing, kicking, sweat burning his eyes. The gravestone snapped the limb high atop the tree.

Thronos's bone cracked—earlier than before! *I can do this, I can reach her!* With one leg freed, he dared a look. "I'm coming!" The next limb down was bowing.

She knew a boulder that big would kill her. She struggled wildly.

"Just hold on!" He bit back yells as he cut, hacking through the bloody calf muscle of his other leg. Taking too much time, too much!

The boulder plummeted like a juggernaut, crushing one limb after another until it caught on the one directly over Lanthe, not twenty feet above her head.

A final defense.

"Thronos?" She'd gone still, as if she feared making too much movement.

"I'm not letting you go! I'm coming for you! We're not done, Melanthe."

"I wish things had been different," she said, voice thick with tears.

"They *will* be! Fight, Lanthe!"

Their eyes met again. "Tell my sister I love her." Chin raised, Lanthe gave him a salute.

Second leg free! The tree limb was about to go. He took to the air, diving for her; she kept her gaze on him, as if for courage.

Craaaack. The boulder crashed down. He collided with it. An instant too late.

"NOOOOOOO!"

He dug his claws into the stone; using his wings for propulsion, he shoved with all the strength he had left. *Ruined my second chance!*

He directed his five hundred years of hate—at himself. *I am the enemy.* He'd had three fleeting nights with his mate, and he'd taken every opportunity to frighten her, to shame her, to hurt her. As if hundreds of years fleeing his kind hadn't been enough pain.

I squandered what I was given, never comprehending the treasure.

She's dead.

Another shove. Another. And another. And another. He gave an agonized roar, clawing at the stone in a frenzy. As he rammed his horns into it, madness threatened, his thoughts taking flight in odd directions. He recalled the end of that encounter he'd had with her mother. . . .

"Melanthe will never be what you need her to be. You can't break my daughter, and that's the only way she'd love you."

Thronos sputtered, "I-I don't want to break her!" Melanthe was perfect as she was!

"Then you'll have to break yourself, hawkling."

Perfect, if only? Melanthe would be perfect.

If only she were alive.

As blood poured into his eyes, he closed them. *Please, gods, give me just one more chance.*

"Something's behind me, isn't it?"

Thronos's eyes shot open. Melanthe was before him, heartbreakingly beautiful, not a mark upon her. The sun was starting to rise, purple clouds in the background like a halo over her black hair.

The hound's howl marked the beginning.

Hell conspired.

Minutes later, the boulder was poised to fall above Lanthe.

Thronos was missing a wing and a leg. Slashes and puncture wounds covered him. The reptilian predators in the brush that had snatched the first hellhound had come for *him* this time.

Shouldn't have ignored that direction. Won't next time.

What if he didn't get a next time? What if three was the limit?

He prayed to any gods listening: *I will do this until I get it right. I will do this for eternity if I have to, but I will save her. . . .*

THIRTY-THREE

Lanthe toed Thronos's convulsing body, then hopped back. Her gaze darted from one marble marker to the other, looking for the threat.

One minute, she and Thronos had been arguing. The next, his eyes had rolled back in his head and he'd dropped like a rock. He was now unconscious, seizing on the ground as if afflicted by a supernatural malady.

What zone had he crossed into? The nightmare sector? The noxious-air belt? The markers were inscribed with those weird glyphs, and her translator was currently writhing, out cold on the path.

Lowering clouds closed in, darkening the morning. A soft rain began to fall; lightning streaking above. What to do? Despite his dickitry, she couldn't just leave him like this.

It was almost as if she felt the same kind of loyalty to Thronos that she did to Sabine. But Sabine had never hurt her the way Thronos continued to do.

Even so, Lanthe would drag him out of the zone. All seven feet of him.

"Thronos, you are such a pain in my ass," she snapped at his unconscious form. "Here I am—saving yours yet again! I want this noted."

Careful not to cross the markers herself, she reached for his feet, lugging him toward her. The instant she'd pulled his head out of the zone, his eyes shot open, locking on her. "Melanthe?"

She dropped his feet; he scrambled to stand. With his irises fully silver, he jerked his gaze around, as if danger was on the horizon. He scented the air.

Under his breath, he grated, "Not real?" The crazed look on his face had her backing away from him.

Then he turned to her. "*Not* real." He eased closer.

"Um, what's happening, Thronos?"

"You're here." In the light rain, he reached for her, cupping her face with hands that shook. His thumbs brushed along her cheekbones. His brows were drawn together, lips thinned.

She'd seen this yearning expression before—after that three-day absence when she'd called him a demon. So long ago, when he'd finally returned to their meadow, his eyes had told her, *I've been pretty much lost without you.*

"I want your future, Melanthe," he rasped now. "I don't care about the past. We'll work out the fucking details."

Where was this coming from? Why had he changed—

His lips descended on hers. As in her dream, his pained groan rumbled against her mouth. He sounded like he'd die if she didn't return his kiss.

A claiming kiss. A no-going-back kiss.

Despite her issues with him, she found herself parting her lips beneath his. He groaned again, as if she'd conceded far more than a kiss. When his tongue dipped, her eyes slid shut in bliss.

His lips slowly slanted, his tongue sensuously tangling with hers. For someone with so little practice, he was turning into a devastating kisser. Her hands twined around his neck, her toes curling as they began sharing breaths.

When he drew back, he left her dazed, blinking up at him. "Thronos, I think that's the best conversation we've ever had."

He didn't release Melanthe, just kept his quaking hands on her cheeks.

She was brimming with vitality, sorcery, *life.* He savored the beating of her heart, the coursing of her lifeblood.

Each wondrous breath she took.

Though she'd initially looked stunned—and pleased—her brows were drawing together. "What's going on with you?" She dropped her hands, ducking from his grip. "You have a seizure, and now you're thinking clearly? You've suddenly realized how stupid it is to obsess about my past?"

"I almost lost you." He bit out the words, unable to process what had just happened—what he'd seen and *felt.*

"What are you talking about?"

"You . . . you dragged me out of it." He opened and closed his fists, needing his hands on her. "Delivered me from it."

"From what?"

"Hell. I was in my personal version of hell."

"Hell changed your mind about my past?"

He nodded. "You talked about traps when we first arrived, about repeated labors. I believe I was in a loop of some kind. In each repetition, no matter what I did, I couldn't save you. You . . . died. You were crushed by stone."

She arched her brows. "Typical. The harlot got stoned to death."

His voice hoarse, he said, "Don't talk like that. *Please.*" He took her hand in his, never wanting to let it go.

She gazed up at him as if she was measuring the emotions in him—the ones he didn't bother to hide. How asinine he'd been! He wanted to make a life with her, a marriage and family. To have all those things, he need only look to their future. It was there—for the taking!

She was.

Unless he'd already ruined things beyond repair.

"What do the markers say?" she asked.

"Pain confesses all. And Time cares naught." He now comprehended that what he'd just gone through wasn't real.

But the lesson had been.

"What does it mean?"

"Time cared naught when it allowed itself to repeat." With his free hand, he tucked a lock of raven hair behind her ear. "And pain clarified my thoughts about us."

"That sounds . . . intense."

You have no idea. "We need to move away from the edge of this zone. If we'd both crossed into it, we could've been there for eternity. And I'd rather spend forever with *the pest that is.*" He brushed the backs of his fingers along her delicate jawline, vowing to all the Lore, to all the gods, that he would protect this woman for eternity.

"You haven't stopped touching me, Thronos."

"You'll have to grow accustomed to that—"

A demon war bugle sounded from not far in the distance.

She gazed over her shoulder. "They wouldn't be signaling a charge during the day . . ."

"Unless they're coming for those keys. Let's put some distance between us and them."

"Where? We can't go back. And we don't know which way this zone's edge extends."

He craned his head up to the sky, biting out a curse. "We can't go up."

Outlined by bursts of lightning, a pack of Volar demons hovered above. An advance contingent? Their position pinned Thronos and Lanthe against the hell zone.

Their backs were against an invisible wall.

THIRTY-FOUR

"If I take you into the air, they'll rip you from me," Thronos grated as the ground began to vibrate beneath their feet.

"More are coming!" Lanthe cried. Just beyond the brush, demon foot soldiers were charging toward them.

"I'll have to fight them here."

She'd seen him victorious against a number of ghouls, but demons were cunning.

With reluctance, Thronos released her hand, bringing his wings in tight to strike. "Stay behind me—right at the edge of those markers. The demons won't go near them."

She edged back.

"But don't cross the line, Lanthe—"

The first wave broke from the brush. So many of them!

In a blur, swords arced out, whistling all around Thronos. He struck with both wings. Heads rolled across the ground like horned bowling balls. Jugular blood painted the silver grass red.

More demons advanced. More died. When Thronos's wings whipped like sails, billowing the air, a fine mist of crimson sprayed over her face.

Any demon who attacked paid with his life. Thronos decapitated with a ruthless efficiency.

But they kept coming. Even the demons at the back started firing on Thronos, lobbing a hail of spears and daggers, fire and ice grenades.

He had to use one wing as a constant shield against the sky as more warriors closed in, swarming like ants from a kicked mound. He deflected the volleys, but he was getting slower, expending so much strength. He couldn't stall them for much longer.

Only a matter of time.

Then he would die, and she'd be captured. Unless she did something. *When in trouble* . . . Portal!

She had some power, but was it enough to create a gateway to a different world, under pressure, just two days after her last one?

It'll never happen.

Still, she raised her hand, dispelling sorcery right at the edge of the hell zone. As she labored to split the seam of this reality, Thronos must have felt the energy; he turned to her with his blood-wetted wings splayed, a warning in his eyes: *Do not run from me.*

She gasped. In the lightning flashes, he looked like a . . . legend.

Like an avenging angel.

From hell.

Every inch of his skin was coated with others' blood, his own as well. Gashes sliced his flesh, bisecting ancient scars. Stark against the crimson, his eyes were fully onyx—and locked on Lanthe as he began fighting his way toward her.

A rift was opening, drawing her attention from him! *Come on, portal! Come on!* Almost big enough for her to step through. *Rothkalina, Rothkalina, Rothkalina,* she repeated like a mantra.

There was nothing to stop her from leaving Pandemonia. *Could* she abandon Thronos to save herself? To return to her family?

After that kiss . . .

Look back over your shoulder at him again, and you'll regret it. Still, at the threshold, Lanthe bit her lip and turned back.

"Don't!" His voice was rife with pain—as if he already *knew* she would leave him behind. "Don't run from me, lamb!"

Lamb.

He hadn't called her that since they were children. She remembered their last day together as they'd sat beneath his wings. She'd sighed that she loved him. His voice had been thick when he'd replied, "I-I love you too, lamb."

Damn him! She couldn't leave him.

Though demons dogged his heels, she bit out a curse and waited for him. *I can't believe I'm doing this!*

He looked as shocked as she felt. Yet then he cast her that determined expression of his, the one she now recognized. It meant he believed he was about to beat all odds and triumph.

He continued fighting to reach her, but with his attention divided, his strikes weren't as efficient. She could see demons circling him in the air—and on the ground. Some lay in wait between Thronos and Lanthe.

He'd never reach her. And malicious gazes had already turned to her. Demons ready to kill. Or worse.

Think, Lanthe! She couldn't use persuasion on this many, especially not the ones farthest back. She frowned. Did she even need to?

As Sabine had told her: *Illusion is reality.*

Lanthe yanked off the chain around her neck, holding it in a fist above her head. The pieces clanked loudly. "Look what I've got!" A few demons locked their gazes on the shining keys.

Infusing her command with sorcery, she yelled, "Look, Pandemonians, *look.*" Blue light coiled all around her, until she was radiating as brightly as the lightning above.

More warriors stilled, hushed murmurs floating over the crowd. In the lull, Thronos backed toward her.

She jostled the keys above her. "Do you want these?" Her sorcery was reflected in the eyes of the closest demons. "Or should I simply disintegrate them—with my deadly blue light?" *Ha!*

Audible gasps sounded.

"I am a great and terrible goddess, the Keeper of Keys and the Queen of Hell." She pointed at Thronos. "He is the mighty . . . Reader of Words." (Best she got.) "Cease fighting him!" Another command.

The demons closest to her disengaged at once.

Brows raised, Thronos hastened to her. He mouthed, *Reader of Words?*

Lanthe wasn't done yet. She told the crowd, "Though we leave you now, I will return with these keys"—return for more gold—"but *only* if you achieve peace here." *Geopolitical stability makes for easier treasure transpo.* "Understood?" She slipped the necklace back on.

When the unsteady threshold began to waver and shrink, Thronos sprinted for her. Would the space be wide enough for them to squeeze through?

He tucked her against him on his way to the portal. "You *awaited* me. For the first time, you didn't run from me!" At her ear, he rasped, "You will never regret this." Clasping her tight, he dove for the opening at the last second.

The rift sealed behind them as they barreled headlong into a new world.

THIRTY-FIVE

"*Ahh!*" Lanthe screeched to find herself under a pounding waterfall in waist-high water.

She swiped her forearm across her face, sputtering. Thronos was before her, filling her vision.

He pulled her from the cascade, shaking out his dark hair. "Where are we?" The demon blood that had coated him had been scoured clean.

Turning to survey their surroundings, she blinked against the brightness of the day. The sun was a blazing golden ball in the sky. Past a field of bloodred wildflowers, she saw pink sand and a placid sea the color of new grass. This huge waterfall and pool were the same shade.

I know this pink beach. I know this scent. The air was sultry, smelling of . . . Hawaiian Tropic, flowers, and sex.

Oh, no, no, this couldn't be!

Yet then the sun began to twinkle. Feveris was usually sunny because its clouds were translucent; when they passed in front of the sun, they made it glimmer like a star. "Oh, my gold, this is Feveris."

"We're in the Land of Lusts?" Thronos said in the same tone a human might say, "For real, we're Powerball winners?"

"This can't be—I aimed for Rothkalina!"

"How long will it be till we're robbed of control?" His voice was growing huskier.

"Less than ten minutes. That's how long I was here before I had my servants drag me back. I'd just wanted to see if the rumors were true." She lost track of what she'd been saying—because Thronos was smiling.

And it was *glorious.*

Twinkling sunlight struck his eyes, setting his irises aglow, molten silver. His firm lips curled, revealing more of his even, white teeth and those fangs. She felt the mad urge to tap one of those points—with her tongue. With his face relaxed, his scars seemed to fade.

The first time she'd seen him smile since he was a boy.

Struggling to collect her thoughts, she asked, "Why do you look so pleased with yourself?"

"For one, you're *alive.* More, you saved me from a demon army—and waited for me. For the first time! And *then* you brought us to Feveris. Maybe you wanted to come here with me as badly as I did with you? I think I'm growing on you."

She wanted to deny it, but couldn't. Something had happened in Pandemonia, a shift in her feelings for him. Had a fragile sprout of affection poked its head above snow?

Illusion *was* reality. *Act like partners long enough, guess what you'll become. . . .*

Stupid sprout.

"Already I feel the effects of this place." He raked his gaze over her body, making her skin flush.

"I do too," she admitted. Out from under the cascade, the water of this pool was balmy and soft. Warm breezes caressed her face, soothing her.

Before, she'd worried about letting go with him. She'd worried what he would think about her. Now the decision had been taken from her. *Had* she subconsciously steered them here?

"Why did you await me, Melanthe?" He reached forward to smooth his fingertips along her cheekbone, casting her a proud smile. "Why did my brilliant mate save me?"

Because this entire journey felt bigger than the two of them? Because when he'd called her *lamb,* her heart had ached from missing their friendship? "I just did, okay? But I didn't intend to come here!"

At her tone, his smile dimmed, and she wanted to call it back. What was happening to her? She just needed time to think!

She tried to march away from him in the waist-deep pool, but her boots were water-logged. With a curse, she pulled off one, then the other, tossing them to the bank.

He must've seen this as an invitation to shed his own clothes. He dragged the remains of his shirt over his head. Faced with the body he was revealing, she couldn't quite disabuse him.

"I thought Sorceri were hedonists?" Off went his own boots. "We're in a plane devoted solely to pleasure. You should be gladdened."

"If we lose control and have sex, it would be disastrous! I might get pregnant." She could ask him to pull out at the last second, but she doubted a virgin would have the willpower necessary—especially when his instinct would be clamoring for him to break his demon seal and spill his seed.

He closed in on her. "Would it be so bad to have a child with me?"

"You mean a bastard?" she countered. "Look, I know you're really gung-ho about having kids and all. But to me, getting pregnant would feel like getting trapped." She reminded herself that Sorceri were unfruitful in general. The odds of it happening were overwhelmingly against.

"Honestly, I'm not as *gung-ho* as I was," he said. "Before, I thought our young would be the only thing we had in common, and raising them our sole occupation. Now I've realized there's much else for us to do." He brought her hand to his groin, to the stiff shaft straining against his sodden breeches.

In a heartbeat's time, she was just as aroused. "Like sex?" Typical male. And this one didn't even know what he was missing!

"Not only sex. You could teach me all the references I don't get. We could travel over realms together, exploring worlds." With each of his deep raspy words, her willpower dwindled. "You liked exploring with me, didn't you?"

She *had.* Their wild-and-woolly adventure in Pandemonia had exhilarated pampered Lanthe.

But there was more to consider! "What about our history? Our families? The war between our factions? We haven't resolved anything between us." Even as she expressed her worries, her hand had begun stroking his length.

"We will," he said, biting back a groan. "But now is not that time. Right now, we're in Feveris, together, after surviving Pandemonia. We desire each other. Denying pleasure between us would be like squandering our coins." He curled his finger under her chin. "And that's something we don't do."

Irresistible demon. Her anxiety was diminishing, Feveris's spell taking hold. Still she fought it. "Turning my words against me?" She dropped her hand—and regretted it immediately. "If we succumb to the magics here, how will we ever escape?"

"Once we've burned off the worst of the lust, you can persuade me to feel no Feveris effects. I'll keep us focused until you can create another portal."

"And again, you want me to use my power on you."

"We don't have a choice. I'm already losing control. For now, lose it with me."

"Thronos—" She felt a sudden sharp twinge across her entire shoulder. *What the hell?* But when she glanced down there was no mark, and the pain ebbed. It was forgotten when he reached for her breastplate, unfastening the clips.

He tugged off the piece, tossing it to shore like a Frisbee.

Sunlight met her bare breasts. She couldn't stop herself from arching toward the warmth, rolling her shoulders. Lingering misgivings receded like the lazy waves of the nearby sea.

When her breasts bobbed with her movement, Thronos was transfixed, as if he was witnessing a miracle. "Melanthe, I've never wanted anything like I want this." With his black claws curling, he reached for her skirt. It soon joined her breastplate. "I must claim my beautiful mate." He tried to remove her panties, but in his haste, the lace gave way.

Once she was stripped of everything but her necklace, his eyes roamed over her greedily. He never took his gaze from her as he started removing his breeches, fumbling with the laces.

How nervous he must be! Did he worry how he'd measure up to her past lovers? Despite his uneasiness, he wore his determined look. He knew what he wanted—and he knew he was about to get it.

He shoved off his breeches, lobbing them to shore as well, the soaked leather making a *fwap* sound.

And then he was naked. Mist from the waterfall dotted his tanned skin, drops clinging to his lean muscles. Just beneath the surface, Lanthe could see his shaft pulsing.

She probed his thoughts, finding his blocks wide open. He craved to feel her sex, to taste it.

To claim it.

His gaze met hers. *And he wants me to know these things.*

Maybe they could just release some steam without consummating anything?

She stiffened when she felt pain on her forearm, like a fresh burn. She broke away to search for a mark, finding none.

"What is it?"

"Nothing." Probably residual hell-plane stress. "Absolutely nothing."

He looked to say more, so she reached for his cock, curving her fingers around it, which apparently robbed him of thought. His lips parted, and he couldn't keep from bucking to her grip.

When she traced her thumb across the taut head, his shaft jerked in her palm, continuing to grow.

"You're really big," she said as she fondled him from base to tip.

He had to clear his throat to manage: "Females like big."

"Only if they're prepared for it, and it's deployed properly."

Worry creased his brow. "How should I prepare you?"

"I'll make sure you get me ready." Because sex was inevitable? It was beginning to feel that way.

She continued to stroke him as he rocked to her fist, but when she cupped his testicles, he went stock-still. *"Melanthe,"* he grated, grasping her wrist to stay her hand. "I've many things I'm dying to do to you. I want to last."

"Hmm. What things?" By the way he was staring at her eyes, she knew they must be glittering.

In an anguished tone, he said, "Readying you?"

"Bite off your foreclaw."

Without a word, he did.

She took his hand in both of hers. When she guided his forefinger into her core, his lids went heavy. Eyes on his, she gave a soft moan.

"My gods," he choked out, his horns straightening fully. She caught his thought: *How will I ever fit inside her?*

Fit? No, they didn't have to have sex! She told herself this, even as she was motioning for him to move his finger. Once he began to thrust with it, they both shuddered.

Her clitoris swelled for attention, her lips plumping around his finger. Soon she was panting, kissing and licking the warm skin of his chest.

Yet then he drew his hand away. Lifting it to his mouth, he sucked his forefinger down to the second knuckle, his eyes hooded.

"Oh!" Her breath hitched. Who was this sexy male? "Ohhh."

When he'd taken all of her taste, he released his finger. "I want more of that, Melanthe."

Should she broach oral sex with him? He might want more, but it was an offendment. Feveris's spell made her feel reckless: *Bring it up. He'll totally love it!* "Speaking of readying me? I think oral sex would help—"

In the space of a heartbeat, he'd seized her in his arms. Striding through the water as if something chased them, he carried her to the bank of the pool. Scrambling out, he strode toward the sea, setting her down on a mat of flowers beneath swaying palms.

His gaze seemed to follow the drops sluicing down her body as he joined her. Soft rays of sunlight filtered through the palm fronds, glinting off her necklace.

With a questioning glance, he reached for it. Though she was loath to remove it, even for a minute, she didn't want anything to distract her from this male. She nodded, and he set it close by.

"I truly was going to give this to you, as a courtship gift."

"You risked your life for a gift?"

He grinned. "When it's the one your mate's set her heart on . . ." Then he moved between her legs, clasping her behind her knees, lifting until she brought her feet up.

She rose up on her elbows, needing to see his every reaction. Judging by the intent look on his face, nothing could stop him from this.

He laid his roughened palms on her inner thighs, spreading them till her knees opened wider. A breeze blew sultry air against her slickened sex.

Even if she hadn't known it was his first time in this position, the way he stared in fascination would give him away. His smoldering eyes were rapt, his expression saying, *Mercy.*

His thoughts drifted into her mind: *—Her exquisite flesh . . . so delicate. Want to set upon her . . .* — When he licked his lips in anticipation, the sight of that pointed tongue made her tremble.

In a barely recognizable voice, he said, "I had my turn in the glade. You'll have yours now." His gaze bored into hers. "See that it happens."

It? Her orgasm? He was telling her in his own way to guide him—because he'd never done this before.

When she gave an unsteady nod, he eased in to press his mouth to one of her thighs. With a tender lick, he told her, "Hold back nothing, Melanthe. . . ."

When he'd sampled her taste on his finger, Thronos had known what forbidden thing he would do. And then for her to suggest it? That she wanted his kiss aroused him like nothing he'd ever imagined.

He could scarcely think past the ache in his shaft. His horns had straightened and were aching along with it.

He knew only two things for certain:

His mate was incomparable, her glistening sex a thing of beauty.

And he was the luckiest male alive.

Yet then he frowned when he felt a stabbing pain low on his torso. He glanced down, spied no matching injury, just old scars.

His pain was forgotten when she rolled her hips, as if to attract his mouth. He gently eased her pink folds apart with his thumbs, riveted by the shadowy dip he uncovered. Her entrance. While he wondered again how he'd ever fit that tiny opening, his shaft jerked, straining for it.

Brows drawn with absorption, he rubbed the dip with his finger, breaching her slick core. Her cream was more slippery than water, and sweet.

The intoxicating taste of his mate.

As his head descended, his sensual female was panting in anticipation, her blue eyes shimmering like metal.

She cried out when he delved his tongue right at her opening. Now that he'd taken her taste into him, he didn't understand how he'd lived his entire life without it. He licked his lips, shuddered, then set back in with a ravening hunger.

"Oh, ohh!" As she undulated, he followed her sex, piercing that slight dip with the tip of his tongue.

He gazed up to gauge her reaction. Her hands had found her lush breasts and started to squeeze. Her expression was lost. When the breeze blew, she arched her back, her nipples stiffening even more.

He rubbed his palms up her thighs, pressing her legs even wider. As he gave her seeking licks, she thumbed those stiff nipples, the peaks he would soon suckle at his leisure.

His hips had begun rocking, his erection hanging down like a steel rod. The pressure within it surged. Even still, his lips curled against her. Because Melanthe seemed to be going out of her head with pleasure.

He was as well. How could he not when her flaring folds grew ever wetter against his tongue?

Between kisses, he murmured, "Lanthe, I can't ever go back."

To life without her. Without sharing this.

She curled one arm under her head like a pillow. Her free hand descended down her flat belly, her palm curving over her mons. Brows drawn, he pulled back, his breaths ragged against her rosy flesh.

She caught his eyes, then grazed the pad of her forefinger over the little bud at the apex of her sex. "If you lick my clitoris like this . . ." She slowly masturbated it, rubbing back and forth as her tongue moistened her lips.

Telling him how she wished to be kissed.

Then her hand wandered back to her chest, to nipples so hard they looked like they throbbed.

He eagerly leaned in, tonguing her clitoris as she'd instructed.

"Yes, Thronos! Just like that," she cried out, earning herself another slick lash. "Now your finger. Put it back inside me while you kiss."

He penetrated the gripping heat of her channel, thrusting his finger in and out as he licked.

"Ah! It's so good!" She reached forward to grasp his horns.

At the contact, he yelled out against her.

She released him as if burned. "Sorry."

Sorry? The idea of her handling him was unbearably erotic. "Take hold of me again!"

Once she tentatively did, he quaked from her grip, assailed by the same currents that sparked whenever their skin touched. Voice low, he commanded her, "Stroke them while I feast."

In a wondering tone, she breathed, "Who—are—you?" But she dutifully rubbed her fists, slaying him with pleasure.

Stroking him thus made her even wetter! He growled and lapped. "You like that too." It wasn't a question.

"More," she panted, rubbing him faster.

His light licks grew fiercer. As her little bud swelled for him, he groaned with amazement. *Maybe I should . . .*

He suckled her clitoris between his lips—

"Oh, my gods!" she screamed, tearing an answering yell from his lungs.

When she bucked for more, he almost came. He started sucking on her bud like a luscious candy, his groans vibrating it.

She went crazy, her head thrashing, her breasts quivering. She made a string of insensible sounds, then managed: "Don't stop that, Thronos. So close! Oh. OHH!"

Pride. *It's happening.*

She ground against his mouth, moaning, "You're about to make me come . . . so hard . . . for you."

Her movements—her words—made his shaft jerk, threatening release. He'd just felt her sheath tighten around his finger when she keened with ecstasy; sorcery shot from her eyes and hands, enough to light a night sky.

As soon as he tasted her orgasm . . . thought left his brain.

THIRTY-SIX

Lanthe gasped on a final, bone-melting spasm. She'd never loosed sorcery like that!

Probably because she'd never had such a cataclysmic orgasm.

He'd suckled her so divinely, penetrating her so deeply . . . but it was more.

It's Thronos. It's all him.

Yet he kept licking her too-sensitive flesh, continuing to finger her. When she tugged on his horns to pry him away, he shook his head, so she pulled harder. He nipped her thigh in warning!

Heaving breaths through his slickened lips, he grated, "Not done with you, woman." Then he set back in.

"I can't! Not so . . . soon . . ." She trailed off—because his strong tongue was licking her into submission. His mouth was conquering.

Soon she'd reach a point where he could do anything to her.

And Lanthe thought he knew it.

She rose on her elbows again, watching in bewilderment as his eyes turned to full black. Maybe she oughtn't to have wished for a demon lover? "Thronos?" She swallowed with trepidation and desire. Was Feveris bringing out their most primal selves?

When his remaining claws seized her ass, lifting her to his mouth, her head fell back into the flowers. With a savage growl, he buried his face between her thighs, tonguing her furiously.

"Oh! Ohhh!" Her control gone, she arched her back like a total wanton. "Yes, Thronos!" With each of his ruthless licks, sorcery filled her again. Swirls of it tickled her skin and caressed her face. She tightened her grip on his horns, about to come for this male. Again.

For Thronos Talos.

Shameless, she snatched down on his horns as she bucked upward.

It was as if she'd lashed him with a whip.

She could barely hang on as his head moved, thrashing back and forth as he licked, a wild demon maddened with lust.

Lanthe wanted to savor his abandon, to remember this forever, but she couldn't fight her mounting orgasm.

"Don't stop, need to come . . ."

He growled between her legs, "Yes, yes, give me more of it." Then he set back in—

Rapture crashed into her. The force of it wrenched the air from her lungs. She caught her breath just to lose it again on a desperate scream. *"Thronos!"* Her body writhed, her vision blurring. With each spasm, her sheath squeezed his thrusting finger.

Consciousness dimmed, her thoughts blanking until her heart finally slowed its frantic beat.

With soothing kisses along her thighs, he released her at last. She thought she heard him rasping against her skin, "Never go back."

Oh, Thronos. Her devastating demon lover.

Still catching her breath, she rose to her knees before him. He sat back on his heels, his thick cock jutting upright, rigid as granite, the head bulging. He inhaled deeply, as if to regain control of himself. In one instant, he looked like a demon about to die from need. In the next, he appeared proud, thrumming with masculine satisfaction.

He should be proud. He'd just wrung from her *two* mind-shattering orgasms.

But Feveris's spell was potent. She wasn't sated. As she gazed at his engorged shaft, desire bloomed once more. Another breeze blew; could he feel the cooling air on that tight, aching part of him?

He shuddered, answering her question. A translucent bead rose from the slit. He looked shocked to feel moisture there.

"It's pre-cum," she murmured. "Is this the closest you've ever been to ejaculating?"

His brows drew together. "Yes."

Because he was with his mate. Only for her would he release his seed, only *inside* of her. But it seemed a drop had escaped. Her tongue twirled in her mouth for it. She couldn't tell which part of her was hungrier for his shaft: her sex or her mouth.

"Melanthe, I need to claim you," he bit out.

She'd wondered if they could simply burn off steam, averting intercourse. How ridiculous that seemed now. He was going to be inside her today. But that didn't mean she couldn't first kiss him in a like fashion.

She wanted to give him that pleasure because he'd just delivered her to unknown heights—but also because she was experiencing feelings for him.

Feelings that demanded an outlet.

She needed to lavish kisses on the scars he hated. To thank his invincible heart for never succumbing. "Can we do that in a bit, Thronos? I thought I could taste *you* now."

"Taste?" His voice was hoarse.

"Will you lie back?"

He wordlessly nodded, eyes widening a touch when he fully comprehended what she was offering. The proud look he'd sported had turned to one of disbelief.

Once he reclined with his wings spread out over the field, she settled between his legs. "Are you ready?"

In answer, he impatiently bucked his hips, his muscled torso flexing, his mouthwatering cock bobbing—the most erotic sight she'd ever witnessed.

Lust jumbled his thoughts.

Thronos wanted to take his mate, but after what he'd just experienced . . . he'd never last.

He was rattled by how much he'd *needed* to pleasure her like that. What male wouldn't be uneasy when he'd just discovered something he was certain he'd die without?

She started kissing down his chest, holding his gaze with her shimmery eyes. She pressed her lips to the scar over his heart, remaining there for long moments. As she nuzzled her smooth cheek against his marked flesh, he thought he heard her breathe, *"Invincible."*

Did she mean . . . his heart?

He'd been confused before. Now? He didn't know how he should react, what he should say.

She continued lower, sending his mind into turmoil. Her hair had begun to dry in silken curls around her face and shoulders. When the winds made locks dance over his skin, he could perceive each tendril.

Enchantress . . .

He felt like he was watching some kind of mystery being played out, something he'd known occurred—without any idea of the inner workings.

Hands shaking, he grasped her head, barely checking the urge to guide her down to his aching member.

Yet then she descended to . . . his thigh? He jerked in surprise when she pressed more loving kisses along the length of that scar.

As in the dream she'd described, he wanted more. He'd never thought she could convey affection with this act.

She kissed his damaged ankle and calf, sources of grueling pain for him. In the beginning, he'd wanted her to suffer guilt, to regret.

No longer.

There were a thousand things he wanted to tell her. "Melanthe . . ." But he fell silent when she moved to his erection, taking hold of him.

His shaft pulsated in her soft grip. Moisture glistened across the crown. Would she mind that? When she was about to kiss him there? To his way of thinking, it seemed almost *impolite* to her. He was shocked at how little dominion he had over his body. He was literally in her hands—

She daubed the hot bead with her tongue.

A dumbfounded breath escaped him. With a shudder, he gave her another drop.

Her lips curled, as if he'd pleased her. Not impolite? *Erotic.* She liked it. She used that bead to thumb the head in mind-numbing circles. "Does this make you feel good?"

"Lanthe, you *know* it does." She was teasing him? Now?

He stared down at the seductive curve of her red lips. He wished he could read *her* mind.

Because he feared he was about to lose his.

She rubbed him until his head swam, lust firing inside him. His claws dug deep into his palms when visions arose . . .

Of thrusting into her mouth. Of lifting her by her hips and planting her on his throbbing shaft.

Of tossing her to the ground so he could cover her, shoving deep within her tight, wet sheath.

Not visions. *Impulses.* Gods help them if he lost control.

Suddenly he felt her tongue—against his sensitive sac. *"Unh!"* His knees fell wide, allowing her free rein to do as she would.

She gave a light suck to one of his testicles, then the other, nearly ending everything! He didn't breathe as she rose up over his shaft.

With her hand wrapped around the base, she guided the head toward her mouth to run the tip across her red lips. Then came her moist little tongue to circle the flared head. He couldn't stop an astonished grunt.

Yet then he frowned to feel pain sear over his arm, as if the skin was burning. When he glanced at it, there was nothing, soon forgotten.

She tongued the crown, darting flicks to the underside, making him growl her name. He'd barely recovered from that new delight when she closed her lips over him—with sublime suction.

"Gods almighty." His hips shot up. Her mouth slid even farther down. . . .

The only thing that could make this better would be if she was straddling his own tongue at the same time.

When she glanced up then, she caught him licking his lips for more of her taste. Her brows drew together. Moaning around him, she took his length even more aggressively. Deeper.

Finally a *deep* he craved.

As his restraint deteriorated, he cupped her face to give shallow thrusts between her lips. He lifted one wing, using a flare to cup her ass. When he rubbed those supple curves, she shivered.

His heavy testicles tightened as his body prepared to release. No way he could hold back. "Don't stop, Melanthe! I need more of this." More of her shimmering eyes, her teasing lips. "Close, sweet. So close." His head tipped back, eyes sliding shut.

Wait. She'd stopped? He faced her again.

She'd taken away that hot wet suction! "Melanthe?!"

She leaned forward to kiss his navel, leaving him racked with need and confusion. Yet then he felt her plump breasts pillowing each side of his erection. Desperate for the contact he'd lost, he rolled his hips. His shaft glided along her cleavage. *"Good gods."*

Another rock of his hips, and he grew nigh once more. "I'll release like this . . . between your perfect breasts . . ."

She tilted her head, gauging his expression. Then, with a sensual grin, she dragged her chest down his body to return to her kiss, adding the stimulation of her hand.

With her fist pumping the base of his dampened shaft, she sucked him with greedy, spine-tingling pulls.

"Ahhh!" Nothing could feel this good. Nothing, *nothing* . . . "I'm about to come!"

As she sucked and pumped, she cupped his testicles with her free hand, giving them an electrifying squeeze that brought him right over the edge.

Pleasure erupted. He threw back his head and roared—a sound that could never be contained.

Against her clever tongue, his length pulsed again and again, his back bowing in time.

She wrung every last shudder from him, forcing him to ride that pleasure . . . over and over. . . . A culmination so heart-stopping, it was almost fearsome.

He gave her only a drop or two of seed, but she hungrily drew on him for more. As if she'd been waiting forever to take him into her.

When she'd rendered his body boneless and his mind boggled, she gave him a last sweet kiss, then curled up against his side. As they both caught their breath, she laid her hand upon his chest, drawing her thigh up over his.

Time passed. Disbelief and satisfaction waged war in his hazy thoughts.

Melanthe began lazily dragging the backs of her nails up and down his chest. Breezes drifted over them as he floated without pain, discovering what bliss was. *I'm to experience this with her for the rest of my eternal life?*

And he hadn't even claimed her.

He was eager to, but resting with his mate like this was an ecstasy all its own. He wondered how long it took for a female's desire to stir anew. He wondered how many times a day she would let him attend to her. After he claimed her, once he'd found that home, how could he ever force himself to leave it?

Were these now to be his concerns? At the thought, he grinned up to the sky. He drew her closer, pressing his smiling lips against her forehead.

When they'd been young, they'd fallen into a ready camaraderie. Being with her had proved effortless—their interplay filled with rapport and affinity, with *ease.*

Now, after sharing pleasure with her, he believed they could become that close again, that they could rekindle the connection they'd shared.

And more.

When a ray of light wavered through the palm trees, he lifted her raven locks to the sun, just to watch them shine. . . .

"Sometimes I feel so comfortable with you that I forget our pasts," she said in a languorous voice. "Sometimes I feel as if nothing had separated us, and only yesterday we were gazing up at clouds together."

"I was just thinking about our camaraderie. It's still here between us."

"Hmm. *Something* is," she murmured.

As if an alarm had sounded, he picked up on the subtle change in her tone. When her hand started to dip, tension renewed within him.

Because Feveris wasn't satisfied. He remained erect, and his mate's hips began to move, rubbing the slick heat of her sex against him. *Bliss.*

"You're hard as iron."

"You make me thus." He turned to her, cupping her face. "Are you ready for more? I can give it to you."

Worry crossed her face, but she still nodded. "I have to feel you inside me."

Even as his shaft strained demandingly, his chest twisted with emotion. "I don't want you to regret this."

She lay back in the flowers and reached for him, her hair like a cloud around her head, night-black curls against bloodred petals. He knew he'd never forget this sight for the rest of his immortal life.

"I can barely think past this fever for you." Her eyes were luminous, telling him things he didn't have the experience to recognize.

He sensed a vulnerability in her that he wouldn't have expected.

As he knelt between her thighs, he said, "Worry not, Melanthe. I'll be good to you. I'll be true to you."

"If we do this, we might be taking a step there's no turning back from."

"Tell me you want this."

She bit her bottom lip. "I do."

Then it will be done. He was to take his mate.

At the thought, his gaze was drawn to the smooth column of her neck. His fangs ached, as if to *mark* her.

Vrekener males didn't bite their mates upon claiming. Defeating the compulsion, he fisted his erection, swiping his thumb over the head as he aimed it toward her tiny opening. "I don't want to hurt you."

"Go slow at first." With a smile in her tone, she said, "Be tender for as long as you can."

He tilted his hips toward her. Just as dampness kissed his sensitive skin, she gave a moan, undulating, sending the crown slipping up and down her wet folds.

A growl rose up from his chest. He wanted her arousal all over him. On his tongue, on his fingers, covering his shaft.

He placed his hands on either side of her head, easing his hips forward. Uncontrollable urges tormented him, and he had to gnash his teeth to keep from plunging inside at once. He'd delved just an inch into her core when his entire body gave a shudder. *"My gods!"* Another inch. "Melanthe, I will want this every hour of the day. You are—"

"Sweet!" a female said from not ten feet behind them. "Hot interspecies action! And I didn't even have to subscribe to this channel!"

THIRTY-SEVEN

For a brief second, Lanthe wondered if Thronos would ignore the interruption and keep going.

Gazing at the intense hunger on his face, she could tell he was debating it. . . .

But then protectiveness or propriety made him stop. With a surprisingly vile curse, Thronos pulled out. As he stood, he dragged Lanthe up as well, tucking her back against his front as his wings enfolded their bodies.

Lanthe narrowed her eyes at the dark-haired female who'd come upon them. It was none other than Nïx the Ever-Knowing. "Why are you in Feveris, Nïx?"

"Am I in Feveris? Are we?" Her voice was melodious, her amber eyes amused. She had a freaking bat perched on her shoulder. "What if we're not?"

"I've been here before and know what it looks like." Lanthe could hardly believe she'd just been caught beneath a Vrekener. Would Nïx tell Sabine? Stressing the words, Lanthe said, "Not to mention that we've been *bespelled* with unending desire."

"Yet you two have no urge to do me?"

Lanthe muttered, "Maybe a little." Nïx was a dish.

"Hey!" Thronos yanked Lanthe closer.

"Understandable." Nïx twirled her long hair. "You two get dressed, and then we'll talk."

When the Valkyrie turned from them, Lanthe eased around within the circle of Thronos's wings to face him. "We *were* bespelled." They might not have been bespelled.

"Of course," he said solemnly.

"We must have been." Otherwise, Lanthe had so very nearly let Thronos Talos claim her—during her most fertile time. And she'd been about to shove her hips up to get him inside her faster!

If she got pregnant with a Vrekener's baby . . . with *his* baby . . .

His expression was inscrutable. Was he angry at himself for their offendments? "Of course," he repeated. "The Valkyrie must be mistaken."

"Uh-huh." *Untruth.*

He released Lanthe so they could find their clothes. She darted for her necklace right away.

The Valkyrie sauntered back to them as soon as Lanthe and Thronos were dressed. Nïx herself wore a T-shirt that read: *I lost my heart on Immortal Island!*

Recalling how Nïx had helped Thronos, Lanthe narrowed her eyes. "You told him how to capture me. Why would you betray me?"

"Did I?"

"I've been running from him for centuries." Or she had been. *Act like partners long enough* . . .

"Have you?"

"Will you stop answering questions with questions?"

"Will I?"

"Ugh!" Lanthe wanted to strangle her!

"You both have roles to fulfill."

"What roles?" Thronos grated.

Nïx waved her hand in an arc above her as she breathed, "*Future* ones!"

Wait . . . *immortal island*? "You were on the Order's prison island, weren't you?"

"Was I?" Nïx asked with a coy smile.

"*You* talked to me when I was unconscious!" Lanthe flashed a look of realization. "You hit me in the face with a log!"

"You dare accuse me of such a thing?!" Nïx snapped, her Valkyrie emotions producing lightning above. "Outrageous! I would never!" Then she abruptly frowned. "I *might* have hit you in the face with a log."

"You talked to me about realms and fires. Why?"

"You were in the mortal plane, then Pandemonia, now here, and soon . . . there. You really are the cutest wittle devilkin of a catalyst!"

"Catalyst? You've been steering my portals! You—you rigged my subconscious." Hadn't Lanthe felt like this journey was bigger than just her and Thronos? Had Nïx wanted them in Pandemonia to shake up those demons? To bring peace to hell? After all, what could those armies fight over now?

Or did Nïx want the dainty keys Lanthe now wore? *Not without a fight, Valkyrie.*

Nïx murmured, "In one realm, hurt. In one realm, leave. In one realm, cleave. In one realm, *shine.*"

Lanthe had hurt in Pandemonia, as if the festering wounds of the past had been sliced open. *At last to heal?* "So here, I'm supposed to leave?"

Nïx smiled blankly.

"What are you playing at, Valkyrie?" Thronos sounded like he was struggling not to lose his temper. He must be regretting their actions as much as Lanthe did.

Ignoring him, Nïx asked Lanthe, "How's your power coming, sorceress? You look at it as if it's a pot that needs to be filled. When in fact, it's a muscle that has been flexed very little."

This news was exciting! "So the more I use it, the stronger it'll be?"

"Use, use, rest. Use, use, use, rest. Use, use, use, use, rest—"

"I get it!"

To Thronos, the Valkyrie said, "How did you like your vacay in Pandemonia? Glad you saved up sick days? Did you feel all . . . liberated? And swagger-y? I bet that plane made your soft parts tingle."

"Once and for all, tell me, woman: Are Vrekeners demons?"

"Tell me, man: Does it matter?" she said with a roll of her eyes.

"Yes! Absolutely. Are we a demonarchy?"

"What would be the difference between your life now versus if you were a demon? You'd be able to trace. Big deal."

Lanthe could sense his steep disappointment. Because he still didn't have the conclusive answers he sought? Or because Nïx hadn't denied Vrekeners were demons?

"I'll make you a deal, Thronos," the Valkyrie said. "I'll tell you where you really are if your mate stores something for me."

"Stores what?" Lanthe didn't even have a bag with her.

Nïx plucked up a curl of her lustrous dark hair, peering down at it. "This is the one, you know."

Lanthe didn't know. "Which one?"

"The one that enslaves all the Valkyries. The tipping point with the Scourge."

"Okay," Lanthe said slowly. "Your hair enslaves?" She turned to Thronos, as if he could make sense of Nïx's ramblings.

The Valkyrie nodded. "Quite." Baring her foreclaw, she sliced off the curl, then glanced around, muttering, "What to tie it with?" She beamed at the bat, who now had a length of string in its creepy little maw. "Why thank you, Bertil!" Nïx tied the end of the curl tight, handing it to Lanthe. "In your pocket, if you please."

Lanthe patted down her outfit. "I don't have a pock—" Sure enough, there was a concealed pocket in one of the leather bands of her skirt. "Okay, give it over."

"I'm ready for an explanation, soothsayer," Thronos told Nïx. "Melanthe and I both felt the influence of this place; there was no denying it."

The Valkyrie's eyes flashed like her lightning. "Or maybe you two simply wanted an excuse to have each other. Here, you were able to get around your premarital sex rule. Here, Lanthe reasoned that you couldn't think badly of her because she would have no control over her actions."

"Then where are we?" Thronos demanded.

A sudden rank smell wafted over Lanthe, like . . . vomit. Where had *that* come from?

"Very well. I'll tell Thronos alone." Nïx sauntered up to him, standing on tiptoe.

When he leaned down to accommodate her, putting their faces close together, a spike of irritation hit Lanthe. Jealousy? No, of course not. Still, she pointed out, "Hey, I'm part of this too!"

Whatever Nïx was whispering made Thronos's eyes widen. When she'd finished, he straightened, looking paler than Lanthe had ever seen him. His scars whitened.

Nïx turned to her. "As much as I'd like to stay and discuss my plans for the Accession—hint: there will be wearable party favors!—I have a meeting that was penciled in one hundred and twenty-five years ago. Do take care with my lock, Lanthe." Then the Valkyrie gazed up at the sky, her eyes swirling like mercury. A split second later, a bolt of lightning struck her.

When the smoke cleared and their eyes readjusted, Nïx was gone.

Loreans had long wondered how Nïx traveled the world(s). Lightning bolts. Who knew?

Thronos hastened to Lanthe, grabbing her shoulders.

"What's going on?" She winced as that pain in her side flared up again. She began to feel more burns up and down her legs.

"You need to wake up with me."

"What is *wrong* with you? I'm not asleep." She glanced past him. Had the fields of flowers wavered? Her nose was now burning with that ghastly smell.

His hands tightened on her. "None of this is real. It's a shared hallucination—so that we don't fight our captivity."

"Captivity?"

"That last portal took us to . . . to a treacherous place. Into the belly of a beast. It will want to keep us—immortals are a source of constantly replenishing nourishment—but we're going to fight."

Was he saying she was something's *food*? One of her worst fears. "Y-you're scaring me."

"I'll get you free, but you'll have to create a portal directly after, or we'll be drugged and trapped once more."

"This isn't funny!"

In a gallows tone, he said, "No, Lanthe. It isn't."

THIRTY-EIGHT

Thrymheim Hold, Northlands
Home of Skathi, goddess of the hunt
Goddess council convening
Agenda: Petition for godhood submitted by Phenïx the Ever-Knowing, firstborn Valkyrie

Nïx, you've known about this meeting for decades and decades," Riora, the goddess of impossibility, said. "Couldn't you have prepared better?"

Nïx blinked at Riora as they made their way through the rumbling halls carved into Godsbellow Mountain, a peak continually shaken by thunder. "I don't take your meaning."

"You're wearing a T-shirt and flops, you're carrying a sleeping bat, and you reek of what can only be gastric acid." The bat burped in its sleep, expelling a puff of green mist. Then it smacked its lips. "This is a formal affair. Kali is wearing *twelve* skulls."

Nïx's eyes went wide. "I should've vajazzled!" Her excitement woke the bat. It clawed its way up her T-shirt to perch on her shoulder. With a shrug, Nïx opened her backpack, retrieving sheets of paper.

Riora looked approving, expecting a résumé of Nïx's great works and deeds, a divine CV to advance her cause—then frowned when the Valkyrie turned to post a flyer for a "barely used" Bentley on one of Thrymheim's sacred walls. "As your friend, I have to tell you that the atmosphere in Skathi's meeting hall is contentious. Most of the deities think you reach above your station. The questioning will be intense." From within the hall, they could hear goddesses debating whether Nïx had "the juice."

"Who's here?"

"Most goddesses. Standing, levitating, and astral projection room only."

"How're you liking my chances?" Nïx asked.

Riora tilted her head. "Nothing is impossible with you, which is why I've always liked you."

Nïx nodded thoughtfully. "Aside from a few other deities, you've always been my favorite."

Riora pursed her lips, and she and Nïx entered.

The focus of the room was a grand wooden table with three concentric rotating disks. One disk measured all times. The second was a perpetually changing map of the mortal world and connecting domains. The third monitored celestial acts taking place across all realms. The center of the table was hollow, with a dais in the middle.

A number of goddesses, or their dimensional likenesses, were in attendance. In the flesh were the witch deities Hekate and Hela; Lamia, the goddess of life and fertility; Wohpe, goddess of peace; Saroh, the goddess of the Jinn; and the Great She-Bear, protectoress of shifters. Among many more . . .

With a nod of encouragement, Riora left Nïx and took her saved spot at the table.

The legendary Skathi presided. She looked exasperated, not bothering to hide her feelings about Nïx's petition.

The Valkyrie didn't seem to notice the goddess's displeasure. With that bat on her shoulder, she nonchalantly made her way toward the dais in the center of the rotating table. As she approached, a path opened up, the wood disappearing, then reappearing behind her, like a wake.

Atop the dais, Nïx turned to Skathi. It was known that if one gazed into that goddess's eyes, he or she would experience all the fear and sorrow of Skathi's prey over the ages; yet Nïx boldly met her gaze. Which appeared to surprise the goddess.

Clearing her throat, Skathi called the meeting to order, then took her seat. "We will dispense with formalities to limit the duration of this meeting. We convene because Phenïx the Ever-Knowing is petitioning to join our ranks in the pantheon of goddesses." Skathi steepled her fingers. "Tell us in your own words: Why should we welcome you into our blessed number?"

Bright-eyed and breathless, Nïx said, "Well, I can mime"—she demonstrated as Riora dropped her forehead to the table. "I'm a mistress of keg stands"—Nïx looked around for a keg with which to demonstrate—"two of my three parents *are* gods, and I have a goddesslike power."

Skathi raised her brows. "Your talent for mime notwithstanding, you have an obvious mark against you: human blood. One of those three parents of yours was mortal."

"Doesn't seem to slow me down." Nïx hiked a thumb at herself. "After all, just this Accession, I orchestrated the death of Crom Cruach." The god of cannibalism. "Hmm, Skathi, wasn't he *your* curse to deal with? Right, then." She brushed off her hands matter-of-factly. "We'll settle up at the bar."

Skathi glared, and the flames of her temple climbed higher. Yet then, a bout of thunder shook the mountain, seeming to soothe her. "A goddess is measured by the company she keeps. Yet you're close to Loa, the voodoo priestess, a mere shopkeeper who grows to be a practitioner of the darkest arts?"

"Loa prefers to be known as the *Commerce*nary."

"You do realize the power she wields?"

Nïx sighed. "Counting on it."

Seductive Lamia observed, "Under your direction, La Dorada the Queen of Evil has arisen."

"Dora and I are like this." Nïx spread her arms wide. "Now, I'll be the first to admit she's not without faults. Very grumpy when she wakes up. And with Dora, it's always *me me me, ring ring ring*."

"Why would you resurrect her?" Skathi demanded.

"No one else was going to do it!" Nïx said, just as her bat leaned in beside her ear. The soothsayer nodded to it, then murmured, "Meet me at the lightning bolt." She gazed on fondly as the creature flew away with a screech.

"Your attention!" Skathi snapped.

"What were we talking about? Let's be quick, then. It's past Bertil's bedtime."

Jaws dropped at Nïx's temerity.

Speaking to no one in particular, Nïx said, "And because we're going to need her."

"Who?" Lamia asked.

"Dora." As if speaking to a child, Nïx said, "You asked me why I'd resurrect her, and I'm answering your question." She narrowed her eyes. "Are *all* of you inebriated?"

"Continuing on," Skathi intoned. "You claim a goddesslike power, styling yourself *ever-knowing*, yet you can't even find your sister Furie."

"Find? As in *bring to light*?" she asked, leaving the pantheon to puzzle over her words.

Hekate said, "You've been working to ally factions of immortals for the Accession, assisting Loreans of different species to find their mates. From what I understand, we're to have a rash of halflings in future generations."

"Halflings are formidable," Nïx pointed out. "Think of Queen Emmaline of the Lykae, Queen Bettina of the Deathly Ones, and Mariketa the Awaited, leader of your House of Witches. Plus, Valkyries have a soft spot for halflings, since we have three vastly different parents. I guess you could call us *triflings*." Broad wink.

"Why are you tirelessly seeding halflings and renewing ancient alliances?" Hekate asked. "To battle what foe?"

Nïx breathed, "The Møriør."

The other goddesses tensed at the mention of the Bringers of Doom. They didn't speak of the Møriør lightly.

The Valkyrie seemed unaware of the stir she'd caused. "All the harbingers are there. They descend upon us. Though the Accession exists to cull the immortal population, mortals and gods alike should fear this one."

Lamia offered, "Nïx would sense them first," and earned glares.

Skathi's flames grew and grew. "You took it upon yourself to plan a defense against the Møriør? You toy with the fate of the entire Lore, Valkyrie!"

"Not defense. *Offense.* Why come out of the dugout for anything less? I'm not interested in a farm league. Which is why I'm here. Only a divinity—with this pantheon's resources—could unite all of the factions."

"You believe *you* can lead the charge? Against *them*?"

"Review: transcript of this meeting. See: farm league comment."

Skathi drew her head back. "All of your sarcastic—"

"Multilayered."

"—answers will not help your cause. You're very flippant about these proceedings."

Nïx's playful demeanor vanished in an instant, her amber irises swirling, mercurial. "Because I've already seen the outcome."

"And what is that?"

"You'll move to dismiss my petition, telling me that I must have a cause—an area of power, a specialization of sorts. After all, you are goddess of the hunt, the Great She-Bear is goddess of shapeshifters, Lamia is goddess of some-some."

When Lamia scowled, Nïx shrugged. "I calls 'em like I sees 'em." Then she addressed all the goddesses: "You believe that this area of power must be a critical one. Since foresight has been taken—hat tip to the goddess Pronoea—you expect I'll come up short. Yet, in fact, I'm going to reveal my specialization, and all of you will comprehend the inevitability of it."

Skathi pursed her lips. "Thrall us, Valkyrie."

Nïx paused dramatically. "I will rise from the ashes of the old ways to become Phenïx, the goddess of . . . accessions."

THIRTY-NINE

In the belly of the beast, stygian darkness was interrupted only by glowing green filth.

Thronos had awakened to find himself trapped against a pulpy surface, held upright by meaty tentacle-like veins that snaked around his arms and legs.

Oozing cavities covered each vein; at that moment, one secreted green sludge onto his disintegrated clothing, his skin, his wings.

Pain flared, smoke rising. Acid! The putrid air was noxious, scalding his lungs. He thrashed—the need to fly surging inside him—but he couldn't get loose.

Nïx had given him just four minutes to get himself and Melanthe free.

He darted his eyes to his right. *Lanthe.*

She was in the same predicament as he—attached to what looked like a stomach lining, surrounded by sizable glowing pustules. She remained unconscious, no doubt believing them still in Feveris.

Acid had eaten away parts of her skin as well, even most of her metal breastplate. The indestructible dragon gold around her neck had protected her to a degree.

A pustule burst beside her, thicker tentacles emerging from the sore to sweep up bits of her pale flesh.

To consume her.

With a bellow, Thronos thrashed with all his might, yanking at his arms. As the tentacle trapping his right arm stretched, he gazed out, spotting thousands more immortals ensnared, unconscious. The stomach walls seemed to go on for miles.

In a rush of bile, the tentacle vein around his arm ripped open. He used his claws to slash another. At his legs, he hesitated, peering over his shoulders and then down. Hundreds of feet below him, a bubbling pool of green acid awaited his fall. How damaged were his wings?

Praying they could support him—and Melanthe—he freed his legs. He plummeted, unfurling his wings, grimacing in pain. But even in the dense miasma, he was able to ascend the wall back to her.

Though he heard eerie moans from a legion of beings, he couldn't think about anyone but his mate. Nïx had told him that this stomach was too thick to slash through, that he'd be drugged again before he could fight his way free. She'd warned him he had only two hundred and forty seconds from the time he awoke until a poisonous mist would be dispersed, wiping away his memories and sending him back to the place of his most coveted dreams.

He darted a glance over his shoulder. On the opposite wall of the stomach, some kind of bulbous gland, at least twenty feet in diameter, was swelling. To emit the mist?

Running out of time! A portal was their only hope. He flew to Melanthe.

Thronos wished he didn't have to wake her until he'd taken her from this place—he'd heard of Loreans faced with such horror that they never recovered their faculties—but he had no choice.

Gripping the tentacle vein coiled around her arm, he slashed at the rubbery surface, pointing the acid-dripping end away from her body.

Her eyes shot open. She sucked in a breath—then released it in an earsplitting shriek.

He redoubled his efforts, attacking another tentacle.

"No, no, this isn't happening." Her face crumpled. "Tell me it's not eating my skin!"

"Melanthe, you have to calm yourself. You've got to create a portal."

Her head thrashed against the putrid lining, searing strands of her hair clear away. "That's why it felt like I was burning in Feveris!" Once he'd freed her and taken her into his arms, she latched onto him. "M-make this stop! I'll do anything. Just make me wake up!"

"We are awake. But if we don't leave this place, we'll be here for eternity. In Feveris, you restored your power."

"You said that wasn't real!"

"Didn't it feel real?" He wished to the gods it had been. "You have power, right now. I need you to use it. Remember, it's a muscle."

She darted her gaze at her surroundings, a series of cries bursting from her lips. That gland swelled, threatening to burst.

"No, look at *me*!" He pinched her chin. "I know you can do this."

Her tears threatened to spill, wrecking him.

He rasped, "You can do this, lamb."

At that, she said, "I-I'll try."

When her eyes began to glitter, he murmured, "That's it." He felt her tensing in his arms. Despite her terror, she called up her power; he could perceive it welling, unstoppable.

Could others? Unconscious captives moaned louder.

Sorcery sparked around her, growing and growing, blazing out from her like dawn—pure, pristine blue overwhelming rancid green.

Dimly, in the back of his mind, he wondered how he'd ever considered the light of her sorcery anything but . . . wondrous.

Heartbeats passed.

She sagged against him.

"I did it," she gasped.

"Where?" He spun them in circles. No opening. The mist would come at any second.

"It should be here! I made a portal. I felt it happening."

The gland erupted, spewing a green fog. "Damn it, no!"

Relaxation stole through Lanthe's body. "This is better." She grinned up at him as her eyes slid closed.

"No, stay with me!" Another turn. Nothing. "Where is the bloody portal?"

With dread, he looked down. A narrow tear in this reality lay waiting—one surrounded by piping acid.

When the portal started to close, he muttered a prayer, wrapped his wings around Lanthe . . .

And dropped.

As they plummeted through the rift, he realized some being had followed.

FORTY

Lanthe woke to the resounding silence of the sea.

When she opened her eyes, she saw murky ocean pressing down all around her and Thronos. In the dim light, his face was set with pain as he struggled to hold on to her and get them to safety.

They'd been freed from that nightmare—only to reach another one.

She clasped him tighter, so he could use both arms to swim. The water was lightening. At least there was a surface!

They were halfway there when her lungs reached their limit. She clawed him, needing air . . . about to involuntarily breathe water. He swam even faster, his heart pounding against her ear.

They breached the surface into a stormy day, sucking in misty breaths as they rolled on giant swells. She blinked against sea spray, trying to get her bearings.

"Where are . . . ?" She trailed off when Thronos's head craned up. She twisted to look over her shoulder, saw water all the way up to the sky.

Inconceivably high. About to crash over them.

He'd already kicked for propulsion, shooting into flight. But if he couldn't get high enough . . .

Her mind couldn't accept the size of the wave—like a mountain of liquid toppling over. "Faster, Thronos!"

His jaw was clenched, his heart sounding like it'd explode. "Don't let go of me, Lanthe!"

When the swell began to crest over them, he rotated in the air, wrapping his wings tightly around her. The wave collided with them so fast the water became as solid as brick.

The momentum hurtled them toward the coast, a jagged stone cliff. When they crashed into it, the rocks tore his wings like a monster with fangs, trying to rip her away from Thronos.

They clung to each other.

The wave sucked them back out to sea.

They clung harder.

The force raked them over coral reefs—before catapulting them back against the wall.

But when it receded the second time, they . . . remained.

Somehow Thronos had clung to the cliff with one quaking hand.

Gritting his teeth, he leapt higher, pulling them out of the wave's reach. The next crest slapped just beneath their feet, foam licking their legs, but it couldn't catch hold of them.

He hauled them up until they'd made the top of the cliff. At the edge, he shoved her ahead of him onto solid ground, then followed.

They lay on the stony ground, heaving breaths, coughing seawater. Beneath them, the cliff shook with each crashing wave.

"Melanthe, speak to me," he said between gulps of air. "Are you hurt?"

She shook her head. Again, he'd kept her cocooned for the most part. "Just some wounds from . . . from where we were." Swatches of her skin had been loosened by the acid, then sucked away.

She'd been food. Still would be, if not for Nïx. Except that the Valkyrie had sent them there in the first place! *Why, why, why?*

Most of Lanthe's breastplate was gone; the scant remains of her skirt clung to her hips. "How long do you think we were in . . . there?"

"Could've been hours or days," he answered. "Even weeks. I doubt our conception of time in Feveris corresponded to the actual duration."

"Right." She would never have words to convey to anyone else how horrific it'd been. Only Thronos could understand those tentacles, the pus, the burning.

Lanthe shuddered. She simply couldn't think about that place right now without losing her ever-living shit.

When he rolled toward the edge of the cliff, scanning the waves as if searching for something, she noticed that one of his wings looked worse than normal, those scale mosaics even more skewed.

"How bad off are you?"

Over his shoulder, he said, "I've got a forearm and a wing snapped. I might've cracked my skull. Nothing major."

That all? "What are you looking for?"

"I think someone—or something—followed us out. It was difficult to see in there, but I believe I spied a being."

"Anyone who followed is probably dead. No one could break free of that current." She frowned. "How did you?"

"I'm not as weak as you think me." As if to prove his point, he lumbered to his feet. His shirt had been either eaten away or torn free; most of his leather pants had disintegrated from acid. "I'm an immortal male in my prime."

"And that was the equivalent of an *immortal* current. Our bodies should have been dashed to pieces."

"Well, they're not." He reached a hand down, helping her stand.

As he steadied her, she asked, "Do you think we had supernatural assistance?"

"Is it so difficult to believe I did that on my own?" He stared down into her eyes as he said, "Maybe you make me strong."

He looked so earnest about this, she decided not to argue the point. "In any case, thanks for getting me to safety. We keep saving each other's asses, don't we?"

"That's the way it should be, no?" He seemed to be asking more than just that simple question, so she changed the subject.

"Where do you think we are?"

"I have no idea."

She turned her attention to herself. Though her necklace was unharmed, her breastplate was beyond salvage, the irregular edges cutting into her already damaged skin. She unfastened the last stubborn clip, then dumped it. Not that she cared, but her hair was long enough to cover most of her breasts. In the back, her locks had been eaten away, an involuntary bob cut. Her boots looked like acid had been drizzled over them, but at least the soles covered most of her feet.

Her skirt had only a few leather strands left. For Thronos's sake, she shifted the garment to cover her front, which gave her an ass-less skirt.

He flicked his gaze over her torso. "You're burned worse than I thought. You need to rest and regenerate."

"Where? We have no idea what dangers surround us."

"Then we need to get to higher ground while my wing heals." He surveyed the horizon.

She saw only flat terrain, a sheet of slate-gray stone that matched the dismal sky. "If there *is* higher ground." But he could see farther than she could.

"Come on." He took her hand in his.

Though the rock had countless craters—just ideal for her acid-eaten stiletto boots—she said, "I can walk on my own."

"I know you can." He kept her hand. After that Pandemonian hell zone, he seemed to have a constant need to touch her.

Still fearing something would take her away from him?

Whatever he'd seen had changed this man. So what would happen to him once they ultimately separated . . . ?

For now, hand in hand, they set off, wending around larger holes.

"What if this is another dream?" she asked. "That hallucination was so realistic." *You know, Thro, the one where we were having hot interspecies action.*

He nodded. "I feel as if I've *known* you. Almost."

"We're lucky that none of it happened. You didn't commit any offendments. I didn't almost get pregnant."

"If we weren't bespelled, then why did we feel such frenzy for each other?"

She didn't have to read his mind to know that the *guy* in Thronos wanted the two orgasms he'd given her to, well, count. "Placebo effect maybe? All I know is that Feveris—or faux Feveris—changes nothing."

"I think I'm your mate just as much as you are mine." Cocky Thronos was back.

She repeated her standard reply. "Sorceri don't have mates."

When he opened his mouth to argue, she held up her free hand. "I'm too tired for this, Thronos. At least wait until all my skin regenerates before you hassle me."

With a scowl, he started forward once more, toward a horizon of *nothingness.*

Nïx had told her to set worlds aflame. What could Lanthe possibly affect in a place like this? And she hadn't exactly been a torch in that belly.

Lanthe had thought she could at least learn from this experience, from her travels. All she'd learned from faux Feveris was that Thronos could be sexy as sin, and that he had a very talented—pointed—tongue.

Oh, and that being intimate with him had been life altering.

For *her.*

When they'd lain in each other's arms . . . as if nothing had ever torn them apart . . .

As the terrain grew even more challenging, he took her arm, helping her along. Gods, her awareness of him had gone through the roof. She could not, could not, *could not* be falling for Thronos.

Doomed did not even begin to describe a future together with him.

If she told Sabine, "I want to be with a Vrekener," her sister would have no doubt that Lanthe had been brainwashed. Which would make Sabine and Rydstrom murderous.

How could Lanthe keep them from killing Thronos? Oh, wait—she *couldn't.*

A briny gust of wind howled over the flats, chilling her bare skin. To escape her current dismal reality, she lost herself in thoughts of her sister and their new extended family, bracing for homesickness. She missed Sabine to the point of pain. She missed Rydstrom, their bedrock of stability. She missed her gurgling nieces with their downy blond hair and wide violet eyes.

The elder by seconds was called Brianna, Bri for short, and the younger was Alyson, or Aly. Cadeon and Holly had wanted to name their girls after loved ones, but in the end, the appeal of three-syllable names that could be shortened to three-letter nicknames was too overwhelming for Holly (she had an OCD thing for threes, thwarted in itself by twins).

Aly and Bri were little badasses. Everyone had been worried about the Pravus making attempts on their lives—as the vessel of this Accession, Holly had certainly been besieged by them—but there'd been no cause for alarm.

Lanthe's nieces were super brilliant, could already trace. If they sensed danger—or bath time—they would simply teleport their diapered butts away.

When hungry, they traced right to their mother's breast, which still freaked out the rather staid Holly. Cadeon thought it was uproarious, would croon praise to them. The twins *and* the boobs.

Rydstrom's ne'er-do-well mercenary brother had finally done well, abandoning his soldier-of-fortune past to build a life and start a family with his mate. Like Rydstrom and Sabine, Cadeon and Holly were as opposite as they could be.

Maybe the differences kept things interesting. Lanthe's gaze was helplessly drawn to Thronos.

But none of their factions were at war. None of their siblings would want to murder significant others.

She felt . . . despairing over the future. Because she couldn't have Thronos? She wished she didn't know how warm his chest was when he held her close—or what it would be like to make love to him.

Lanthe was a sorceress who wanted what she wanted when she wanted it. . . .

Not to be.

Despair promptly turned to resentment. Thronos had done this to her.

Made her wonder. Made her imagine more.

After several minutes of silence, he said, "I can't stop thinking about Feveris."

She yanked her hand from his. "Try!" When another gust hit them, she glared at her surroundings and kicked a stone. "This whole ordeal is like motherfucking *Time Bandits,* and I'm over it!"

"Don't know who those bandits are, Lanthe."

"Of course you don't." Because he'd never watched a movie in his eternal life.

They had nothing in common, except for some shared childhood experiences and recent hallucinatory orgasms.

Extremes.

Thronos now knew what it would be like to lose Melanthe forever, powerless to save her, forced to watch her die.

But he'd also glimpsed what it would be like to claim her as his woman. Neither experience had actually happened, which made him question if he were truly here with her even now. And she wondered why he kept touching her?

In their last two realms, he and Melanthe had been tested together—making him feel closer to her. Yet she was drawing away.

The situation wasn't helping. Her skin was wounded. She must be freezing from regeneration, and still half shocked over where they'd been.

She was probably starving as well. He had no idea when they'd last eaten. *How many days or weeks were we within that beast?* Already, he'd suspected Pandemonian time moved differently. He could only guess how long he and Melanthe had been missing.

He helped her over a gulley, his thoughts ricocheting among four things: concern for her immediate safety, reliving her death in those harrowing loops, recalling his pride as she'd manipulated those demons to save him—and relishing how she'd responded to him in their dream of Feveris.

For the latter, he lowered his mental shield, letting her hear his musings loud and clear.

He replayed her wet heat kissing the head of his shaft . . . the pressure of her sex beginning to squeeze the crown as he inched inside . . . her pulse racing because she'd needed him too . . .

"It wasn't real!" she insisted.

"It feels bloody real!" No one got his wings up like she did! "Damn it, I know your taste. I know your moans. Why are you so eager to deny what we felt?"

It was as if she considered herself weak because she'd surrendered to it. *And all I feel is strong.*

"Because it never happened!" Brows raised in challenge, she said, "If that hallucination truly took place, then shouldn't Nïx's lock of hair be in my pocket?" She dug into the waterlogged leather strip, one of the last remaining.

She pulled out a lock of Valkyrie hair.

He gaped. *Could* Feveris have been real?

Melanthe pinched her brow with confusion. "No, no. Nïx must've planted this on me when she attacked me on the island. She could've slipped this in when I was unconscious. Or maybe she was in the beast herself?" Melanthe shoved it back in her pocket. "Don't look at me like that!"

"Like I made you scream with pleasure?" He closed in on her. "Face it, sorceress, I nearly claimed you as mine—and you *loved* it." They were toe to toe. "You wanted me inside you. You wanted more. Nothing can ever take that away."

"That would've been disastrous!" She looked half enraged, half wary.

He reached forward to brush his thumb over her bottom lip. "I want to get us back to where we were before we got interrupted."

"A male wanting sex from me." She jerked away from him. "How novel."

"You know I want more than just sex." He grabbed her upper arm, drawing her close once more. "I want *everything* from you."

Her lips parted, but then she seemed to collect herself. "Just because Sorceri don't dwell on regrets doesn't mean we set ourselves up for them either. What you want to happen between us just . . . can't. We're too different. Our families and factions would never accept this."

"Maybe a relationship between another sorceress and a Vrekener would prove impossible. But we've been through too much. We've *earned* each other. You can't deny that. If you took away all the strife surrounding us, could you accept me?"

She didn't reply, wouldn't meet his gaze.

"Look at me, Melanthe."

When she eventually faced him, he stared into her eyes, seeing that same vulnerability he'd beheld when he'd been about to claim her.

He thought he was beginning to understand it. . . .

In Pandemonia, he'd discovered his mate yearned for love. She'd never found it with another—and she clearly wouldn't settle for anything less. She'd told him she would give her heart only to the right male.

I'm that male.

Looking at her now, he comprehended that she felt vulnerable—because her heart was *already in play.* He believed he could make Melanthe fall in love with him, claiming something from her all his own.

"Let me go, Thronos."

"And if I say never?" In that moment, he realized exactly how he should handle her sorcery in the Skye. The solution was so blindingly obvious, he almost slapped his forehead.

With a groan of frustration, she kicked his shin; he cupped her nape, pulling her close for an overdue kiss—

A metal net descended over them.

He yelled, splaying his wings, snaring himself in the weighted lines.

"Oh, gods, it's like the tentacles!" She dropped to the ground, cringing away from the mesh. "Get it off, get it off!"

"Trying!" When he clawed the metal, sparks erupted. Mystically protected.

Just as he scented foreign creatures over the sparks, Melanthe cried, "Stheno sentries!"

Before he could reach her, she'd been snatched out from under the net. He lunged for her, thrashing to get free, until one of the towering creatures propped Melanthe up like a doll to hold a trident at her neck.

They were surrounded by a dozen vicious Sthenos, nine-foot-tall gorgons with crimson sea snakes for hair. Each sentry carried a trident.

"Release us," Melanthe commanded, blue light emanating from her eyes and hands. Nothing. *"Release us now!"*

The largest Stheno, and obvious leader, said, "Your powers will not work on us, sorceress. We have been divinely shielded."

Time to fight, then. His gaze flicked as he calculated his next several moves—until the Stheno holding his mate threatened her with more than a trident.

Sea snakes coiled down to drape over one of her graceful shoulders, their fangs bared, forked tongues twitching.

Melanthe swallowed. "Their poison . . . I might not recover from it."

He froze, holding up his hands.

The leader said, "You've erred by trespassing in Sargasoe, kingdom of Nereus."

"The sea god?" Melanthe asked.

"The deity Nereus, our lord and master. You will attend him in his keep, where he holds feasts of celebration. Depending on His Highness's mood, you will either be guests—or the entertainment."

FORTY-ONE

The Sthenos had bound and blindfolded their captives, making the descent from towering cliff to sea level even more perilous for Lanthe. She wanted to tell them that she could never, ever find her way back to Nereus's keep. But they hadn't exactly been chatty.

—What is this god like?— Thronos asked her on their unending trek along a beach.

Lanthe supposed the Vrekener was getting over his telepathy hang-up. *—Nereus is a party-hearty trickster, like a cross between Pan and Loki. He's notorious for his games and manipulations.—*

—What happens if we're "entertainment"?—

—Probably something that'll make you want to take a boiling shower and scrub your skin with steel wool. Let's just put it this way: I don't think I'll be able to twerk my way out of this.—

—Don't know what twerk means, Melanthe.—

Sigh. *—I've heard that Sargasoe is a hidden realm on the human plane.—* Like Skye Hall. *—The goal should be to get Nereus to transport us from here.—*

Without sacrificing too much of themselves . . .

—Do you think you can ensorcel him?—

—If he can shield the Sthenos from my power, there's not a chance. And he'd likely kill me for trying.—

Thronos fell silent, seeming lost in his own thoughts.

Though Lanthe's skin was gradually healing during their long walk, she was drained from keeping up with the fast Sthenos. Their lower halves were fat snake coils, kind of like Cerunnos, except Sthenos gorgons were all females. Plus they had hypnotically wavering snakes for hair. Oh, and brass hands and claws.

Whenever Lanthe tripped in the shifting sands, her Stheno personal guard would heft her up, those claws digging into her arm.

After the belly of the beast, this was nothing. Right?

Wrong.

A blast of ocean wind buffeted her. When Lanthe tottered and got clawed yet again, she snapped, "Watch the claws, bitch!"

—Melanthe?— She could all but see Thronos raising his eyebrows. Just because he was cool and collected didn't mean she had to be. He'd had his tantrum—his *man*trum—on the Order's island, and it was now her turn.

—I have no more fucks to give. Okay, Vrekener?— She'd hit her limit. She was sick of portaling, sick of getting captured, sick of being food or potential food.

—We're going to escape once more. Worry not.—

—Why are you *so calm?—*

He was quiet for long moments. *—It's my nature. What you saw those first nights and days was not . . . me.—*

She'd figured calm was his default setting. So to all his other attractive attributes, she could add *not psycho.*

Finally, their entourage slowed, entering some kind of echoing space. A sea cave?

They descended for what must be miles. When pressure made her ears pop repeatedly, she realized they were deep beneath the ocean. No flying for Thronos, even if he got free.

She felt sympathy for him. His fear of depths was like her fear of heights. She couldn't imagine how difficult this must be for him.

Probably as difficult as she would find the Skye. Still, she asked: *—You okay with this?—*

—It's temporary.—

In other words, he wasn't, but he would *handle* it.

In Pandemonia, she'd told him about crazy stuff going down with Sorceri kids, and he'd confidently said, "We can handle it."

We.

She and Thronos *did* work well together.

Gods, she did not need to conclude that the Vrekener would be a good father. Her biological clock cried, *The best. None better!*

Suddenly Lanthe heard gears whirring, cogs clicking, as if a gate was opening. They entered a warm, damp area, and the gears whirred once more. Behind them, a seal closed with a hiss. The scent of brine pervaded everything.

Off went the blindfolds. Thronos swung his head around to face her, as if he'd been hungry for a single look.

—I'm okay. Still standing.—

When he gave a grim nod of encouragement, she dragged her gaze from him to survey Sargasoe, the legendary lair of Nereus.

This hall had been carved from rock with glittering coral-pink and blue striations. A sheen of water poured down all the walls, but it seemed to be by design.

The area was lit with . . . sconces—basically raised glass bowls where luminescent jellyfish shuttled in circles. Rippling reflections abounded, as they did underwater, making the walls seem to sway.

"Forward," the leader commanded, the Sthenos slithering behind them.

As Lanthe and Thronos trudged deeper, huge sections of the stone floor would shift and retract, revealing the sea. The construction of this place was spectacular.

Mirrors abounded. Shadows and light danced for dominance. Glowing eyes peeked out from darkened passageways.

This totally looked like the lair of a capricious deity notorious for his games.

She also sensed a permanent portal down here. How to get Nereus to let them use it?

Their group eventually entered what must be an underwater gallery of sorts. There were enormous rounded windows at intervals, the way paintings might line a museum wall.

When Lanthe passed the first, her eyes went wide. Ships were piled up, as if in a junkyard. She turned to Thronos. —*Are you seeing this?*—

—*It makes sense that a sea god's home would have a vortex.*— A mystical magnet. —*We're in an abyss; everything sinks to this level.*—

At the next window, she squinted out into the dark, seeing gems the size of footballs scattered all over the sand. Schools of mercreature sentries glided by. They were humanoids to a degree, but instead of legs, the mermaids sported fishtails, the mermen collections of tentacles.

The next window revealed a submarine with Russian lettering on its hull, and what looked like part of an aircraft carrier. This was too wild!

For all the suffering Lanthe had borne just to reach Sargasoe, she was excited to behold such an exotic place. But what was in store? Nïx's prediction echoed in her mind: *In one realm, hurt. In one realm, leave. In one realm, cleave. In one realm, shine.*

So was Lanthe supposed to cleave here? She bit her lip, glancing at Thronos. *Cleave* was a word with several meanings, one of which was *to separate.*

She'd already sensed a portal. What if Nereus offered two different rides: one to the Skye and one to Rothkalina?

Was she ready to part from Thronos? Despite all her blustering and denials earlier, the thought made her chest ache. If only a relationship between them didn't pose so many insurmountable odds.

When they passed a mirror, she turned away, not wanting to see her reflection. Yet suddenly all the injuries over her body began mending. The restraints around her wrists disappeared, and she felt as fresh as if she'd recently bathed. With a gasp, she peered down at herself.

She now wore a black leather skirt, mesh hose, and leather boots. Her top was a halter woven of gold and silver strands—with denser weaves of metal over the front to conceal her breasts. Sleek metal gauntlets covered her hands and forearms, and she detected a mask over her face.

Sorceri formal dress! Her hands flew to her necklace. Still there!

She whirled around to the mirror. Her mask was sapphire blue, accentuating her eyes. Her hair had been twined around a substantial gold headpiece, with wild braids framing her face. No more bob cut in the back—long locks had grown out, left to curl down her back.

She felt more like a sorceress—less like food. She was starting to enjoy Sargasoe's amenities! She turned to Thronos, and her lips parted.

The Vrekener was . . . drop-dead gorgeous.

His recent injuries had disappeared, and he was dressed in new clothes. Leather breeches and boots. A wide leather belt to highlight his narrow hips.

A crisp, white lawn shirt molded over his muscles and wing stems as if tailored. Which she supposed it had been, by a divine hand.

She was entranced by her tall, built, devilish, demon lover. Or would-be lover. He had the physical attributes to attract any female—but Lanthe also admired how he stood so proud and stalwart, ready to do battle once more.

She and Thronos continued to be challenged; they continued to overcome, protecting each other. Maybe he was right; maybe they *were* the Vrekener/Sorceri couple who could beat those odds.

"Is *this* real?" he asked, gazing back at their guards. "Between the loops and Feveris, I'm unsure."

She was used to magics like these, Thronos not so much. "I think it is."

"Follow the sounds to the feast," the Stheno leader said, using her trident to point down the corridor. "Do not entertain ideas of escape. For your kind, there is only one way out of Sargasoe."

When the cadre turned to slither away, a thought occurred to Lanthe. "Wait! Where are my clothes from before? There was a lock of hair—"

"Your offering has been received," the leader said, her head snakes wavering. "It's the reason you live yet."

"Oh." And then Lanthe and Thronos were alone. "Hope Nïx didn't need that back."

When he canted his head at her, Lanthe realized he hadn't seen her looking this put-together in forever. "Sooo, what do you think?"

"Your garments are revealing. It won't bother you to attend a feast half-naked?"

Before Melanthe could answer, a covey of scantily clad sea nymphs began to rise up from one of the floor cutouts. Nereids. The females were all ethereally stunning, and dressed in nothing but short sea-foam skirts.

Each time a nymph emerged from the water and flipped her hair back, she seemed to move in breathless slo-mo.

The Lore held that Nereus had been trapped in Sargasoe either by another power—or by his own agoraphobia. His loneliness had driven him to create a new species of nymph to serve as his concubines and servants.

The females stopped and stared at Thronos, pointing at his wings with admiring looks and giggling flirtatiously behind their hands. Lanthe supposed he could be the first male with wings that they'd ever seen. Not many sky-born Loreans would journey to the bottom of the ocean.

Before Lanthe's eyes, the nymphs' flirtation transformed to brazen desire.

What would Thronos think about their interest? As they raked their gazes over him, she delved into his mind, but found his shields up.

Because he was thinking lustful thoughts about them and didn't want her to know?

Dick. Typical male.

So this is jealousy. How had Thronos lived with it for so long?

She glared daggers at the females. *Back off, nymphos. He's mine.*

Mine?

Mine.

Merely thinking that word was like a gunshot triggering an avalanche of emotion.

She and Thronos had literally been through hell together. *Act like partners* . . . They'd become a team, and the idea of parting from him—or sharing him with nymphs—*hurt.*

When the gaggle of Nereids finally sashayed away, Lanthe said, "Perhaps I should go without this top? Since the nymphs wear none, I don't want to be overdressed."

He drew closer to her. "That is not going to happen."

"You sure? You seemed as taken by them as they were by you." Jealousy *sucked.*

His expression was inscrutable. "Did I? Hmm."

What did that mean?

Thronos changed the subject. "If we've been healed and dressed, have we escaped a fate as 'entertainment'?"

"No, not necessarily." She didn't need to be hissying over Thronos; she needed to be plotting. "This could be part of the setup. Be wary. I've heard that if guests bore him, Nereus smites them down."

As she and Thronos neared the sounds of revelry, she squared her shoulders, feeling like she was going to a court event in Castle Tornin.

Under the reign of Omort the Deathless.

Intrigues, plots, and machinations had been constantly in play. To lower one's guard could mean a stolen power—or death.

She was ready for this, had been honed in a war zone like no other.

Outside an arched doorway, she murmured, "Our goal is to get him to transport us. Just follow my lead. Remember, nothing can get in the way of escape. Okay?"

"I understand." He pinned his wings as much as he could, until they jutted only slightly past his broad shoulders.

"And, Thronos, this sea god considers himself a Casanova. I'm going to have to flirt, and you've got to roll with it."

"Of course," he said, even as he draped an arm over her shoulders. "Lead the way."

They stepped into the hall to find the feast in full swing. The area was resplendent with shimmering shells and garlands of sea grass. Pearls the size of bowling balls adorned the walls and ceilings. There were more floor cutouts revealing the sea; serving nymphs emerged from them with bubble-encased platters and pitchers.

Hundreds of guests were in attendance. Their species ran the Lore gamut from oceanfolk to woodland beings—but none from the air.

In addition to the mercreatures, she saw selkies with their seal-skin coats, tree nymphs, and satyrs. Kobolds and gremlins scurried about underfoot. Lanthe even spotted a no-nosed *fuath*—one among an evil species of water spirits. It had webbed feet, a blond, shaggy mane down its back, and a spiked tail.

They all looked *wasted.*

The dining table was immense, a weighty glass surface laid over coral tubes. The chairs were made of polished driftwood. Smiling Nereids served drinks to guests. Others danced and played instruments.

One blew on a conch to signal their arrival, announcing them as "Melanthe of the Deie Sorceri, Queen of Persuasion, and Prince Thronos of Skye Hall and all Air Territories."

"Welcome, my honored guests!" a male called from the head of the table.

Must be Nereus. He was strikingly tall. His long red hair and beard were streaked through with blond. He wore only the bottom half of a toga, displaying the brawny muscles of his oiled chest, arms, and shoulders. Gold bands encircled his beefy biceps.

His emerald-green eyes roved over her with such intensity that Thronos's arm tightened around her.

Nereus waved them over. On the surface, he seemed in a joyous mood. Yet there was an undercurrent of something in his gaze, something that turned his handsome mien almost creepy.

She could handle creepy. Lanthe cast him a bright smile. *Showtime.*

FORTY-TWO

Once the god had greeted Melanthe and Thronos, all the revelers stared.

Though not as intently as Nereus himself had ogled Thronos's mate!

Out of the corner of her mouth, she said, "Just smile and wave, boys. Smile and wave."

As she was speaking to a single male, Thronos figured this was another cultural reference he didn't understand.

The entire trek here, he'd worked to remain calm because he'd sensed that Melanthe was nearing her breaking point. Perhaps she had been, but no longer.

Now she looked like a knight about to enter a fray: focused, confident, yet aware of the stakes.

"Join me here," Nereus called. At the far end of the table, he pointed to a pair of chairs just to the right of his throne.

Why would he seat them in such a place of honor?

The festivities ramped up once more, the music restarting. The nymphs' song was strangely relaxing, but Thronos knew he needed to stay sharp.

He assessed his environs. Exits: only the doorway and floor cutouts.

Adversaries: unknown. So he'd consider every single being a potential enemy—except the harmless nymphs.

Disadvantages: they were deep beneath the ocean, not exactly his preferred battleground. A week ago, he would have said this was his worst nightmare.

Now he knew that losing his mate was.

As he and Lanthe made their way down the length of the table, Thronos worked to limit his limp—in hostile situations, opponents always scouted for weaknesses. Though his arm and wing had been healed, his old injuries still plagued him.

Other guests were already seated, some Loreans he'd never seen before. Most wore skimpy togas, their heads decorated with wreaths.

Thronos counted himself lucky to be dressed in traditional Vrekener attire.

At some sections of the table, water-filled tanks had been pulled up for the comfort of mercreatures. They drank heavily from shell goblets. Though the tanks were transparent, tentacles groped or . . . probed.

That's just not right. But Thronos showed no reaction.

Farther down the table was even more lechery. Nymphs perched across knees or astraddle males, their hands busy beneath the glass tabletop. The way one nymph was writhing over a satyr's furry lap, Thronos figured the male had to be inside her, concealed by her sea-foam skirt.

Melanthe cast him a look from under her lashes, probably thinking he couldn't handle the iniquity of these scenes. After Inferno, he was growing more accustomed.

As he and Melanthe passed, revelers cast amorous glances at her. How could they not? None of the females here could hold a candle to his. She was a sensual sorceress, blessed with unmatched beauty.

He hadn't seen her dressed like this in ages. Her glossy braided hair shone in the hall's light. Her eyes were sky blue behind her mask.

He pictured her wearing these garments in the Territories. Compared to the bare-breasted Nereids strolling Sargasoe, Melanthe appeared almost demure. Thronos supposed everything was relative—a startling realization for an all-or-nothing thinker to have.

Nereus told the crowd, "Everyone, partake heartily of libations, feast on rich foods, and fill my hall with merriment!"

Melanthe murmured to Thronos, "Libations? Rich foods and merriment? In other words, this is your special kind of hell." She made him sound like a killjoy. She'd *called* him a killjoy.

He could be merry if he wanted. If it was so bloody important to her . . .

Yet with each new detail he registered in this hall, he became more certain that "feasting" would never be a favorite activity. He was used to action, used to searching for Melanthe.

Now he merely wanted to begin a life with her.

Once they'd seated themselves beside Nereus with formal greetings exchanged, the god snapped his fingers and two serving nymphs arrived.

They poured wine for her and ale for Thronos, again showing a perplexing degree of interest in him. Earlier, he'd noted Melanthe's displeasure over this. When he'd felt her delving, he'd shielded his thoughts, wanting her to wonder what *he* was thinking about for once.

"My dear travelers, this is a time of celebration," the sea god explained—to Melanthe's breasts. "Though a foe breached our walls last month, he didn't seek any of my offspring! Only wanted to settle a small debt."

"Felicitations, Nereus," Melanthe said warmly, raising her goblet.

Nereus finally met her gaze. "And now I have new and interesting visitors at my table. My dinner guests have been so boring of late." He stroked his lengthy beard. "I have to execute them just to salvage the night!"

Still smiling serenely, she asked Thronos: *—Now do you understand the stakes?! We've come this far. I don't want to die in Sargasoe.—*

—I'm rolling with it, aren't I? Even though his gaze has scarcely left your chest.— Thronos's wings tensed with the need to lash out against the male, his fangs and claws readying to rend flesh.

As a demon's might. But he bridled his rage.

"A toast is in order!" When Nereus stood, Melanthe coughed, her wide eyes on the god. What was she looking at?

Oh. Nereus was grossly endowed, so much so that when he'd stood, his member had swung like a pendulum beneath the thin fabric.

Melanthe gawked. *—It's his very own kickstand! You could snuggle it like a body pillow.—*

Thronos clenched his jaw. *—Got an eyeful?—*

—And then some! No one will believe me when I tell them about this.—

"To our castaways," Nereus said, with a grand gesture toward them. "May they find *everything* they seek in my domain."

His tone made Thronos's wings twitch, but when Melanthe elbowed him to raise his goblet, he played along. Yet he couldn't shake the feeling of a threat.

—Drink it. Nereus can make you if he wants to.—

Scowling into the cup, Thronos took a drink, and found the ale . . . delectable. He'd downed the goblet's contents before he'd realized it.

At once, a Nereid crossed to him with a pitcher, shoving her breasts into his face as she poured.

Naked breasts in his face, and all he could think was: *I hope Melanthe is seeing this.*

Lanthe would soon have to walk a very fine line.

She needed to intrigue and arouse Nereus, a debauched libertine. And she needed to do that without inflaming Thronos's jealousy beyond his control.

Easy as easy pie; except it wasn't.

When Nereus turned his full attention to her, she felt like footlights had just lit up. "Do you like your Sorceri wine? The vintner assures me it's sweet enough to please a sorceress's tongue."

Lanthe took a sip. "Scrumptious! It's not often that I get to enjoy it away from home."

"How did you come to be upon Sargasoe's coast?"

"Oh, it's such a long and boring tale."

—Boring? The hell it was.—

—Pipe down. I need to concentrate here.—

—Then go on, weave your spell. I could almost pity the sea god.—

She laid her hand over Nereus's. "Instead, let's talk about *you.* It's not every day I get to meet a divinity."

"What would you like to know, sorceress? Am I attracted to your charms? Absolutely. Next question."

She grinned at Nereus, even as she sensed Thronos turning away, refusing to watch their interaction. "What enemy dared to descend on Sargasoe?"

"A vampire," Nereus answered. "You might know him—Lothaire the Enemy of Old. I'd been indebted to him, but no longer!"

"I suspect half of the Lore is in his infamous book of debts." Unfortunately Rydstrom was; he and Sabine had been hunting the diabolical vamp over the last year, figuring a dead leech couldn't collect. As of a few days ago, Lothaire had been an Order prisoner, obviously escaped now.

In the past, Lanthe had considered the Enemy of Old to be one of the sexiest males in the Lore. But now . . .

Her gaze slid over to Thronos. He didn't even act like he was with her, just sipped from his goblet, glowering at his surroundings. *—Easy with the booze, tiger.—*

—Just get this over with.—

She turned back to Nereus, inwardly frowning as a thought occurred. The god had said his foe *Lothaire* had come *last month.* Between Pandemonia and the belly, how much time had she and Thronos lost? Sabine must be out of her head with worry!

Nereus observed, "I wouldn't have expected to see a sorceress and a Vrekener as traveling companions."

"Cheap airfare," she said with a wink.

He smiled, revealing straight, white teeth. A nice smile. Fangs would make it better. "Yes, but I sense that you are a hedonist like myself. And the Vrekener is *not.*"

"Interestingly, he and I share a fated connection."

—*You. Are. Mine.*—

—*Thronos, come on!*— She reached for her wine again.

Nereus waved her statement away. "I detect a great many things about you. You're a sensual connoisseur, are you not?"

She paused over the rim of her goblet.

"From one hedonist to another," he continued, "I find it refreshing when women know their way around the bedroom. A humanoid female who happens to be a connoisseur of males is a most coveted creature in nautical realms."

"Not so much in other realms."

In a bemused tone, Nereus asked, "Why is sex the only endeavor where a male hopes his partner is a rank novice?"

Lanthe couldn't stop the grin that spread over her face. "Why indeed?"

Nereus gazed at her smiling lips for long moments, then leaned in with a get-down-to-business look. "You want to get to know me, but I want us to get to know *each other*." He might as well have cracked his knuckles. "So tell me, what is the favorite pastime of a sorceress like yourself?"

"Drinking wine and watching TV." She illustrated the first with a deep draw from her glass.

"Admirable. And how would you react if you developed gills?" he asked, as if he was ticking off a mental list of questions.

"I'd wonder how to accessorize them."

"Your stance on sharing males?"

"Generally not a fan." The dick was speed-date interviewing her! "I'm high-maintenance, usually more than one male can handle."

Thronos snorted. He might as well have said, "Preach."

"In five years, where do you see yourself?" Nereus asked. "With more than a dozen spawn? Or fewer?"

"Absolutely fewer than a dozen."

"Pets in the bed. Yay or nay?"

"Depends on the pet."

"For instance, a pod of Nereids."

—Yes, Melanthe, tell us. How would you feel?—

—Gold preserve me.— "Do I get a pass?"

Nereus hesitated, then let her off the hook on that one. "If you could meet any Lorean, alive or dead, who would it be?"

Finally a question that wasn't laden with skeevy undertones. In all honesty, she would have liked a chance to talk to her mother.

She wished she could tell Elisabet that she now understood how difficult it must've proved to be the vessel of an Accession, to be banished from her Deie Sorceri family, to leave her home and all she'd known.

To beget a child like Omort.

Lanthe now knew Elisabet had done the best she could. Their father, too.

But Lanthe could never answer honestly. So she glibly said, "Naturally, it would be you, Nereus."

If the god noticed that her mood had changed, he didn't indicate it. Yet she felt Thronos's penetrating eyes on her.

"Flattering sorceress," Nereus fake-chided, but she could tell he was pleased. The questions resumed. "What's your favorite art and music, across all planes and worlds?"

She felt herself relaxing. This was an easy subject for her. "For art, I enjoy the Helvitan masters. The way those vampires use ground bloodroot on a canvas of cured flesh is nothing short of inspiring. For music, I like a mortal genre called *top one hundred.* Or, of course, classical Draiksulian. Those fey know how to compose a jaunty tune. I noticed earlier that your Nereids were playing thirteenth-century sirenades. Lovely."

"They were indeed! I hadn't thought anyone would notice." He narrowed his green eyes. "You are clearly well educated. How are you at trivia?"

Sometimes she would play trivia games with Sabine, Rydstrom, Cadeon, and Holly, going from third wheel to fifth wheel. "I guess I'm not too bad. When I was young, I'd often read to pass the time."

"Then answer this: Who was the leader of the Three-Century Rebellion in the Quondam realm?"

She'd expected a trick question from a trickster god. "Actually, that rebellion was in the *Quandimi* realm. The leader was Bagatur the Battlecrafter."

Nereus gave a robust laugh, his oiled chest rumbling. "I thought I would stump you."

"My sister and I studied ruthless leaders to pick up pointers. We were convinced we would rule the worlds in one great co-queendom."

Out of the corner of her eye, she saw Thronos cast her a quizzical look. *—You know a great many things.—*

—Maybe I earned *my idle pastime of TV viewing? I'm not an empty-headed bimbo. Which is why I didn't take kindly to your suggestion that I study Vrekener history and spend time in contemplation.—*

—Fair enough.—

Nereus too was impressed with her knowledge. "I find you to be quite learned about art and culture and the ways of the world. I've made my decision." His hand landed on her knee. "With your beauty and sexual prowess, you would be ideal for spawning."

He *had* been interviewing her. She glanced down, saw Thronos's arm muscles bulging as he clenched his fists.

—You said you'd roll with this!— She sipped from her goblet to buy time.

Thronos drained his. *—If you'd been alone, would you have received Nereus?—*

—Anatomically, I would have concerns.— So how should she lead Nereus off this spawning path? Bait and switch? Whom could she throw under the bus?

It came to her in a flash. "My dear Nereus, while I'm humbled that you would think of me for such an honor, I fear I can't betray my queen." Morgana was a big girl. She could handle an infatuated god.

"I don't understand."

Lanthe peeled his hand from her knee. "Surely you know of Morgana's interest in you? She constantly rhapsodizes about your prodigious . . . intellect."

"I was not aware of this."

"For me to cross the Queen of Sorceri in this would be a fatal mistake." Actually, crossing her in anything would prove fatal.

Morgana was a queen in two senses. Just as Lanthe was the Queen of Persuasion, with a persuasive ability greater than that of any other, Morgana—the Queen of Sorceri—possessed the ability to control her subjects and their powers absolutely. Plus, she was also the *regent* of the Sorceri.

"Is Morgana so fearsome, then?" Nereus asked.

"We are all fairly much helpless before her." Well, except for her archnemesis La Dorada—who, incidentally, had risen for this Accession. "Taking something Morgana wants would be a treasonous act."

He stroked his beard. "I will have to think on that."

Had Lanthe done enough to deflect him?

An army of Nereids began serving the main course: lobster still in the shell, with sea vegetables as an accompaniment.

"This looks amazing!" Lanthe said, though she would never touch the lobster.

"Enjoy, my winsome sorceress." When Nereus rose, she jerked her gaze upward before she got another eyeful. "Allow me to circulate so that my other guests don't accuse you of monopolizing me. I'm not the only one who considers smiting a solution to social blunders."

"Of course. Take your time." She waved bye-bye, then turned her attention to Thronos, who was presently slouched in his chair, wings slack, regarding everything with a gimlet eye. Probably pondering how to kill a god.

"When Nereus gets back, I'm going to ask him about the portal."

Thronos's knuckles were white on his goblet when he drank.

Under her breath, she said, "I don't have a choice in this. I refuse to die here, and I refuse to be trapped as some spawner beneath the ocean. I'm doing the best I can in a honey/vinegar situation."

"I know this!" Thronos exhaled, then said in a lower tone, "I know. And that was clever to throw Morgana into the mix."

"Let's just hope it works."

Appearing to shake away the worst of his ire, Thronos raised his goblet before her. "Taste this ale." He seemed almost buzzed. "It's delicious."

She took a sip from his cup, then handed it back with a grimace. "Are you crazy?"

"What?" He downed a large gulp.

"That's demon brew." Loved by demons and hated by most others in the Lore.

He swallowed loudly, nearly choking on the liquid. He must know that this drink left one steadily tipsy, until abrupt drunkenness hit like a sledgehammer.

"Why would they serve me demon brew?" he demanded.

Lanthe gave him a *bless your heart* look.

He bit out a harsh laugh. "So the evidence continues to mount? And Nïx wants to know if it *matters* that we might be demons."

"How much have you had, Thronos?"

"Three or so goblets."

"Three? You're going to be tanked." Though she'd only had a little more than a goblet of wine, she would taper off, just in case.

He gazed at her mouth, his lids heavier. "My impending drunkenness should please you, no?"

"You've misunderstood me. I don't care if *you* drink or not; I just don't want you to tell *me* not to. But tonight, I'll take it easy, so one of us is on guard."

A Nereid squeezed between them to fill his goblet. The female all but pressed her voluptuous breasts in his face, before traipsing off.

Even though he was buzzed, he kept his mind blocked.

As her glare followed the Nereid, Lanthe told him, "If she shoved her breasts any closer to your ear, I believe you could've heard the ocean."

"Compared to the belly of the beast, this situation is a vast improvement," he said nonchalantly.

She turned her glare on him. "Because the belly of the beast lacked topless nymphs? Talk to management."

"You're *jealous.*" He leaned in closer, the electricity between them sparking. "I knew I was growing on you." With a crooked grin, he said, "After all, you loved hallucinated sex acts with me."

Had she ever! She sipped her wine to cover her reaction to him.

When she licked her lip, Thronos muttered, "Lucky lip."

Lanthe's fine line had just gotten finer. The brew would hit Thronos soon. "You need to eat something." She pointed to his platter of lobster. "A full stomach might forestall some of the effects."

He had to be starving, but he was clearly at a loss. "Crustaceans are not something I've much experience with. What I wouldn't give for a nice haunch of venison." He looked around as if to see how others were handling their lobsters. The mercreatures ate the entire thing, including the shell, probably throwing up that part later. He turned back to her. "I've got nothing."

With a look of commiseration, she started on the salad of seaweed, sea lettuce, and kelp. She found it surprisingly tasty.

Once Nereus returned, Thronos turned surly straightaway.

The god noticed. "You show no interest in my lovely nymphs?"

"Melanthe is my mate," Thronos said with unmistakable pride. "I have interest in only one female."

Nereus's gaze was shrewd. "Ah, but does the interest run both ways? Well, sorceress? Are you as besotted with the Vrekener as he is with you?"

I might be falling for him.

But the next step in their relationship was her accompanying him to Skye Hall, an all-in scenario. Going with him to heaven would be the craziest thing she'd ever done. Yet as she peered over at him, she realized that wasn't true.

Letting this one go might be.

How proud Thronos had sounded when he'd said, "Melanthe is my mate," declaring interest only in her. For years, she'd imagined what it would be like having a male to prize her and hold her hand in public. To take her to court events.

Instead of into the shadows for whispered assignations.

Thronos would never wince at his watch, claiming, "Got a really early morning tomorrow, sweet." He would never, ever blaze.

The situation with him—with their families and factions—was anything but ideal. Yet Thronos, the man, was getting there.

"We're taking it day by day," she finally told the god, earning a black look from Thronos. "So, let's get back to you." Resting her chin on her hand, she gazed at Nereus with—seemingly—utter absorption. "Won't you tell me about the Marianas Trench siege? That was supposed to have been a doozy!"

She planned to go in for the kill soon. Would Nereus let them leave immediately? Or make them wait till after the feast? She wanted to get Thronos out of here as soon as possible, before the brew hit him.

"I remember that one," Nereus began. "I was only a millennium or two in age. . . ."

Once he'd recounted the tale, she sighed, "The stuff of legend. Nereus, your hospitality has been as fabulous as your spectacular realm. I can't wait to tell my fellow Sorceri all about you, as well as my friends among the witches and Valkyrie. The Vertas alliance will know of your generosity. . . ." She trailed off, frowning at a nearby wine pourer.

The nymph was giving Thronos another assessing glance.

No, not *assessing*. Something darker.

Lanthe gazed around, saw other nymphs with the same expression. They looked . . . proprietary.

As if they already owned him.

—Stop drinking, Thronos. We might be in trouble.—

—This ale is hitting me hard, Melanthe.— Even telepathically, his words were slurred.

When fogginess overtook her as well, she knew it wasn't only the demon brew affecting him. *—I need you to fight it.—*

At once, she scented blood. He was digging his claws into his palms. But it was a losing proposition.

She swung her head around at Nereus, and almost toppled out of her chair. "What are you doing?" she snapped, her words sounding far away. The Nereids weren't the only ones looking proprietary.

As her head lolled, she heard Thronos murmur aloud, "Lanthe?"

Black dots swirled at the edges of her vision. The last thing she saw was Nereus throwing back his head to give a loud laugh.

And then nothing.

FORTY-THREE

Lanthe woke in a cavernous chamber, atop a bed with a shell canopy.

"Where am I?" she asked groggily. "What happened?"

She was having a hard time marshaling her thoughts, felt like she was riding waves—or beset by that spinning-bed feeling. Had she drunk that much wine? Had she wandered into the wrong room, then passed out fully dressed?

She wished she could say that had never happened. But then, Lanthe liked her wine. So where was Thronos?

With bleary eyes, she regarded the room. Along one wall, a waterfall cascaded; scenes from under the sea played across the surface, like a TV.

Wait, was that Nereus crossing toward her?

Everything came crashing back. She and Thronos had either been drugged or bespelled!

"You're in my private chambers, sorceress." Nereus was leering like a kraken about to take his sacrifice. As he stalked closer, his shaft swayed under his filmy toga.

"I must have accidentally found my way in here," she said to give him an out, though she knew he wasn't about to take it.

A giggle sounded from beneath her.

"What the—"

Oh, for the love of gold! Lanthe wasn't atop a mattress; she was atop a collection of curvy Nereids. They lay on their bellies, tightly nestled together.

Did Nereus sleep on them? *Make love* atop them?

She scrambled to her feet. "Are you kidding me?" she cried, trying to shake off whatever the god had roofied her with. "I need to get back to Thronos. He's going to be wondering where I am." When he woke. *Wherever* he woke.

Nereus kept advancing on her. She backed away from him, darting a glance out the round underwater window to her left: no help there. She was about to turn from it—until she heard a muffled shriek that vibrated the glass.

Chills broke out on her skin as she scanned the depths. A field of glittering gems drew her gaze. Her lips parted with shock.

Like the rays of the sun, the gems radiated out from a female . . . who was shackled to an anchor at the bottom of the ocean.

Her long black hair streamed across her naked body and floated above her head. The strands were coated in phosphorescence, illuminating her pale, corpselike face, her haunted violet eyes.

It was the queen of the Valkyrie, Furie, so named because she was part Fury—a fire-winged Arch-Fury. Rumor held that she'd been captured by the old vampire king, who'd cursed her to this existence, trapped alive underwater, hidden from her Valkyrie sisters and allies.

As a Lorean, Furie would drown every few minutes before her immortality revived her; she'd been missing for more than fifty years. Five decades of breathing water into her lungs.

Lanthe had almost drowned earlier—once—and it had been horrifying.

The Valkyrie locked eyes with her. Furie's violet gaze was filled with madness—but also *blankness.* As if she couldn't comprehend where she was or how she'd gotten here.

Flames ignited behind her—Furie's unique fire wings splaying.

Only to be extinguished.

Lanthe had been wrong. There *was* another sky-born here at the bottom of the ocean.

Realization dawned. As with the other realms, Nïx had wanted Lanthe here. She was the planted spy, conducting Valkyrie recon.

"Do you like my new acquisition?" Nereus asked, as if he'd just pointed out a vase. "I found her along the ocean bed."

Lanthe turned to him. "Truly an original," she managed to say with Sabine's composure. "But really, I need to get back to Thronos."

"He's occupied at the moment. You'll remain with me."

The god's ominous tone filled her with fear. "Nereus, I don't want this."

"Of course you do. You think I cannot sense such a thing?"

"If you've sensed anything, it was my need for Thronos."

"A shame he doesn't return it."

She straightened. "What does that mean? I know he does. He has for centuries."

"He's with Nereids right now."

"That's not possible."

"They're seducing him as we speak. For those centuries, how many times has he prayed to be free of the bonds of matehood? To collect his own sexual experiences, as you have? I'm merely answering a prayer."

Nereus and his games. He'd known Lanthe and Thronos's story all along.

"Here in Sargasoe, matehood holds no sway. The Nereids now exude your scent. His body and instinct are as free as if he'd never met you."

So, physically Thronos could stray. That didn't mean he would. In Feveris, he'd told her he would be true to her.

Except Feveris wasn't real. *You said so yourself, Lanthe.* Still . . . "He won't go through with it."

"No one has ever resisted them."

The god didn't understand; if there was any male out there who would prove loyal, it was Thronos. He was upstanding, principled, and forthright. He made tough choices. He was going to try to rehabilitate his evil brother, for gold's sake!

Lanthe straightened her mask. Sorceri were gamblers. She would bet on Thronos to be, well, *Thronos.* "Care to make a wager on that score?"

Nereus raised his red brows. "I would. If the Vrekener succumbs to their considerable charms, you will spend the night with me. Willingly and lustily."

"And if he doesn't?"

"I will release both of you, giving you use of Sargasoe's portal to travel wherever you choose."

"How will we know?" she asked.

Nereus waved a hand, and a new scene played on the waterfall.

Lanthe could see Thronos lying on a bed, much like the one in which she'd woken—with Nereids for a mattress. He was slowly coming to.

A dozen more nymphs loomed over him. The sea-foam skirts they'd worn at the feast had disappeared. Their made-for-sex bodies were completely unclothed, their eyes lambent with desire.

Naked nymphs in obvious heat surrounded Lanthe's male.

This situation would be any man's most fevered fantasy—yet Thronos looked agitated. "Where's Melanthe?" In the face of such splendor, his first thought was of her.

Because he's mine.

He pushed them away, and her heart soared. He was so handsome, so strong. So . . . good.

"I'll take your bet," Lanthe told the god in a smug tone.

Nereus's smile was unctuous. "Then we have a pact, sorceress."

Yet before Thronos could reach the door, the nymphs fell upon him. Pale hands roamed all over his body, stroking his wings, his chest, his horns, their touch seeming to daze him. "I just want to find . . . it's important to find her," he murmured.

"Find *us,*" they purred, as if with one voice. "We desire you so deeply."

Over her shoulder, Lanthe snapped, "They're bespelling him! That wasn't part of the deal!"

Nereus shrugged. "A worthy male, one who intends absolute fidelity, could shake off their spell. Otherwise he'll succumb, and once he does, he'll never want to leave. In fact, he'll go into a murderous rage if separated from his harem."

Lanthe's stomach lurched as the females led Thronos back to the bed, ripping off his shirt on the way.

"Where is she?" he demanded, but his resistance faltered with each expert caress.

"She doesn't want you," they chorused, coaxing him to lie back. "Not like we do."

I do! Faced with losing him, Lanthe was rocked by a yawning loss. She'd already been having possessive feelings toward Thronos, but now . . .

I want him so much.

Since she could remember, she'd pined for a male who would adore her above all things. Yes, there was a vicious history between her and Thronos, but she'd believed he would eventually fall in love with her.

True love. Which was more than she could say about any other male she'd met in her lifetime. . . .

Off went his boots. "All your life, you've pursued and endured," the Nereids murmured, "while she enjoyed other males. You longed for the freedom to choose who you desired. Now you can, but only here, where there's no such thing as matehood."

How could he resist that reasoning? He'd felt "cuckolded." He'd *tried* to stray. And now in this realm, he was finally free to.

No longer was Lanthe his bitter necessity.

Just days ago, he'd told her she was lacking, that he would never desire someone like her.

But things *had* changed between them. He'd told her he wanted *everything* from her. Maybe if she'd given him any kind of encouragement, any definitive signal that her own feelings had changed, he would've stayed faithful.

When one of the Nereids began undoing Thronos's pants—with her teeth—Lanthe was staggered by the tears spilling from her eyes. "Let me go to him and stop this. Please, Nereus!"

His mien darkened, growing more piscine. She heard doors shutting and locking to prevent her escape.

Even after the nymphs had stripped Thronos naked, he gave one last struggle, so they deepened their spells to knock him out completely.

One nymph told another, "He'll wake in my mouth."

Then it was as good as done. No male alive could wake to a nymph blow-job and deny the female.

Crying, sick, Lanthe turned her back on the scene. *I should've locked Thronos down. I should've fought for him when I had the chance.*

Now she would have to face his murderous wrath when she tried to steal him back from the nymphs.

If she somehow could, would Thronos even want her after she bedded Nereus?

"My dear sorceress, if it's any consolation"—Nereus patted the "bed" by his side—"he resisted them longer than any other male I've seen."

She was too heartbroken to react much to her own predicament. The overly endowed god wasn't known to be a gentle lover.

She wanted to blame Thronos for her situation, but of course she couldn't. She was responsible for her fate. If she'd given him any sign . . .

With leaden feet, she crossed to Nereus—

A bellow sounded.

She whirled toward the waterfall screen, saw Thronos shoving away Nereids, sending them flying across the room. "Where's my mate?" he yelled, wings flaring, his naked body magnificent. "Begone from me, you foul witches!"

She smiled through new tears, cheering him as he yanked his pants on. Snatching up his clothes, he stormed away—from a carnal paradise.

For me.

She beamed with pride. By denying those nymphs, he'd gone against his instincts—and his ego.

Nereus released a stunned breath. "Amazing. Go to your Vrekener with my blessing." In the distance, doors began to clang, unlocking for her. "I'm sure you can sense the location of Sargasoe's portal." Giving her a salacious grin, he added, "But you have no idea what you're missing."

"Uh, thank you. We'll be off."

"And by the way"—out of thin air, he produced a lock of shining black hair, scenting it—"tell Nïx that she asks much. Quelling a tsunami is no mean task."

Whatever. "Will do, Nereus, will do," she assured him, sprinting for the door.

FORTY-FOUR

What did I do with them?

Thronos recalled little of what had happened in that room, just knew he'd woken with no clothes on and naked Nereids kissing his body—while more had been layered beneath him.

"Melanthe!" he bellowed as he strode down the corridor, hastily dressing as he went.

Those nymphs had whispered that there was no matehood in Nereus's realm. Thronos would be free to partake—as he'd wanted to for ages.

But that had been before.

I was unfaithful.

He'd gotten drunk on demon brew, then betrayed his lovely, brave, intelligent mate. All of his laws, all of his righteousness, all of the grief he'd given her about her behavior—and he was the one who fell.

How could he tell her?

If he'd been seduced by nymphs, then what in the hell was happening to her? Was Nereus ravishing her? *If the god touches her* . . . "Melanthe!" His fear for her, his blind panic, burned away much of his inebriation. "Answer me!"

He heard, "I'm here!" just before he saw her speeding around a corner.

She ran for him, face ecstatic. *My incomparable mate.* So bloody beautiful.

"We're free, Thronos! We can leave now."

He gave a curt nod, looping his arm over her shoulder. "I want to get far away from this wretched place."

"The portal's near." She led him down a shadowy passageway.

As they hastened along it, sweat beaded on his lip. *What did I do?* "Where were you?" he asked.

"Uh, looking for you."

"Nereus didn't hurt you?"

"No, he kept his hands to himself."

You're going to have to tell her. The only thing worse than his infidelity would be hiding it. How would she react?

At the end of the corridor was the portal. Living coral framed the rippling surface.

"What's wrong with you?" she asked. "I can all but hear you grinding your molars to dust. We're here, we're finally here."

"Melanthe, my instinct tells me to do anything I can to get you to the Skye." Only a coward would confess afterward. "But I must be honest with you."

"What is it?"

He wanted to rail at himself, to tear at his hair. His fist shot out, connected with the wall. Stone cracked, and a trickle of water seeped through it. "Lanthe, I . . . I was unfaithful to you."

She raised her brows. "With whom?"

"Nereids."

"Plural?" She seemed to be vibrating with some kind of tension.

"Yes."

"I thought you couldn't stray," she pointed out.

"They smelled like you."

"And what did you do to them?"

"I was . . . drunk." An excuse he'd never expected to give, an excuse that shamed him. "I tried to fight off the effects, but at one point I lost consciousness. I woke unclothed." He cleared his throat. "With their mouths upon me. I don't know what I did or how long I was out."

"You look sick about this."

"I am! I want only *you.* It will always be this way." He scrubbed his hand over his face. "I don't understand how this could happen. If you knew how badly I desire you . . ."

"And you decided to confess this to me now?"

"I want you to come to my home. But I won't trick you to get you there."

"I know about the Nereids." She looked unperturbed. "Nereus set it up so that I could see all of it."

"But you're not . . . upset? You don't even care, do you? What would it take to make you give a damn?"

"They bespelled you, and you still didn't do anything. You're the first male ever to shake off their magics."

That relieved some of his guilt, but his chest felt hollow at her lack of reaction. She'd witnessed those nymphs seducing him; if he'd ever *seen* a male's hands on her naked body, it would have annihilated him. "You suffer no jealousy?" She might as well have sunk a sword into him. "Maybe I should've indulged them!"

She went up on her toes and grabbed his face. "When I thought you were going to succumb, I cried."

After all the times he would've expected her to cry in the last week? Even in the belly of the beast, she'd somehow stemmed her tears. "You cried over me?" he asked gruffly.

She nodded. "And not just because of the bet I'd made with Nereus."

"What are you speaking of?"

"I bet Nereus that you couldn't be seduced. If I won, we'd go free. If I lost, he'd bed *me.*"

Nereus would've taken my mate this very night! But Thronos had proved stronger than even the Nereids' spells, and now he and Lanthe would be rewarded.

He seized her hands. "Then come with me to the Skye."

She bit her bottom lip. "We could go to Rothkalina."

"I need to return home to get something settled with Aristo. Changes must be made."

"You still plan to rehab him?" She drew away.

He reluctantly released her. "I told you. I will make him see reason. You will help me. Once he understands what we have together, what we've overcome, he'll have to conclude that his views are mistaken."

"Why do you think I won't use my power for ill while I'm up there?"

Earlier, he'd thought of the solution. "I have ways."

"Tell me, Thronos."

"I'm going to trust you *not* to. I'm going to take you fully empowered to my home, because I trust you."

Clever, clever demon.

Of all the things he could've said . . .

"You are trusting me to deal with my brother," he told her. "I'm trusting you to use your sorcery in a way we both can live with."

"That's your plan?"

He lifted his chin. "That's my plan. I *know* you, Melanthe. You're a good person."

"Lower your voice!" Her eyes darted. "If that got out . . ."

"Come, take this step with me."

"You think King Aristo will let me stay empowered in the Skye?"

He quirked his brow. "If anyone tries anything, then I'm sure you can persuade them not to."

"You're giving me leave to protect myself?"

"I know you won't harm anyone unless you must do it in self-defense."

Was this a good-with-the-bad situation? If a sorceress wanted a man who would stay faithful even when bespelled and accosted by nymphs, then she had to support that man even when he believed he could rehab his douchelord brother.

But Lanthe and Thronos had so many issues unsettled between them. She didn't see how these things could be improved in the realm of the Vrekeners. To her, going there would be like going into the belly of the beast. Having actually *been* in the belly of the beast, she didn't think this lightly.

He curled his finger under her chin. "In Pandemonia, you accused me of wanting something from you. I do. The opportunity to protect you and treasure you." She parted her lips to argue, but he stopped her. "Not only because of my instinct."

"I'd like to believe that. I would. But . . ."

"Do you want to know what Nïx's advice was concerning you? One sentence: 'Before Melanthe was this, she was that.' I figured it out two worlds ago."

"Tell me."

"Before you were my enemy, you were my best friend."

Just as it had centuries ago, her heart ached with yearning.

"You still are," he told her. "And *that* is why I want you to come with me."

He was nothing like Felix—or most other males she'd met.

Thronos was a good man. He was *her* man.

Hadn't she wished for the opportunity to give him encouragement? She replayed the yawning loss she'd felt when she'd thought he would succumb. Now, she needed to say something, anything, but her thoughts were tangled.

He must have sensed she was on the ropes. He inched closer to her. "When we were children, we made big plans in that meadow, expecting every happiness to follow. I want to look back one day and say that our plans went awry for only the first five hundred years, but not for the following millennia. Lanthe, if you come with me, I'll want to wed you. This very day."

Marry him today? The word *cleave* had another meaning. *To bind.*

In a flash, she understood: on this night, she would either separate from Thronos or bind her life to his.

If she went with him, she would be all-in, committed to him, to them. She would do her damnedest to make a future with Thronos.

But could she abide Skye Hall? Could she bring her family around? And survive his?

He released her and moved to the edge of the portal, the threshold of something more, and awaited her.

She swallowed. All-in?

With his eyes gone molten silver, Thronos Talos—a fierce, sensual demon—offered his hand, inviting Lanthe to her idea of hell, to become his bride.

Like a fool in love . . .

She took it.

FORTY-FIVE

It was night in the Skye.

With Thronos leading the way through the portal, he and Lanthe stepped onto a cobblestone path in the Air Territories. He didn't release her hand.

She'd asked him to go first—after all, she hadn't had the best run of luck with portal directions. And she had to admit she still might be conflicted about this on some level.

Though she'd never been so high up, her gaze was drawn even higher. The stars were sparkling brilliantly, arcing above them like a diadem. "Wow."

"That's how I feel right now." He squeezed her hand.

She lowered her face to behold just as wondrous a sight: Thronos smiling down at her with starlight reflecting in his eyes.

Just like that, the apprehension she'd felt at crossing that threshold began to fade.

When she could drag her attention away from him, she observed her surroundings with interest. They were in a shallow, sandy vale, with treeless mounts and hills rising up on all sides. White, sun-bleached buildings covered those heights, connected squares or rectangles of various sizes—like one might see on a cliffside along the Mediterranean.

Bordering the structures were cobblestone streets and walkways, all seeming to be straight and narrow, all leading down to this clearing.

"What do you think?" he asked.

"It's certainly . . . uniform." And monochromatic. "How far are we from the edge of the island?" She'd expected her fear of heights would have kicked in by now, but she felt no different than if she were standing on terra firma.

"We're about in the center."

"It truly is warm."

"The climate extends for miles around the Territories."

"Where is everyone?" Not a soul could be seen.

"I believe it's the middle of the night. Morning comes very early here." He pointed toward the largest building in the area, one elevated above all the rest. "That's Skye Hall."

"I never knew it was an actual hall." The seat of Vrekener power.

The grand edifice was the only building with the slightest ornamentation; Corinthian columns fronted it, but like all the others, it apparently had no roof. What might be this island's only trees grew around it.

"The building was constructed against a ridge. The assembly rooms front the elevation, while the royal residence is above it."

After all she and Thronos had been through, the prospect of entering that hall and facing Aristo left her queasy. "Can we wait till tomorrow to talk with him?"

"Yes. We must be wed first," Thronos said decisively.

Shit just got real.

"He might not even be in residence," Thronos pointed out. "He often travels."

Busy, busy Aristo. *Wonder what he's up to now* . . . "Okay, then, show me your digs." Even if there was some kind of air mojo up here, she was getting dizzy from the altitude, having gone from miles below sea level to miles above it.

"Don't know what digs are, Melanthe."

"Where's your place?"

"*Our* place." She knew the exact moment when he comprehended he was truly going to claim her—and soon. He swallowed, his Adam's apple bobbing, his piercing gaze sweeping over her body—as if he was deciding what he wanted to do with it first. He didn't block his thoughts, but she didn't delve.

In a huskier voice, he said, "We live there." With his free hand, he pointed out another structure high on a cliffside, at the edge of the village. Though unconnected to the other structures, it wasn't more than a hundred yards or so from them.

"Hmm." They started toward it.

"*Hmm* what?"

"I guess I was expecting a palace or something. *Our* roofless house is really close to other roofless houses, huh?" *How 'bout those wedding night sex acoustics?*

"We're not without problems in our kingdom, Lanthe. We live immortal lives, yet our lands are finite. We face overpopulation."

Interesting. "When we talk to Aristo, you can tell him we're going to go found a Vrekener offshoot colony in a different realm. We'll call it *LantheLand.*"

"As appealing as LantheLand sounds, I don't see it happening. The Vrekeners will always live together. Our unity is our strength." Thronos stopped to gaze down at her. "So eager to leave? When you just got here?"

"I fear things won't turn out with your brother as you expect them to."

"Maybe I don't expect a resolution. Maybe I just need to say I tried."

That she could accept. She nodded, and he continued leading her toward . . . *their* home.

On the way, he pointed out a trio of obelisks of differing heights. "I learned to fly by dropping from those columns—the smallest one when I was but two or so."

She imagined him as a toddler, fearlessly leaping into a parent's arms, wearing the determined expression she knew so well; maybe that look had been born there. His wings would probably have been oversized for his little body. "I'll bet you were absolutely adorable." A thought struck her. "Does your mother still live?"

"Most Vrekeners don't go on without their mates."

So Sabine had essentially killed *both* of his parents. Were Lanthe and Thronos kidding themselves?

He swiftly changed the subject. "On the other side of Skye Hall is the bastion, an area where we eat and socialize. It used to be a prison, but we had to reclaim the space."

"Vrekeners socialize?"

"Of course. There's a gathering hall on each island."

"How does that work, if you can't drink or gamble? I'm guessing dancing is out?"

"We have sporting events and contests. Those of a more studious bent gather to read and debate."

Bully. When all the dust settled, Lanthe would be portaling to Rothkalina weekly, just to tie one on. She'd force Thronos to come with her. "I'm sure your people will be overjoyed to have someone like me living among them."

"At first they might not know what to think. But they'll come to see you as I have. It will happen." His utter certainty reassured her, his confidence proving contagious.

They started up a steep walkway with a series of switchbacks. "I'm surprised you guys bother with steps."

"We do have Sorceri who live here. And injuries occasionally happen to the wings of the young."

A very generous way of putting the latter. He was doing everything possible to make her comfortable.

"How many islands are there? How many Vrekeners?"

"Tens and tens of thousands are spread over one hundred and seventy islands."

She'd had no idea there were so many of them. But it made sense that an immortal faction would thrive in a hidden realm.

"I'll take you over the entire kingdom in the coming days," he said as they reached the landing in front of his—*their*—place. The wooden door was of simple construction, with a rustic latch and no lock. He opened it, ushering her inside.

Filled with curiosity about the man he'd become, she took in details. The best word to describe the area: spartan. The few pieces of furniture were no-frills—a table with a couple of backless benches, additional benches in a sitting area. Just as with the rest of the realm, there was no color.

And no freaking roof. This lack had looked weird from the outside but was even weirder from within. The structure felt like a dollhouse, as if they were being watched from above. No wonder Vrekeners were so concerned with private behavior.

Thronos led her along a hallway, past a study lined with books; she decided to come back later and investigate at her leisure. With limited space in his home, every tome he kept must be important.

"Where's the kitchen?"

"We eat in the bastion."

"So no servants?"

"Not in the Skye."

Ugh.

Past a surprisingly modern-looking bathroom was a spacious bedroom, with just a nightstand, a chest of drawers, and an enormous bed. The mattress was larger than a king-size, probably because of wingspan considerations.

When her steps teetered, he grabbed her elbow.

"Lanthe?"

"Sorry. I'm light-headed after coming from the bottom of the ocean."

"You should lie down." He led her to the bed.

She sat at the edge. "In the legendary Bed of Troth?" It'd been crafted of a dark wood and looked sturdy. In a head-on collision with a truck, this bed would dominate. The headboard and footboard were carved with mysterious Vrekener markings. "So this is where we'll do the deed?"

As if the words were pulled from him, he said, "I will wait until you feel better. I've waited this long."

Since he'd been a teenager. Lifetimes of curiosity and building lust.

"Thronos, I'll be fine if you give me a few minutes to get used to the altitude."

She could hear his pulse accelerate as he said, "So tonight, we'll . . ."

All in, Lanthe? Accompanying him to heaven meant marriage. Marriage meant possible pregnancy.

Which was a lot for any sorceress to have to decide in one night. Was she really going to take this step?

She'd told him that if he ever gave her a loving expression like the one that Volar had sported, she'd consider giving it up.

She regarded his face and found herself saying, "I figure I'll go ahead and claim you."

He grinned. "Then I need to retrieve something from the Hall. I'll be right back. Make yourself at home—because it is your home." At the doorway, he turned back. "I'm reluctant to let you out my sight. I feel like I should be chasing you, or we should be saving each other from some calamity."

"I'll be here waiting for you." When he exited with a look of longing, she reclined to gaze at the stars. *I'm in Thronos's bed.*

Weird.

How many times had he lain here and thought of her? He'd told her he'd dreamed of her for hundreds of thousands of nights. How many of those times had been in this bed?

Now she began to get nervous. Because he was a virgin (her first and only virgin), she felt even more pressure to make this unforgettable.

But how could the reality possibly measure up to five hundred years of fantasy?

FORTY-SIX

Thronos was tempted to fly to the Hall, but didn't want to deal with that grinding pain right now. So he ran, withstanding a lesser agony in his leg.

He was actually going to claim Melanthe tonight! He'd been so close in Feveris—or in his hallucination—yet then he'd had that bliss wrenched away from him.

He couldn't shake the feeling that something would befall them before he could return to her. He resolved to avoid Aristo. Though his brother might be away, Thronos entered the Hall quietly.

He passed the sorcery power vault and the sacred scribe's room, where the extensive list of offendments was kept. This close to the hallowed writings, he experienced a twinge of guilt for all the things he'd done with Melanthe before they'd been wed.

Some things couldn't be helped. They would marry this night, a proper wedding.

He headed toward his family's storage room. Inside, he combed through boxes of ancient mementos and books. By the time he'd located the specific case he sought, in the most out-of-the-way spot, he was covered in dust.

Whoever had organized this closet clearly hadn't thought Thronos would *ever* get married.

Case in hand, he hastened back to his mate. Though pain coursed up his leg, he found himself growing hard in anticipation of this night. He could feel his horns straightening, becoming more sensitive—

He froze. Had the distinct impression of being watched. Rubbing the back of his neck, he turned and scanned the shadows. Spied nothing.

Surely any Vrekener or Sorceri ward drifting about would hail him, and no one else could find this place.

He shrugged off his disquiet by the time he'd reached the house. He swallowed nervously as he unlatched their front door. When he passed the bathroom, he saw her mesh top hanging beside the shower, with her skirt and hose folded atop a hamper. Her blue mask dangled from a towel hook.

Seeing her things here gratified him to a staggering degree.

She'd showered. Should he? Another delay. He glanced down at himself, at the dust.

With an impatient curse, he set down the case, ripping off his garments. Under the water, he rested his head and hands against the wall. Though the temperature was ice cold, it did nothing to diminish his erection.

He recalled his mate's tightness . . . would he last long enough even to get inside her? Would he hurt her?

She'd taught him how to get her ready. He bit off his foreclaws. Thinking better of it, he took the next ones over as well.

When he returned to the bedroom, he had a towel wrapped around his hips and the case at the ready.

His heart stuttered a beat. She was kneeling at the end of the bed, running the pads of her fingers over the footboard. She wore her long shining hair loose, and she'd donned one of his shirts, rolling the sleeves up to her wrists. The sight of her clad in something that belonged to him affected him in inexplicable ways, made him want to squeeze her in his wings, to rub his horns all over her trembling body.

Mine, all mine.

Melanthe in his bed, awaiting him. She was *too* beautiful.

He watched her gaze leisurely take in his face, his chest, lower. . . . She parted her lips on a sigh, and her little tongue wetted them. *Gods almighty.*

Her eyes glittered with appreciation—for him.

She mightn't even be real. Feveris hadn't been, nor those time loops.

Soon he'd wake from slumber, aching for her, greeted by his customary pain—always more excruciating in the morning. He would clench his fists, renewing his determination, resuming his search. . . .

With a grin, she waved at his blatant erection behind the towel. "Are you doing your Nereus impression?"

A laugh escaped him before he even realized it. "You really are here." Her mischievous smile got him tied up in knots, always had. "I never thought I'd see you in this bed."

"That makes two of us." She had removed her prized necklace, setting it on his nightstand. On *their* nightstand. "By the way, the hot water's broken."

"Oh?" Probably not a good time to tell her that there was never any hot water for showers.

"So what's in the case?"

He sat beside her, opening it to reveal the claiming sheet sewn for him ages ago. The material carried the pleasant scent of preserving herbs.

She unfolded it with a frown. "This is what you had to retrieve? It won't be big enough for your bed."

"We're expected to keep that sheet between us. It's tradition."

"How is that going to work . . . ?" She trailed off when she found the stitched opening in the middle of the material. "Well, how kinky. But isn't this supposed to be rubber?" She poked her forefinger through the gap, waggling her eyebrows at him.

He blinked at her. "Why would it be rubber?"

She sighed. "So many things I'll have to teach you. I'm all for tradition, but do you really want something between us?"

He pulled her onto his lap, wrapping his arms around her. "Somehow we managed to get to this bed before sleeping together. I want to do this right. A proper marriage."

"This claiming business is important to you, huh?"

"It is." His forehead rested against hers. "But, Melanthe, you must be certain of this. We haven't been together for long. And while I can't have others—obviously wouldn't even if I could—you could find someone else." He began stroking one of her supple thighs. "If we take this step, you'll have to pick me over all the men you'll meet in your eternal life. Because I won't ever let you go." *As if I would now . . .*

She laid her silken hands on his face. "I picked you over all others when I walked through that portal with you. I want to be *your* wife."

His heart felt too big for his chest. "My wife." He dipped down, rubbing the base of one horn up and down her neck. *Mine.* She had to know he was marking her with his scent.

When she tilted her head away to give him more access, to let him do as his instinct commanded, he wanted to kiss her until her little toes curled.

"Just one last consideration," she murmured absently. "I'm probably not even in season anymore, right? We could've been in the belly of the beast for weeks."

He raised his head. "Though I'd wanted to impregnate you so you'd feel bound to me, I can't lie. I scent you're in season. It's waned, but still there."

"Then our already slim odds waned too." She pressed her lips to his neck, then his jawline, then to the corner of his mouth. "You amaze me, Thronos. I wonder if I'll ever get used to your honesty."

"You're going to have to. Because I'm about to marry you." Season or not, she still wanted this. He turned to slant his mouth over hers.

Lanthe's lips parted, welcoming his tongue as it slipped toward hers. She loved how leisurely he took their kisses, working the slow build—despite the tension in his massive body.

Despite the scorching hardness of his shaft beneath her ass.

As they tangled tongues, he reached higher between her thighs, his fingers trailing upward. There was something so erotic about wearing his shirt, his hand moving unseen beneath the fabric.

Against her lips, he rasped, "Need to get you ready."

Seeing his gorgeous physique in that towel had already primed her pump. But who was she to disappoint the Vrekener? "I told you: I look at your body and mine grows wet for it. Anything else will be a bonus." She spread her thighs for him.

He took the invitation, gently cupping her sex, pressing the heel of his hand against her sensitive clitoris.

With his other hand he started to rub her stiffened nipples, one, then the other.

Lightly pinching. Thumbing the very tip. Rolling each peak between his fingers . . .

When he dipped down to suckle her through the fabric, she gasped, threading her fingers in his damp hair. With each pull of his lips, she arched to him for more.

"Love suckling you. Could do it for hours."

She was moaning when he moved to her other nipple, his breaths hot against the sensitive tip. As he sucked, he eased his finger inside her, groaning to find her so aroused.

The electricity that always sparked between them grew like a lightning storm. His finger was just a tease, a precursor to the delight she'd almost experienced with Thronos before—when he'd started to wedge his huge shaft into her.

At the thought, she rocked to meet his thrusting finger, her ass rubbing over the hardness she'd soon enjoy.

He grated, "This will be over before it starts."

She was ready for him. She cupped the back of his neck. "Then get inside me. Quick, before something interrupts our wedding."

His brows shot up. "My thoughts exactly." He moved her from his lap, laying her back on the bed. Once he'd stripped her of the shirt, he dropped his towel, revealing that mouthwatering erection.

She took her time admiring all seven feet of his warrior's body. His wings were unfurled, her demon's sexy backdrop. His horns had gone ramrod straight.

When he'd run those lengths against her before, her sex had clenched in reaction. He'd marked her with his scent—and she'd loved it. She wanted to kiss and stroke those horns. Then lick his firm lips. And his flat nipples. She wanted to run her mouth along the rigid edges of his pec muscles before following his goodie trail down. . . .

What was her type? *Voilà.*

He moved to kneel between her legs. Because they were about to do this. Without protection.

Her biological clock was screaming: *Roll. The. Dice.*

Yet then he spread that sheet over her. It was about eight feet square, with a strategically placed slit. The politics of this rankled. She didn't get contraception, but he got this barrier?

No, no, this was important to him. Her self-help books told her compromise was vital to a developing relationship.

Then she lit on an idea, a way for them both to be happy with the sheet; she decided to play along for now.

As he aligned the opening with her sex, he asked, "Are you sure you're ready?"

"If you go slow."

He levered himself above her, resting on one straightened arm. "Slow?" His gaze fell upon her nipples jutting against the sheet. "I fear I won't last. I've craved you for too long." With his free hand, he gripped himself, aiming for the sheet's gap.

She rested her hands on his broad shoulders as she awaited that first contact. When the bulbous head bumped right at her hungry core, she moaned in readiness. "I might not last long either!" Blue sorcery shimmered from her hands, tendrils of it swathing them.

He hissed in a breath, determinedly pressing against her. "My sensual sorceress." He gazed down with possessiveness ablaze in his expression.

His silver eyes were telling her he was about to claim her, that nothing could stop him.

When he'd raised himself up on both arms, she kneaded his shoulders. "Can you feel how slick I am? How wet for you?"

"Lanthe . . ."

"When we were in the glade, I imagined what your shaft would feel like plunging inside me." Her words were throaty. "Tonight you'll show me."

A shudder strangled whatever he'd been about to say.

His unpracticed reactions, the *honesty* of his responses, ratcheted up her arousal to a shocking degree.

Honesty was a turn-on. Who knew?

Subtly rocking to his pulsing rod, she murmured, "You couldn't be sexier, Thronos."

He canted his head, as if he didn't believe her. But whatever he saw in her eyes convinced him otherwise. Whatever he saw made his shuddering grow worse.

By the time he'd planted the crown inside, he was sweating. His voice broke lower as he said, "You're so tight around me. Never knew you'd be so hot." The wonder in his tone made her toes curl.

The sheet rose and fell with her shallow breaths. She arched her back so that her nipples strained against the material, which seemed to bespell him more than the nymphs had. "Don't you want to bare my breasts at least?"

The dilemma was clear on his face. He finally tugged down the sheet just past her breasts. "Too lovely to cover."

And she lost a little bit more of her heart to him.

Eyes rapt on the pebbled tips, he licked his sensual lips. He'd expressed a particular pleasure in suckling her. If he did now, this might truly be over before it started. To distract him, she rolled her hips—

Which impaled his shaft even deeper.

She gasped at the sudden fullness; he grunted, *"Tight."*

His gradual pace was the only reason she hadn't cried out. "Slow is good, Thronos."

With a solemn nod, he fed her sheath more of his throbbing length. Already he waged an obvious battle not to come. His wings were furling and unfurling like a fist opening and closing. Sweat slicked the breathtaking swells of his brawny chest, the rippling muscles of his rock-hard torso.

As he sank ever deeper, a drop of his clean sweat splatted over one of her swollen breasts, making her shiver—and undermining her own control.

"Sorry," he bit out.

"For driving me crazy?" She cupped his nape, arching up to graze her breasts across his chest—sending the sheet to her waist, sending him deeper inside her.

"I feel your nipples . . . so stiff . . . *ah, gods*—" His hips bucked forward in an uncontrollable rush, till he was seated deep within her, a growl wrenched from his lungs.

Her own lungs were squeezed for breath. His body was inside her, surrounding her, seeming to vibrate from his struggle to regain the control he'd lost.

"Lanthe! I didn't mean—have I hurt you?"

She wriggled beneath him, adjusting to his length. "Just give me a second." Deep within her, she could perceive his cock pulsating to the beat of his heart. His invincible heart. "I'm good, Thronos. All good."

He clasped her face in his big hands, touching her with *reverence.* "I just wed you," he rasped, making her melt.

I've waited my entire life to see that look. "Since I'm also engaged in the act"—she shimmied beneath him, eliciting a groan—"I'd say we just wed each other."

With a pained smile, he grated, "That sounds fairer."

She couldn't stop grinning back at him. As if they'd pulled off a stupendous achievement. Which, she supposed, they had.

But their amusement receded when he began to withdraw. The friction of his cock and that flared crown wrested a plaintive cry from her.

Before he gave his first thrust, he said, "Ready?"

She nodded.

When he tilted his hips forward, he threw his head back, the muscles of his neck bulging. "My Lanthe!" Then he faced her once more, to gaze at her—with awe.

He was still swelling inside her, much more than she'd expected. Apparently, he was a show-er *and* a grower. She did her best to stifle a wince. Brave little soldier, and all that.

Lanthe had always thought the term *joined* was hyperbole in a sexual sense. Now, so much of his body was within hers, she *did* feel joined to him. If she could just get herself accustomed . . . "Stir yourself in me."

"Stir?" He circled his hips, grinding against her sensitive clitoris.

"Oh, *yes.*" Pleasure seared her with the intensity of flames.

A sharp exhalation escaped him. *Puh.* His expression was thunderstruck.

In the quiet of the night, his heart pounded like a drum. His wings were stretched wide, the pulselines glowing like shooting stars from the diadem above.

His starry eyes, gazing down at her, outshone them all.

He stirred himself again, stretching her, filling her thoroughly. Bliss suffused her, warmth coursing throughout every inch of her. She felt brimming with him, with emotions.

Replete.

But her emotions confused her. Amid the tenderness she felt for him, she also experienced gratitude, relief—and even *joy.*

With her hands meeting around his nape, she murmured, "Thronos . . ." *I'm yours. You're mine. You confuse me. This confuses me.* She hadn't even orgasmed, and it was the best sex she'd ever had. Never had sex felt like coming home to someone.

Like she was being showered with fate's gold coins.

He laid his big palm on the side of her face. "I don't recognize . . .

what your expression's telling me," he admitted in a gravelly voice. "But I think I like it."

"I'm trying to tell you a thousand things at once. I'm telling you I'm ready—to be taken by you." Not only was she accustomed to him; his cock now felt so critical that she wondered how she'd survived without it. "I'll give you anything you need." Her hands moved to his ass, digging into the flexing muscles. "Do you need to thrust?"

"By all the gods, *yes.*" He drew his hips back, sinking himself more slowly.

Ecstasy surged inside her. Her lids fluttered as she moaned.

Another painstaking thrust. "Is it always like this, Lanthe?"

"Emphatically no." She couldn't stop writhing on his hardness, wanting ever more of it. "More, Thronos!"

"The way you move . . . *maddening.*" He clamped her restless hips, his body driving forward. Then again. Each time he hit the end of her sheath, her clitoris got a shot of delicious stimulation. Her orgasm mounted.

"You're squeezing me so tight." His pace quickened. "I can't hold out!"

"No, don't come," she said, feeling her sorcery rising. "I won't let you." The air blurred near her lips.

Had she just used her power on him?

He thrust hard, groaning as if in pain. *"Lanthe . . ."* His skin sheened with sweat, his muscles corded. Just looking at him like this—her steady Vrekener in the throes, a massive warrior about to unleash centuries of need—brought her right to the edge.

She was going to come for this male, and she could almost fear the intensity of the escalating pleasure.

"Need to . . . thrust harder. Can't go slow."

"Don't. Take me as you need to."

With a groan, he shoved into her body. Again. And again, until he was railing between her legs, to her delight. His hands dipped beneath her, his remaining claws biting into the curves of her ass—a primal sign of possession that sent her spiraling.

So close, so close.

He gave a frustrated yell, confusion flashing in his eyes. "Lanthe, I *can't* come."

"I might have . . . commanded you." Though she'd been tripping headlong toward her climax, she sucked in a breath and resisted it, wanting to torment them both.

"Undo it!" His tendons stood out with strain, his mighty body toiling to free its seed.

"Hmm. We're going to have such fun tonight. . . ."

FORTY-SEVEN

This was anything but *fun*! Thronos could feel a knot of semen trapped right beneath the crown, and he couldn't release it.

His body knew exactly who he was claiming, knew it was to spill seed for her womb. The pressure of it made his erection throb like a hammered thumb—worse than it ever had before because he had semen welling for her.

Her hot channel clutched him so tightly, seeming to demand it. He wanted to savor his first time, to savor *her,* but he could hardly think past that damned violent throbbing.

He gazed down to where their bodies joined. Mistake. Through the slit in the sheet, he could see her rosy flesh gloving his engorged length.

When he saw his mate was wetting the material with her arousal, his shaft jerked within her, as if panting for her. "About to lose my mind!" She'd told him that if he was ever inside her, there would be no doubt; he would be broken down at a molecular level, altered irretrievably.

She'd gravely understated.

Their crackling electricity now scorched him, as if lightning bolts detonated between them. The feeling of connection overpowered him, awed him. Physically, his body was wracked—he labored to ease the pressure and claim his pleasure—but he also needed to give his fated mate his seed, to leave something of himself inside her.

He gazed down at her face; her eyes were luminous, speaking to him in a language he didn't yet understand. "Release me, Melanthe!" His voice was strangled, the pain unbearable.

Even as it felt so damned good.

In answer, she leaned up to kiss his neck. With her ethereal, blue sorcery coiling all around them, she licked his pulse point, the same way she'd taken gold dust from him. It drove him just as crazy. When she started sucking on his neck, he wondered if she *sought* to unhinge him.

"I'll release you," she murmured against his skin, "once you release me."

Comprehension hit his lust-addled brain. He had to bring her to orgasm before she'd let him come.

He ran his arms behind her back, scooping her up, arching her breasts to him. His mouth grazed one nipple, then the other. He took them with his tongue, then his lips, rocking between her legs as he sucked.

Against one plump breast, he yelled, "Release me!" Rocking, suckling, rocking her. *Losing my mind.*

"Thronos, I can't hold back any longer . . ."

"Hold back?" This was all deliberate?

"I'm close!"

"Tell me what you need . . . to get you there."

"Your kiss—take my lips!"

Their heads shot forward, teeth clicking before he slanted his mouth over hers. Their tongues tangled, flicking licks. They traded breaths, her moans and his groans. She was thrashing against him as wildly as he plunged into her.

Just as he reached a crisis point—when he couldn't think past *pressure,* and *wetness,* and *heat*—she broke away to whisper at his ear, "When you feel me coming around you . . . give me your seed." Sorcery swirled with her command.

Between gnashed teeth, he hissed, "Gods almighty."

"And you might want to cover my mouth, because you're about to make me scream." She held his gaze. "Thronos, *now*!"

He used his palm to muffle her abandoned scream. Her back bowed beneath him, her little body surprising him with its strength.

His own body stilled, stunned when her sheath clenched him like a fist. To milk him of the seed he could finally provide? With that first contraction around him, his shaft gave an answering pulse, primed to ejaculate. His seal about to break.

His wings snapped wide as he began pounding between her legs with all his might.

Like an animal. Like a demon.

Then . . .

In a scalding rush, semen *erupted.* His hot essence for his mate alone.

Before his bellow shook the night, he sank his fangs into her neck, roaring against her skin.

Just before he'd latched onto her neck, Thronos's starry eyes had turned black as night.

Then had come his fangs, claiming her flesh. When Lanthe had felt him *marking her*—as a demon would—sorcery exploded from her like a bomb blast.

Her orgasm ramped up all over again, until she was screaming into his palm, thrashing beneath him as he fucked like a piston. His cock forced its way even deeper inside her as he pumped his sizzling come into her.

As jet after jet of his seed filled her, his muscles tightened all around her, his claws digging into her skin, his wings shuddering.

Brutal, beautiful demon.

He thrust till he'd emptied himself dry, till she'd grown lax and dazed beneath him. . . .

He removed his hand from her mouth and collapsed atop her, releasing his bite with clear reluctance. As he licked his mark with his pointed tongue, he loosed a long groan of utter satisfaction.

Then he seemed to wake up. He rose on his arms above her. "Did I hurt you?"

"Hmm. Your bite *might* have hurt, but I was too busy coming to feel it." She nipped at his chest. "You were tender for as long as you could be."

He relaxed, lowering himself to his elbows. "More evidence that I'm a demon, then? Lanthe, nothing could've kept me from marking you as mine." He brushed her hair from her forehead. "But no other Vrekener males do it."

"That you know of. My skin will be healed by morning. Who's to know what we've done?"

He still looked uncertain, so she said, "Maybe Pandemonia liberated the demon in you, but I don't care. Whatever you are—it doesn't matter to me. What just happened was mind-blowing and shattering and *perfect.* I wouldn't change an instant of it."

The corners of his lips curled with pride. Such a *guy.*

"I felt you coming." He didn't bother trying to keep the amazement out of his voice.

With a grin, she clenched her sheath around him; his eyes went wide.

"I felt you, too." She supposed she should be worried about him spilling inside her, but she was still high from their sex. She was addicted to this male. Not just physically, but . . . emotionally.

His honesty had affected her, coaxing her to lower all her guards. Tonight she'd learned that, for her, trust was the strongest aphrodisiac.

His eyes gleamed with excitement. "I always thought my seed would, I don't know, *flow* from me. I had no idea the pressure would be so intense. When it releases, it's almost . . . violent—but in the best way."

Already his shaft stirred for more. She grinned, realizing her Vrekener was only getting warmed up for the night. "So, was I worth the wait? I talked a big game."

"You'd every right to, sorceress. Just as you said"—he dipped a kiss to her lips—"you broke me down at a molecular level."

FORTY-EIGHT

Thronos was a male transformed, with too many thoughts for his mind to handle, too many emotions to be contained.

He remained inside her, still hard. He could feel the dampness of his semen in her—and that satisfied him so deeply. "I never want to leave," he told her. Like him, she seemed in no hurry for their bodies to part. "Can we sleep like this?"

She nodded. "I could lie over you. Though I think sleep would be the last thing we'd be interested in. Speaking of which, when can you do it again?"

"I'm pretty sure I can do it as much as you like," he said with a thrust.

"That's the best news I've heard all night." Her eyes were merry.

He reached out, stroking his thumb over her silken cheek. She turned her head into his palm, drawing his thumb between her lips to suckle.

"Uhn." How could that enflame his entire body so fiercely? The jolt of sensation was startling—not to mention the memories she conjured, of when she'd sucked his shaft thus . . .

Now that he had seed to give her, would she take it between her lips? Spending semen like that was an offendment, but if Lanthe would drink, he'd give and give till she'd had her fill.

Just like that, he was desperate for her, his hips beginning to pump into her hot glove. When she released him with a last lick, he cupped her nape, drawing her closer—

"Wait!" she cried. "Let me up, let me up."

He jerked back. "Have I hurt you?"

"Roll onto your back."

With a frown, he did, reversing their positions.

Once she was on top, she gracefully dismounted, leaving the sheet's opening to ring the base of his shaft.

She'd turned the claiming sheet around on him.

His eyes widened at his rampant erection protruding from the sacred sheet. "Lanthe, this . . . this might be blasphemy."

"You did it to me, and I'll do it to you. That's what our marriage will be like—equal and a little subversive to both of our factions. But it'll work for us."

His heart pounded. Though he was convinced, her certainty surprised him. "*Will* it work for us?"

"That depends on how much grief you give me about the freaking sheet."

Realization struck him with the force of an anvil. If they continued to make concessions for each other, they would not only be wed forever, but wed *well.* She'd traveled here for him—no other reason—and she'd surrendered much; he would meet her halfway. "No grief, wife."

"Good man," she said softly. "So are we done with the sheet now?"

"Yes. But only because we're married." He enjoyed saying that. "It's served its purpose."

She tugged the material off him, tossing it to a far corner of the bed. "Back to business, then." With a smile, she straddled him, kneeling up above his shaft. "So, this is what I like to call Thronos and Lanthe's Pandemonian position."

His grin faded when she began to slip down his length. He could only stare as her sex swallowed him inch by torturous inch. . . .

Altering.

Once she'd taken him as deep as he could go, he gazed up at his exquisite wife. Her hair was a glossy tangle all around her heartbreakingly lovely face, her sorcery shimmering. He dimly noted that her swollen nipples were the same shade as her curving lips.

While he beheld her, she'd been gazing at him. "Look how big and hard your body is. And it's all for me. The greedy sorceress in me is well pleased."

Gods, she made his chest bow with pride.

She rasped one of his nipples with a nail, and the jolt of pleasure was as unexpected as when she'd suckled his thumb!

Then she pressed her hands on his shoulders to rise up. . . .

The night air cooled his heated testicles, the base of his wetted shaft. When his hips bucked, chasing her tight heat, she dropped down at the same time.

His eyes rolled back in his head.

He roused when she began to slowly ride him, her breasts bouncing for his enthralled gaze. Mesmerized by the way they moved, he fought the urge to knead them. "So damned lovely—"

His words were cut off. As she slipped up and down his length, she squeezed it—from the inside.

"Lanthe!"

"Do you like that?" she asked in a siren's voice.

"Never want this to end!" Part of him still disbelieved he was inside her. He realized it would take him a while to accept this turnaround.

To accept that his dream woman was in their bed sating her lusts with his body, as he did the same.

She bent her arms over her head, crossing her wrists as she snapped her hips. The way she writhed atop him robbed him of breath. Hypnotic female.

Her hands glided down, one to cup a breast, one to masturbate her sex. In the future, he would watch her self-pleasure; for now, he brushed that hand away. When he stroked the swollen bud with his forefinger, she threw back her head.

The ends of her hair tickled his thighs; added sensation for a male awash in it. The more he rubbed her sex, the harder she writhed. Rubbing her, petting . . . "I grow nigh again!"

She faced him. "I won't do anything to stop you this time."

He grated, "Good to know." He had another urge to contend with. The need to wrap his protective wings around her was overwhelming.

He'd marked her with his horns—and his fangs. She'd accepted his most primal drives. So he leaned up to take her in his arms. As his wings closed around her, she grew even slicker, her tempo increasing.

"I think you like my wings."

She nodded breathlessly. "You are such a surprise to me. Everything about you . . ."

When he enfolded her against him, she wrapped her arms around his neck, and the satisfaction made him quake. It was just the two of them, cocooned against the world, bodies lit by his pulselines.

Her nipples raked up and down his chest. "So when I scream—soon—do you think anyone could hear me past your wings?"

He rose up on his knees, cupping her ass. Pinned on his length, she tightened her legs around him.

"Maybe that's how the others keep quiet? One way to find out."

In an urgent whisper, she told him, "I'm so close, Thronos." She leaned in to suck on his neck in that maddening way, bearing down on him at the same time. When he realized his mate was grinding her needy little bud against the base of his shaft, he spontaneously . . .

Came. *Hard.*

His roar reverberated within his wings as he bucked furiously against her, grinding back as he started pumping his seed.

"It's so hot!" She rode him faster, sending him into a frenzy. "I'm coming, Thronos! You make me feel so—" She tensed against him, her thighs trembling around his sides. Her head fell back against his wings, her climax wrenching a scream from her.

He experienced something like euphoria when her channel demanded its due once more. He eased his thrusts just to feel her spasms rippling up and down his length, her pleasure wringing his so perfectly.

He groaned his lingering disbelief. "My Lanthe . . ."

When her orgasm subsided, he continued to quake—as if his release had generated aftershocks.

With her head tucked against his shoulder, her breaths on his neck, she patted his heaving chest. "There. I claimed you too."

Late in the night, Lanthe and Thronos lay facing each other, wrapped in his wings. As they'd done when young, they murmured secrets.

All those years ago, he'd told her that he'd be her husband. How right he'd been!

Lanthe had been *claimed.* She'd lost track of all the times he'd taken her, how many times he'd brought her over the edge.

The sheet separating them had been tossed by the wayside. *All* the sheets had. His wings kept them plenty warm.

Now, seeing him with his hair ruffled, looking relaxed and drowsy, made her heart ache.

"Was it like you expected?" she asked.

"Not really, lamb."

"Tell me."

He frowned, as if searching for words. "When we first met, I took your scent into me—sky and home. When I'm inside you, I feel like I've found the sky for the first time, or returned home after an eternal absence. It's as if every want and need I've ever had, or ever will have, is fulfilled. I hadn't expected the . . . totality of it."

Though his admission was one of the most moving things she'd ever heard, he exhaled and said, "I make little sense. Woman, you've addled me." He turned the question on her. "Was it like you expected?"

"No, but in a good way."

"How so?"

How to explain what she'd felt and learned? "I discovered things tonight, Thronos. So many things." She stroked his hair from his forehead.

"I felt safe with you, connected *to* you. And those feelings heightened everything. It's addictive."

He nodded. "I feel the same. I sometimes wonder what I wouldn't do for more of you."

"Exactly. Let's put it this way—I'm so happy I took your hand earlier."

Even as his lips curled, his lids grew heavier. She'd never seen him sleep. He hadn't in weeks, but now that he'd released tension and was back in his own bed, she hoped he could. "You should rest." She motioned for him to go to his back, then draped herself over his chest. His strong arms twined around her. "We have a big day tomorrow." Words she'd despaired of ever saying to a significant other.

"I'm reluctant to sleep." He pulled her even closer to him. "Fear you won't be here when I wake."

His gruff words made the ache in her heart worse. "We're married now. I'm not going anywhere." And she meant it. He was her husband, her lover, her prince.

Thronos was her best friend.

Though she worried what tomorrow would bring, she believed in *them.*

As he was drifting off, he said, "With all my dreams having come true, what will I dream of now?"

Oh, damn. Lanthe gazed at his face in sleep. *I just fell in love with him.*

FORTY-NINE

The brightest sunlight Lanthe had ever encountered blazed down on her. The harsh light of day—and she had zero regrets. Still, she grumbled, "I feel like Private Benjamin!"

"Don't know who that is, Lanthe."

She could *hear* the grin in his voice. "Turn off the light!"

"I can't turn off the sun."

She cracked her eyes open to find him sitting at the edge of the bed, looking like a boss. "Well, aren't you happy with yourself?" His smile was brilliant against his crisp linen shirt. *Glorious male.*

He nodded. "I woke this morning, disoriented, convinced last night had been a reverie. Then I gazed down and your head was upon my chest. I comprehended that we are wed." He gazed deeply into her eyes. "There has never been a better morning."

This was a world away from her typical morning-after scenarios. "How long have you been sitting there?"

"Couple of hours. I enjoy watching you sleep."

With anyone else, Lanthe would have found that creepy, but not with her new husband.

In any case, she couldn't talk since she'd mooned over his relaxed, sleepy face until she'd dozed off. Then she'd been out like the dead. No nightmares. No restlessness.

"Come, I'm eager to introduce you to our people."

Bully.

"We'll find you a grand breakfast. Apple tartlets, maybe? Or honey bread?"

She *was* hungry. "Okay, okay. I need a shower first." When she rose and knotted her hair above her head, his gaze fell on her breasts, his brows drawn tight. As she padded into the bathroom, she knew he was ogling her ass so she put an extra spring in her step.

His growl made her grin. She'd wager she wasn't leaving this house before he took her again.

She checked her appearance in the mirror. Her eyes were bright, her cheeks pinkened. She felt a tinge of regret to see that his claiming mark had healed.

In the shower, she called, "Hey, can we get the hot water fixed?" She'd turned the single lever all the way right, but the water never approached warm.

"In the Territories, there is no hot water for showers," he called back.

To herself, she muttered, "You've got to be shitting me." She sucked in a breath and stepped under, screeching, "This isn't right—I didn't join the army!"

He came to gloat, leaning against the doorway with a barely checked grin. "We Vrekeners find cold water's good for the mind and body."

"Oh? That's a shame—because hot water's good for morning sex."

His eyes flickered. "I'll warm you up. . . ."

Some time later, when they emerged, Lanthe was a cold-water convert. Now *she* was grinning like a boss.

After she dried off, she reached for her clothes from the night before. Full regalia. Including the mask.

The beauty of metal and leather garments? Easy cleaning. She tugged on her skirt.

"Shall I find you some gowns?" he asked as he dressed again.

She studied his face. "You can, but I won't wear them until I have them altered." Lanthe had lived through the Victorian age; out of necessity, she'd learned how to transform a high-necked, floor-length, long-sleeved gown into a proper sleeveless minidress. Or, rather, to give directions for someone else to. "I'll feel more comfortable in my own clothes."

He parted his lips, hesitated, then said, "Very well."

Good man, she thought again. "I feared we were about to have our first married fight." She slipped on her top. As far as Sorceri clothing went, the outfit wasn't even *that* provocative. Her hemline almost reached her knees. Her boots did, so little of her legs would be exposed.

"I know how much you compromised to come here with me," he said. "I want to meet you halfway. Besides, if you scream at me, it should only be because you're about to erupt/explode/die with ecstasy."

"In other words, later today?" She reached forward to cup him between the legs, loving how he rocked on his toes to her hand.

When he groaned, she released him with an affectionate pat.

She donned her boots and gauntlets, then did a quick job braiding her hair. Thronos watched her every movement with undisguised fascination.

"Grab my necklace?"

He hastened to get it, returning to lace it over her head. "I kick myself for not giving you this sooner."

"Well, we were a mite preoccupied with dragons and demons and pests and all. I treasure it as if you presented it to me—since you put your life at risk to retrieve it. Even if it weren't silisk gold, it would always be my favorite."

"Sorceri exchange rings with marriage, do they not?"

She whirled around. "Yes, I want a ring! A gold one, with extra gold."

His lips curled. "When my mate sets her heart on something, who am I to deny her?"

With an answering grin, she slipped on her mask. "Okay, then, let's go get this over with."

He offered his hand; she proudly took it.

The moment they walked out the door, a Vrekener male greeted them, as if he'd been loitering just outside. Tall and broad-shouldered, with a rangy build like Thronos's, he had olive-green eyes and sandy brown hair tied in a queue.

Lanthe stiffened when she saw his silvered talons. A knight. She wondered how many Sorceri he'd killed. Or neutered?

"Greetings, Jasen!" Thronos said. "I didn't think anyone knew we'd arrived."

Lanthe frowned at Jasen's reaction to Thronos; the male's pensive expression had turned to one of abject relief, the way one might look when handing over a ponderous weight—or a rabid animal.

"Melanthe, this is Jasen," he said, introducing the man to her first, showing her deference. "Jasen, this is Princess Melanthe, my bride."

"You . . . you *have* her."

Lanthe didn't offer her hand. Because it was glimmering blue behind her back.

After a moment, Jasen appeared to shake away his shock at this development. He turned to Thronos. "My liege, the knights have assembled in the Hall for an important security meeting. Will you attend?"

"Is my brother here?"

"No, my liege, I'm afraid he's not."

Thronos was calm and cool on the outside, but now that she knew him better she could see that his scars were a touch lighter, which meant his face was tense.

—I'm sorry, Thronos. I know you'd wanted to get something settled with Aristo.—

—Gods only know what he's up to out in the worlds.— To Jasen, he said, "Melanthe and I will attend." Hand in hand, they followed the knight down the steps to the sandy vale. *—In this assembly, I will not tolerate disrespect to you. Remember that you are their princess.—*

Talk about a trial by fire! She drew her sorcery close. *—I don't think it's a good idea for me to go. What if the meeting is about my presence here? What if I'm in danger?—*

He glanced at the power swirling around her. *—You can take care of yourself. Just try not to hurt anybody.—*

—Ha.—

—You know I'd slay them all before I let them touch a hair on your head.—

On the hills above them, Vrekeners stopped their daily routines to stare down at her.

What would Sabine do in this situation? Her sister would put her shoulders back and never let anyone forget she was a noble daughter of the Sorceri. Lanthe would do no less. To those who stared the most boldly, she inclined her head with a regal air.

Of course, she could understand their interest. Her garments must shock them, plus she had sorcery around her. Not to mention her one-of-a-kind, priceless necklace. She defied any female not to secretly pine for it.

The Vrekener males all wore white lawn shirts and leather breeches. Each female's dress was drab and baggy, revealing only her face and hands. Their wings were pinned so tightly, one would think the Vrekeners were embarrassed by them. These people absolutely looked like they had quiet, boring sex.

They were the anti-Sorceri.

But then, Thronos had once been too—before she'd gotten ahold of him. These Vrekeners had no idea that Hurricane Lanthe had just made landfall in the Skye. *—Are Vrekeners always so somber?—* If she didn't know better, she might have thought someone had ensorcelled their land with misery.

To be fair, she would've expected shrieks as mothers shoved their kids back into their weird roofless houses. But the people were steady and unflinching.

Unsmiling.

—Not usually this *tense. I'm keen to find out what's going on.—*

The moment he'd come within sight of his people, Thronos had clenched his jaw and worked not to limp, which must be killing him. She had used her powers on him last night; maybe she could try to help with his pain.

But pain obliteration was a command that could seriously backfire. As she debated the pros and cons, she realized what was missing from this picture. —*Where are the Sorceri?*—

—*Good question. I'll soon have answers for you.*—

Then the grand Skye Hall loomed over her and Thronos. Last night she'd gazed upon it and marveled that she was that close to the seat of Vrekener power.

Now she was about to enter. Sabine would never believe it!

As Lanthe and Thronos climbed the stairs, his wings rippled, as if he was preparing for battle.

They entered what looked like an anteroom of sorts. The construction was awing, but she couldn't quite wrap her mind around it. Without a roof, it seemed like a ruin—or an arena. Yet it was pristine.

From there, she and Thronos crossed through a double doorway into a larger room with a giant round table. Forty or so males were seated about it in backless chairs.

Shocker, it was a sausage fest. Not a single female knight. *Ugh.*

There was no throne or dais. The arrangement looked like one of those town-hall kinds of settings where royalty acted like they were just normal folks, and no one got elevated above others (though the royals were the ones whose heads would roll if shit went down).

All the males appeared astonished to see Melanthe.

"My wife and princess." Thronos held up her gauntleted hand. "Melanthe of the Deie Sorceri."

She peered up at him, and her heart thudded. He gazed at her with absolute acceptance. *My husband.* When her sorcery sparked with her pleasure, several hawk-eyed gazes locked on it, but no one said a word. They probably assumed it was just sorcery left over—after Thronos had harvested her power.

If so . . . *psych!*

The Vrekeners who recovered quickest shot to their feet, in respect for their prince at least. The ones who hadn't stood received a murderous look from Thronos until they did.

"My wife and I are eager to hear news of the realm."

When all the males took a step away from the table and began to kneel, Thronos's scars grew even lighter—and Lanthe got a sick feeling in the pit of her stomach. . . .

FIFTY

My brother is dead.

These males would kneel before only one male in this domain or any other. Their king.

Thronos said one word: "Aristo?"

Jasen answered, "He has recently passed on, my liege. I apologize for not saying something earlier, but I couldn't reveal any details out of the assembly. And there is . . . much to be explained."

—I'm sorry, Thronos.— Melanthe looked as shocked as he felt.

Working to make his tone even, Thronos said, "Be seated." He led her to a chair, taking the one beside her. "How did he die?"

"He was murdered," Jasen said. "By the king of the Deathly Ones demonarchy."

Murdered?

"There is no king of that demonarchy," Melanthe said. "I'm friends with Bettina, their princess. She's half Sorceri. As of a few weeks ago, she was unwed."

Jasen told her, "We understand that the male who wed their princess is a Dacian vampire who won her in a recent tournament."

Thronos cast her a questioning glance. —*Dacians actually exist? I thought they were a myth.*—

—*I've always believed they did. Thronos, I fear we've been gone for longer than we thought.*—

—*As do I.*— Aloud, he asked the others, "What reason had this king to murder another?"

"There are those who say the act was purportedly carried out in retaliation for some perceived violence done to his Bride."

Thronos frowned at Jasen. "Perceived violence?" Compared to Melanthe's straight-from-the hip talk, this deferential speak grated.

With regret on her face, she told him, "A few months ago, Bettina was attacked by four Vrekeners. Though she's a young, ninety-five-pound waif who's never harmed anyone, they broke every bone in her body. Then they doused her with spirits, about to burn her alive. She was rescued just in time."

He recalled Melanthe telling him that she and Sabine weren't the only ones brutalized. Thronos expected denials from the knights. Any second the warrior males would staunchly reject the idea that a Vrekener could be capable of such a craven act.

The silence that reigned gave Thronos chills.

All eyes turned to Jasen to continue. Thronos supposed the male had assumed the role of leader in the absence of a king, which was surprising. Thronos would've expected Cadmus, their general knight of war, to lead. Yet Cadmus sat quietly, as if biding his time.

Jasen said, "The vampire took your brother and three of his knights."

"From where?"

Around the table, eyes darted.

"From *here*. The male traced to Skye Hall."

A leech had located this kingdom. "How is that possible? A vampire can only trace to a place he's previously been. And what about our wards?"

"We have no idea how he did it—or if he'll lead more vampires or demons back here. We've posted extra sentries."

Hidden guards. So that was who'd watched Thronos last night.

"We're ready to take more action. My liege, this has understandably sent shockwaves through the populace."

All Thronos had wanted to do was wed Lanthe and come to an understanding with Aristo, or to endeavor to. Now . . .

I am king. The last of his line.

He could scarcely process that his brother was dead—and that the welfare of all these people rested on his shoulders. "Why would the vampire target my brother so specifically?"

Jasen said, "There might . . . there's a chance King Aristo was one of the four who inflicted those injuries upon Princess Bettina, not understanding who she was."

His brother might have tortured a tiny young sorceress, intending to burn her alive. Aristo's voice sounded in his head: *"Death to every last one of them!"* Though Thronos felt like he couldn't get enough air, he fought to keep his expression neutral.

"My liege, there's more. The vampire stole your brother's fire scythe."

"This is a grievous loss, but there are three others." And Thronos didn't intend for the knights to use the scythes for sorcery harvesting in the future.

Because my word will be law.

"The vampire turned it over to Morgana. She perverted its purpose, using it to loose the powers from the vault. She has reclaimed them all."

"She *emptied* the vault?" What else could she do with a scythe?

Jasen nodded. "She sent some of the powers out into the ether to reach their original possessors. We know this because a few of the Sorceri here received theirs."

Melanthe asked, "Where are they?"

"They fled. As far as we can tell, one of them reclaimed a teleportation ability. The rest left with him."

Fled. So they had been as miserable as Melanthe had said, escaping at the first opportunity.

Thronos gazed at her. *—You were right. About everything.—*

Lanthe didn't necessarily *want* to be right, now that she'd signed on for life above the clouds. Nor was she pleased about being queen of the Vrekeners.

Queen of any other faction? Sure, why not!

But these people?

Another male rose to speak, another knight. Melanthe didn't like the looks of him. He was waxy-skinned with light hair and eyes. He had one of the beefier builds among the males. Where the other Vrekeners struck her as still-waters-run-deep types, this guy seemed smarmy—like some of the Sorceri courtiers she'd known.

"My liege, four factions of the Lore have declared war on us. If we count the Sorceri's age-old declaration, that brings the total to five."

Just weeks ago, Lanthe would've been heartened by this development. Now she was part of the *us.*

Even when Thronos was faced with this news, his shoulders remained squared. And she wanted to kiss him for it. "Tell me, Cadmus."

"The rage demons, the House of Witches, the Dacians, and not unexpectedly the Deathly Ones." Though conveying distressing news, Cadmus sounded almost thrilled.

Did war turn him on?

Thronos's eyes narrowed. "What do we know about these enemies?"

"Not as much as we'd like, my liege," Jasen answered. Lanthe supposed that Vrekener wasn't too bad. Compared to Cadmus, Jasen struck her as a levelheaded font of reason. "The Dacians live in a secreted realm, but they have very recently begun opening up communications with outside factions. Their newly crowned king is Lothaire, the Enemy of Old."

Lothaire? Like a bad penny!

Thronos turned to her. "You know him."

"I do. If we can deliver a missive to him, I will try to establish a dialogue."

Thronos told her, "We have a station on the ground, with messengers awaiting."

"Good. I don't know why he would declare war. It seems random."

Jasen answered, "The new king of the Deathly Ones is a Dacian royal. We believe Lothaire is backing his relative."

"I expected the rage demons to declare war," Thronos said. *Because of me.* "Now it becomes clear why the Deathly Ones and the Dacians have. But what of the House of Witches? Are they not in the Vertas alliance? The House has always maintained an uneasy truce with the Vrekeners, no matter how closely their faction is related to the Sorceri."

Historically, witches and Sorceri hadn't been chummy. Unlike Lanthe and Carrow.

Cadmus shrugged. "We don't know why they call us enemy."

Lanthe did. She'd bet Carrow had survived the island and was still trying to get Lanthe's back. *I knew I liked that witch.*

Cadmus said, "It's my recommendation that we strike back against the vampire who stole into our kingdom, sending Vrekener might to crush the Deathly Ones. If the Dacians want a war, we can give them a reckoning."

Thronos intoned, "You're quick to want war for a kingdom in flux."

Cadmus's lips thinned. "King Aristo was given no death rites—because the vampire made a gift of your brother's head to the princess in that sick demon tournament," he said, again seeming to relish delivering the gruesome news.

Lanthe squeezed Thronos's hand. He had to be freaking inside, but he appeared undaunted.

Turning to Cadmus, she said, "You want to crush the Deathly Ones? Those demons garner strength with each kill they make. In other words, they get *more* powerful as a war drags on. Plus, their kingdom is specifically warded against Vrekeners. As for the Dacians, they're fairly much supervampires, with unearthly might and cunning. Lothaire alone is millennia old." And immortals grew stronger with age.

"The Sorceri seek to war with us," Cadmus said, addressing Thronos as if Lanthe hadn't even spoken. "Yet now we have one of them as queen? How can we be sure where her loyalties lie?"

Oh, it's on. "My loyalties lie with Thronos," Lanthe declared. "I'll do everything within my power to protect him and his interests." *—By the way, Cadmus is an asshole.—*

—We are in agreement.—

"So the sorceress says now."

Blue light began to swirl around her just as Thronos snapped, "Your queen has spoken, and you will not doubt her."

Cadmus choked out a breath. "That's not residual sorcery flowing from her. You left her empowered?" Others looked stunned by this as well. "When I've felt *her* very sorcery compelling me against my will?"

What was this tool talking about? *—When has he felt my sorcery?—*

—He was with me in Louisiana when we ambushed you last year. Jasen as well.—

Oops.

Cadmus pounded his fist on the table. "She must be disempowered to walk freely in our realm. It's the law!"

In an eerily calm voice, Thronos said, "Obviously I just *changed* that law, General Cadmus. Get up to speed."

When Cadmus looked like he was about to go off, Jasen hastily said, "We have burdened our regents with much unwelcome news." He turned to them. "Your new apartments in the Hall have been readied."

Thronos hesitated, so she said: *—Cadmus will get what's coming to him. But for right now, Thronos, our army of two needs to regroup* off *the battlefield.—*

With a kingly air, he stood. "I've much to think about. We'll reconvene later."

As she and Thronos walked from the assembly room, again hand in hand, the knights lined the aisle, lifting their wings above it like an arc of swords. Even Cadmus.

She might enjoy Thronos's wings; didn't mean she could tolerate anyone else's.

—*Easy, Lanthe.*—

She held her breath until she'd gotten out from under those jagged flares and glinting talons. . . .

The adjoining royal residence was built on a higher protrusion of rock, a wide stairwell leading to it. Inside, there were more roofless rooms and they were larger, but the space was still fairly bare.

As Thronos showed her around, his thoughts obviously preoccupied, she removed her gauntlets, settling in. *Home sweet home.*

He escorted her to a balcony, stopping just short of it. "From this height, you can see all the way to the edge of the island. I don't want you to be afraid."

"I'm not scared when you're around." At the risk of sounding mushy . . . sustaining a fear of heights was difficult when she knew he would always catch her.

He led her to the railing, then draped a protective arm around her shoulders.

In the distance, the blindingly blue sky was dotted with other islands, each with its own city. Below them, a thunderstorm hovered, lightning flashing.

The sight was remarkable, but she and Thronos had work to do. She turned to survey his face. "I was proud of you in there."

"For what reason could you possibly be proud?" He led her back inside, heading for a sitting area.

"Though you were repeatedly kicked in the ballbag, you didn't look like it."

"Thanks?"

"Perception is important. When Omort's rule crumbled, it was because no one believed in him any longer. His powers were still intact, godlike even, but he lost his followers through his behavior, his lack of leadership. I can't believe I'm telling you this, but . . . these Vrekeners need a strong king right now. They need you."

He let out a breath. "I never wanted to be king."

"I always dreamed of being a Vrekener queen."

He raised a brow at that. "And what about now—can I look as though I've been repeatedly kicked in the ballbag?"

"With me, of course."

He sank into a chair, rubbing his swollen leg. Then her upstanding Vrekener muttered, "Fuck."

She pulled up a chair beside him, leaning in. "We're going to get through this."

"You were right all along. Things are not as I'd imagined them. I had this idea of black and white, and now I'm immersed in gray."

"I regret that you lost your sibling"—best she could muster—"but you'll make a great king."

"I can't believe Aristo is gone. I know he did evil things—he hurt *you*—yet I'm still conflicted. Just when I add one member to my family, I lose another." He pinched the bridge of his nose. "*Was* he the one who did those things to Queen Bettina?"

"She told me that she thought the group acted with impunity, as if they were outside of the normal Vrekener command. Who besides Aristo would dare such a thing?"

"You believe him capable of such an act?"

"If you'd seen him as my sister and I have . . ."

Thronos shut his eyes. "Did Cadmus speak the truth about my brother's ultimate fate?"

She hesitated, then said, "It's likely. The Deathly Ones are a warrior breed. If the vampire was trying to impress them, that would be just the way. Plus, he was probably venting some serious rage. The vampire's young Bride was . . . savaged."

Thronos opened his eyes. "How did Aristo become like that? Your brother was destined to become evil, but mine seems to have rushed headlong toward it."

She had no answer for him. He didn't seem to expect one.

He motioned for her to come to him; she gladly went into his arms, sitting on his lap. "I'm the last of my line, Melanthe."

"After last night, there's a chance—slim to none, but still a chance—

that you aren't." Lanthe's overwrought biological clock gave a sigh of hope.

Thronos stared at her with eyes gone silver. Kind of like he loved her. Then he said, "How am I to fix all that my brother's broken?"

"We've *got* this. My sister is very good friends with Bettina. We can extend an offer of peace to the Deathly Ones. You might have to apologize on behalf of your brother."

"That won't be a problem. I'm bloody eager to."

"Normally, it wouldn't be easy to get her to the table. She kind of became a shut-in after her attack. If you even utter the word *Vrekener,* she runs away, sobbing and stuff."

"My gods."

"But there's an upside. Bettina's not only a gold fanatic like me, she's a gold*smith.* She would do just about anything for this." Lanthe held up the silisk medallion. "So we'll offer it as a present to celebrate peace between our factions. Depending on how much sway she has over her new king, this could be a lock."

"You told me earlier that the necklace is your favorite. You'd give up your most treasured gold for the Vrekeners? For this kingdom?"

She made a scoffing sound. "Not in a million years. But I'd give it up for you. Because that's what we do—we save each other's asses." She let that sink in. "So by neutralizing the Deathly Ones, we'll be taking care of the Dacians as well. As for the House of Witches, I think that's all Carrow. The good news is that she survived the island. The bad news is that the last she saw of us wasn't . . . ideal." When Thronos had been dragging Lanthe down a tunnel as she'd spat and cussed.

Thronos winced at the memory. "Lanthe, I—"

"Look, you can make that up to me by biting your tongue when you first meet my sister. For now, we can't worry about anything other than getting this kingdom out of the crosshairs. I'll write to Carrow and explain to her that I'm with you voluntarily. Same with the rage demons. The only reason Rydstrom declared war is that he doesn't know I'm in Skye Hall of my own volition." She frowned. "Did I really just say that?"

"So you're to be my ambassador queen?" Thronos curled his finger under her chin. "I don't want you to have to fight my battles."

She leveled her gaze on his. "We are *partners.* We'll be *co*-ruling this joint, and we'll play to our strengths. I'm pretty good at stuff like this. Nïx said that I was to shine in this realm. So just let the sorceress do like she do."

He exhaled a long breath. "Then I'm heartened. And grateful for my co-ruler."

"But there's one faction that I can't guarantee. My own. If Morgana drained the powers from the vault, she will have kept the choice ones. She was already a force in the Lore before, so I can only imagine how dangerous she's become."

In the past, Morgana had been impossible to reason with. Her ego was so colossal, it outstripped even Sabine's. And now that Morgana's adversary Dorada had risen, who knew how the queen would react about anything?

"I can extend an olive branch," Lanthe said, "letting her know that Skye Hall is under new management, and that fifty percent of the royals here are Sorceri. But I make no promises. She's about as predictable as Emberine. Thronos, she could strike down everyone here with a snap of her fingers."

"Assuming she can find us."

"If the vampire breached these wards, what's to stop him from teaching Morgana how to do the same? We already know the two were working together to some degree since he gave her the fire scythe. Morgana won't stop until the vampire tells her everything."

"Will she be so bent on reaching us?"

"I don't mean to heap bad news upon bad news, but Bettina is her ward. One of the few people in existence that Morgana cares about. Now that Bettina's married a Dacian royal vampire, I don't see how your brother could have targeted a worse victim." Aristo had screwed up, well, royally.

"What about your presence here? Will that not influence your queen?"

"I'm sure she thinks I've been abducted and brainwashed. Even if I convinced her I'm here by choice, I'm only one among her many subjects.

She and Sabine have a bond of sorts, but Morgana wouldn't forgo any of her plans for Sabine—and definitely not for me."

"Perhaps if I make amends to Bettina, it would lessen Morgana's hostility?"

Lanthe shook her head. "It infuriates Morgana that this place is hidden, that she's been unable to retaliate for all the harm done to her subjects. She'd love to strip the wards here completely, leaving the Territories defenseless. Imagine if she enlisted Portia and Emberine. These islands are made of rock. Portia could send them colliding like bumper cars. Emberine is packing the firepower—literally—of dozens of fire demons. She'd be lying in wait to burn anyone who thought to escape to the air."

With Lanthe's every word, Thronos grew more tense. She hated that, but she wouldn't sugarcoat the problem.

Or hide the sheer magnitude of it.

"There are other Sorceri with powers just as catastrophic," she said. "Morgana doesn't even have to get them to sign on—she can simply control them. That's her sorceress power: the ability to control others' powers."

"If they attacked in that manner, humans would be able to detect us," he pointed out.

"Some Loreans don't care."

"What do you suggest?"

"The sorceress in me is wondering how all these Vrekeners can get scarce really quickly."

"I don't understand," he said, the idea of fleeing completely foreign to a warrior like him.

"Do you have an evacuation plan in effect? Everybody, even the strongest species, needs a contingency, a plan B, a rabbit hole." A harsh reality she'd learned by running from Vrekeners. *Fate is weird.* "Is there some place where these people could go?"

"When the Territories reside over Canada, there's a remote forest we visit to hunt. A permanent fog bank cloaks the tops of the trees, so some have built cabins in the mist. It's an outpost of sorts."

"Perfect. Maybe we could head that way? Oh, and can you and your guys devise a security alarm of sorts? Like a first-warning system that would encompass all the islands?"

"I can see."

"Okay." She stood, cracking her knuckles. "We've got shit to do. I need pen and paper."

"Parchment and quill?"

"How did I know you were going to say that?"

FIFTY-ONE

SPLAT.

"Ugh!" Another inkblot on an official Vrekener queen document. Lanthe laid down her quill and examined her stained fingers. She looked like she'd been finger painting.

Occupational hazard, she supposed, now that she was pretty much the royal letter writer. For the last five days, her quill (because of course it *was* a quill) had been her sword.

Lanthe wasn't saying she'd do murder for a Bic; but she wasn't *not* saying that either.

Her first letter had been to Sabine. In it, she'd vowed to gold that things were well and that she was happy to have wed Thronos. She'd written that she was now a queen and included a plea to get Morgana to enter into talks with her.

Lanthe had known there was a risk in sounding like she adored it up here—everyone would think she'd been brainwashed—so she'd tried to sound as much like herself as possible.

She'd had that letter delivered immediately. Then she'd set about contacting all the factions who'd declared war on them.

To Carrow, she'd explained that Thronos had turned out to be a wonderful surprise.

Kind of like Malkom Slaine turned out for you, if I'm not mistaken? Do you remember how everyone in the prison cell disbelieved you'd wed him, but you refused to deny it? Though no one will believe I willingly married Thronos, I need you to. So, a couple of things, Crow: Say hi to Ruby, and please get the witches to back off.

To Bettina, she'd written:

The old Vrekener king was a vicious fiend who got what he deserved. Kudos to your new vamp husband for a well-played assassination and tournament victory.

Lanthe had also written that the *new* Vrekener king would like to personally make amends to Bettina with a gift of priceless dragon gold.

In her letter to Lothaire, Lanthe had reintroduced herself, then related that heaven was under new management. The Vrekeners wanted only peace with the Dacians, so could the two factions reach an accord? She hoped the missive would get to the Enemy of Old; the contact details for the newly revealed kingdom of Dacia were sketchy. But Thronos had a trusted knight who had yet to fail on a delivery.

She'd also written to Nïx:

From Nereus's bedroom window (don't ask), I saw Furie, trapped at the bottom of the ocean. She's alive and doing as well as can be expected—i.e., cataclysmically bad. I assume you and the Valks are going to bring the pain to Sargasoe soon? P.S. We sure could use some foresight up here in the Skye.

With all those letters written, Lanthe had struggled with a more lengthy explanation for her sister. She'd started—then wadded up—more than a dozen of them. She hadn't been able to decide how much to reveal of her past with Thronos.

It was one thing to tell her big sister to her face: "Well, I kind of misled you for centuries." It was quite another to write it out.

How to explain what Thronos had come to mean to her?

Yesterday she'd decided to start from the beginning, the day she'd first met him. Now it was late afternoon, and she'd only just gotten to the—heavily edited—faux Feveris part. She'd given herself a deadline of one more day. . . .

She gazed up from her desk, scanning the sky for Thronos. He'd be home soon to take her to the bastion for dinner.

He'd been meeting with his knights, tirelessly strategizing their defenses and implementing their new evacuation plan. Yesterday they'd organized their first drill. There'd been some hiccups, so today, they planned to "calibrate" things.

His body was paining him until he could barely conceal the agony in front of others. The stress of leading a realm on the brink of war wasn't helping anything. He was exhausted from all his duties, exhausted from his conflicted grief.

In Pandemonia, he'd told her that when he'd realized his father had killed her parents, he'd looked up at the man and seen a stranger. He felt the same way about his brother—

She heard the now familiar swoop of Thronos's wings. When she was with him and they were able to close out the world, life could be sublime. When she wasn't with him . . . not so much. Unable to hide her customary jolt of excitement, she leapt up from the desk. "You're home—"

He seized her hand. Without a word, he headed straight for their bedroom to fall face-first atop the bed—his big body was like a tree gone *timber.*

"Your day was that good, huh?" She climbed onto the bed, rucking up her skirt. "Scooch your wings." When he parted them, she straddled the small of his back.

He turned his face to the side. "I had more fun with the pest." Clearly, he was not in the mood to go dine with others right now.

Oh, darn. They'd have to miss eating in the grim dining hall? Not a problem. She'd been stockpiling fruit, surprisingly tasty breads, and divine cheeses—for just such an occasion.

When she began to knead his muscles, he gave a deep groan. "You're a gods-send, lamb."

"I know," she said though she'd just gotten ink prints all over the back of his shirt. Oops. "Um, how did the calibration go?"

"The alarm does work. Unfortunately, the only place to trigger it is in the Hall. Every island needs this ability to sound the alarm."

"It'll come." She pressed her thumbs round and round into his fatigued muscles.

"Tell me your day was better than mine."

"Mine was okay." Lanthe found it funny to be having this "How was your day, dear?" conversation with him. As if they were a long-wed couple.

But the two of them *had* started to fall into rhythms. Each night after dinner, they assailed each other—even if he'd managed to drop in a few times over the day. During those stolen daytime trysts, he'd take her hard against the wall or atop her desk, with his hand over her mouth to mute her desperate moans. He'd sink his fangs into his forearm to stifle his own bellows.

Every time he brought her release, he grew more sexually confident. More cocky.

Which was hot as hell.

If he came before her, he'd drop down and use his mouth to bring her over the edge. The first time he'd done this, she'd cried, "Oh! Ohhh . . ." and felt obligated to say something before he tasted his own seed.

He'd answered, "It's unavoidable. Throughout every day and night, I will fill your sheath and kiss it at every opportunity. Besides, it's me mingled with you—never deny me that."

Wicked, pervy Vrekener.

Once the worst of their need had been slaked, they would read correspondence together. He always wanted her opinion on things. More than once he'd told her, "When you said you wanted to co-rule, I took that very seriously. Tell me what you think. . . ."

Now he asked her, "Did you pick up your new clothes?"

"I did!" Her second day here, she'd realized that she needed lots of new garments, and that they should be fabulous since she was a queen and all. Even if her subjects were lame.

After giving designs for metal garments to the smithy, she'd crashed a group's sewing circle with instructions for strapless dresses. Lanthe figured she would split the hemline difference with Thronos—mini instead of micromini.

"How did the females treat you this time?" he asked. "Did they, um, throw 'tude?"

There'd been no pushback from the sewing circle—by now everyone knew their sorceress queen could bespell them—but Lanthe had gotten some attitude.

After she'd faced down the females of Omort's court and vanquished a sorceress like Hettiah, those Vrekeners had been a cakewalk. "No, I shut that down." Remembering one of Sabine's favorite sayings—*if one shows me fear, he shows me respect*—Lanthe had returned the 'tude and then some.

In other words, her clothes had been rush-ready! The dresses were plain white, but when she wore them with the necklace . . .

Not too shabby.

Of course, her current dress was white—and ink. "Anything new about Aristo?" Every day, more Vrekeners found the courage to divulge horror stories about the previous king and his three trusted knights. Those four had been a scourge on the Lore, hiding behind a cloak of righteousness.

"It's everything you warned me of."

As king of a people who believed in chastity until marriage, total sobriety, and forthrightness in all instances, Aristo had kept several love nests, drunk like a fish, and lied about his behavior.

She'd thought she would feel vindicated when Thronos comprehended these things. Instead she hurt for him. He was ashamed of his blood relative, feeling responsible.

"Things can only get better, right?" he asked.

"Speaking of which, I got a response from Bettina today." The queen of the Deathly Ones had reported progress with her Vrekener phobia, but she'd still been less than enthusiastic to meet with one.

That hadn't stopped Bettina from inquiring about the dragon gold. "She requested a detailed description of the medallion with a weight estimation and a photo if possible. So we've got her on the hook. Go, peace!"

Though his eyes remained closed, his lips curled. Yet then he tensed up again. "I regret that you have to give up your treasure."

At least she'd still have her silisk gold keys.

"As soon as things settle down here," he continued, "I'll replace the medallion with something even greater."

Another queen might have said, "Oh, you don't have to do that, my goodly monarch, for I reap satisfaction just from assisting whenever I can."

Lanthe? She cried, "Okay! And that has to be *in addition* to the ring you already promised me." She worked her hands to the edges of his broad shoulders, massaging there, making his wings ripple from pleasure.

"Duly noted," he said wryly. "And your letter to Sabine? How far have you gotten?"

"Only to Feveris. I might have spent a *bit* of time describing the gold temple. In any case, I want the Reader of Words to scan it before I send." She bent down and pressed a kiss to his neck. "Our story's pretty epic."

But she had a chapter she wanted to add: the "Thronos's Eternal Pain Ends" part. She couldn't change the past, couldn't magically transform their current circumstances—but could she make his old injuries better?

She'd hesitated to use power on him; ensorcelling his pain away would be a huge risk. For instance, in combat he might need pain to recognize how bad an injury was, or to remind him of blood loss so he could adjust his tactics for weakness.

Lanthe would have to straight-up heal him. Though she'd become an expert at this when she was a girl, she hadn't needed to use those commands for ages.

Plus, back then, Sabine hadn't been frozen into her immortality yet; she'd been more . . . malleable.

With Thronos, Lanthe would need to take her time. An unresisting patient would be ideal.

Her sorcery heated the air when she whispered at his ear, "Sleep, Thronos." He passed out at once, body gone lax on the bed.

She rose to remove his boots, inspecting his lower right leg. The muscles on the inside of his ankle were contorted, as if he'd sprained them to a supernatural degree. Even with his body at rest, the tendons were knotted so tightly, they pulled his foot inward.

His calf was equally bad. She probed the bunched muscles with her fingers.

Total healing? She cracked her knuckles. She had to at least try.

Blue sorcery began to shimmer in her ink-stained palms as she brushed them over his flesh. "Heal," she commanded as she massaged him.

Heat sprang from her hands, seeping into him. She could see currents of it beneath his skin, blue swirls. *"Heal."*

Beneath her fingertips, she felt the tiniest twinge. Had some tension eased?

Massaging. Sorcery. Massaging. "HEAL."

His muscles . . . started to relax! His foot was returning to a normal resting position!

With a delighted laugh, she turned to his left wing. She grasped the gnarled joint, repeating the process. *"Heal."*

In a rush, his wing scales rippled, like a racetrack betting board refreshing. With a snap, Thronos's skewed mosaics settled back into their natural spellbinding alignment.

She lovingly traced the pads of her fingertips over those metallic scales. After repeating the same treatment on his right wing, she surveyed the rest of his big body.

If she knew her Vrekener, she'd bet he had other aches that he would never mention. So she gave him a sorcery-powered full-body massage.

Because he was a transitioned immortal, she didn't know if these changes would stick. Most alterations on an immortal, such as a tattoo, would disappear within a day or so. But as long as her sorcery was flowing, she could do this every day.

Time to find out how her patient was doing. . . .

Thronos roused from a deep, ensorcelled sleep.

He shot to his feet, scowling at Melanthe. "Damn it, woman, why would you knock me out?"

Wait. Having bounded out of bed with no care—as opposed to his usual gradual rising—he should be feeling a chorus of anguish starting in his feet, shooting through his legs and torso, stabbing into his back and neck, before clawing through his wings.

Where is the pain?

He frowned down at his feet; they lined up perfectly. A sight he hadn't seen in ages.

"You were saying?" she remarked from the bed, buffing her nails.

He tentatively unfurled his wings, groaning with relief. Holding his breath, he tried to pin them . . .

They folded and compressed, just as they were supposed to. "How? How is this possible?"

"Lanthe's Sorcery Massage. Tee-em."

"Don't know what *tee-em* means," he said with a grin. "You fixed my pain?"

Her own smile faded. In a voice laced with sadness, she said, "The least I could do since I gave it to you."

And then she took it away. In no imagining had he dared to envision this. "Your powers are growing, lamb."

He felt no pain; she was regenerating her abilities. They were both healing from the wounds of the past. He would allow no sadness on this night.

The Sorceri were right: dwelling on the past injured the present.

"Thronos, I don't know if this is permanent. But I can do it every day if I have to—" She didn't get to finish because he'd already taken her into his arms, and into the air.

"Are you okay with this?" he asked.

"I am." She rested her head on his chest, her braids dancing over him. "I trust you."

He swooped his wings as hard as he could, taking them far from the Hall, from worries, from responsibilities. Under the stars, he couldn't contain a laugh. "I feel no pain!"

"It might only last a day."

"So you'll have to massage me daily?" Her hands all over him? Just like that, he was stiff for her. "Lucky *me*. But I must be awake next time. And I'd prefer to be on my back, sorceress."

Her gaze glittered as her hand dipped. She parted her lips when she found him fully erect. "Take me home."

"There's no time like the present." He adjusted her to their Pandemonian position, with her legs around his waist and his arms clasped securely around her.

"In the air?" Her eyes widened with excitement. "My weird, pervy Vrekener. I love it!"

FIFTY-TWO

Thronos was barely listening as Jasen and Cadmus argued over further security. A group of knights had met on one of the outermost islands, assessing weaknesses—and quarreling about defenses.

Thronos and Melanthe had been here only a week, but already the kingdom was more secure. He and the knights had implemented a successful alarm. In time, they'd install an emergency lever on every island. For now, Vrekener sentries patrolled the perimeter of the entire realm.

As a plan B, Thronos had ordered that the Territories begin their inexorable journey toward the Vrekeners' forest outpost. After days over the ocean, they'd passed the tip of Greenland and were now crossing a wintry gulf far in the northeast of North America.

At first, the idea of an evacuation system—and an unscheduled move—had sat ill with the assembly. At least until Thronos had described some of the Sorceri power he'd witnessed on the Order's island.

Jasen agreed with Thronos that the Vrekeners couldn't have enough measures in place.

Cadmus believed that his king was discounting the might of their warriors—because Cadmus had never met a being like Portia and could never conceive what she was capable of until he'd seen it with his own eyes.

On the one hand, Thronos had to convince others how malevolent some Sorceri could be. On the other, he wanted them to respect his queen and worked ceaselessly to smooth her way among his people. He'd been quick to tell the assembly of Melanthe's part in the assassination of Omort. He'd lauded all her work to neutralize threats from other factions.

Already, the House of Witches had declared peace. Once Bettina of the Deathly Ones had received Melanthe's description of the red gold medallion, she'd promptly agreed to future talks.

The Dacian ruler, Lothaire, had responded with a terse missive written in blood:

Vrekeners actually exist?
L, The King

Which might have been a joke? Thronos decided it was a good sign.

As for the rage demons, Rydstrom had written Thronos a personal message that still left him grinding his teeth. . . .

Thronos,
You are fucking up mightily, son.

My queen and I received Melanthe's letter, and based on your history with her, we can find no truth in it.

Gods only know what you're doing to my sister-in-law up there. Release her within the week, or court war with all of my vast kingdom.

Since I know Lanthe is your mate, I also know that you'll never release her, despite my threats. If anyone had tried to force me to relinquish Sabine, I would've laughed in his face.

The only thing that can save us from bloody conflict is if Lanthe convinces her sister that she is with you of her own free will.

Your best bet is to make your mate so deliriously happy that she can give a glowing—and believable—report. If you're willing to try, then take my advice, because I've been right where you are.

You don't have to understand *Sorceri ways; you just have to* accept *them. Allow her to be as she needs to be.*

Sabine has told me of your animosity toward all Sorceri, so unfortunately, I don't have high hopes that you can content Lanthe. I ready for war. I recommend you do as well.

Vrekener, harm my sister-in-law in any way, and I will find you on the battlefield. Your last sight will be of me, laughing as I take your head with my bare hands.

R

Of course Thronos had shown Melanthe the letter; she'd read it with wide eyes. "So my first letter was a Patty Hearst bust?"

He'd had no idea what that meant. "Advise me in this," he'd told her. "Do you want to meet with your sister?"

"I'm scared she'll use her sorcery to take me from you. Or Rydstrom will attack you. Let me try one more time." She'd bitten her lip. "Are you going to write him back?"

Thronos had given the matter much thought. As he'd watched Melanthe sleeping last night, he'd penned a response, sending it this morning. . . .

Lanthe's work had mitigated danger from three formidable sources, and most of the assembly was grateful. But Cadmus and his contingent remained suspicious of their queen and disgruntled that Thronos had left her empowered.

He could understand their doubt—because he'd initially contended with it himself. He'd had to go through hell before he'd appreciated Melanthe.

Pain had confessed all.

In Pandemonia, he'd resisted his feelings for her, bent on returning to the Hall, to reason and sanity, to find his anchor.

Now that he was here, he'd realized *Melanthe* was his anchor.

In any case, sanity and reason had proved in short supply for his brother. When had Aristo become so twisted? How? And how had he found three other males who'd shared his proclivities?

Thronos feared that the rules of their culture were so strict, the specter of offendments so pervasive, that some grew warped under the strain.

Should one truly be punished for something so harmless as a kiss?

Thronos had failed to follow the letter of Vrekener law; how could he expect others to be bound by them?

During his and Melanthe's tour of worlds, he'd learned that his all-or-nothing, inflexible thinking was a liability. As she'd told him, "Up in heaven, I'm sure things make sense and everyone acts as they're expected to and surprises are few. But outside of heaven, life can be confusing and heartbreaking and dire. So most of us take pleasure where we can find it. And we don't judge anyone who does the same."

In "heaven," surprises had been many. Thronos's brother had not acted in expected ways.

Life had proved utterly confusing.

Perhaps Vrekeners should judge less and enjoy more, taking pleasure where they could find it—especially since dire threats now surrounded them. Eternal life could be grindingly long, or heartbreakingly short.

Once the Territories were "out of the crosshairs," he would discuss social reforms with his co-ruler. . . .

The debate between Cadmus and Jasen was winding down, the day coming to a close, which meant he could soon return to her. Every second he wasn't with Melanthe, he wished he were.

For the public, he maintained what she called his *poker face.* At home with her, he could relax. Thanks to her generous infusion of sorcery, he remained pain-free, even days later. Still, she wanted to do a maintenance massage tonight, just in case.

Lucky, lucky me.

How could he have handled this time without her? She made him laugh. She forced him to shuck off some worries and most regrets. He was insatiable for her. To his remarkable fortune, she was just as much so for him.

He'd started taking more control, which she'd seemed all too happy to relinquish. Two nights ago, he'd positioned her on all fours, mounting her from behind, using his pain-free wings to propel his thrusts. When he'd felt her coming around his length, he'd reached forward to cover her mouth, then followed her, biting down on his forearm.

Late last night, he'd been gripped by an erotic dream about her, despite their many couplings. Just as he'd once hoped, he'd awakened with his shaft buried deep inside his wife, his hips pounding between her thighs.

When he'd realized what he was doing, he eased his movements, dumbfounded.

Until he'd felt her nails dig into the muscles of his ass. "Don't stop, Thronos. So close! I'll be quiet. . . ."

Over these days, he'd done things that he could tell had surprised her. She'd cry, "Oh!" then follow it with a breathy, *"Ohhh."* To tell him she liked it.

Just as she'd promised in Inferno, she always let him know what she needed.

When he thought about how eagerly his lusty mate took his seed with her body, her hands—and yes, her mouth—he couldn't prevent the grin that spread over his face.

Until he realized that all attention was on him.

"What do you think, my liege?" Jasen asked.

About? Thronos coughed into his fist. "I think we'll pick this up tomorrow. I know most of you have families awaiting you."

I have a family. He and Melanthe were an army of two.

He could fly, without pain, to meet his wife in their home. Gods, how things had changed in the weeks since he'd taken her. He smiled more often. So did she, casting him that mischievous grin.

As a girl, Melanthe had snared his heart with it.

As a woman, she owned his heart—invincible no longer.

I have her had become *I love her.*

Thronos would tell her tonight. He couldn't be certain how she'd react, but he would never again keep something so important in his pocket.

FIFTY-THREE

Having completed her and Thronos's history, Lanthe was tweaking her opening to Sabine. The letter would go out in one hour—and would prove even more important than she'd thought.

Sabine and Rydstrom still thought she was a prisoner.

Lanthe had begun . . .

My dearest sister,

How I do adore Skye Hall! I now enjoy cooking and cleaning, tasteful jokes, and demure clothing. Why, I hardly miss my sorcery or gold at all!

JK JK! I wouldn't know if I like any of that shit, because I've never tried it. My lust for gold is as strong as ever, my sorcery even stronger.

Your little sis is quite a boss.

And she's totally in love with a Vrekener.

In Inferno, Thronos had asked her if she'd ever been in love. She'd answered, "I've never known romantic love." True. But as a girl, Lanthe *had* loved Thronos—fiercely.

Deep down, maybe she'd never stopped. Maybe it'd always been there, waiting to bloom into a different kind of love. The fragile sprout of affection that she'd copped to in faux Feveris had grown into . . . a moonraker.

And her feelings for him were so strong, they'd even started coloring how she viewed Vrekeners.

Lanthe could still call them lame—but if anyone else did, she'd shut that down.

Sabine, when you read the rest of this letter, please keep an open mind. I'm not brainwashed, and I never will be. Just as you're bringing change to Rothkalina, I plan to here. Once all the dust settles, you can give me queenly pointers!

When Lanthe felt a vibration of power, she frowned, laying the quill down. She sensed sorcery—not hers.

She leapt to her feet. Something was approaching, a threat to the people here. She raced for the assembly hall.

Where was everyone? Was it dinnertime already?

Lanthe hastened toward the vibration, out the front doorway of the Hall. A portal was opening, right before her eyes.

On the freaking steps of Skye Hall.

Her jaw dropped when Sabine emerged. "Ai-bee?" Her sister was in full war regalia, with a broad gold headdress atop her flame-red tresses. A metal breastplate served as her top, and a jade mask adorned her face.

Sabine was a jolt of color in this monochrome realm.

"What are you doing here?"

"I'm rescuing you," Sabine said blithely as she traipsed onto Vrekener land. "Look at your necklace—is that red gold? To die for! It almost makes up for that dress."

"I don't need rescuing!"

"As I feared, the Vrekeners brainwashed you, just like so many Sorceri before you. But I vow I will get you back. When we return to Rothkalina, I'm enrolling you in cult deprogramming."

"You're not *hearing* me. I want to stay with Thronos."

As if Lanthe hadn't spoken, Sabine said, "The stress of all you've been through isn't helping. I know about the Order, about your fight to stay alive. About your capture and imprisonment *here*."

"I'm not imprisoned! Why would I still have my sorcery if I were a prisoner?" Nothing. "How did you find the Skye, Sabine?" *Can others?*

"The same way that Dacian vampire did: with a one-of-a-kind scry crystal. It's been tucked away in hidden Dacia for ages. Anyway, the leech let us borrow it. And then we used a portal power similar to yours."

"We?"

With a wave of her hand, Sabine used her sorcery to make Lanthe's necklace invisible. "I wouldn't want that to be taken from you. She'll think I merely gave you a glamour."

"She . . . ?" Lanthe trailed off, swallowing with fear when Morgana emerged from the threshold, also in war regalia.

Her pale blond hair was interwoven throughout her gold headdress. Her irises were the color of a bottomless pit. Sorcery of differing colors swirled around her. Lanthe had never perceived so much of it in one being—Morgana was overflowing with reclaimed powers, *laden* with them.

Like a snake who'd recently fed.

The queen glared at her enemy's domain with a vicious eye.

Lanthe held up her unlit hands, a gesture of yielding for Sorceri. "Now, let's just talk about this, Morgana. Can we do that?" Lanthe glanced around; the people were all gathered in the bastion, which meant no targets at hand for Morgana to smite. For now.

But this also meant Thronos would return soon. . . .

"We shall talk," Sabine said. "Back at Rothkalina. Come, Lanthe, we're on a bit of a clock here."

"Tick tock," Morgana sneered. "I've seen more than enough."

When Lanthe vowed, "There's no way I'm leaving here," Sabine clamped her arm in her gauntlet, turning her toward the portal. On the other side, visible through the threshold, was Lanthe's tower room.

"Behold, sister, your room in Rothkalina." As if speaking to a baby, she asked, "Do you *remember your room*? All your fabulous clothes, luxuries, servants, and self-help books are just beyond this threshold. Your TV and vault of gold await you. That is where you belong."

Lanthe fought to throw off her grip. "I *belong* here. What can I do to make you believe I'm not brainwashed! I'm not going anywhere—"

"Nooo!" Thronos had caught sight of them from above. "Don't touch her!" His wings snapped close to his body as he dove for them.

An enraged Vrekener was attacking, expression grim, eyes deadly.

A reckoning.

"Stay away!" Lanthe screamed. He was the embodiment of physical power, Morgana of mystical. Despite all the strength in his mighty body, and all his battle-hardened centuries, Thronos couldn't match that queen. "She will *kill* you!"

He didn't even slow; the rage in his eyes . . .

Morgana raised one hand. As if a giant fist had seized him in the air, he was brought up short, held in place—though he grappled to reach Lanthe.

"Don't hurt him!" She started drawing on her own power.

Morgana squinted at her as if she were an insect in need of a good crushing. "Careful, little girl, I'll snatch that persuasion from you before you could ever wield it against me." She turned her attention back to Thronos in the air. With another wave of her hand, the queen began lowering him in front of her for a better look.

Lanthe turned to Sabine. *—Ai-bee, please, please help us! I love Thronos.—*

Behind her mask, Sabine rolled her eyes. *—You cannot be serious.—*

—I've loved him since I was nine. I have so much to tell you, but if Morgana kills him, she'll be killing me!—

—I don't believe your brainwashed babble. It makes no sense!—

—What if there's even a chance it's true? Imagine if Morgana was about to murder Rydstrom. Imagine how you'd feel. This is HAPPENING to me, right now.—

—How could you possibly love one of . . . them?— Sabine flicked her hand in Thronos's direction.

Lanthe wanted to strangle her. *—If I'm brainwashed, you can always kill him later. For now, HELP US!—*

—*I suppose that* is *true.*—

When Morgana brought Thronos to the ground, to his knees, he grated, "Release my mate, and begone from these lands." Gnashing his teeth, he fought her sorcery enough to stand.

Morgana appeared surprised by his strength. But when Thronos again tried to reach Lanthe, the queen redoubled her hold, halting him in place. "This one had the audacity to abduct one of my subjects." Prismatic wisps of sorcery coiled around her. "Actions against Sorceri will now have swift and severe consequences."

"Morgana, I wasn't abducted! I made a conscious decision to come here!"

The queen merely ignored her.

—*Ai-bee, please!*—

—*Fine. My gods.*— Sabine's insouciance never faded as she said, "Morgana, though this is tiresome even to bring up . . ."

"What is it?" she demanded.

"I wouldn't slay that one if I were you." Sabine peered at her gauntlets, rapping the claws with boredom. "Why wouldn't you take him as prisoner?"

Morgana's eyes sparked ominously, glinting like obsidian. "Do you comprehend how long I've waited for this?" She squeezed her fist harder until Thronos labored to breathe. "My *ward* was brutalized by his *brother.* This Talos will pay as well!"

Lanthe tried to get between Morgana and him, but the queen's magic was an impenetrable leash from her to her prey. "Please, Morgana! Thronos was disgusted by what happened to Bettina. He's already in talks with her. Just speak with her! But for now, spare him. Please!"

At once, the air blurred around Morgana's body. Above her headpiece, her blond braids wavered like a gorgon's serpents. *"Spare him?"* she bit out. "*SPARE him?* Are you jesting with me? You and your sister have been running from him and his brother for ages! Now that your queen is in a position to mete out justice, you cower from what must be done?"

Before Lanthe could say anything, Morgana cut her off. "Do you know how many powers I pulled from the Vrekener vault? Do you know how many attacks those powers represented? How many of my subjects were victimized?" Voice rising with every word, she yelled, "The fact that I don't torture every godsforsaken Vrekener individually is my GIFT to them!" Sorcery whipped about her, coils electrified by her rage. "Thronos Talos will be *punished*!"

Sabine said, "I believe that's about to happen, no? In moments."

Lanthe's dread intensified even more. "What does that mean?"

Ignoring her, Morgana raked her fathomless gaze over Thronos. Though his skin reddened from lack of oxygen, he still struggled against her power.

But Morgana was just too strong. "I believe this being loves you, Melanthe." The queen smiled, as if in anticipation—one of the most bloodcurdling sights Lanthe had beheld. "What a weakness he's delivered to us. If I spare his life, he'll suffer a worse fate." Morgana could be diabolical, seemed to love devising twisted punishments for those who crossed her.

"Please, my queen—" Lanthe's words were cut off when she felt Morgana pulling on her persuasion. "What are you doing?"

"Controlling your sorcery. Your root power should be the one that curses him."

"Curses? Please stop this!"

Lanthe's blue light started to emanate from Morgana's hands. "Thronos, brother of Aristo, heed my voice and obey my commands. You will forget Melanthe."

He stole enough air to bellow, *"Never!"* Muscles all over his body rippled with strain as he fought the order.

Lanthe cried, "Morgana, I'm begging you!" She couldn't fight the queen now, but at least Thronos would live. In the future, Lanthe could reverse this! *—Thronos, I'll return for you! I'll make you remember me. Just stay alive!—*

Morgana commanded him, "Forget her, forget her, forget her! All memories of Melanthe are gone!"

Thronos's eyes met Lanthe's just as blue sorcery exploded out from Morgana, striking him like a bolt.

—I'm coming back for you, Thronos!—

It was already too late; once he'd recovered from that strike, he gazed blankly at her. Zero recognition.

She swallowed past the lump in her throat. If the queen forced her from the Territories, Lanthe would create another portal right back here and fix everything. But that didn't mean it wasn't killing her to see Thronos like this.

Morgana wasn't finished with him. "Your love for her will remain. The yearning you would feel to be parted from her will endure. Yet you won't understand the never-ending ache, won't comprehend the source of your misery. Should anyone speak to you of your queen, you'll react with anger, then forget the conversation. And, Thronos, should you live past the next two minutes, you'll forget we were ever here."

Lanthe swung her head around on Morgana. "What happens in two minutes?"

The queen looked like revenge personified as she said, "The mighty shall fall."

Tick tock? *Mother of gold* . . . "What have you done?" Somehow, Morgana was going to bring the Territories down.

"With access to their power vault, I turned their infuriating defenses against them. Their magics will destroy all that was long guarded and shrouded. Tick tock goes the clock."

Sabine began shoving Lanthe toward the portal. —*This is a done thing. I have to protect you.*—

Lanthe broke away from Sabine and lunged for the security lever just inside the doors of Skye Hall. The alarm roared to life, blaring across the Territories.

From the bastion, Vrekeners shot upward in a flood, wings spread as they evacuated according to plan.

At once, the late-day sky turned to night. The air grew chill.

Across all islands, they soared. Except for Thronos, who was still trapped by Morgana.

With her chin lifted, Lanthe turned to face her queen, to accept her wrath.

Morgana seemed to boil with fury, the very ground shaking beneath her. The rainbow colors of her powers merged to . . . black. Raising a hand, she hissed, "Ill-advised, sorceress."

When Sabine lunged in front of Lanthe, Morgana hesitated, then seemed to rein in the worst of her rage. "I'd punish you for this—and them for fleeing—but I haven't the time." With another wave of her hand, Lanthe was propelled toward the portal.

"No, leave me here!"

Sabine snapped, "Not going to happen!"

As Lanthe clung to the edge of the invisible threshold, she screamed, "Thronos, leave this place!"

Though Morgana's hold on him had eased—he could breathe once more—he continued to stare at the spot where she'd been standing.

"FLY AWAY!" Lanthe commanded.

But her persuasion had been drained from Morgana's catastrophic use of it.

Sabine peeled her fingers away. "We're running out of time, Lanthe!"

"Leave, Thronos!" With her grip loosened, Lanthe was sent careening into her room. "Please, GO!" she sobbed as the threshold closed behind them. . . .

The blaring alarm roused Thronos.

He blinked again and again. Why was he standing on the steps of Skye Hall, staring at nothing? He shook his head hard.

Vrekeners had surged upward from the islands, flying in the direction of the outpost. Why was he not moving with them? He wondered if this was another drill, until he heard explosions coming from the outer islands.

One blast after another detonated along the lines of the monoliths. Fires erupted, overrunning the islands in blue and white flames—an unnatural fire.

An immortal killer.

Burning rock shot upward—and downward, cascading toward the gulf far below them.

The warded and protected Territories were being annihilated by some unseen force.

Act, Talos. Move! He tensed to fly—

A white flash fire roared from the Hall itself, engulfing him just as his wings reflexively shielded his body. The mystical flames consumed both wings; the explosive percussion hurtled him down to the vale.

Which had disappeared.

The island had . . . disintegrated.

Thronos plummeted amid the fiery rubble. Blood poured from his ringing ears. Wind snapped what was left of his still-burning wings. They were useless.

My lands, my people. He was helpless to do anything for them.

He couldn't fly. Could only fall.

He knew he had fallen as a boy. Though he didn't remember why, he hadn't used his wings all the way down.

As now.

Once more I fall.

His back was turned to the world below—so he could keep his eyes on the sky. Time seemed to slow.

Traces of malevolent sorcery eddied around crimson and purple clouds. Lightning fractured those clouds, illuminating all the debris raining down around him.

Scorched plaster. Burning books. A charred cradle.

For mere days, he'd been king. Now his realm had died.

You've lost something else, something even dearer. His heart twisted. What could possibly be more treasured than a kingdom?

What was it he'd lost?

He finally dragged his eyes from the heavens and gazed below him. The water rushed ever closer. Blue and white flames soared from the gulf. Thronos had no shield from the heat. When he hit, he would be incinerated.

His life had been long and unfulfilling, his dream of finding his mate unrealized. Perhaps he was meant to have died after his first fall. Perhaps fate sought to right that misguided mercy now.

He turned to the nearby mountainside and spotted . . . Vrekeners. Thousands of them. They'd gathered on a plateau above the gulf to watch their home perish.

Thronos had never named a successor. His people were more vulnerable than they'd ever been. For them, he had to survive.

Wasn't there a way? He couldn't remember it!

What couldn't he remember?

Once more I fall. . . .

FIFTY-FOUR

On a mountaintop far across the gulf from the gathered Vrekeners, Nïx the Ever-Knowing and Morgana, the Queen of Sorceri, watched the Skye fall.

One female had allowed it; one had caused it.

Nïx's lightning crackled all around her—and the bat she carried. Morgana's usurped powers were so volatile that the color streams of her sorcery had morphed to a permanent black.

As the two immortals bore witness, they sparked off each other like negatively charged ions.

"I foresaw the Queen of Persuasion desperate to stay with King Thronos," Nïx said, never looking away. The water was already aflame with soaring plumes of otherworldly fire.

Morgana too kept her gaze trained. "As soon as I left her and Sabine in Rothkalina, Melanthe probably created a portal back. To *nothing*." Black swirls danced from her lips, as if a contagion was trying to escape her body. "If the Vrekener survives, the memory of his wife will not—"

The giant monoliths crashed into the flames, displacing miles of water, generating towering tsunamis.

"I suppose the mortals will know of this now," Morgana said, tone inscrutable. "Of *us*."

"Not quite yet. . . ."

From the gulf, the sea god Nereus rose up like a mountain himself, visible only to the immortal pair. With a monstrous inhalation, he sucked all the flames into his lungs.

Then he brandished his divine triton, raising it over his head to subdue the waves. The tsunamis paused, their terrible surge arrested in midswell—

Yielding to his command, they gradually subsided, slipping to acquiescence.

The surface was still, the fire defeated. Before Nereus sank to the depths once more, his smoldering gaze lingered on Morgana.

She frowned, but that was the least extraordinary thing she'd seen this day.

A reviled realm—the bane of her entire life—had perished by fire and been entombed in the sea. Her heart was glad.

The Valkyrie soothsayer turned to the sorceress queen. "For better or worse, it's begun. . . ."

FIFTY-FIVE

1. ~~Portal to Vrekener outpost~~
2. ~~Adjust directions, portal to outpost~~
3. ~~Adjust directions again, portal to outpost~~
4. ~~Offer demon mercenaries gold to scour Canadian forests for difficult-to-find Vrekener outpost~~
5. ~~Offer witches gold to scry for Thronos~~
6. ~~Contact Loa, re: Hail Mary option—send gold deposit~~
7. FIND NÏX
8. Keep from losing your ever-living shit because he needs you
9. Contact oracles and witches in more worlds—offer gold
10. Save up power for tomorrow

"What have I told you about chasing after boys?" Sabine drawled, sashaying into Lanthe's substitute suite.

Her former residence was still being repaired, nearly a week after the Territories had fallen.

Lanthe glanced up from her desperate letters and lists, allowing Sabine see her panic, her despondency. Both grew with each minute. "Thronos is not a boy—he's *my husband.* And I want him back."

"You look like hell. Would you like me to weave an illusion over you?"

As if Lanthe could be bothered with her appearance—when every other thought in her head was *YOU'RE RUNNING OUT OF TIME TO FIND HIM!*

How was Thronos dealing with the destruction of his kingdom? How was he coping with his feelings of loss? What if he thought he had nothing to live for and was careless in some battle? What if Cadmus staged a refugee coup?

"You're pushing yourself far too hard, Lanthe." Sabine reclined on a nearby divan. "Since when have you been able to create portals so frequently?"

After Lanthe had failed to locate the outpost that first day, she'd reasoned that Nïx had actually been talking about *all* of Lanthe's powers behaving like muscles. She'd been able to shave down the time between her portals to once a day, but that was the limit.

Use, use, use, use, use—and no *rest?* Accuracy . . . suffered.

"You need to dial down the thresholds," Sabine warned.

"I haven't created one today." Holding off was one of the hardest things she'd ever done.

But she was about to go for broke, to try to reach a realm that could be light-years away.

"That's only one of the things I'm here to talk about."

She'd known Sabine would want a sit-down soon. Lanthe heard the whispers in the castle growing louder and more numerous. They said that Thronos had surely perished.

She supposed they had reason to believe that. . . .

As soon as Morgana had left Rothkalina to go watch her handiwork from some vantage like a ghoulish spectator, Lanthe had slashed open a rift to get back to Thronos.

In time to catch the blast.

Sabine had shoved her out of the way, taking the full brunt—a force strong enough to send her flying across the room. Her impact had buckled a tower wall. Luckily Sabine had been wearing scads of metal.

Lanthe hadn't been able to create another portal until the next day. With a suitcase full of clothes and big hopes, she'd portaled to Canada, using the just-in-case directions Thronos had given her to the Vrekeners' outpost.

Past Lanthe's threshold, there'd been nothing but rocks and trees, not a trace of Vrekeners. She'd been greeted by a herd of deer so tame they'd approached her. Clearly, no winged hunters had been in that area stalking them, though Thronos loved venison.

Either she'd gotten the directions jumbled (as she had every other time in her life, in which case, she sucked) or her portal had gone awry (in which case, she sucked).

While she'd been recharging for another futile go at Canada, Sabine and Rydstrom had told Lanthe that even an immortal like Thronos couldn't survive a fire born of sorcery like Morgana's. Sabine relayed to her that Morgana had watched it all—after the blast, the islands had simply crumbled into flames and plunged.

"Yes, but Thronos's wings are fireproof," Lanthe had argued.

Sabine had said, "Even his wings would be vulnerable to an unnatural fire."

Lanthe had reasoned, "Someone could have swooped in to save him."

With grave hesitation, Rydstrom had pointed out, "But hadn't everyone already evacuated, Lanthe?"

Whatever. Thronos had survived. Period. Lanthe had promised herself that she would never underestimate him again. He was an extraordinary male who would prevail in any situation.

Besides, her husband had one more trick up his sleeve. Granted, he wouldn't quite *know* he had it. . . .

"We can talk later," she told Sabine now. "I'm busy." She waved at the stack of missives she was penning to witches and oracles all over the worlds.

The afternoon of her first ill-fated Canada trip, Lanthe had gotten one of the castle guards to trace her to the Louisiana chapter of the House of Witches. Carrow and her super-powerful friend Mariketa had scried for

Thronos, but some of the Vrekeners' ancient magics still held. The same cloaks that had hidden them from humans lingered.

The witches couldn't locate an entire populace.

So Lanthe had dispatched Cadeon's former band of mercenaries to manually search Canuck forests. "Which ones?" they'd asked.

All of them. Because I suck.

From the divan, Sabine picked up one of the maps that Lanthe had spread over every available surface. "Too busy with your search to inquire after my healing? I'm right as rain, by the way."

Lanthe felt a twinge of guilt.

"Busy or not, you won't get rid of me so easily." Her sister rang for wine.

Powerless Sorceri servants known as Inferi promptly answered the call, then vanished once more.

"Rydstrom made me promise to talk to you because he thinks I'm upset about this tiff between us." Sabine sipped from a golden goblet. "So here I remain because, weirdly, I keep promises to him. By the way, Morgana wanted me to ask you why the sea god Nereus sent her a coral tube carved to look like a humongous cock. Apparently he mentioned your name in a very naughty gift card."

"Long story, meager payoff."

Sabine sighed. "You're still angry with me. Though surely you know I couldn't have convinced Morgana to call off her attack. Fearing for your life, I went to her, trying to do just that. She suggested the use of that scry crystal to evacuate you. I did what I thought was right. And I do believe my actions prevented Morgana from simply smiting the Vrekener outright."

Lanthe put down her pen. "You want credit for that—even though you think he's dead anyway?"

No, she couldn't have expected Sabine to defy Morgana any more than she had. But Sabine didn't seem to regret what the queen had done, even after Lanthe had told her everything about Thronos, about all that she and the Vrekener had been through together.

The pages Lanthe had written of their history had been erased from existence—just like their history had been erased from Thronos's mind.

Sabine had been shocked to discover that Lanthe truly loved him, and probably had since she was a girl. But she hadn't embraced the idea of her little sister wed to an enemy Vrekener: "Especially one who doesn't even have a house, much less a kingdom," Sabine had said, making Lanthe want to punch her in the tit.

Sabine had been more worked up about Emberine daring to cut off Lanthe's tongue: "She will pay dearly for that. I plot for her very soul!" Sabine had also raised a fuss over the dragon gold: "I didn't conceal your necklace from Morgana just so you can throw it away willy-nilly! Let me handle Bettina. I know her pressure points. Consider their declaration of war null and void."

In an attempt to distract Lanthe from her search, Sabine had invited Cadeon and his family to stay for a few weeks. Lanthe had paused only to press a kiss on each babe's downy head, greet their parents, and ask Holly if she knew where Nïx was ("No earthly idea"). So Lanthe had gotten back to work.

The entire royal family pitied her. Yesterday Lanthe had gone to Tornin's library for more maps. Rydstrom and Cadeon had been down in the courtyard, conversing amiably in their deep demon voices and *Sith Ifrican* accents. With a swaddled babe in each arm, Cadeon had crowed, "I've got a trio of females who all adore me. Life is rich, brother!"

Spying Lanthe above, Rydstrom had motioned for Cadeon to keep it down.

They shouldn't pity her. Because Lanthe was going to fix this. She needed to get her husband back for more than just—

"Are you sending out even more gold?" Sabine said now, setting away her goblet. "Lanthe, you've spent a fortune!"

In their childhood meadow, Thronos had tickled Lanthe, teasing her, "You like me far better than gold."

I do. I really do. "As if you wouldn't do the same for Rydstrom."

"But Thronos is a *Vrekener.* They're despicable!"

"Those are my subjects you're talking about!" Lanthe could call them names all day long, but if anyone else did . . .

"I insult our age-old foes, and your eyes glimmer with outrage? Up is down, down is up."

"Just leave, Sabine. I don't have time to make you understand."

"Kicking me out, when I have in my possession a letter from Thronos to Rydstrom, sent before the collapse of the Territories?"

Lanthe's eyes went wide. "Why didn't you say anything before?"

"We've only just learned of it today, because I *allegedly* ordered the Vrekener messenger to be waylaid and interrogated—in defiance of Lore law. Which *allegedly* delayed the letter a bit." She tugged a folded sheet of parchment from inside her gauntlet. "I make no apologies. Based on the information I had, I was desperate to find you."

"Open it!"

When Sabine patted the divan beside her, Lanthe nearly tripped on her feet to join her there. "You haven't read it?"

"No. Rydstrom has, and he suggested we read it together."

Lanthe saw Thronos's handwriting and seal, and tears welled. She didn't trust her voice, so she circled her hand in the air, *come on, come on.*

Ever dramatic, Sabine took her time unfolding it. "I wonder how your Vrekener will respond. Rydstrom's letter to him was by no means gentle, so I can only imagine what this rebuttal will contain." Finally Sabine held up the letter, and together they read:

King Rydstrom,

My first reaction when I received your message was anger. Who the hell are you to advise me on how to treat my beloved wife? To make her happy?

Beloved wife? Lanthe's tears spilled down her face, making Sabine roll her eyes. They read on. . . .

I think you and Queen Sabine have a mistaken impression of Melanthe's life in the Territories.

She roams the kingdom freely, fully empowered—because I trust her implicitly. She wears whatever garments she chooses and worships gold, of which I plan to provide her ever more.

She doesn't do these things because I allow *her to, or because she* demands *to—this is simply the way things are in our life.*

We co-rule our kingdom. Our marriage is a partnership.

It works.

Lanthe gave a sob.

"Thronos truly understands about the gold?"

"He m-met Mother when he was a boy. He understands the importance."

Sabine didn't look surprised, but then she'd long since woven an illusion over her face.

However, upon further reflection over your letter, I realize that my only response to you can be gratitude. Melanthe is not only my wife and queen, she is my most treasured friend. You helped free her from the tyranny of Omort, and you've pledged your protection since.

Because of this, I am deeply in your debt. I wish for no war between us.

If you can agree to terms, I propose a meeting that would include you with your wife, and me with mine.

Melanthe has been against this course, fearing that you or Sabine will take her from me against her will.

I look upon my powerful queen even now as I write this, and confidently dare you to try.

Thronos

Lanthe choked back her next sob. If he hadn't written of her being a powerful queen, she'd probably be curled up in a ball, her tears wetting the divan upholstery.

"That was . . . big of him." Sabine folded the letter. "Perhaps we Sorceri *oughtn't* to have blown up his kingdom?"

Lanthe whirled around and punched her sister in the tit. Regrettably, Sabine was wearing a metal breastplate.

As Lanthe shook out her hand, Sabine snapped, "You should've told me about your history with the Vrekener!"

"I didn't know what to make of it back then! For so long, it only brought pain. I was embarrassed. It seemed like all I ever did was confess my poor judgment to you."

"Can you not understand what it looked like to me? I thought you'd finally been caught by a fiend. I was just trying to protect you."

"I don't need your protection anymore! I don't need your worry! Sabine, I stole keys to the gates of hell and convinced demon hordes that I was a goddess." She held up her necklace, the red gold nearly mesmerizing Sabine. "I somehow made a portal under duress in the belly of a beast! Thronos and I prevailed over a deity."

"I can't simply *stop* worrying about you or stop protecting you. Short of your commanding me not to, it will never happen."

"Then fine, don't stop. But support me in this." She took her sister's face in her hands. "For me, Thronos is all the gold in the world. He's my next heartbeat."

Sabine was bewildered, and let her sister see it. "Well. Way to sum up your feelings." At length, she exhaled with defeat. "All right, then, consider me . . . supportive—if you'll forgive me, and stop being cross. I can't stand having discord between us." She opened her arms. "You know I only want what's best for you."

Lanthe hugged her for long moments—she'd hated the discord too.

Sabine was teary when they broke away. "You know, the Queen of Zephyr is a very disagreeable sorceress. In the future, if you'd like to spend some quality sister time together, we could ambush her and steal her power of flight. In case Thronos wants a flying wife, or whatever."

Lanthe smiled through her own tears. "QT with my big sis? I'd really like that."

"Also, if you're out of leads, you could renew my search for the Hag in the Basement." After Omort had died, Hag had delivered those antidotes for the morsus, then fled Tornin. "She's rumored to be working for *King* Lothaire in Dacia. Wrap your head around that for a moment, will you?"

Hag possessed locating powers! "You've stopped looking for her?"

"We sought her—only to find her partner in crime, Lothaire, and his hateful book of debts. No longer. It's rumored that he gave the book to La Dorada for some reason."

Then Rydstrom owed the Queen of Evil a blood debt? That didn't bode well. And he and Sabine already had a lot on their plate.

Because the mysterious Well of Souls was . . . stirring.

"Hag's a great idea," Lanthe said. "I'll send a dispatch to Dacia right away."

"There's one more idea. Cadeon came up with it. . . . If Thronos truly is a demon, it might be possible for you to summon him."

A female who slept with a demon of certain breeds could summon him at any time—if she knew the rites and possessed the esoteric ingredients. The demon would uncontrollably teleport back to her.

Lanthe had contemplated this—was preparing for it—but had decided to save the idea until she'd exhausted all others.

Despite the amount of gold she'd offered Loa the Commercenary, the priestess couldn't get the ingredients to Lanthe for another three weeks.

In any case, the situation with Thronos was . . . tricky. He wasn't going to remember Lanthe when he saw her. As far as he'd know, she might be an enemy sorceress. Plus, she wasn't sure whether he'd ever fully accepted he was a demon.

Being involuntarily demon-summoned by an unknown Sorceri would have to spook him.

"Of course, some breeds are immune," Sabine continued, "and I can't imagine anyone having tried it on a Vrekener."

"Tell Cadeon thank you from me. But it's my last-ditch option—since I have Thronos's memory issues to consider."

Sabine narrowed her gaze. "You've got another plan up your gauntlet.

You never used to keep secrets from me." She snapped her fingers. "Oh, wait. You did for five hundred years."

"I'm saving up my sorcery till tomorrow, so I can create a portal all the way to Pandemonia." She'd attempted it yesterday and had accidentally opened a rift back to the belly of the beast. She'd slammed the portal door in an instant, but her room had still smelled like gastric acid.

Surely if Lanthe rested her threshold muscle, she could reach that demon plane. "I think he'll be there."

"How? Does he have a portal . . . Ah! You think he can trace! That's why you're so confident he lives."

Lanthe shrugged. Nïx had mentioned it in faux Feveris: *You'd be able to trace—big deal.* Thinking back, Lanthe realized the Valkyrie might have been saying that in earnest.

Tracing *was* a big deal. It could save a demon's life.

Even if Nïx had said nothing, Lanthe would believe. "Sabine, you'd have to know Thronos like I do—he always beats the odds. He wasn't supposed to survive his fall as a boy. He did. He wasn't supposed to fly again. He does. He was never supposed to catch me or win my heart. How could I ever bet against him?"

"So why Pandemonia?"

"I think his subconscious will take him back there. Or his demonic blood will, or vestiges of our history. Pandemonia is where Thronos and I made a fresh start." *Melanthe, let's begin with a kiss.* "There's a glade we rested in, where we had our first real connection." Or *re*connection.

"Then Rydstrom and I will accompany you," Sabine said. "I'm very interested in that realm's dragons. We have an extraordinary female here who needs her own stable of males; she's basically a basilisk rock star—"

"I'm going alone. If Thronos sees two Sorceri and a rage demon, it'll put him on guard. And even with no memory of me, he might remember you as Morgana's henchwoman."

"It's too dangerous."

"Pandemonia's really not that bad once you know the zones. Some parts were even hauntingly beautiful. The dragons can be a problem, but

I'll figure it out." Lanthe didn't expect to arrive there on the same day he did. Which was why she'd packed a bag—and a tent.

She wasn't leaving hell without her man. Melanthe, of the Deie Sorceri—late of the lavish Castle Tornin—was going to . . . *camp out.*

"Say he lives, Lanthe. Say he can trace. Then say he goes to Pandemonia. If you can somehow find him, how will you handle him? He might be so enraged at Sorceri that he'll kill you first and ask questions later."

"He would never hurt me."

"You won't be able to undo Morgana's curse with a wave of your hand. You'll have to be fully empowered. She amped up the voltage of your sorcery to astronomical levels."

"I'll figure it out." Lanthe's persuasion had been strengthening once more, but would it be enough?

"Are you sure you should restore his memory?" At Lanthe's glare, Sabine said, "Based on what you told me, he had some issues with how you've lived your life. Why not let him be blissfully ignorant? You two could meet and date, as if it's the first time."

"He changed; those issues are resolved. And even if I had no problem lying to him—which I do—I have to let him know that we were together."

"Why?"

"So he doesn't fall over in shock when I have a halfling in a few months." The witch Mariketa had been the one to sense it, telling her: "You do know you're totes preggo, right?"

Lanthe's biological clock had cried, *That's right, bitches, remember my name!*

Her first reaction had been a muttered "Fuck," à la Thronos. But with each passing hour, she'd had time to grow accustomed to the idea. She was now officially elated—or she would be.

As soon as she located her kid's father.

"Amusing, sister." When Sabine saw that she wasn't joking, she gasped, "Mother of gold."

FIFTY-SIX

He must've damaged his head in the fall. He's . . . different."

"His wings were wasted by flame."

"So how did the king come to be on that mountain?"

As Thronos completed his nightly patrol of the outpost, he heard his people's whispers, had been hearing them for a week.

Some believed he'd traced to the mountain, as a demon might. Some believed he'd been ensorcelled with a protection spell—though Thronos had no idea what would make them think that.

All of his subjects were wary about their king and their future, and he couldn't blame them—he wasn't confident in either of those things himself.

My mind is not well. . . .

He descended through a profuse bank of fog, splaying his wings. Since they'd regenerated, flying had become excruciating once more, such a change from the inexplicable reprieve he'd enjoyed.

Gritting his teeth, he dropped to the landing of his elevated cabin, one of many in their outpost. Trees housed thousands more.

Jasen was already there awaiting him. Each night the two of them met to discuss the day's events. The male appeared as exhausted as he felt.

Inside, Thronos took his place at his rough-hewn desk. "Any new developments today?"

"None." Jasen sat on a simple wooden bench. "The people remain unsettled. They feel like we're living on borrowed time."

Thronos gazed out his sole window into the night; as usual he could see little past the blanket of mist that enveloped this forest.

But eventually the humans would find them here. Their wards would not screen them forever. A horde of Vrekeners couldn't live in the mortal world. Not all together.

And our unity is our strength.

"There is some talk of dividing our numbers, my liege."

"That will *not* happen."

Jasen looked relieved by Thronos's unequivocal reaction. "But in one thing, many agree—they want revenge for what we've lost. Cadmus stirs the pot for war."

Thronos had heard those rumblings as well. "Revenge against a revenge?" he asked. "Did Aristo's actions not deserve reprisal?" Thronos was more conflicted about that than most. After all, it was his brother who'd brutalized Morgana's ward. It was his brother who'd waged a silent and relentless predation on her subjects.

"You're saying we deserved this?"

"No, I'm saying that everything isn't black and white. I'm saying that revenge is a zero-sum game. Especially for immortals. If we start it, we'd better be prepared to play it for eternity." He exhaled. "Even if we come to decide on war, now is not the time."

Thronos was in no shape to lead them. He'd been injured in the explosion, and had suffered some kind of damage to his mind—yet it wasn't healing. He still had gaps in his memory, and his temper had grown short.

He could remember a meadow in the Alps of the mortal realm, where he'd played as a boy—but he couldn't recall what he'd been doing ten nights ago.

When his thoughts wandered, they always turned to the demon plane of Pandemonia. He knew he'd been there for some reason, narrowly escaping with his life. There'd been dragons, hellhounds, and demon hordes.

In his daydreams, Thronos mused on the realm's paths, like **The Long Way.** He'd avoided it—as most would.

Unless one was looking for something. . . .

Thronos could remember with precise detail every glyph he'd read there—from **Behold a temple unequaled** to **The pest that WAS**—but he couldn't determine how he'd traveled into the belly of a beast.

Nor how he'd come to be in the lair of a sea god.

Asides from all these gaps, Thronos felt like he'd forgotten something *critical,* and that memory churned so close to the surface—maddeningly—like a word on the tip of his tongue that refused to reveal itself.

His chest ached with a loss so marked that he sometimes thought he'd go insane. He felt as if the glass shard that had so grievously wounded him in his boyhood had again lodged itself beside his heart, but he couldn't remove it. When he was alone, his claws constantly found his chest and flayed his skin—

"When will it be time?" Jasen asked.

Thronos glanced up, nearly startled by the male's presence.

"For war?" Jasen prompted. "I understand you're hesitant because of your queen."

"I don't *have* a queen," Thronos grated, wondering if his knight had suffered head damage as well.

"You said the same when I asked if she had survived the explosion. My liege, I'm a simple soldier—I don't understand pretext as you do. Are we to behave as if she never existed? By your actions, it seems you want to forget she ever lived—but why?" Jasen scrubbed his hand over his face, looking genuinely upset, while Thronos was baffled—and angered—by this outburst.

"We know she wasn't involved in the attack," Jasen continued. "A few even spied the queen at the lever. Only because of her did we have the alarm in the first place, and then she warned everyone. It could be argued that she saved our species."

Thronos grasped for patience, saying slowly, "I don't know what you're talking about. I—have—no—queen."

"Very well, my liege." Jasen sounded rocked with disappointment. "I won't mention it again."

"See that you don't. See that no one does!" Thronos regretted his tone immediately. He knew he was on edge, his ire ever at the ready. Yet moments later, he could never recall what he'd been angered about. "As for Cadmus and his warmongering, no longer are we hidden and immune to harm. We live in an indefensible outpost. We must approach this coolly. Jasen, if we war, we risk not only defeat—but our very extinction."

He was about to pinch his aching temples, but then lowered his hand. Eyes were on him. He needed to look like a competent leader. "Until we find a place to call home, we should focus on nothing but that."

What if we took the long way home . . . ?

Thronos cut off the idea before it even fully formed. *Too far-fetched.*

"Have you considered seeking asylum with another faction?" Jasen asked. "One within our alliance?"

"I've thought about asking Rydstrom the Good of the rage demonarchy for refuge in the Grave Realm." The badlands of Rothkalina, filled with outlaws and dragons. After Pandemonia, dragons no longer gave Thronos pause.

This seemed to surprise Jasen.

"I corresponded with him recently." Though Thronos didn't remember about what, or even what had been said. All he remembered was that he'd come away with the idea that Rydstrom was irritating but honorable.

"You're speaking of colonization on a *demon* plane?"

The vaguest memory arose. He could hear a muted voice, a female saying, *We're going to go found a Vrekener offshoot colony in a different realm.*

At the memory, Thronos fought the urge to take his head between his hands and squeeze till something cracked. *My mind, my mind . . .*

"What do we do for now, my king?"

With effort, Thronos kept his tone even. "We recover. We plan."

Jasen opened his mouth, then closed it. Thronos knew what question the knight had been trying to pose all week—but he didn't know how he'd answer.

"My liege . . . will you tell me how you came to be on that mountain?" Jasen finally dared to ask. "Hundreds saw you simply appear."

As Thronos had fallen, he'd desperately wanted to reach his people. Air had shrilled over him, his heartbeat booming in his damaged ears. Suddenly a wave of dizziness had overcome him, so fierce he'd had to close his eyes. When he'd opened them, he'd been standing amongst the others.

I traced for the first time.

Over the last week, he'd debated revealing his talent. If he had the ability, others would too.

After his journeys, he'd begun to suspect their blood might be demonic. Hadn't he recognized that strange script in Pandemonia, as if from a genetic memory? Hadn't he felt at home in that plane's harshness? Why was he still so drawn to its untamed and tumultuous lands?

The ability to trace could be a priceless talent in any upcoming war. But his people had recently lost their king and then their kingdom; Thronos didn't believe it was the time for them to learn of their demonic origins.

After arriving at the outpost, he'd given himself just one night to explore his new talent. He'd envisioned the temple of gold. That dizziness had struck him; an instant later, he'd traced there. As he'd run his fingers over the bricks, the feel of that invisible shard in his chest had returned with a vengeance.

When he'd flown over an eerily silent battle plateau and a river of lava, deeper went the glass.

And then, arriving in the forest glade—the oasis where he'd rested between his trials—he'd been nearly debilitated by the pain in his chest.

With a bellow, he'd traced back to the outpost, resolving never to return.

He'd only made it until the next night, drawn back to Pandemonia. . . .

"I will tell you this, Jasen," he said at length. "You alone for now."

"Yes, my liege?"

"If you want to reach something badly enough, you *will*."

Jasen's eyes lit with excitement. "Very good, sir." Before he left, he turned and said, "I'm glad that you are our king."

Thronos wanted only to be a worthy one.

No, that wasn't true. He wanted something else, craved it with a blistering intensity. Yet he couldn't identify what it was.

Alone, he made his way to his simple cot, telling himself that he needed to sleep in order to heal. He lay back, the pain in his body flaring even worse at rest.

Sleep proved elusive. He felt he should be somewhere else, anywhere but here. *Agitated* didn't begin to describe the turmoil inside him.

His shaft started to harden with insistent pulses, as if it had every expectation of releasing. The pressure only aggravated Thronos's restlessness.

Perhaps he should make just one more trip. . . .

The lure proved too great to resist. He closed his eyes and pictured the forest glade, then tensed to trace there.

From the coolness of his cabin, he teleported into warmth and sprinkling water. He gazed up at towering moonraker trees, marveling anew at the floating bubbles, the drops that couldn't seem to decide whether to travel up or down.

Lucky drops.

Why would he think that? He waved his wing, fanning the bubbles. Such a whimsical gesture, yet for some reason it *grieved* him. The glass shard was back, gouging through his flesh down to his godsdamned spine. He snatched at his hair, then twisted around to punch the trunk of a moonraker.

Leave this place of pain. Return to the outpost.

He made a vow to himself then: he would not ever come back here—until his mind had healed.

Pandemonia isn't going anywhere. . . .

Lanthe sucked in a steadying breath. "I'm ready," she told the group that had assembled in her room.

Rydstrom had his brawny arms crossed over his chest. Cadeon would have as well if he hadn't been holding a baby. Holly, also holding a baby, looked worried for Lanthe. Sabine did too, having forgone her illusion of indifference.

Rydstrom said, "It's too dangerous, Lanthe." They still wanted to accompany her.

All of them. Well, except for the twins. Though those little badasses would probably think Pandemonia was great fun.

"We've been over this," Lanthe said. "If Thronos sees huge demons, a Valkyrie, and two Sorceri, it'll put him on the defensive. Face it, we look like a marauding gang. One more time, guys, I will be fine."

Assuming she could even *get* to Pandemonia, Lanthe was as prepared as she could be. Sabine had insisted she borrow her ability to talk to animals. If a dragon wanted to chat, Lanthe was ready.

Another loaner? Lanthe wore her sister's most battle-tested breastplate. As Sabine had grumbled, "You need extra insurance for my halfling niece or nephew." Lanthe was also wearing more sensible boots (no stilettos this time) and a pair of second-skin leather pants—might as well squeeze into them while she still could!

"You're not going to simply run into him there," Sabine said. "What if you miss him?"

Lanthe marched over to her camping backpack. "That's why I'm staying there."

Jaws dropped.

Cadeon recovered first. "You? Camping?" He snorted. "Much less camping in hell!"

"Cade." Holly slapped his chest.

He muttered, "You gotta admit that's funny."

Lanthe piped her lip and blew a braid out of her eyes. Apparently everyone here had forgotten that she'd *already* camped in hell. Granted, she hadn't been alone. . . .

Sabine said, "I was opposed to you going by yourself for just an hour or so! Now you want to go indefinitely? And if you tell me it's really not that bad there one more time, I might scream."

"I've set everything in motion here that I can. In a few days, I'll check in for news."

"And to provide proof of life," Rydstrom said.

Cadeon gave him a *damn straight* look.

"If I haven't found Thronos in three weeks, I'll return to summon him. And, Sabine, it's really not that bad there."

When Sabine parted her lips to argue, Lanthe said, "This baby bird's gotta fly, sis."

"Great," Sabine drawled. "She's already speaking in avian metaphors."

Holly chuckled, then made her face serious once more.

Lanthe gazed at her sister, hating that she worried. But there was nothing she could do about it. "It's time for me to go. I'm recharged, resolved, and ready to do this—on my own."

Rydstrom drew Sabine close. "She's got a point, *cwena*." Demonish for *little queen,* his nickname for her. "There comes a time when you just have to trust. I had to do that with Cadeon."

"Only took him fifteen hundred years," Cadeon remarked. Aly blew a bubble and tugged on her pointed ear at the same time, which Cadeon clearly thought was a marvelous feat.

"At least leave the portal open," Sabine said, "until we can be sure you even got to the right realm."

In a grousing tone, Lanthe muttered, "Fine. Just so you won't worry so much."

"Don't forget what we talked about, Lanthe," Rydstrom told her. Now that he knew what Thronos was really like, he was cordially offering refuge in Rothkalina to every Vrekener. Sabine was grudgingly co-offering it.

"Thank you for that." But Lanthe had another idea. It was so crazy, she hadn't mentioned it to a soul. . . .

Dreaming of reuniting with Thronos and restoring his memory, she felt sorcery coursing through her. She raised her hands and began to open a rift.

For me—and for our halfling.

Lanthe directed the door straight to the glade (in theory). Squeezing her eyes shut, she inwardly begged that she'd find floating bubbles—and not a giant stomach.

FIFTY-SEVEN

Thronos's pain continued to escalate.

He'd decided to leave, but at the last moment he'd felt as if he was on the verge of remembering something. *So pain be damned.* He remained in the forest glade.

Thronos *knew* pain. He could handle it.

The day was beginning its long, slow fade to twilight. Considering this realm's sluggish passage of time, he'd already been away from the outpost far too long. But leaving this place would be cowardly. And he was no—

Movement behind him? He twisted around.

In the center of this glade, the air blurred. A gap opened, a *portal.*

Cautiously stepping from it was the most breathtaking female Thronos had ever seen.

Long raven hair. Plump red lips. Eyes as blue as the skies he'd lost when his kingdom fell.

That raw emptiness, that maddening absence began to . . . ease? As if some magnet were pulling him toward her, his feet started to close the distance between them.

But she was dressed as a sorceress, with a metal headdress and breastplate, an unusual gold necklace—and leather trews that lovingly molded to her generous curves. He scrubbed his palm over his mouth, needing to focus; difficult when treated to such a sight.

A sorceress might fear he meant her harm. After Morgana, he supposed he should be suspicious of this one as well.

If he announced himself, would she run back into that portal, lost to him? At the thought, panic seized his chest. Why did he feel like she would run?

She caught sight of him, and her gaze widened, as if with disbelief. She dropped the bag she was carrying, taking a quick step forward, body tensed, those red lips parted.

He could almost swear she'd been about to leap into his arms before she'd stopped herself. Which couldn't be right. A trick of the mind.

Raising his palms, he quickly said, "My name is Thronos Talos, and I mean you no harm, sorceress."

"I know." Her eyes started to shimmer with a blue metallic gleam. "I don't mean you any harm either," said the tiny female—who looked like she couldn't hurt a fly.

But with Sorceri, appearances were deceiving.

Her friendly demeanor emboldened him to step closer to her. He struggled not to limp in front of such a beauty.

"I'm Lanthe." She looked like running from him was the last thing on her mind. Again, he got the curious impression that she was barely holding herself in place.

She also showed no surprise at her surroundings, as if she'd been to this glade before. Thronos had half believed he was the only one who knew of it.

All around her, surreal drops floated and bubbles bobbed, but she never took her eyes from him. When she tilted her head, her black hair swept over her shoulder, sending tendrils of her scent toward him.

He inhaled greedily. His muscles shot tight with tension.

Sky. Home.

This exquisite creature was . . . his mate. A sense of déjà vu wracked him. "Will you not close that threshold and speak with me, Lanthe?"

She nodded, turning back to the portal. She leaned over to poke her head back in. Gods, the body on that female! He didn't know whether he wanted to kiss her—or crush her in a hug.

All he knew was that the shard was slowly withdrawing from his chest.

Lanthe seemed to be speaking to someone on the other side. Was there another who would yank her back through? Who could ever let such a female go?

His face fell. How could a woman this incomparable have no mate?

"Yes, right this very minute!" she said to someone unseen. "Not twenty freaking feet behind me!" Pause. "Because maybe I *don't* suck." Another pause. "For the love of gold, I don't need an illusion," she said in an exasperated tone. "I look *fine.* I'll portal soon!"

Relief rushed through him as soon as the threshold closed.

"My sister." Lanthe rolled her eyes. "For someone so cool, she's turned into a mother hen. Weird. So where were we?" She seemed *nervous.*

"Why are you in a place like this, sorceress?" A dark thought arose. "Perhaps you've come to spy on me for your queen?" Maybe Morgana sought their total annihilation.

"I vow to you that I have no loyalties to Morgana. She's taken much from me."

"Then we have that in common."

"I'm so sorry about your kingdom, Thronos."

"How much do you know of the situation?"

Seeming to choose her words carefully, she said, "I believe that I'm versed in both sides of the conflict."

"Then you know Vrekener actions could have prevented the attack. *I* could have. I should have paid more attention to the former king and his actions."

"You blame yourself?" she demanded, as if indignant on his behalf.

"Of course."

"How about this: Let's not blame anyone. Let's just fix the situation as best as we can."

He liked this sorceress! Playing along, he said, "How shall we fix it, then?"

"I'm working on it even as we speak. But first, tell me—why are you here? What do you hope to find in Pandemonia?"

"I . . . I can't lie." He ran his fingers through his hair. "I've been unwell. In the explosion that destroyed my home, I somehow injured my mind, and I'm not healing. Some of my memories were lost." Why did he find it so easy to talk to her? Just because she was his fated one? Yet she also felt familiar to him. "I recall traveling to this place, but it's like looking at a puzzle with half of the pieces missing. Incomplete. I come here in the hopes of remembering." Sharing these things with her felt like shucking weights from his shoulders.

"Maybe I can help with that?" she said softly, her voice like a balm.

Surely this sorceress had to be taken by someone. And even if she wasn't, the idea of a female like *her* choosing *him* was implausible.

He was scarred, his body and mind battered. He had no wealth, no real home, nothing in the worlds to offer her.

But I want her. He'd still try. Because he also had nothing to lose.

Yet when she sidled closer and he drew more deeply of her scent, he detected the faintest hint of . . . another.

Recognition slammed him, along with a misery so weighty he felt that his knees would buckle. Voice gone hoarse, he said, "Sorceress, you're expecting." She *was* taken. "Where's your man?" *I will challenge him for her.* And since the other male would fight to the death for a female like this . . . *I will kill him.*

Her eyes misted as she murmured, "I fear the man I knew is lost to me forever."

The depths of sadness she conveyed roused a seething jealousy inside him. He wanted her to feel so strongly about him—only him!

But if the other male was lost . . .

Then I can have her for my own.

Lanthe had just probed his mind—and nearly wept.

She'd found *nothing* of herself in Thronos's thoughts, not past today. His blocks were down—he might not even remember that he had them—so she'd searched, and found . . .

Not a single fleeting memory of a girl named Melanthe.

A wife. A queen. A best friend.

How could she make him recall what was no longer there?

His thoughts troubled her as well. Though he was filled with fury toward the man she loved—unknowingly himself—he was struggling to choke it back so he could speak to her with his full attention, because his "mind was not well."

Already, he'd scented that she was his mate. He neared, tentatively, so as not to scare her away. He had no idea he'd never be rid of her.

When drops from the canopy kissed her face, he drew his wings over his head, creating a shelter. "I've always room for you too."

Don't cry, don't cry. As she met him halfway, she gazed up at him, taking in his exhausted mien, his troubled gray eyes. He didn't look like he'd eaten or slept since they'd been separated, and his wings had reverted to their gnarled and twisted state. She'd noticed him trying to conceal his limp in front of her.

Because she wasn't *his* Lanthe anymore. She was a mysterious woman—his fated one—and he longed to impress her.

Yes, she would start over with him and tell him about their past, but how could she adequately put their journey into words?

Overcoming impossible odds. Defying death and learning to trust. Coming to love each other again.

Reminded of all they'd beaten, she set her jaw. *I'm getting my Vrekener back.* She would juice him with all the power in her body if she had to.

She'd done it for Sabine; she'd do it for him. When he stood before her, Lanthe said, "Thronos, if I tell you something crazy, could you try to believe me?"

"Sorceress, in these last few weeks, I've seen crazy. I've lived it."

No kidding. "What if I told you that we were well acquainted with each other? But you were bespelled to forget me?"

She debated telling him upfront that they were married (oh, and having a kid!), but decided against it. She didn't want him to believe she was a lock, didn't want him complacent. For now, she needed him to ache for her—as badly as she did for him.

"I don't see how I could ever forget you. Lanthe, I believe that you are my mate." He eased even closer to her. "You don't look surprised by this news?"

She shook her head. "Before Morgana destroyed your kingdom, she erased all your memories of me." Voice going throaty, Lanthe said, "But, Thronos, we *knew* each other."

He was in disbelief. "I've *known* you?" As if testing the waters, he tentatively smoothed her hair behind her ear, his hand trailing down to her face . . . to her neck . . . to her collarbone . . .

When she didn't stop him, in fact arched to his touch, a shocked breath escaped him.

Puh.

"That's right, Thronos. I want to make you remember that and everything else. Because our story is epic."

"How is this possible? It would explain so much. . . ." He swallowed thickly, as if he were starting to believe—to *hope.* "How would you restore my memory? Understand me, sorceress: I can't express how fiercely I covet these memories. How I covet *you.*"

She laid her palm on his chest; his heart thundered. "I'll need to use my sorcery on you." It radiated from her palms. "Can you trust me to make this right?"

Ever brave, he squared his shoulders. "Do as you will, Lanthe. I've nothing to lose."

She shook away any thoughts about her on-the-fritz power or her sorcery limitations. Yes, Morgana was stronger. Yes, the queen had packed one hell of a persuasive punch.

But love would triumph.

Right?

Lanthe pressed her alight palm over his chest as she commanded, "Remember me, Thronos. Remember." Her sorcery burned brighter, coiling around them, *through* them. "Remember."

The air grew warmer. Subtle tremors rippled beneath their feet. Floating drops of water began to rocket in haphazard directions. *"Remember me."* Her voice sounded altered, vibrating with power.

Sadness seeped into his expression. "I . . . don't."

"We're only getting started, Vrekener. Just open your mind as much as you can."

He got that determined look, the one she'd seen hundreds of times before, the one she couldn't love more. "I will."

"Remember me. *Restore your memories.* Shake off what Morgana did to you." *To us.*

When he still evinced no recognition, she bit her lip, deciding to reveal more of their past. "Do you feel the need to enclose us in your wings?"

"Overwhelmingly. But I don't want to scare you."

"You don't."

Again, as if he were testing the waters, he gradually wrapped his wings around her, enfolding them both completely. His pulselines were lighting like crazy. Her poor Vrekener must be a bewildered mix of nerves and anticipation. "Thronos, when we're like this, we tell each other secrets. Do you want to know some?"

He nodded.

"We were best friends as children," she told him. "Just as we are now."

"Friends?"

"Yes," she murmured. "But we're so much more. You love me. And I love you."

"You? Love *me*?"

"Wildly. Madly." Maybe a kiss would remind him. Maybe she needed to spur his body as much as his mind. She rose on her toes, cupping his face between her glowing hands, drawing him to her. Within his wings, her iridescent sorcery lit his eyes, joining his surreal pulselines. "Can I kiss you?"

His brows drew tight. "By all the gods, *yes.*"

Just as he had kissed her after those time loops—so she would kiss him.

A claiming kiss.

A no-going-back kiss.

He went motionless as she brushed her lips over his, once and again. When she slanted her mouth across his, he parted his lips.

She deepened the contact, slipping in her tongue to tease his. He met her with a groan, and she grew encouraged—as if he'd conceded far more than a kiss.

He began one of his slow-build love affairs with her mouth, sensuously licking her until her eyes slid shut.

Her hands shook on his face as their tongues slowly twined. His arms wrapped around her. He palmed the back of her head with one hand, his other dipping toward her ass, as if he couldn't help himself. His wings tightened around her back even more, squeezing her closer.

Once they were sharing breaths, she drew back to whisper against his lips, "Remember me, love." The ground tremors intensified, until even the immense trees shuddered. She felt like a sorcery reactor, stronger than she'd ever been.

Because I've never wanted anything like I want him.

"Remember"—she commanded between seeking kisses—"Thronos, please, remember me. I'm waiting for you. *Remember, remember, REMEMBER!*" Sorcery blasted from her to him.

Breathless, she drew back.

His eyes were heavy-lidded, vivid silver. Flickering remnants of blue light sparked around them.

"Anything?"

He shook his head. "Though I'd like to repeat this process to be sure."

He tenderly brushed the pad of his thumb over her bottom lip. "Shall we try again, lamb?"

He frowned; she beamed.

Voice roughened, he murmured, "I . . . smell magics on you?"

Her eyes misted again. "Those were the first words you ever said to me."

His brow creased as he clearly recollected. "I remember you!" Recognition flared in his gaze. "My Lanthe." As they had so long ago, his eyes told her, *I've been pretty much lost without you.*

"Um, there's a part in the middle. . . ."

"I've already skipped past it," he told her. "We don't dwell on things that have no consequence, and I'm not one to squander my golden"—he kissed her forehead—"coins."

She grinned up at him. "I've been looking everywhere for you! I never would've given up."

"I love you, Lanthe. I knew it before, was going to tell you that night . . ." He trailed off. "And you love me too?"

"I do. I love us together. I want you back."

"I'm here." His smile was glorious. "You're right. Our story is epic." He buried his face in her hair, inhaling—

His muscles went tense. "Wait. I'm to be a father?" His wings fluttered open—as if *they* were stunned. "We're having a baby?"

"What were the odds, huh?" she asked wryly. "Now we'll be an army of three. And I have it on good authority that we can handle this."

He swooped her up, spinning her around. Then he slowed, his face falling. He set her back on her feet, his hand dipping to her belly. "I have nothing to offer you. You—and our babe." His hand shook over her as he said those words. "I have no kingdom. No home. What would you want with a displaced king and faction, living on borrowed time in a mortal forest?"

"*Our* faction could live here in Pandemonia. You felt something for this realm, I know you did."

"It's true. But the land is rife with danger."

"Because of the demon hordes?" She waved that away, tugging her necklace up. "Don't forget that I'm the Keeper of Keys and you're the Reader of Words. We'll open both gates and air this place out a bit. Oh, oh, I can speak Dragon now! So we could negotiate some kind of treaty with them—we might have to offer them a hottie Rothkalinan dragoness, but that's okay." Lanthe walked her fingers up his chest. "I'm not saying we, like, *own* Pandemonia. But I'm not *not* saying that either."

He caught her hand, pressing a kiss to her palm. "You'd live with me here?"

"Of course! I'd rather live in hell with you than in heaven without you."

"The Vrekeners will think we're mad."

"I believe they'll feel a pull to this place, just like you did. In any case, we'll convince them. I know it's a bit of a fixer-upper"—she motioned around her—"in need of Vrekener TLC. But it's nothing that a bucket of paint and some lava dams can't spruce up!" She stood on her toes, wanting more of his kiss. "We've *got* this, Thronos."

He leaned in, his eyes telling her he was about to kiss her till her toes curled. Just before his lips met hers, he rasped, "If my mate has her heart set on Pandemonia, who am I to deny her?"

FIFTY-EIGHT

"What if there's an even better place than the demon valley?" Thronos asked, his voice roughened from his many bellows to the proverbial rafters. After Lanthe had healed his old injuries once more, he'd made love to her until well after the sun had gone down. Now they lay within the cocoon of his wings, telling secrets. "What if we were to lead the Vrekeners to something even greater?"

"What do you mean?" She stroked the backs of her fingers over one of his cheeks.

"I keep thinking about one of the paths here: The Long Way. I can't *stop* thinking about it."

"Then it must mean something," Lanthe said, excitement filling her. "Let's go see what awaits us at the end!"

He cupped her face. "Exactly my thoughts."

After dressing, they set off hand in hand into the night. They stepped upon The Long Way—which was anything but straight and narrow.

Together, they followed its many twists and turns.

With each league away from the fuming lava and the miasma of the swamp, the air grew cleaner. The sun was beginning its long, slow rise when their army of two (soon to be three) arrived at a lush plain. In the center was a colossal gray-stone mountain wreathed in white clouds and moonrakers. A babbling brook meandered around the trunks.

The temperature was cooler here, the morning sun brighter.

The sky was a dazzling violet.

"Oh, my gold," Lanthe whispered. "It's so beautiful."

Gaze still on her, he said, "Beautiful."

She grinned. "And what do you think about the mountain?"

Thronos turned to take it in, canting his head.

Lanthe saw his chest bow, as if it were filled with too much emotion to be contained.

He tugged her back against his front, draping a possessive arm over her. "It smells like you."

"Oh, yeah?" She sank into him, luxuriating in his warmth. "How's that?"

Pressing a kiss into her hair, Thronos murmured, "It smells like sky. And *home*. . . ."